Dreams of Alchemy

Jason Holloway

Contents

CHAPTER ONE

Ash and Ember

The Phoenix Stone pulsed against Lyra's palm with unexpected warmth as she slipped through Sylvanthia's morning mist. The forest path ahead twisted like a half-forgotten memory, its edges blurred by fog that clung to ancient trees with pale, grasping fingers. Dawn had barely broken, the sky above a watercolor wash of lavender and gold that struggled to penetrate the dense canopy overhead.

Seven years. Seven years since fire had devoured her childhood home, since shadows with steel had stolen her parents and left nothing but questions that burned hotter than the flames. Seven years of searching, of dead ends and false hopes—until now.

Lyra adjusted the worn leather satchel at her hip, feeling the reassuring weight of the ancient tome inside. Its weathered pages contained the first real lead she'd found, a fragile thread connecting her parents' murder to something larger and more sinister than she'd dared imagine. The Syndicate—a name whispered in

Alchemoria's darkest corners, a shadow organization whose tendrils reached into every aspect of power and commerce.

She paused at a fork in the path, consulting the crude map she'd sketched based on the tome's descriptions. The Temple of Elemental Harmony should be less than a day's journey northeast, hidden in a grove where the boundaries between worlds grew thin. If the text was correct, the Phoenix Stone—the artifact her parents had died protecting—waited there, along with answers she'd spent years hunting.

A twig snapped behind her.

Lyra spun, her hand instinctively reaching for the vial of corrosive solution strapped to her belt. Her fingers curled around its smooth glass surface, ready to unleash its contents at the first sign of threat.

"Easy there, doom-gloom. It's just your favorite alchemist," came a familiar voice, followed by the appearance of a woman with flame-red hair and a smile that promised either salvation or catastrophe, depending on the day.

"Mira," Lyra exhaled, releasing her grip on the vial. "I told you to meet me at midday. The sun's barely up."

Mira shrugged, the numerous vials and pouches attached to her belt clinking softly with the movement. "Sleep is overrated when your best friend is about to storm an ancient temple. Besides, I figured you'd try to leave without me if I actually showed up when you asked."

Lyra couldn't deny the accusation. The thought had crossed her mind—not because she didn't value Mira's skills, but because the path ahead promised danger she was reluctant to share.

"I work better alone," she said, the lie tasting stale on her tongue.

"Spectacular falsehood," Mira replied cheerfully, falling into step beside her. "Remember the Crimson Alley incident? You'd be decorating some collector's shelf as a peculiarly gloomy statue if I hadn't been there with my dissolution spray."

Lyra winced at the memory. "That was different."

"It's never different," Mira countered, her green eyes suddenly serious despite her light tone. "We're partners, Lyra. Have been since that tavern brawl in Lower Alchemoria when you saved me from those Syndicate thugs."

"You'd already poisoned two of them," Lyra reminded her.

"Details," Mira waved dismissively. "The point is, whatever's waiting at this temple, whatever this Phoenix Stone thing is—you don't face it alone. Not when I've got a fresh batch of explosive solutions just begging to meet some ancient guardian's face."

Before Lyra could respond, another voice cut through the morning stillness—deep, rough, and decidedly unwelcome.

"The Phoenix Stone isn't something to be trifled with, alchemist."

Both women turned sharply. A man stood several paces behind them, his broad frame silhouetted against the misty path. He stepped forward, and Lyra's breath caught. His face was a battlefield of scars, some faded to silver, others still angry and red. Despite this, there was a strange nobility to his features, accentuated by eyes gray as storm clouds and a jawline that could have been carved from granite.

Lyra's hand returned to her vial. "Who are you?"

"Someone who's been tracking the Syndicate longer than you've been hunting answers," he replied, making no move toward them. "The name's Kael."

"That tells us nothing," Mira said, her fingers already wrapped around what Lyra recognized as her most volatile concoction—a brilliant blue liquid that could freeze a man solid in seconds.

"It's all you need for now," Kael replied evenly. "What matters is that we share a common enemy. The Syndicate took someone from me too—my sister, Lirien." A muscle in his jaw tightened. "Seven years ago."

Lyra felt a chill that had nothing to do with the morning air. "The same night they came for my parents."

"Yes." Kael's eyes met hers, and she saw in them a reflection of her own pain—a void that no amount of time could fill. "The same night they took many things from many people. A coordinated strike across Alchemoria and beyond. They were searching for something."

"The Phoenix Stone," Lyra said, the words barely above a whisper.

Kael nodded. "They believed your parents knew its location. Just as they believed my sister, an apprentice at the Grand Archive, had uncovered texts revealing its powers."

"And did she?" Mira asked, her usual flippancy subdued.

A shadow passed over Kael's scarred features. "I don't know. By the time I reached her, the archive was in flames. I found nothing but ash."

The word hung between them, heavy with shared grief. Ash—the only legacy the Syndicate had left them all.

"Why are you here now?" Lyra finally asked, her suspicion not entirely quelled.

"Because the Syndicate is moving again," Kael said, stepping closer. In the strengthening daylight, Lyra noticed the sword at his hip—well-worn but meticulously maintained, its hilt wrapped in leather darkened by years of use. "They've been searching the ruins of temples throughout Sylvanthia. Whatever they're planning, it centers on the Phoenix Stone, and it's happening soon."

"Convenient timing," Mira remarked, still not releasing her vial.

"Not convenience. Necessity." Kael's gaze returned to Lyra. "I've been watching you, tracking your movements since you left Alchemoria. You found something in that tome—something that led you here. I need to know what it is."

Lyra hesitated. Seven years of searching had taught her caution, especially with strangers claiming common cause. Yet something in Kael's eyes—the raw, unhealed grief that mirrored her own—gave her pause.

"The tome speaks of the Temple of Elemental Harmony," she finally said. "It claims the Phoenix Stone was hidden there after the Great Sundering, when the Aethyr Order still guarded the boundaries between worlds."

"The Aethyr Order," Kael repeated, surprise evident in his voice. "They've been gone for centuries."

"But their temples remain," Lyra countered. "And if the text is right, so does the Phoenix Stone."

A moment of silence passed between them, broken only by the soft calls of birds awakening in the forest canopy. Finally, Kael spoke again.

"I'm coming with you."

It wasn't a request. Lyra bristled at his presumption, but before she could object, Mira stepped forward.

"What skills do you bring besides that oversized letter opener?" she asked, nodding toward his sword.

The faintest hint of a smile touched Kael's lips. "I've spent years studying the Syndicate's movements, learning their patterns and weaknesses. I know their methods better than anyone outside their ranks. And," he added, his hand resting on his sword's hilt, "I've killed seventeen of their agents in the past three years. The 'letter opener' works well enough."

Mira raised an eyebrow, clearly impressed despite herself. "Seventeen? That's practically a hobby."

"It's a debt," Kael corrected, his momentary levity vanishing. "One I intend to pay in full."

Lyra studied him, weighing the risk of trusting this scarred stranger against the potential advantage of his knowledge. Finally, she nodded. "Fine. But at the first sign of betrayal—"

"—I'll turn him into a very surprised ice sculpture," Mira finished cheerfully, finally returning her vial to her belt.

Kael inclined his head in acknowledgment. "I would expect nothing less."

With that uneasy alliance formed, they continued along the forest path, the mist gradually burning away as the sun climbed higher. Lyra led the way, consulting her map at each junction, while Mira followed close behind, occasionally murmuring to her vials as if they were beloved pets. Kael brought up the rear, his vigilant gaze constantly scanning their surroundings.

As they walked, Lyra found herself stealing glances at their new companion. His movements were fluid and purposeful, despite his size—the practiced economy of someone who had learned to survive by being aware of every potential threat. The scars that mapped his face told stories of battles survived, though at great cost. She wondered how many had come from his encounters with the Syndicate, and how many were from before—from the night he lost Lirien.

"You're staring," Kael said without looking at her, his voice low enough that Mira, who had moved ahead to examine a peculiar flowering vine, couldn't hear.

Lyra didn't bother denying it. "Seven years is a long time to hunt the same shadow."

"Not long enough," he replied simply.

She understood then, with perfect clarity, that Kael's quest was not merely about justice or even vengeance. Like her own, it had become his purpose—the thing that defined his existence when everything else had been reduced to ash.

"My parents were alchemists," she found herself saying, unsure why she was sharing this with him. "Not the showy kind that populate Alchemoria's market squares, turning water different colors for applauding crowds. They were researchers, obsessed with the fundamental nature of reality."

Kael nodded, encouraging her to continue.

"They never spoke of their work, not in detail. But sometimes, late at night, I'd hear them arguing—about boundaries and balances, about powers that shouldn't be disturbed." Lyra's hand unconsciously moved to her satchel, where the ancient tome rested. "I was seven when they came. Men in dark cloaks, their faces hidden. They demanded something—I couldn't hear what from where I was hiding. Then there was fighting, screaming..." She swallowed hard. "Fire."

"They burned my sister's quarters too," Kael said quietly. "A signature of sorts. The Syndicate likes to leave nothing behind."

"Except us," Lyra said, meeting his gaze.

"Except us," he agreed.

The moment was interrupted by Mira's return, her hands full of delicate purple blossoms. "These are perfect for my newest concoction," she announced, carefully placing them in one of the many pouches at her belt. "Three drops of extract mixed with powdered moonstone, and you've got yourself a solution that can temporarily phase through solid matter." She grinned wickedly. "Imagine the possibilities."

"I'd rather not," Lyra replied dryly, grateful for her friend's timely distraction from darker thoughts.

They continued through the forest, which grew denser and more ancient as they progressed. The trees here were massive, their trunks wider than three people could encircle with joined hands. Moss hung from branches in thick curtains, and the undergrowth teemed with plants Lyra had never seen before—some with leaves that seemed to shift color as they passed, others that emitted soft, bell-like tones when brushed against.

"We're getting close," Kael observed, his voice hushed with what might have been reverence. "These are old woods—older than Alchemoria itself. The kind of place the Aethyr Order would have chosen."

Lyra consulted her map again, though she was increasingly certain they were on the right path. The forest itself seemed to be guiding them, the undergrowth thinning in places to reveal clear passages that hadn't been visible from a distance.

By midday, they reached a clearing unlike any Lyra had seen before. Perfectly circular, it was carpeted with moss so vibrant it seemed to glow from within. At its center stood a ring of stone pillars, each carved with symbols that shifted subtly when viewed from different angles. Beyond the pillars, partially obscured by vines and the natural growth of centuries, rose the Temple of Elemental Harmony.

It wasn't the grand structure Lyra had imagined from the tome's descriptions. Rather, it was elegant in its simplicity—a series of interconnected chambers built directly into the face of a cliff, their entrances framed by stone arches that bore the same shifting symbols as the pillars. Four main doorways were visible, each marked with a different elemental sign: a flame, a wave, a leaf, and a spiral that could only represent air.

"It's beautiful," Mira whispered, for once subdued by the sight before them.

Kael nodded in agreement, but his expression remained vigilant. "And likely protected. The Aethyr Order didn't leave their treasures unguarded."

As if in response to his words, the air in the clearing seemed to thicken, becoming harder to breathe. The symbols on the pillars began to glow with a soft blue light that pulsed in a rhythm reminiscent of a heartbeat.

"We're being watched," Lyra said, her hand moving to her vial once more.

"Not watched," Kael corrected, his eyes fixed on the temple. "Tested."

Before Lyra could ask what he meant, the ground beneath them trembled. From the base of each pillar, lines of light spread outward, connecting to form a complex pattern across the clearing's floor. The moss, which had seemed merely unusually vibrant before, now revealed its true nature—thousands of tiny crystalline structures hidden among the green, each catching and amplifying the light until the entire clearing blazed with radiance.

In the center of the pattern, directly before the temple's entrances, a figure began to coalesce—not solid, but formed of light and shadow, its features constantly shifting between those of an elderly man and a young woman.

"Seekers," the figure spoke, its voice neither male nor female but something in between, resonating not just in their ears but in their very bones. "What brings you to the Temple of Elemental Harmony?"

Lyra stepped forward, drawn by an instinct she couldn't name. "We seek the Phoenix Stone."

The figure's form rippled, like the surface of a pond disturbed by a stone. "Many have sought the Stone. Few have been worthy of its power."

"I don't seek its power," Lyra replied, surprising herself with the truth of her words. "I seek answers."

"Answers," the figure echoed, its tone unreadable. "And what questions do you bring, child of ash?"

The title sent a chill through Lyra. How could this entity know of the fire, of the loss that had defined her life? Yet somehow, she was certain it did.

"Who killed my parents," she said, her voice steady despite the emotion welling within her. "Why they died. What they were protecting."

"And if the answers bring not peace but greater burden?" the figure asked. "What then, child of ash?"

Lyra hesitated, feeling the weight of Kael and Mira's gazes upon her. This was the moment she had worked toward for seven years—the threshold between not knowing and knowing, between the quest and its resolution. What if the truth was worse than the void she had carried all this time?

"Then I will bear it," she finally said, lifting her chin. "As I have borne everything else."

The figure seemed to study her, though its shifting features made it impossible to read its expression. Then, slowly, it turned its attention to Kael.

"And you, child of steel? What do you seek from the Stone?"

Kael's hand tightened on his sword hilt, but he did not draw the weapon. "Justice," he said simply. "For my sister. For all those the Syndicate has harmed."

"Justice," the figure repeated, "or vengeance? They are not the same, though many confuse them."

"I know the difference," Kael replied, his scarred face set in grim lines. "I seek to stop those who would use the Stone's power to cause more suffering, not merely to punish them for what they've done."

The figure nodded, then turned to Mira, who had been uncharacteristically silent throughout the exchange.

"And what of you, child of chaos? What brings you to this sacred place?"

Mira straightened, her usual irreverence tempered by the solemnity of the moment. "I'm here for her," she said, nodding toward Lyra. "Because she's my friend, and she needs me. No grand quests or revenge plots—just loyalty."

The figure's form stabilized briefly, taking on the appearance of a young woman with eyes far older than her face would suggest. "Honesty," it said, and there might have been approval in its tone. "A rare gift, and one the Stone values."

With those words, the figure dissolved into motes of light that drifted toward the temple entrances. As they watched, the four elemental doorways began to glow—fire burning red, water shimmering blue, earth pulsing green, and air swirling with silver light.

"The way is open," the figure's voice echoed, though its form was gone. "But be warned: the Temple tests all who enter. The Stone reveals truth, but truth has a price. Are you willing to pay it?"

Lyra exchanged glances with her companions. Mira's expression was resolute beneath her usual cocky smile, while Kael's scarred features betrayed nothing but determination. Whatever awaited them within the temple, they would face it together.

"We are," Lyra answered for all of them.

The light intensified briefly, then settled into a steady glow that illuminated the path to the temple doors.

"Then enter, seekers," the voice said, fading like the last notes of a song. "And find what you have come for."

Lyra took a deep breath, feeling the weight of seven years of searching culminate in this moment. With Mira and Kael at her sides, she stepped forward, crossing the clearing toward the temple that held the key to her past—and perhaps her future.

As they approached the four elemental doorways, a new challenge presented itself: which path to take? Each entrance pulsed with its respective element's energy, offering different ways into the temple's heart.

"The tome didn't mention this part," Lyra murmured, studying the symbols carved around each archway.

Mira circled the entrances, her alchemist's eye analyzing the patterns. "Four elements, three of us. Not the best math."

"We don't split up," Kael said firmly. "That's exactly what the temple wants—to separate and test us individually."

"Or maybe that's exactly what it doesn't want," Lyra countered, a realization dawning as she examined the symbols more closely. "Look at how the patterns connect between the doorways. They're not separate paths—they're aspects of a whole."

She pointed to where the carvings from one archway flowed seamlessly into the next, creating a continuous circuit around all four entrances.

"The Aethyr Order believed in balance," she continued, recalling passages from the ancient tome. "Not just between the elements, but between people. No single person could master all elements—that kind of power would corrupt. Instead, they worked in harmony, each contributing their strength to the whole."

Kael studied the carvings, understanding dawning in his eyes. "So we each choose the element that speaks to us most strongly."

"Exactly," Lyra nodded. "Together, we create the balance needed to reach the Stone."

Mira grinned, already moving toward the doorway marked with a spiral of air. "Dibs on air. Unpredictable, impossible to contain, and everywhere at once—sounds like me."

Kael considered the remaining entrances before stepping toward the one marked with a flame. "Fire," he said simply. "For Lirien. For everything that was lost in the flames."

Lyra found herself drawn to the doorway marked with a wave. Water—fluid, persistent, capable of wearing away stone given enough time. Like her search for answers, flowing around obstacles rather than trying to smash through them.

That left the earth doorway untended. For a moment, Lyra hesitated, wondering if their theory was flawed.

"Earth represents foundation, stability," Kael observed. "Perhaps it's meant to be the ground we all share, rather than an individual path."

"One way to find out," Mira said with her characteristic impatience. "On three?"

They positioned themselves before their chosen doorways, each glowing with elemental energy that seemed to respond to their presence, growing brighter as they approached.

"One," Lyra began.

"Two," Kael continued.

"Three!" Mira finished with enthusiasm.

Together, they stepped through their respective entrances. Lyra felt a momentary resistance, as if passing through a waterfall, then a sensation of rightness as the temple accepted her. Through the doorway, she found not a separate chamber but a corridor that curved gently to the right, its walls lined with symbols that glowed with a soft blue light.

She could see Mira and Kael in parallel corridors to her left, separated by walls that were somehow translucent from this angle, allowing them to maintain visual contact while following their individual paths.

"It worked!" Mira called, her voice slightly muffled but audible. "This place is incredible!"

Kael nodded in agreement, his scarred face illuminated by the red glow of his corridor. "Stay alert. The test has only begun."

As if triggered by his words, the temple shuddered. The translucent walls between their corridors became opaque, cutting off their view of each other. Simultaneously, the floor beneath Lyra's feet began to ripple like the surface of a disturbed pond.

Water—her chosen element—was manifesting in a very literal way.

The ripples grew stronger, the solid stone beneath her transforming into a surface with the consistency of thick liquid. Lyra struggled to maintain her balance as waves began to form, pushing her toward the corridor's end where darkness waited.

"Mira! Kael!" she called, but there was no response. She was on her own, facing the temple's first real challenge.

The waves grew higher, more insistent, threatening to sweep her off her feet and into the unknown darkness. Fighting against them was futile—the more she resisted, the stronger they became, like a riptide pulling her inexorably toward depths she couldn't fathom.

Understanding dawned. This wasn't a test of strength but of acceptance—of flowing with the current rather than against it. Just as water found its way around obstacles rather than trying to break them, she needed to adapt, to yield without surrendering.

Lyra took a deep breath and stopped fighting. She allowed her body to move with the waves, using subtle shifts in weight and balance to guide her direction without opposing the water's fundamental nature. The waves responded, becoming less violent though no less purposeful in carrying her forward.

As she approached the darkness at the corridor's end, Lyra felt a moment of primal fear. What waited in those depths? But she had come too far to turn back now. Seven years of searching, of carrying the weight of questions unanswered—she would not falter at this threshold.

With a final surge, the waves propelled her into the darkness. For a breathless moment, Lyra felt herself suspended in nothingness, neither falling nor floating, simply existing in a void where direction had no meaning.

Then, with a gentleness that belied the force that had brought her here, she found herself deposited on solid ground in a circular chamber illuminated by a soft, ambient light that seemed to emanate from the walls themselves.

In the center of the chamber stood Mira and Kael, looking as disoriented as she felt.

"That," Mira declared, brushing what appeared to be actual feathers from her clothing, "was simultaneously the most terrifying and exhilarating experience of my life. The air literally carried me here—I was flying!"

Kael's experience had clearly been different. His clothing bore scorch marks, and there was a new, small burn on his left cheek to join his collection of scars. "Fire tests through pain," he said simply. "Through the willingness to endure."

Lyra nodded, understanding. Each of them had been tested according to the nature of their chosen element—Mira through air's unpredictability, Kael through fire's purifying pain, and herself through water's insistence on finding its own path.

But their individual trials had led them to the same place: this chamber at the heart of the temple.

And at the chamber's center, rising from a pedestal of stone carved with all four elemental symbols, was the Phoenix Stone.

It wasn't what Lyra had expected. Rather than a gem or crystal of obvious power, the Stone appeared almost ordinary at first glance—a smooth, amber-colored river stone that could have been plucked from any streambed. Only when she looked more closely did she see the subtle glow emanating from within, pulsing like a heartbeat in rhythm with the temple around them.

"Is that it?" Mira asked, clearly underwhelmed. "Seven years of searching, and it's a glorified pebble?"

"Don't be deceived by appearances," Kael warned, his eyes never leaving the Stone. "The most powerful artifacts often disguise their true nature."

Lyra approached the pedestal slowly, drawn by an instinct she couldn't name. As she drew closer, the Stone's pulse quickened, its amber glow intensifying until it illuminated the chamber with a warm, golden light.

"It's responding to you," Kael observed, his voice hushed.

"Or to all of us," Lyra countered, remembering the guardian's words about worthiness and truth.

She reached out, her hand hovering inches above the Stone's surface. "Together," she said, looking to her companions. "Whatever answers it holds, whatever truth it reveals—we face it as one."

Mira moved to her right side, Kael to her left. As one, they reached for the Phoenix Stone.

The moment their fingers touched its surface, the world exploded into light and memory.

Lyra saw her parents in their workshop, arguing over a scroll bearing symbols she now recognized from the temple walls. She saw Kael's sister, Lirien, discovering a hidden text in the Grand Archive, her eyes widening with shock at what she read. She saw the Syndicate forming centuries ago, a cabal dedicated to harnessing powers beyond mortal understanding, corrupted by their own ambition.

And she saw something else—a figure of shadow and flame, imprisoned beyond a barrier that was growing thinner with each passing year. Veyra, a name whispered in the oldest texts, a power that had nearly destroyed the world once before.

The Phoenix Stone had been created to seal that barrier, to prevent Veyra's return. And the Syndicate sought to break that seal, believing they could control what lay beyond.

The visions faded, leaving the three of them gasping, their hands still touching the Stone, which now glowed with a steady, brilliant light.

"My parents," Lyra whispered, tears streaming down her face. "They were trying to hide the Stone, to keep it from the Syndicate. They knew what would happen if it fell into the wrong hands."

"And Lirien discovered the truth in the archives," Kael added, his voice rough with emotion. "She was trying to warn someone—anyone—when they came for her."

Mira, for once, had no quip or jest to offer. Her face was pale, her eyes wide with the weight of what they had seen. "This is bigger than revenge or answers," she finally said. "This is about stopping something terrible from happening."

As if in response to her words, the temple shuddered violently. Dust rained from the ceiling, and the glow of the elemental symbols along the walls flickered like candles in a strong wind.

"We're not alone," Kael said, drawing his sword in one fluid motion. "The Syndicate has found us."

Lyra's hand closed around the Phoenix Stone, lifting it from its pedestal. It felt warm against her palm, alive in a way she couldn't explain—as if it had been waiting for her, recognizing in her the same determination that had driven her parents to protect it with their lives.

"Then we do what my parents died trying to do," she said, her voice steady despite the tears still drying on her cheeks. "We keep the Stone safe, and we stop the Syndicate from breaking the seal."

The temple shook again, more violently this time. From beyond the chamber, they could hear voices—harsh commands being issued, the sound of boots on stone.

"Four elements, four doorways," Mira said, already pulling vials from her belt. "But only one way out, I'm guessing, and they're blocking it."

Kael moved to the chamber's entrance, his sword ready. "I'll hold them off. You two find another way out."

"Not happening," Lyra said firmly. "We came in together, we leave together."

The Phoenix Stone pulsed in her hand, as if in agreement. Its light spread, enveloping the three of them in a golden glow that seemed to strengthen as their resolve solidified.

"The Stone," Kael realized. "It's responding to our unity."

Lyra nodded, understanding dawning. "The Aethyr Order believed in balance—in harmony between elements and people. The Stone was never meant to be used by a single person, but by those working together."

"Great theory," Mira said, eyeing the entrance where sounds of approach grew louder. "But unless it can magically teleport us out of here, we're still cornered."

As if in response to her words, the Stone's light intensified, spreading to illuminate the chamber's walls. Symbols that had been invisible before now glowed with golden fire—a complex pattern that spiraled across the stone surface toward a section of wall directly opposite the entrance.

"There," Lyra pointed. "Another way out."

The wall in question appeared solid, but as they approached, the Stone's light revealed what their eyes had missed—a doorway, hidden by arts beyond mere physical concealment, its outline now visible in the Phoenix Stone's revealing glow.

"How do we open it?" Mira asked, running her hands along the seam without finding any mechanism or handle.

The answer came not in words but in understanding, a knowledge that seemed to flow from the Stone itself into Lyra's mind. "Together," she said, placing her free hand against the center of the hidden door. "Each of us, with the element we chose."

Mira and Kael joined her, placing their hands beside hers on the stone surface. As they did, Lyra felt the Phoenix Stone grow warmer in her grasp, its light flowing through her and into the door where their hands met the rock.

The hidden doorway responded, glowing with the combined light of all four elements—fire's red, water's blue, earth's green, and air's silver—before sliding silently open to reveal a narrow passage leading deeper into the cliff face.

"Go," Kael urged, as the sounds of their pursuers grew louder. "I'll be right behind you."

Lyra hesitated, unwilling to leave him even for a moment.

"Promise," he insisted, meeting her gaze with an intensity that brooked no argument.

She nodded, then plunged into the passage with Mira close behind. The tunnel was narrow but not cramped, its walls smooth as if worn by centuries of flowing water. It curved gently downward, leading them deeper into the cliff.

Behind them, they heard shouts of anger and the clash of steel—Kael engaging the first of the Syndicate agents to reach the chamber. Lyra's grip tightened on the Phoenix Stone, its warmth a reassurance that they had chosen the right path.

After what felt like an eternity but could only have been minutes, they emerged into daylight once more—not in the clearing where they had entered, but on the far side of the cliff, overlooking a valley lush with vegetation unlike any Lyra had seen before. The plants here seemed more vibrant, more alive, as if nourished by the same ancient power that had built the temple.

"Elara's Grove," Mira breathed, recognizing the location from old tales. "The heart of Sylvanthia's enchanted forest."

Before Lyra could respond, they heard footsteps in the tunnel behind them. Both women tensed, ready to fight or flee, but it was Kael who emerged, his sword bloodied but his expression triumphant.

"They won't follow immediately," he said, sheathing his weapon. "I collapsed part of the tunnel behind me. It won't hold them forever, but it gives us time."

"Time for what?" Mira asked, already scanning the valley for potential escape routes.

"Time to understand what we've found," Lyra replied, opening her hand to reveal the Phoenix Stone still nestled in her palm. "And what we need to do next."

The Stone's glow had subsided to a gentle pulse, but Lyra could feel its power—not as something separate from her, but as an extension of her own determination, her own quest for truth. It had shown her the past, revealed the connection between her parents' death and a threat that spanned centuries.

Now it offered something else: a path forward.

"The Syndicate will keep coming," Kael said, cleaning his blade before returning it to its sheath. "They've invested too much in finding the Stone to give up now."

"Let them come," Mira declared with her usual bravado, though there was a new seriousness beneath her smile. "We've got a magical rock, a warrior with anger issues, and an alchemical genius—that's me, in case you were wondering. What could go wrong?"

Lyra couldn't help but smile at her friend's irrepressible spirit. "Everything could go wrong," she said. "But for the first time in seven years, I feel like we have a chance to make something right."

She looked out over the valley, then back at the Phoenix Stone in her hand. Its amber surface caught the sunlight, transforming it into a miniature sun that warmed not just her skin but something deeper—a place within her that had been cold since the night fire took everything she loved.

"My parents died protecting this," she said softly. "Lirien died because she discovered its importance. We owe it to them to finish what they started—to stop the Syndicate from breaking the seal and releasing Veyra back into the world."

CHAPTER TWO

Fragments of Power

D awn broke over Sylvanthia in ribbons of gold and amber, casting long shadows through the ancient trees. The forest awakened with a symphony of sound—birdsong cascading from the canopy, the soft rustle of creatures stirring in the underbrush, and the distant murmur of a stream tumbling over moss-slick stones. The air carried the sharp tang of pine resin mingled with the earthy perfume of damp soil and the faint sweetness of wild honeysuckle.

Lyra sat on a fallen log at the edge of their makeshift camp, the Phoenix Stone cradled in her palms. Its warmth seeped into her skin, pulsing with a gentle rhythm that matched her heartbeat. She'd barely slept, too consumed by the weight of what they'd discovered in the Temple of Elemental Harmony. Her mouth still tasted of the bitter herbs Mira had brewed for their evening tea—a concoction meant to ward off fatigue, but which had left her mind racing through the night.

The Stone wasn't just an artifact—it was a key. A key to understanding her parents' deaths, to unraveling the Syndicate's plans, and perhaps to something even greater.

As her thoughts drifted to her parents, a sharp pang of grief struck her heart. The Stone responded immediately, its amber glow dimming to a mournful blue that cast eerie shadows across her hands. Lyra blinked in surprise, watching as the color shifted with her emotions, responding to her pain like a living thing.

"You look like you're having a staring contest with destiny," Mira said, dropping onto the log beside her with characteristic lack of ceremony. Her red hair was disheveled from sleep, but her green eyes were alert, studying Lyra with barely concealed concern. "And destiny's winning."

The Stone's light warmed again, threads of gold weaving through the blue as Lyra's mood lightened at her friend's presence.

"Just thinking," she replied with a tired smile.

"Dangerous habit, that. Thinking." Mira stretched, joints popping as she worked out the stiffness of another night spent on hard ground. Her words tumbled out in their usual rapid-fire cadence, punctuated by expressive hand gestures that seemed to physically shape her thoughts in the air. "Especially when there's breakfast to be made and miles to cover before the Syndicate catches our scent again. Not that I'm opposed to thinking, mind you—some of my best explosions have come from excessive thinking. Usually right after the excessive drinking."

She rummaged in her pack, producing a small tin of dried herbs that released a sharp, citrusy aroma when she pried off the lid. "Been saving this blend for a special occasion. Makes even stale water taste like it came from some fancy noble's table." She winked, tapping the tin with a fingernail that bore traces of various alchemical stains. "With the added benefit of sharpening reflexes. My own invention. Nearly blinded myself getting the proportions right, but that's progress for you."

Lyra glanced back at their camp. Kael was already awake, methodically checking his gear with the practiced efficiency of a career soldier. His scarred face betrayed nothing of his thoughts, but the tension in his shoulders spoke volumes. He hadn't fully relaxed since they'd left the temple. The metallic rasp of his whetstone against his blade created a rhythmic counterpoint to the morning birdsong.

"Do you think we lost them?" Lyra asked, though she already knew the answer.

Mira snorted, a sound entirely lacking in delicacy. "About as likely as me brewing a potion that doesn't explode. They want that rock too badly to give up now." She nodded toward the Stone. "Have you figured out how it works yet? Besides the whole glowy-mood-ring thing?"

"Not entirely," Lyra admitted, turning the Stone over in her hands. Its surface shifted with inner light, amber deepening to gold, then flaring with touches of crimson that reminded her of sunrise. The Stone felt warm against her skin, but not uncomfortably so—like holding a cup of tea that had cooled to the perfect drinking temperature. "It responds to intention, I think. When I focus on protection, it grows warmer. When I think about finding a path forward, the light changes direction, like it's pointing the way."

To demonstrate, she concentrated on the need for safety, picturing a shield around their small group. The Stone pulsed strongly, its glow extending outward by several inches to form a faint dome of light that hovered over her hands for a moment before fading. The air within the dome briefly carried the scent of something like cinnamon and woodsmoke—comforting and warm.

"Handy," Mira said, her skepticism visibly wavering in the face of such a clear demonstration. "A magical compass that reads minds and moods. What could possibly go wrong? Not that I'm complaining, mind you. Better than my last invention. Tried to create a potion that could identify poisons in food. Worked perfectly! Except it turned out to be more poisonous than most of the things it was meant to detect."

Before Lyra could respond, a twig snapped in the underbrush—a sharp crack that silenced the nearby birdsong. Both women tensed, Lyra's hand instinctively closing around the Stone while Mira reached for one of the many vials strapped to her belt. The Phoenix Stone flared bright crimson in response to Lyra's sudden alarm, its heat intensifying against her palm until it nearly burned.

Kael was on his feet in an instant, sword half-drawn with a soft metallic hiss, his body positioned between the sound and his companions. "Show yourself," he commanded, voice low and dangerous, each word clipped and precise like a soldier calling formation.

The underbrush parted to reveal a slender figure—a young woman with pale blonde hair and delicate features that belied the determination in her eyes. She wore a simple tunic of faded blue, patched in several places, and a cloak that had seen better days. Most striking, however, were the intricate runes etched along her forearms, glowing faintly in the early morning light with a soft blue luminescence that cast strange shadows across her face.

"Peace," she said, hands raised to show she carried no weapons. Her voice was melodious but hesitant, as if she hadn't spoken aloud to another person in some time. "I mean no harm."

"That's what they all say right before the stabbing starts," Mira muttered, not releasing her vial. Lyra noticed it contained a swirling liquid the color of storm clouds, with tiny flashes of what looked like lightning dancing within. The glass clinked softly against Mira's rings as her fingers tightened around it. "Always with the 'I mean no harm' right before the harm happens. Terribly predictable, really."

The stranger's eyes flickered to the Phoenix Stone in Lyra's hands, then back to her face. "My name is Elara. I've been tracking the Stone's energy since yesterday. The pulse when you claimed it from the temple..." She paused, searching for words. "It resonated across all of Sylvanthia. Like... like a bell struck in perfect silence."

Kael's stance remained defensive. "You're a rune-caster," he observed, nodding toward the markings on her arms. His words emerged measured and even, a soldier's economy in every syllable.

"I am," Elara confirmed, her fingers unconsciously tracing one of the glowing runes on her forearm. "Or trying to be. My training was... interrupted when the Syndicate raided my village three years ago." A shadow passed over her face, grief momentarily eclipsing her composure. "I'm the only one who survived."

Lyra felt a pang of recognition. Another orphan of the Syndicate's cruelty, another life shattered by their ambition. The Stone in her hands shifted from crimson to a deep purple, responding to her mixture of suspicion and sympathy.

"Why seek us out?" she asked, not unkindly. "Why risk yourself?"

Elara reached into her cloak, moving slowly to avoid alarming them. The fabric rustled softly as she withdrew a small cloth bundle and carefully unwrapped it to reveal a fragment of amber crystal that glowed with the same inner light as the Phoenix Stone.

"Because I carry this," she said simply, her voice carrying a faint musical lilt that became more pronounced with emotion.

Lyra felt the Stone in her hands pulse in response, its warmth intensifying. A high, clear note—like crystal struck by silver—rang through the air, though none of them had touched anything that might make such a sound. The Stone's light reached out toward the fragment, tendrils of amber energy stretching across the space between them like seeking fingers.

She stood, taking a step toward Elara. "A fragment?"

Elara nodded. "It was my mother's. She was a Guardian of the Old Ways, keeper of lore about the Aethyr Order and their artifacts." Her words took on a rhythmic quality, almost like reciting poetry. "She died protecting this piece, telling me to run, to hide it from those who would misuse its power." Her voice wavered slightly. "I didn't understand then. I'm not sure I fully understand now, but when I felt the Stone's awakening yesterday, I knew I had to find you."

Kael hadn't relaxed his vigilance. "Convenient timing," he remarked, echoing Mira's earlier skepticism about his own appearance. His scarred fingers remained wrapped around his sword hilt, the leather of his grip creaking softly.

"Not convenience. Necessity," Elara replied, unconsciously echoing Kael's own words from days before. "The Stone calls to its fragments. It seeks to be whole again."

As if in confirmation, the Phoenix Stone flared brightly in Lyra's hands, sending a wave of warmth up her arms. The fragment in Elara's palm responded in kind, its light pulsing in perfect synchronization.

"Let her approach," Lyra said quietly to Kael. Something in her gut told her to trust this stranger, this fellow survivor.

Kael hesitated, then stepped aside, though his hand remained on his sword hilt. The subtle shift of his weight on the forest floor sent a few dried leaves skittering across the ground. Elara moved forward, her steps light and cautious, until she stood before Lyra.

"May I?" she asked, gesturing to the Stone. The scent of lavender and something like rain-washed stone emanated faintly from her skin.

Lyra nodded, extending her hands with the Stone resting on her palms. Elara placed her fragment beside it, and for a moment, nothing happened. Then, with a soft chime that seemed to vibrate through the air rather than sound within it, the fragment melded into the larger Stone, its edges flowing like liquid before solidifying once more. The Phoenix Stone glowed brighter, its inner fire more vibrant, more alive.

As the pieces joined, a rush of images flooded Lyra's mind—a village nestled in a valley, flames consuming thatched roofs, a woman with Elara's features pressing the fragment into a child's hands, urging her to run. The vision was so vivid, so immediate, that Lyra could smell the smoke, taste the ash in the air, and hear the distant screams. She gasped, staggering slightly.

"You saw it too," Elara whispered, her eyes wide. "My memories. The Stone... it's connecting us."

"It's becoming whole again," Lyra managed, still reeling from the intensity of the shared vision. "Just as the legends said."

"What legends?" Mira asked, finally coming to stand beside them, her curiosity overcoming her caution. Her boot heels scuffed against the forest floor as she approached. "What exactly does this thing do besides make pretty lights, share traumatic memories, and give everyone in Sylvanthia a magical homing beacon to our location? Not that I'm complaining about the light show, mind you—quite spectacular—but I prefer my magical artifacts with a side of 'not getting us killed.'"

Elara's gaze remained fixed on the Stone. "The Phoenix Stone was created by the Aethyr Order during the Great Sundering, when rifts began appearing across our world." Her voice took on that same rhythmic quality, as if reciting words passed down through generations. "It has the power to mend these rifts, to restore balance to places where reality has been... damaged." She looked up at Lyra. "But it was broken, its pieces scattered to prevent misuse. The Syndicate has been hunting these fragments for generations, believing that with the complete Stone, they could not just mend rifts but create them—open doorways to other realms, harness powers beyond mortal understanding."

"And your mother was protecting a piece," Lyra said softly. "Just like my parents."

Elara nodded. "Many families have guarded fragments over the centuries, passing them down through generations, moving constantly to stay ahead of the Syndicate. But in recent years, they've become more aggressive, more coordinated in their search."

"Why now?" Kael asked, his tactical mind already working through the implications. "What's changed?" His words emerged clipped and direct, each syllable precisely placed.

Elara's expression darkened. "The rifts are growing. There's one in particular, deep in the Shadowpeak Mountains, that's expanding faster than any recorded in our histories. If it continues unchecked, it could swallow entire regions of Sylvanthia." She hesitated, then added, her voice dropping to barely above a whisper, "And there are... whispers. Rumors of something trying to come through from the other side."

A chill ran down Lyra's spine that had nothing to do with the morning air. "Something like what?"

"The old texts speak of entities that exist between worlds—beings of immense power that were sealed away during the formation of our realm. If the rifts grow large enough..." Elara trailed off, leaving the implication hanging in the air between them.

The Phoenix Stone dimmed in response to Lyra's growing dread, its light receding until it glowed only faintly, like embers banking themselves against a long night.

"Well, that's just perfect," Mira said with forced cheerfulness, her words tumbling out faster than before. "Ancient horrors, world-ending rifts, and a magical rock that everyone wants to steal. And here I thought we were just running from garden-variety murderers." She pulled a small notebook from her pocket, flipping it open to reveal pages of alchemical formulas. The pages rustled crisply as she thumbed through them. "Looks like I need to adjust my brewing priorities. Less 'turn enemies different colors' and more 'banish interdimensional threats.' Though I was quite fond of that purple-skin formula. Made a fellow in Westmarket look like a plum for a week. Couldn't have happened to a more deserving fellow, mind you."

Despite the gravity of the situation, Lyra found herself smiling at Mira's irreverence. It was a gift, that ability to find humor in even the darkest moments. The Stone brightened slightly, responding to her brief moment of amusement.

"So what now?" Kael asked, practical as ever. His stance shifted, weight balanced evenly on both feet—a soldier ready for orders. "We have a fragment of the Stone. Elara has—had—another. How many more are there? And where do we find them?"

"Seven fragments in total," Elara replied, her voice taking on that lyrical quality again. "The number holds significance in the old magics—seven elements, seven realms, seven aspects of balance. With two now joined, five remain scattered."

"And let me guess," Mira interjected, twirling a lock of red hair around her finger, "you have no idea where they are. Typical magical quest nonsense. Always with the scattered pieces and the vague directions. Would it kill these ancient powers to leave a proper map? Or at least a list with checkboxes?"

Elara's cheeks colored slightly. "Not exactly. But the Stone itself can guide us. As it grows stronger, its ability to sense its missing pieces will improve." She turned to Lyra. "Especially in the hands of one it has chosen."

"Chosen?" Lyra echoed, the word settling uncomfortably on her shoulders. "I didn't—I mean, I just found it in the temple."

"The Stone doesn't allow itself to be 'just found,'" Elara said gently, her fingers brushing lightly against the Stone's surface. "It calls to those with the strength to bear its burden and the heart to use its power wisely. That it responds to you, that it shows you paths forward... these are not coincidences."

Lyra looked down at the Stone, its warm glow casting her face in amber light. The thought that it had chosen her, that she was somehow meant to carry this responsibility, was both terrifying and strangely comforting. All these years of searching for answers about her parents, feeling adrift and purposeless in their absence—had it all been leading to this moment?

As if sensing her uncertainty, the Stone's light pulsed in a steady, reassuring rhythm, like a heartbeat finding its strength after a moment of hesitation.

"If the Stone can guide us to the other fragments," Kael said, breaking into her thoughts, "then our path is clear. We find them before the Syndicate does, reassemble the Stone, and use it to seal the rifts." His words were precise and measured, laying out the mission parameters with military clarity.

"Simple as that?" Mira asked, arching an eyebrow. "Just traipse across Sylvanthia collecting magical trinkets while being hunted by murderous zealots? Should be a delightful stroll. Perhaps we'll have a picnic along the way. I do so enjoy dining with imminent death looming over my shoulder—adds a certain spice to the meal." She tucked her notebook away and began reorganizing the vials at her belt, the glass clinking softly as she muttered to herself about "inadequate explosive yield" and "need for wider dispersal patterns."

"No one said it would be simple," Kael replied evenly. "But it's necessary."

Lyra nodded, decision crystallizing within her. "Kael's right. If what Elara says is true, this is bigger than just our personal vendettas against the Syndicate. This is about protecting Sylvanthia itself." She looked at each of them in turn. "But I won't ask any of you to come with me. This is my burden to—"

"Oh, stop right there," Mira interrupted, rolling her eyes dramatically. "If you're about to give some noble speech about going it alone, save it. I've invested too much time keeping you alive to let you wander off on a suicide mission now." She patted a particularly large vial at her hip, the liquid within sloshing ominously. "Besides, I've been working on this beauty for months. It would be a shame not to use it on some deserving Syndicate agents. Turns their own shadows against them—quite poetic, really."

"The Stone has chosen you," Elara said, her melodic voice gentle but firm, "but that doesn't mean you must carry it alone. In fact, the old texts suggest that the Stone's power is amplified by bonds of trust and loyalty. It was never meant to be wielded by a solitary bearer."

As if to confirm this, the Stone brightened noticeably as they spoke of unity, its amber glow extending to touch each of them briefly before receding. The air filled momentarily with the scent of warm honey and summer herbs.

Kael nodded, his expression softening slightly. "Besides, you'd never make it past the first Syndicate patrol without me." The ghost of a smile touched his scarred lips, softening his usually stern countenance.

Lyra felt a lump form in her throat, gratitude welling up unexpectedly. "Thank you," she managed. "All of you."

"Don't thank us yet," Mira said with a wink, the glass of her vials clinking as she adjusted her belt. "Wait until we're actually being chased through the wilderness by those black-cloaked lunatics. You might change your tune. I know I will—probably to something with a lot of creative cursing. I've been working on some new combinations that would make a tavern brawler blush."

They broke camp quickly after that, gathering their meager supplies and erasing all signs of their presence. The smell of damp earth rose as they scattered the ashes of their fire, and the soft crunch of pine needles accompanied their movements. As Lyra shouldered her pack, the Phoenix Stone now secured in a pouch at her belt, she caught Elara watching her with an expression she couldn't quite read.

"Something wrong?" Lyra asked.

Elara hesitated, then shook her head. "No. It's just..." Her fingers traced a rune on her forearm, leaving a brief trail of blue light. "I've been alone since my village was destroyed. I never thought I'd find others who understood, who had lost as I had." A small smile touched her lips. "It feels like finding family again."

The words struck a chord in Lyra's heart. Family. Yes, that's what they were becoming—a makeshift, battered family forged in shared loss and common purpose.

"You're not alone anymore," she said simply, and was rewarded with Elara's smile widening, the sorrow in her eyes receding like shadows at dawn.

With Kael taking point, they set off deeper into Sylvanthia, the morning sun climbing higher as they walked. The forest around them hummed with life—birds calling from the canopy, small creatures rustling in the underbrush, insects buzzing in dappled patches of sunlight. The scent of pine grew stronger as they moved deeper into the woods, mingled with the occasional sweet burst of wild berries. Yet beneath this ordinary symphony, Lyra sensed something else—a subtle vibration in the air, a feeling of being watched by eyes older than the ancient trees themselves.

The Phoenix Stone pulsed warmly at her hip, as if in response to her awareness. She placed her hand over it, feeling its rhythm sync with her heartbeat, and found herself wondering what other secrets it held, what powers lay dormant within its amber depths, waiting to be awakened.

As if reading her thoughts, Elara fell into step beside her. "The Stone responds to intention and emotion," she said quietly, her words carrying that subtle musical cadence. "The stronger your connection to it grows, the more it will reveal of its abilities."

"Have you tried using the fragment you carried?" Lyra asked.

Elara nodded. "In small ways. It helped me sense energies, particularly those related to the rifts. Once, when Syndicate agents were close, it created a kind of... veil around me. They looked right at me but couldn't see me." She frowned slightly. "But it was never predictable. Sometimes it would respond to my needs, other times it remained dormant no matter how desperately I called to it."

"That's reassuring," Lyra said dryly.

"The complete Stone will be different," Elara assured her. "More stable, more responsive. Especially as you learn to channel its energies properly." She glanced at Lyra's face. "I could teach you some basics of energy manipulation—rune-casting techniques that might help you focus your connection."

"I'd appreciate that," Lyra said sincerely. The idea of having more control over the Stone's powers was appealing, especially given the dangers that lay ahead.

Mira, who had been walking a few paces behind them, quickened her step to join the conversation. Her boots made a distinctive pattern as she walked—two quick steps followed by a slightly longer stride, creating an odd, syncopated rhythm. "If we're sharing skills, I could teach you both a thing or two about alchemical defenses. I've developed some compounds that react specifically to Syndicate energy signatures." She grinned, her fingers dancing over the vials at her belt. "Makes for a very targeted explosion. Or implosion. Or occasionally a strange sideways-plosion that defies proper classification. That one was an accident, mind you, but quite effective at removing unwanted doors."

"Is everything an explosion with you?" Kael asked without turning around. His own footsteps were measured and even, almost silent despite his size.

"Not everything," Mira replied cheerfully, gesturing expansively. "Sometimes it's a controlled burn. Or a strategic melting. Or that one time I accidentally turned a man's hair into snakes—temporary, of course, and they weren't venomous. Mostly. I contain multitudes."

They walked in companionable silence for a while, the forest gradually thinning as they approached a ridge that overlooked a vast expanse of Sylvanthia. The scent of pine gave way to the sharper smell of sun-warmed stone and wild thyme growing between the rocks. When they reached the top, Lyra paused, breath catching at the view spread before them.

From this vantage point, the true scale of Sylvanthia revealed itself—endless forests in shades of emerald and jade, winding rivers glinting like silver ribbons in the sunlight, distant mountains purple against the horizon. The wind carried the mingled scents of a thousand different plants and the faint, sweet tang of distant rain. But what drew her eye was a disturbance in that perfect landscape—a patch far to the northeast where the natural colors seemed to warp and blur, as if that section of the world was slightly out of focus.

"A rift," Elara said quietly, following her gaze. "One of the smaller ones, but growing."

"It looks... wrong," Mira observed, squinting at the distant anomaly. "Like someone smudged a painting before the paint dried. Makes my teeth itch just looking at it, and I've seen some properly disturbing things. Created most of them, if I'm being honest."

"That's an apt description," Elara nodded. "Rifts are tears in the fabric of reality itself. What you're seeing is where our world begins to blend with... something else."

Kael studied the horizon with a tactician's eye. "How many of these rifts are there?" His voice remained level, but his hand tightened on his sword hilt, the leather creaking softly.

"At least a dozen that I know of," Elara replied. "Most are small, stable for now. But the one in the Shadowpeaks..." She pointed to the distant mountain range, though from this distance, no disturbance was visible. "That one is different. Older, deeper, and growing at an alarming rate."

"And the Stone can seal them?" Lyra asked, her hand moving unconsciously to the pouch at her belt.

"Yes, though its power is limited while fragmented. Each piece we recover will strengthen its ability to mend the rifts." Elara's expression grew somber. "But we must be cautious. The Syndicate believes the rifts can be controlled, harnessed as gateways rather than sealed. If they obtain the Stone before we complete it…"

"They'll tear the world apart trying to prove their theory," Kael finished grimly, his words clipped and precise.

"Precisely. And what might come through…" Elara hesitated, her voice dropping to a near-whisper that forced them to lean closer. "The texts describe Veyra as a being of pure will, neither good nor evil as we understand such concepts, but utterly alien in her perception of reality. She exists across multiple planes simultaneously, perceiving all possible futures at once. In her mind, our world is merely clay to be reshaped according to her vision—a vision that has no regard for the sanctity of individual lives or the natural order."

"The texts say she once walked among us," Elara continued, her voice taking on that rhythmic quality again. "A woman of impossible beauty and terrible purpose. Those who gazed upon her saw what they most desired, while she saw through them—past flesh, past bone, to the very essence of their being. She spoke in riddles that drove scholars mad and truths that broke the hearts of kings. And when she was finally bound, it's said she smiled—as if imprisonment was merely another path she had foreseen."

Mira whistled low, the sound cutting through the mountain air. "So basically a god with no moral compass and a penchant for interdimensional redecorating. Charming. Sounds like my great-aunt Betrilda, minus the dimensional powers. Though her redecorating was certainly horrifying enough."

"That's… one way to put it," Elara conceded, her lips twitching slightly. "The Aethyr Order managed to bind her once, at great cost. I doubt we could do so again without the complete Stone."

Lyra took a deep breath, the weight of their task settling more firmly on her shoulders. This was no longer just about avenging her parents or thwarting the Syndicate. It was about protecting Sylvanthia itself from threats both within and beyond their world.

"So where do we go first?" she asked, turning to Elara. "How do we find the next fragment?"

Elara gestured to the Stone at Lyra's belt. "Ask it. Let it guide you."

Feeling slightly self-conscious under their collective gaze, Lyra removed the Stone from its pouch. It sat warm and alive in her palm, its inner light pulsing gently. She closed her eyes, focusing on the question in her mind: *Where is the next fragment? Show us the path.*

For a moment, nothing happened. Then she felt the Stone grow warmer, its pulse quickening. When she opened her eyes, she saw that the light within had shifted, concentrating on one side of the Stone and extending outward like a beam pointing southwest.

"That way," she said, indicating the direction. "Toward the river valleys, I think."

Kael nodded, already calculating routes and potential dangers. "Two days' journey, if we maintain a good pace. The terrain is more open there—less cover, but easier travel." His words emerged measured and precise, a soldier plotting a campaign.

"Also easier for the Syndicate to spot us," Mira pointed out, her fingers dancing nervously over her vials. "But I suppose we can't be picky about where magical rock fragments decide to hide. Would be nice if just once they'd be in a pleasant meadow with a tavern nearby. Always with the dangerous, remote locations." She was already sorting through her vials, seemingly taking inventory of her arsenal. "I'll need to prepare some new compounds tonight. River valleys mean water, which changes the effective radius of most of my explosives. Water and fire have such a complicated relationship—rather like my parents, now that I think about it."

Elara studied the Stone's directional glow with interest. "The fragment must be calling strongly to be sensed from this distance. Perhaps it's in the hands of another guardian, like my mother was."

"Or it's a trap," Kael said bluntly, his stance shifting subtly into a more defensive posture. "The Syndicate could have obtained a fragment and is using it to lure us."

Lyra considered this possibility. It was certainly within the Syndicate's methods to use such bait. "Either way, we need to find it," she decided. "We'll just approach with caution."

With their direction set, they began the descent from the ridge, following a narrow game trail that wound through scrubby underbrush and scattered boulders. The day grew warmer as the sun climbed higher, and Lyra found herself grateful for the occasional patches of shade offered by towering pines. The scent of sun-warmed stone gave way to the sharper smells of wild herbs crushed underfoot as they made their way down the slope.

They had been walking for perhaps an hour when Kael suddenly raised his hand, signaling for them to stop. He dropped into a crouch, motioning for the others to do the same. The soft crunch of their footsteps on the rocky trail ceased abruptly.

"What is it?" Lyra whispered, crouching beside him. Her heart hammered in her chest, loud enough that she worried the others might hear it.

"Tracks," he replied softly, pointing to marks in the soft earth of the trail. "Fresh. Not animal." His voice had dropped to barely above a whisper, each word delivered with careful precision.

Lyra studied the footprints. They were clearly human—booted feet that had pressed deeply into the soil, suggesting someone of considerable weight or carrying heavy equipment. The pattern indicated a purposeful stride, not the wandering path of a lost traveler.

"Syndicate?" she asked.

Kael nodded grimly. "Most likely. A scout, judging by the spacing and depth. Moving fast, traveling light."

"How far ahead?" Mira asked, her hand already reaching for one of her vials. Gone was her usual torrent of words, replaced by focused intensity.

"Not far. The soil is still settling in the deepest prints." Kael's scarred face was set in hard lines as he scanned the trail ahead. "They're moving in the same direction we are."

"That can't be coincidence," Elara murmured, her runes glowing faintly as she sensed for magical energies. The blue light cast strange shadows across her delicate features. "The Stone's awakening must have alerted them. They're seeking the same fragment we are."

"Then we need to move faster," Lyra said, determination hardening her voice. "We can't let them reach it first."

Kael held up a cautioning hand. "Rushing blindly will only get us killed. We need to be smart about this." He studied the terrain ahead, his tactical mind working through options. "The trail forks about half a mile ahead. One path follows the ridge, more exposed but faster. The other cuts through the valley, more cover but slower going."

"The valley," Elara suggested, her fingers tracing a rune in the air that briefly shimmered before fading. "I can create concealment runes to mask our passage. It won't fool them for long, but it might give us enough of an advantage."

Kael nodded in agreement. "Valley it is. Stay close, move quietly, and be ready for anything." His words emerged clipped and precise, a commander issuing orders.

They proceeded with heightened caution, Kael leading the way with his hand never far from his sword hilt. Mira followed, uncharacteristically silent, though the tension in her shoulders betrayed her readiness to act. Elara moved with surprising grace for someone who had spent years in isolation, her steps light and sure. Lyra brought up the rear, the Phoenix Stone a warm presence against her hip, its pulse quickening as if sensing the danger ahead.

When they reached the fork in the trail, Elara knelt briefly, tracing runes in the dirt with her finger. The markings glowed blue, then sank into the earth, spreading outward like ripples in a pond before fading from sight. The air briefly carried the scent of ozone and rain-washed stone.

"Concealment and misdirection," she explained softly as she stood, her melodic voice barely above a whisper. "Anyone following our trail will be drawn to the ridge path instead."

They descended into the valley, where the air grew cooler and damper, heavy with the scent of moss and rich soil. The canopy thickened overhead, dappling the ground with shifting patterns of light and shadow. Birds called to one another in the branches, their songs creating a natural symphony that would help mask the sounds of their passage.

For nearly an hour, they moved in tense silence, each lost in their own thoughts as they navigated the increasingly dense undergrowth. The soft squelch of damp earth beneath their boots and the occasional rustle of leaves against their clothing were the only sounds they made. Lyra found her mind returning to her parents, wondering if they had made similar journeys in their quest to protect the Phoenix Stone fragment they guarded. Had they felt this same mixture of determination and dread? Had they known the true scale of what they were fighting against?

Her reverie was broken by Kael's sudden halt. He raised his fist—the signal to freeze—and dropped into a crouch, his other hand drawing his sword in one fluid motion. The soft metallic rasp of steel leaving its sheath seemed unnaturally loud in the forest's hush. The others followed suit, crouching low among the ferns that filled the air with their earthy, green scent.

Ahead, barely visible through the trees, a figure moved along the valley floor. Even at this distance, the black cloak and purposeful stride were unmistakable—Syndicate.

"Just one?" Mira whispered, her voice barely audible, none of her usual verbose energy present in the face of danger.

Kael shook his head slightly. "Never just one," he murmured back, each word precise and measured. "Where there's a scout, others follow."

As if confirming his words, two more figures emerged from the trees further ahead, joining the first. They conferred briefly, gesturing in different directions before splitting up again, clearly searching the area in a coordinated pattern.

"They know we're here," Elara breathed, her face pale. "My runes should have diverted them. Unless..."

"Unless they have a rune-caster of their own," Lyra finished the thought. "Someone who can sense the Stone's energy directly."

The implications were troubling. If the Syndicate had recruited individuals with talents similar to Elara's, their ability to track the Stone—and by extension, Lyra's group—would be significantly enhanced.

As they watched, one of the agents removed his hood, revealing a face that made Kael tense beside her. The man was perhaps in his forties, with a shaved head and a distinctive scar that ran from his left temple to his jaw, pulling his mouth into a permanent sneer. He carried himself with an air of authority, his movements precise and controlled.

"Dravus," Kael whispered, his voice tight with suppressed fury. "The Butcher of Blackthorn Pass."

The forest seemed to still around them, as if the very trees held their breath. Even the birds had fallen silent, sensing the presence of predators in their midst. The Phoenix Stone grew hot against Lyra's hip, responding to the rising tension. A breeze stirred the leaves overhead, sending dappled shadows dancing across the forest floor, momentarily illuminating the three Syndicate agents as they continued their methodical search.

In that moment, Lyra understood with perfect clarity that their journey had truly begun—and that the path ahead would test them in ways they couldn't yet imagine. The Stone at her hip pulsed with a steady, determined rhythm, as if making a promise of its own: that whatever challenges awaited, they would face them together.

CHAPTER THREE

Temporal Currents

Night had fallen by the time they reached the abandoned mill. The ancient structure loomed against the star-scattered sky, its weathered timbers creaking in the gentle breeze that carried the scent of river water and damp earth. Moonlight silvered the dilapidated water wheel, now motionless in the stream that had once powered it, the current whispering secrets around its moss-covered paddles.

"Charming," Mira muttered, eyeing the sagging roof with professional skepticism. "Nothing says 'safe haven' quite like a building that's one strong sneeze away from collapsing. Should we check for murderous wildlife, or shall we assume they've already claimed the best sleeping spots?"

They'd spent the remainder of the day evading the Syndicate agents, following Rowan's lead through a maze of overgrown game trails and shallow stream crossings that left their boots squelching and their nerves frayed. The cartographer had proven his worth, his knowledge of the valley's hidden paths allowing them to put considerable distance between themselves and their pursuers.

"The structure is sounder than it appears," Rowan said, his voice low but confident as he adjusted the resonance compass on his wrist. The device emitted a soft blue glow, its multiple dials shifting subtly as he turned. "I've used it as a waypoint before. The main supports are stone, and the roof leaks only in the eastern corner."

Kael circled the perimeter, his movements economical and silent, sword still drawn. "Single entrance. Defensible. Windows high and narrow." His assessment came in clipped fragments, the cadence of a soldier evaluating terrain. "Could do worse."

"High praise indeed," Mira quipped, already rummaging through her pack. The glass vials at her belt clinked softly against one another. "I'll set up some alarms along the approach. Nothing explosive—well, nothing *very* explosive—just enough to give us warning if our black-cloaked friends decide to pay a midnight visit."

Elara's runes glowed faintly in the darkness as she traced patterns in the air, her melodic voice barely audible as she murmured incantations. "I can strengthen the concealment wards. They won't hold against a determined search, but they might buy us the night."

Lyra felt the Phoenix Stone pulse against her hip, its warmth a counterpoint to the evening chill. Removing it from its pouch, she found its amber light had taken on a subtle blue tinge, and its surface rippled like water when she turned it in her hands.

"It's responding to the nearby fragment," Elara observed, finishing her rune-casting and coming to stand beside Lyra. The faint scent of lavender and rain-washed stone accompanied her. "The Water Fragment must be close."

"How close?" Lyra asked, watching the blue patterns swirl within the Stone's depths.

"A few hours' journey, perhaps less," Rowan answered, studying his compass with narrowed eyes. The contraption clicked softly as its needles aligned. "The old watchtower stands at the confluence of three rivers. The locals call it Timekeeper's Tower." He glanced up, his expression thoughtful. "They say the water flows differently there—sometimes backward, sometimes not at all. Time plays tricks on those who linger too long."

"Temporal anomalies," Elara nodded, her fingers unconsciously tracing the rune for 'flow' on her forearm. "The Water Fragment doesn't just control the movement of water—it influences the flow of time itself, in limited ways."

"Wonderful," Mira said, returning from her perimeter check. "Because what this adventure really needed was time distortion. As if murderous zealots and interdimensional horrors weren't enough." Despite her words, her eyes gleamed with curiosity. "Though I have to admit, the alchemical applications are fascinating. I've been experimenting with compounds that accelerate or decelerate reactions, but they're wildly unstable. Nearly lost my eyebrows last month."

"Your eyebrows seem to live in a perpetual state of peril," Kael remarked dryly, finally sheathing his sword with a soft metallic whisper.

"The price of innovation, my scarred friend," Mira replied, tapping her temple. "Can't make history without breaking a few facial features."

They settled into the mill's interior, clearing debris from the stone floor to make space for their bedrolls. The air inside smelled of dust and old wood, with undertones of river silt and something sweeter—wild honeysuckle growing through a gap in the wall. Rowan built a small, carefully shielded fire in what remained of the hearth, the flames casting dancing shadows across the weathered walls.

As they shared a meager meal of dried meat and hard bread, Lyra studied their newest companion. Rowan moved with a scholar's deliberation, each action precise and considered. Yet there was an underlying tension to him, a vigilance that suggested he'd learned hard lessons about survival. The wound in his side clearly pained him, though he made no complaint as he adjusted his position to ease the pressure.

"Your compass," she said, nodding toward the device on his wrist. "You designed it yourself?"

Rowan glanced down, a flicker of pride crossing his features. "Yes. Took three years to perfect. The crystalline matrix at its center is attuned to rift energies—it can distinguish between different types of tears and measure their relative strength." His voice took on the enthusiastic cadence of a lecturer as he continued. "The rifts don't just distort space; they create ripples in time as well. Areas near major rifts experience temporal fluctuations—moments that stretch or compress, events that repeat or happen out of sequence."

"You've seen this happen?" Kael asked, his skepticism evident in his tone.

Rowan nodded, his expression sobering. "I was mapping the Silvermere Rift last year when I witnessed a village experience the same sunrise three times in succession. The villagers didn't notice—to them, it was simply morning, every time. But I was outside the effect's radius." He tapped his compass. "This protected me somehow. When I returned a month later, the village was gone. Not destroyed—there was no debris, no signs of violence. Just... gone, as if it had never existed."

A heavy silence followed his words, broken only by the soft crackle of the fire and the distant hooting of an owl.

"The rifts are growing more unstable," Elara said finally, her melodic voice tinged with worry. "The barriers between realms are thinning."

"Which is why we need to find the remaining fragments," Lyra said, her hand moving unconsciously to the pouch containing the Stone. "Starting with the Water Fragment tomorrow."

"About that," Mira interjected, leaning forward. The firelight caught the copper highlights in her red hair, making it seem as though flames danced there. "If we're heading into a place where time might decide to do a little dance, shouldn't we have some sort of... I don't know, buddy system? A way to make sure we all come out the same age we went in?"

"The Stone should provide some protection," Elara offered. "Its purpose is to stabilize reality, after all."

"And my compass has shielded me before," Rowan added. "I can adjust it to extend its influence, though I'm not certain how effective it will be for a group."

"Wonderful," Mira sighed. "So our protection against time distortion is 'maybe this will work' and 'it helped me once.' Very reassuring." She began sorting through her vials, muttering to herself. "Need to modify the duration stabilizer... perhaps a temporal anchor compound..."

Kael, who had been silent for some time, suddenly spoke. "Dravus won't give up easily." His scarred fingers tightened around the hilt of his sheathed sword, the leather grip creaking softly. "He's... persistent."

"You know him well," Lyra observed, noting the tension in Kael's jaw.

"Too well." His words emerged clipped and hard. "He led the ambush at Blackthorn Pass. Twelve of us guarding the mountain route. Thirty of them came at dawn." His eyes fixed on the fire, seeing something beyond the flames. "They didn't just kill my patrol. They made it slow. Made me watch each death."

The silence that followed was heavy with the weight of unspoken horror.

"Why let you live?" Rowan asked quietly.

"To spread the word. To be their message." Kael's hand moved unconsciously to the scar that ran from his temple to his jaw. "Dravus believes in making examples. In leaving witnesses who are... marked." His voice had taken on a distant quality, as though part of him remained trapped in that bloody pass. "He enjoys his work. Takes pride in it. Considers it an art."

"I've seen his handiwork," Elara whispered, her fingers tracing a protective rune that briefly flared blue in the darkness. "In my village. He... collects trophies."

Mira's usual torrent of words had dried up, her expressive face uncharacteristically still. "Then we'll just have to disappoint him," she said finally, her voice soft but fierce. "I've got something special brewing for our friend Dravus. Something he won't see coming until it's too late."

"We should rest," Lyra said, recognizing the darkness gathering in Kael's eyes. "Tomorrow will test us all."

They arranged their bedrolls in a rough circle around the fire, with Kael volunteering for first watch. As the others settled, Lyra found herself staring up at the gaps in the roof, watching stars wheel slowly overhead. The Phoenix Stone rested against her chest, its gentle pulse synchronizing with her heartbeat, its warmth seeping through the fabric of her tunic.

Sleep proved elusive. Her mind churned with all they had learned—about the rifts, about Veyra, about the Stone itself. The responsibility settled heavily on her shoulders, a weight she wasn't certain she could bear. Her parents had carried a fragment of this burden, and it had cost them their lives. What would the complete Stone demand of her?

"You're thinking too loudly," came Elara's soft voice from nearby. The rune-caster had propped herself up on one elbow, her pale hair silvered by moonlight. "I can practically hear the wheels turning."

Lyra smiled faintly. "Sorry. Just... processing."

"It's overwhelming, isn't it?" Elara's melodic whisper carried just far enough for Lyra to hear. "Finding yourself at the center of something so vast."

"Did you ever imagine this?" Lyra asked. "When you were guarding your fragment, did you think about what it might mean to find the others?"

Elara was quiet for a moment, her delicate features thoughtful in the dying firelight. "I didn't dare to hope," she admitted finally. "For years, survival was enough. Finding food, staying ahead of the Syndicate, preserving what little knowledge I had." Her fingers absently traced a rune on her forearm, leaving a faint trail of blue light. "But the fragment... it dreamed of being whole again. Sometimes I would feel its longing, like a song just beyond hearing."

The Phoenix Stone warmed against Lyra's chest, as if responding to Elara's words.

"And now?" Lyra asked.

"Now I have purpose beyond survival." Elara's smile was small but genuine. "And I'm not alone anymore. Neither are you."

Lyra nodded, grateful for the simple truth in those words. Whatever challenges lay ahead, she wouldn't face them by herself. That knowledge, more than anything else, allowed sleep to finally claim her.

Dawn arrived with tendrils of mist rising from the river, wreathing the abandoned mill in ghostly white. The air tasted of dew and earth, with undertones of wild mint growing along the riverbank. Birds called to one another in the surrounding trees, their songs muffled by the fog.

Lyra woke to find Rowan already up, kneeling by the stream with his resonance compass extended over the flowing water. The device emitted a soft blue glow, its dials turning with tiny clicks as he adjusted various settings.

"What are you doing?" she asked, coming to stand beside him. The grass was wet beneath her boots, soaking the leather with morning dew.

"Calibrating," he replied without looking up. "Water carries echoes of time's passage. By measuring the resonance patterns in the current, I can get a more accurate reading on the fragment's location." His fingers moved with practiced precision over the intricate mechanisms. "The temporal distortions are stronger this morning. We're getting close."

The Phoenix Stone seemed to agree. When Lyra removed it from its pouch, she found its amber glow suffused with swirling patterns of blue, like currents moving beneath its surface. It felt cooler than usual against her palm, and strangely fluid, as though it might slip through her fingers despite its solid form.

"Fascinating," Elara said, joining them by the water's edge. Her runes glowed faintly in the morning light. "It's already responding to the Water Fragment's influence."

"Is that good or concerning?" Lyra asked, watching the blue patterns shift and flow within the Stone.

"Both, perhaps," Elara admitted. "It means the fragment is powerful and relatively intact. But it also means the temporal distortions will be stronger as we approach."

Mira emerged from the mill, her red hair wild from sleep but her eyes alert. She carried a small metal contraption that resembled a pocket watch, though its face displayed not numbers but alchemical symbols. "Morning, fellow adventurers into temporal doom," she greeted, her words tumbling out in their usual rapid cadence. "I've modified my reaction timer to detect time fluctuations. Should give us some warning if minutes start deciding to last hours or vice versa. Probably. Unless time distorts the warning itself, in which case we're back to being hopelessly unprepared. But at least we'll be stylishly hopelessly unprepared."

Kael appeared last, his movements betraying no sign of the night's interrupted sleep. He scanned their surroundings with practiced vigilance, his scarred face impassive. "We should move," he said simply. "Daylight's wasting."

They broke their fast quickly with the last of their provisions, then set off along the river path with Rowan leading the way. The mist clung to them as they walked, beading on their cloaks and dampening their hair. The world beyond arm's length was reduced to vague shapes and muted colors, lending an otherworldly quality to the familiar landscape.

"The tower stands at the meeting of three rivers," Rowan explained as they walked, consulting his compass periodically. "The locals avoid it. They say time flows strangely there—fishermen cast their lines and return home to find years have passed, or children wander too close and emerge with gray in their hair."

"Folk tales often contain kernels of truth," Elara observed. "Especially regarding places of power."

"In this case, more than kernels," Rowan replied. "My measurements show significant temporal distortion around the tower. The effect seems to fluctuate—sometimes barely noticeable, other times severe enough to create visible anomalies."

"Such as?" Kael asked, his hand never straying far from his sword hilt.

"Water flowing uphill. Birds frozen mid-flight. Seasons changing in the span of hours." Rowan's voice held the clinical detachment of a scholar, though his eyes betrayed a deeper fascination. "I once observed a sapling grow, mature, die, and decay in the space of a day, only to repeat the cycle again."

"Lovely," Mira muttered, checking her modified pocket watch. "And we're walking straight toward this temporal nightmare because...?"

"Because the alternative is letting the Syndicate get there first," Lyra reminded her. "And we've seen what they do with power."

The mist began to thin as morning advanced, revealing more of the valley around them. The river widened, its current quickening as it was joined by smaller tributaries. The vegetation grew lusher along the banks—willows trailing their branches in the water, beds of river iris unfurling purple blooms, tangles of wild grapevine climbing over fallen logs.

By midday, they reached a point where the main river split around a small island. Rowan halted, studying his compass with a frown.

"Something's wrong," he said, tapping the device. "The readings are... fluctuating. As if the fragment is moving."

"Could the Syndicate have reached it already?" Kael asked, his hand moving to his sword.

"Possible, but unlikely," Rowan replied. "The temporal distortions would slow them considerably without proper protection."

Elara closed her eyes, her runes glowing brighter as she extended her senses. "I feel... echoes," she said slowly, her melodic voice taking on a distant quality. "As if the fragment exists in multiple places simultaneously."

"A side effect of the time distortions?" Lyra suggested.

"Perhaps," Elara conceded. "Or perhaps the Water Fragment's nature allows it to exist in multiple moments at once."

Mira's modified pocket watch began to emit a soft, rhythmic clicking. She studied it with raised eyebrows. "According to this, we're experiencing time at approximately 1.3 times the normal rate. Which explains why I'm suddenly starving despite breakfast being only—" she checked the device again, "—four hours ago. Huh. Felt shorter."

"We need to be careful from here," Rowan warned, adjusting his compass. "The distortions will grow stronger as we approach the tower. Stay close, and if anyone experiences anything unusual—disorientation, memory lapses, physical changes—tell the others immediately."

They proceeded with heightened caution, following the river's course as it curved around a stand of ancient willows. The air grew heavier, charged with an energy that made the hairs on Lyra's arms stand on end. Sounds seemed to reach them from a great distance—bird calls elongated into eerie, drawn-out notes, the rush of the river slowing to a deep, resonant rumble.

The Phoenix Stone pulsed against Lyra's chest, its rhythm no longer matching her heartbeat but following some other pattern, ancient and alien. When she touched it through her tunic, images flashed through her mind—water flowing backward, trees ungrowing from ancient trunks to saplings, clouds racing across the sky in reverse.

"There," Kael said suddenly, pointing ahead.

The mist parted to reveal their destination. The Timekeeper's Tower rose from a small island at the confluence of three rivers, its weathered stone gleaming dully in the midday sun. It stood perhaps five stories tall, its circular design reminiscent of ancient observatories. Windows spiraled around its circumference, following the path of an interior staircase. At its summit, a domed chamber caught the light, the glass panels reflecting blue and gold.

But it was the water surrounding the tower that drew their attention. The three rivers met in a perfect circle around the island, their currents flowing not outward but inward, creating a perpetual whirlpool that somehow never drained. More strangely still, portions of the water moved at different speeds—here rushing in a torrent, there barely creeping forward, elsewhere seeming to stand perfectly still like glass.

"The Heart of Amber," Elara breathed, her eyes wide with wonder. "The Water Fragment."

As they watched, the quality of light around the tower shifted, as if clouds passed overhead—but the sky remained clear. Shadows lengthened and shortened in the space of seconds, creating the impression of days passing in moments.

"How do we cross?" Lyra asked, eyeing the unnatural currents with apprehension.

"There used to be a bridge," Rowan said, consulting his notes. "But it collapsed decades ago. Or will collapse soon. The records are... contradictory."

"Temporal confusion affecting historical documentation," Elara suggested. "Events become difficult to place in linear sequence near powerful time distortions."

Mira had been unusually quiet, studying the water with narrowed eyes. Now she stepped forward, removing a vial from her belt. The liquid inside was clear but seemed to catch the light oddly, bending it around the glass. "I might have something for this. Been working on a compound that stabilizes reaction rates regardless of external conditions. Theoretically, it should create a temporary path of normalized time through the distortion field."

"Theoretically?" Kael echoed, one eyebrow raised.

"Well, I haven't exactly had the opportunity to test it in a time-warped whirlpool before," Mira admitted, her fingers already working to uncork the vial. "But the principles are sound. Probably. It's either this or we try swimming through water that might age us fifty years or turn us into infants."

"I vote for the experimental potion," Rowan said quickly.

"Seconded," Elara agreed.

Mira grinned, a flash of teeth in her freckled face. "Excellent! Stand back, everyone. This might get a bit... reactive."

She approached the water's edge, her movements suddenly precise and controlled—a stark contrast to her usual animated gestures. With careful deliberation, she poured the clear liquid in a line along the riverbank. The compound hissed as it contacted the earth, releasing a faint mist that smelled of ozone and something sweeter, like honey left too long in the sun.

For a moment, nothing happened. Then the mist began to spread outward, forming a bridge of fog that extended across the whirlpool toward the island. Where it touched the chaotic currents, the water calmed, flowing at a normal, consistent rate.

"It's working!" Mira exclaimed, genuine surprise coloring her voice. "I mean, of course it's working. Exactly as I calculated. Definitely didn't expect it to explode."

"How long will it last?" Kael asked, eyeing the misty bridge with professional assessment.

"Based on the reaction rate and ambient conditions..." Mira consulted her modified pocket watch, tapping its face thoughtfully. "Accounting for temporal dis tortion... somewhere between ten minutes and several centuries. But I'd aim for the lower estimate to be safe."

"Reassuring as always," Lyra said with a faint smile. "I'll go first."

Before anyone could object, she stepped onto the bridge of mist. It felt surprisingly solid beneath her boots, though she could see the water flowing normally just inches below. The Phoenix Stone pulsed strongly against her chest, its blue-tinged light visible even through the fabric of her tunic.

"It's holding," she called back. "Come across one at a time."

Kael followed immediately, his hand on his sword hilt, eyes scanning for threats. Elara came next, her runes glowing brighter as she crossed the boundary into the distortion field. Rowan hesitated only briefly before joining them, his compass whirring frantically as he navigated the bridge. Mira came last, muttering calculations under her breath as she carefully placed each foot.

They reached the island without incident, though Lyra noticed with concern that the misty bridge was already beginning to dissipate behind them. The ground beneath their feet felt solid enough, covered in short, silvery grass that seemed to ripple even when no wind blew. Ancient willow trees grew in a circle around the tower's base, their branches moving in slow, deliberate patterns, as if stirred by currents rather than air.

"The fragment is inside," Elara said with certainty, her eyes fixed on the tower. "I can feel it calling to the Stone."

Lyra nodded, feeling the pull herself—a tugging sensation centered on the Phoenix Stone, urging her forward. As they approached the tower's entrance, she noticed strange markings carved into the stone archway—symbols that resembled flowing water but shifted subtly when viewed directly, reorganizing themselves into new patterns.

"Time-script," Rowan breathed, his scholarly enthusiasm momentarily overcoming his caution. "I've only seen fragments in ancient texts. It's a language that exists in multiple temporal states simultaneously, conveying different meanings depending on when it's read."

"What does it say?" Mira asked, squinting at the shifting symbols.

"It's... difficult to translate precisely," Rowan admitted. "Something about guardians and worthy seekers. And a warning about 'those who would bend time to their will rather than flow within its currents.'"

"Sounds like the Syndicate," Kael observed grimly.

The entrance stood open, revealing a spiraling staircase that wound upward through the tower's interior. No doors barred their way, no obvious traps presented themselves. Only the persistent strangeness of time's flow around them suggested danger—shadows that moved independent of their sources, dust motes that hung suspended in air for minutes before suddenly racing upward in a flurry, the sound of their footsteps sometimes preceding their movements.

"The fragment will be at the top," Elara said. "In the domed chamber."

"Too easy," Kael muttered, his soldier's instincts clearly troubled by the lack of obvious defenses.

"Perhaps time itself is the guardian," Rowan suggested. "The distortions would disorient most seekers, possibly trap them in temporal loops or accelerate their aging until they crumbled to dust."

"That's... not comforting," Mira remarked, checking her pocket watch again. "According to this, time is flowing at roughly 0.7 normal speed inside the tower. But it's fluctuating wildly—spikes of acceleration followed by near-stasis."

"The Stone will help stabilize us," Lyra said, more confidently than she felt. "And Rowan's compass. And your device, Mira. Between them, we should be protected."

"Should be," Mira echoed with a nervous laugh. "Two experimental devices and a magical rock against the fundamental forces of reality. I like those odds. Actually, I've gambled on worse."

They began their ascent, the spiral staircase winding ever upward through the tower's heart. The interior walls were lined with more of the shifting time-script, interspersed with mosaics depicting flowing water in all its forms—rivers, oceans, rainfall, mist. But the water in the images moved, flowing continuously in hypnotic patterns.

As they climbed, the temporal distortions grew more pronounced. Lyra experienced moments where her companions seemed to move in slow motion, their voices deepening to impossible bass notes, followed by bursts of acceleration where they blurred around her. The Phoenix Stone grew warmer against her chest, its pulse steadying her when disorientation threatened to overwhelm her senses.

Halfway up the tower, they encountered their first real obstacle. The staircase simply vanished for a section of perhaps ten feet, leaving a gap in the spiral. Below, the stone floor was visible, impossibly distant despite being only three stories down.

"What happened to the stairs?" Mira asked, peering cautiously over the edge.

"They haven't been built yet," Rowan said, studying his compass. "Or they've already crumbled. This section of the tower exists in multiple timeframes simultaneously."

"So how do we cross?" Kael asked, practical as ever.

Elara stepped forward, her runes glowing brightly as she studied the gap. "I think..." she began, her melodic voice thoughtful, "the stairs are still there, just not in our now." Her fingers traced patterns in the air, leaving trails of blue light. "If I can align our perception with the right moment..."

The runes flared brilliantly, then settled into a steady glow. As Lyra watched, the missing section of staircase seemed to fade into view—transparent at first, then gradually solidifying until it appeared as substantial as the rest of the structure.

"Quickly," Elara urged, strain evident in her voice. "I can't hold the temporal alignment for long."

They hurried across the manifested stairs, the stone feeling strangely insubstantial beneath their feet, like walking on packed snow that might give way at any moment. As soon as they reached the other side, Elara released her spell with a gasp, and the stairs faded from view once more.

"That was remarkable," Rowan said, genuine admiration in his voice. "Few rune-casters can manipulate temporal perception with such precision."

Elara managed a tired smile. "My mother taught me the basics before..." She trailed off, then straightened her shoulders. "The fragment is close now. I can feel it."

Indeed, the Phoenix Stone had grown almost painfully warm against Lyra's skin, its blue-tinged light now bright enough to shine through her clothing like a beacon. The air around them felt charged with potential, as if reality itself had grown thin, malleable.

They continued their ascent, passing windows that sometimes showed daylight, sometimes star-filled night, sometimes strange auroras that painted the sky in impossible colors. The tower seemed to exist in all seasons and times at once, a nexus point where temporal laws broke down.

Finally, they reached the uppermost chamber. The domed ceiling soared above them, its glass panels filtering sunlight—or moonlight, or starlight, as the sky outside shifted continuously through its cycles. The circular room was empty save for a pedestal at its center, upon which rested a pool of what appeared to be liquid crystal, contained by no visible barriers yet maintaining its perfect circular shape.

"The Water Fragment," Elara breathed.

Unlike the solid amber of the Phoenix Stone, this fragment existed in liquid form—a pool of flowing light that shimmered with inner radiance. Blues and silvers predominated, but other colors moved within its depths—flashes of gold, ripples of green, currents of deepest purple. It didn't merely reflect light; it seemed to capture time itself, holding moments suspended in its crystalline surface.

As they approached, Lyra saw images forming in the liquid—reflections not of the chamber around them, but of other places, other times. A verdant Sylvanthia untouched by rifts. The same landscape scarred by chaos. Cities rising and falling in the span of seconds. The birth and death of stars.

"It's beautiful," Mira whispered, her usual torrent of words reduced to simple wonder.

"And dangerous," Kael added, his practical nature reasserting itself. "We should secure it quickly."

Lyra stepped forward, drawing the Phoenix Stone from its pouch. It flared brilliantly in response to the Water Fragment's proximity, its amber light now shot through with swirling blue currents. She extended it over the liquid pool, feeling a powerful resonance build between the two pieces—a harmony that vibrated through her bones and sang in her blood.

"They recognize each other," Elara said softly. "Parts of a whole, seeking reunion."

The liquid began to rise from its pedestal, defying gravity to reach toward the Stone in Lyra's hand. It moved with purpose, with awareness, shaping itself into a spiraling column that twisted and flowed like a living thing. When it touched the Phoenix Stone, a chime rang out—pure and perfect, a note that seemed to reset the chaotic timeflows around them.

For one breathless moment, everything stabilized. The shifting light steadied into ordinary afternoon sunshine. The disorienting sense of multiple timeframes collapsed into a single, linear now. In that clarity, Lyra saw the liquid fragment flow into the Phoenix Stone, merging with it completely. The Stone pulsed once, brilliantly, then settled into a steady glow—amber now permanently infused with currents of blue.

"Three fragments joined," Elara said with quiet triumph. "Four remain."

The moment of temporal stability shattered as a slow handclap echoed through the chamber. They whirled to find the staircase entrance no longer empty.

Dravus stood there, flanked by Sybil and Mortimer. The Syndicate commander's scarred face was twisted in a smile that never reached his cold eyes.

"Impressive work," he said, his voice smooth and cultured, at odds with his brutal reputation. "Navigating the temporal maze, retrieving the fragment... you've saved us considerable trouble." He stepped forward, his movements precise and controlled. "Now, if you'll hand over the Stone, we can conclude our business with minimal bloodshed."

Kael's sword rasped free of its sheath, the sound sharp in the sudden silence. "The only business we'll conclude is unfinished," he growled, his scarred face hardening into a mask of cold fury.

Dravus's gaze flicked to him, recognition dawning. "Ah, the survivor of Black-thorn Pass. Still carrying my marks, I see." His smile widened fractionally. "I'm pleased my work endures."

"You'll create no more 'works,'" Kael replied, his voice deadly quiet.

Sybil stepped forward, her flame-red hair bound in a severe braid, her twin daggers already drawn. "Five against three," she observed, her voice a silken purr. "Hardly seems fair." Her eyes, cold as winter frost, fixed on Elara. "I remember you, little rune-caster. You ran while your village burned. I've saved a special place in my collection for your bones."

Mortimer remained silent, but his pale hands began to trace patterns in the air, sickly green runes forming in opposition to Elara's blue ones. The air between them shimmered with conflicting energies.

"The Stone, girl," Dravus said, returning his attention to Lyra. "Give it to us now, and perhaps I'll allow your friends quick deaths. Resist, and..." He shrugged eloquently. "Well, I'm known for my creativity."

Lyra felt the Phoenix Stone pulse against her palm, warm and alive with the power of three fragments. Its light spilled between her fingers, illuminating her face with amber and blue radiance. In that moment, she felt something shift within her—a certainty, a purpose that burned away doubt.

"The Stone stays with us," she said, her voice steady and clear. "And so does Sylvanthia's future."

Dravus sighed, a sound of theatrical disappointment. "As you wish." He nodded to his companions. "Take them."

The chamber erupted into chaos. Kael lunged toward Dravus, his blade a silver arc in the shifting light. Sybil darted forward, daggers flashing as she targeted Elara. Mortimer's green runes flared, sending a wave of disruptive energy across the room.

But something unexpected happened. As the Syndicate agents attacked, the temporal distortions—momentarily stabilized by the fragments' joining—reasserted themselves with violent intensity. The tower shuddered, and time fractured around them.

Lyra saw Kael's blade move both impossibly fast and agonizingly slow, existing in multiple positions simultaneously. Mira reached for her vials in a blur of acceleration, then froze mid-motion for several heartbeats before continuing. Elara's defensive runes expanded outward in pulsing waves that seemed to bend the very fabric of reality around them.

The Phoenix Stone burned in Lyra's hand, responding to the danger with a surge of power that coursed through her veins like liquid fire. Instinctively, she raised it high, and the combined fragments pulsed with blinding intensity.

"Time," she commanded, though she hadn't planned the word. It simply emerged, powered by the Stone's will as much as her own.

The effect was immediate and dramatic. The chaotic temporal distortions coalesced around the Syndicate agents, enveloping them in swirling currents of blue-tinged light. Dravus's face contorted in surprise and rage as his movements slowed to an excruciating crawl. Sybil's daggers hung suspended mid-strike, while Mortimer's runes dissolved into meaningless fragments.

"What's happening?" Mira gasped, her hands still clutching her defensive vials.

"The Water Fragment," Elara breathed, her runes glowing in harmony with the Stone's light. "It's responding to Lyra's command—controlling the flow of time around our enemies."

"It won't hold them forever," Rowan warned, his compass spinning wildly as it tried to measure the localized temporal anomaly. "The distortion is already beginning to destabilize."

Indeed, Lyra could feel the strain through her connection to the Stone. The power required to maintain such precise control over time was immense, draining the fragments' combined energy at an alarming rate.

"We need to go," she said, already backing toward the stairs. "Now, while they're contained."

They fled down the spiral staircase, the tower shuddering around them as temporal currents clashed and rebounded. Behind them, they heard Dravus's enraged roar as he began to break free of the time-lock, the sound distorted and stretched like an echo from a nightmare.

The island itself seemed to be unraveling as they raced across it, the unnatural whirlpool surrounding it churning with increased violence. Trees aged and unaged in rapid cycles, grass withered and bloomed beneath their feet, and the very air tasted of ozone and possibility.

"The bridge is gone!" Mira shouted as they reached the shore, pointing to where her misty creation had completely dissipated.

Lyra clutched the Stone tightly, feeling the Water Fragment's essence swirling within it. Understanding bloomed in her mind—not knowledge, exactly, but intuition guided by the fragment's nature.

"Join hands," she commanded, extending her free hand to Kael beside her. "And whatever happens, don't let go."

As they formed their circle, Lyra raised the Stone once more and focused on the churning waters. "Part," she whispered.

The whirlpool stilled, then divided, creating a path of dry land across to the opposite shore—like ancient tales of seas parting before worthy travelers. Without hesitation, they ran across, the waters towering on either side, held back by the Water Fragment's power.

They had barely reached the far bank when the Stone's energy faltered. The waters crashed together behind them with a thunderous roar, and from the tower came the distant sound of furious pursuit.

But they were across, alive, and the Phoenix Stone—now pulsing with the power of three united fragments—glowed with triumphant light against Lyra's palm.

CHAPTER FOUR

Dreams Between Worlds

T he morning after their escape from the Syndicate agents, they made camp by a small tributary of the main river. Dawn arrived with hesitant fingers of light that pried through the canopy, dappling the forest floor with gold. A

fine mist clung to the water's surface, giving the clearing an otherworldly quality as it swirled and eddied with each breath of wind.

Lyra sat at the water's edge, the Phoenix Stone resting in her open palm. Its light had changed since absorbing the Water Fragment—the amber glow now interlaced with currents of blue that shifted and flowed beneath its surface like tides responding to an invisible moon. When she tilted it, the blue light rippled in ways that defied the Stone's solid form.

"It's beautiful," Elara said, settling beside her. The rune-caster's movements were graceful but cautious, as though she carried an invisible weight. Her blue eyes reflected the Stone's light as she studied it. "The fragments are beginning to harmonize."

Lyra nodded, feeling the Stone's warmth pulse against her skin. "It feels.. . stronger. More alive somehow."

"Three fragments joined," Elara confirmed, her melodic voice tinged with wonder. "The Stone is remembering what it once was."

"And what exactly was that?" Mira called from where she knelt by their small cook fire. The alchemist was stirring a pot of something that smelled surprisingly appetizing, given their limited provisions. Her red hair was pulled back in a messy knot, revealing the sharp angles of her face. "Besides a fancy light show and time-bending paperweight, I mean."

Elara's lips curved in a small smile. "The Phoenix Stone was the Aethyr Order's masterwork—a focus for stabilizing reality itself. When the rifts first began appearing, the Order created the Stone to mend them."

"But they broke it," Kael interjected. He sat on a fallen log, methodically sharpening his sword with smooth, practiced strokes. The whetstone's rasp provided a rhythmic counterpoint to the morning birdsong. "Why shatter something so powerful?"

"To prevent misuse," Elara explained. "The Stone doesn't just mend rifts—it can control them. In the wrong hands, it could tear reality apart rather than heal it."

Rowan looked up from his maps, interest sharpening his features. He'd been unusually quiet since their escape from the tower, his focus divided between his charts and the resonance compass strapped to his wrist. The device had been clicking softly all morning, its needles twitching as it registered distant rift energies.

"That's what the Syndicate wants, isn't it?" he asked, setting aside his mapping tools. "Not to destroy the Stone, but to use it."

"Yes," Elara confirmed. "They believe the rifts are doorways to power—paths to realms where reality bends to will rather than natural law."

"And Veyra waits in one of those realms," Lyra added quietly, remembering Elara's earlier description of the ancient entity.

A solemn silence fell over the camp, broken only by the gentle burble of the stream and the soft hiss of Mira's cooking pot.

"Well," Mira said finally, her voice deliberately bright, "nothing builds an appetite quite like contemplating interdimensional horrors before breakfast. Food's ready, by the way."

They gathered around the fire, accepting the bowls Mira handed out. The stew was simple—dried meat and foraged roots softened in river water—but the alchemist had added something that gave it a rich, earthy flavor that bloomed on the tongue.

"This is... surprisingly good," Kael admitted after his first cautious spoonful.

Mira grinned, the expression transforming her sharp features into something almost impish. "Just because I specialize in things that go boom doesn't mean I can't appreciate the subtler arts. Besides, my third favorite uncle was a royal cook before he accidentally poisoned a duke. Honest mistake—the mushrooms looked very similar."

"Your family sounds fascinating," Rowan remarked dryly, though a genuine smile softened his usually serious expression. He'd set his compass beside him as he ate, and Lyra noticed how his eyes kept returning to it, checking its readings with the attentiveness of a parent monitoring a sleeping child.

"Oh, they were. Entirely mad, of course, but never boring." Mira's smile dimmed slightly. "The Syndicate wiped out our entire village when I was fifteen. Something about 'dangerous alchemical experimentation.' Which, to be fair, wasn't entirely wrong."

The casual way she mentioned such tragedy struck Lyra anew. Each of them carried similar wounds—families destroyed, homes lost, lives shattered by the Syndicate's ruthless pursuit of power. Yet here they sat, sharing a meal in the morning light, finding moments of warmth amid the danger.

"The Water Fragment," Lyra said, returning to more immediate concerns. "What can it do, exactly? I felt something when we faced Dravus and the others—like I could control the flow of time around them."

Elara nodded. "The Water Fragment governs flow in all its forms—rivers, blood, time itself. With it joined to the Stone, you can influence temporal currents to a limited degree."

"Limited how?" Lyra asked.

"Distance, duration, precision," Elara explained. "The closer you are to your target, the more control you'll have. And maintaining temporal alterations drains the Stone's energy quickly."

"So I can't just freeze all our enemies in time indefinitely," Lyra concluded.

"Unfortunately not," Elara confirmed. "Though what you managed in the tower was impressive for a first attempt."

"Speaking of the tower," Kael interjected, "we should discuss our next move. The Syndicate knows we have three fragments now. They'll be hunting us with everything they have."

Rowan spread his map on the ground between them. It was a remarkable piece of craftsmanship—the terrain rendered in exquisite detail, with crystal markers embedded at key points, connected by threads of silver that caught the morning light. Various colored lines overlaid the physical features, representing what he had called "rift energies."

"You made this yourself?" Lyra asked, impressed by the map's intricacy.

Rowan nodded, a hint of pride breaking through his reserve. "Cartography is more than just recording what exists," he explained, his voice warming with enthusiasm. "It's about understanding the relationships between places—how they connect, how they influence each other." His fingers traced one of the silver threads that linked two crystal markers. "These represent energy flows between rifts. The Syndicate believes these connections are random, but they're not."

"You've found a pattern," Elara said, studying the map with new interest.

"Yes," Rowan confirmed. "The rifts aren't just tears in reality—they're forming a specific configuration. I believe they're components of a larger structure, though I haven't determined its purpose yet."

"That's... unsettling," Mira remarked, leaning closer to examine the pattern.

"Based on the Stone's guidance before we reached the Timekeeper's Tower, I believe the next fragment lies here," Rowan continued, pointing to a region in the northwest. "The Cloudspire Mountains."

"Air Fragment," Elara said immediately. "It would make sense—after earth and water, air would be the next element in the traditional sequence."

"What does the Air Fragment do?" Mira asked, leaning forward with interest.

"It governs breath, wind, sound—all things that move through air," Elara explained. "And thought itself, in some texts."

"Thought?" Lyra echoed.

"Ideas flow like currents in the mind," Elara said. "The Air Fragment can influence these currents—enhance perception, clarify thought, even cloud judgment if used... improperly."

"Mind control?" Kael asked sharply, his hand tightening on his sword hilt.

"Not exactly," Elara hastened to clarify. "More like... suggestion. Amplifying existing thoughts rather than creating new ones."

"Still sounds dangerous," Kael muttered.

"All power is dangerous," Rowan observed quietly. "That's why the Stone was broken in the first place." He carefully rolled up his map, securing it with a leather cord. "I've been tracking these patterns for years. My parents were scholars who studied the rifts—they believed the Syndicate's approach was fundamentally flawed. That the rifts should be understood, not exploited."

"What happened to them?" Lyra asked gently, recognizing the past tense.

Rowan's expression clouded. "The Syndicate happened. They refused to share their research, so..." He shrugged, the gesture failing to mask his pain. "I've been continuing their work ever since. Trying to understand what they died to protect."

"And now you're helping us find the fragments," Lyra said. "Why?"

"Because my parents believed the Stone was the key to stabilizing the rifts, not widening them." Rowan met her gaze steadily. "And because I've seen what happens when the rifts grow unchecked. Whole regions swallowed, reality itself warping beyond recognition. If the Syndicate succeeds..." He shook his head. "There won't be a world left to save."

Lyra studied the map, tracing the path from their current position to the Cloud-spire Mountains. "How far?"

"A week's journey, perhaps more," Rowan replied. "The terrain grows difficult as we approach the mountains, and my compass indicates increasing rift activity in that region."

"Meaning more temporal distortions?" Mira asked.

"And spatial ones," Rowan confirmed. "The rifts don't just affect time—they warp space as well. Distances become unreliable, paths shift, landmarks appear and disappear."

"Wonderful," Mira sighed. "Just when I thought magical quests couldn't get more complicated."

"We should leave soon," Kael said, rising to his feet. "Dravus won't stay trapped in that tower for long."

As if summoned by his words, a distant sound reached them—the crack of branches breaking underfoot, voices calling to one another through the trees. The peaceful morning shattered like glass.

"Syndicate scouts," Kael hissed, hand flying to his sword.

"How did they find us so quickly?" Mira demanded, already gathering her vials.

"The Water Fragment," Elara realized, eyes widening. "Its energy signature is distinctive—especially after joining with the Stone. They must be tracking it."

Lyra felt the Stone pulse against her palm, its blue-tinged light brightening as if in response to the threat. "Can we mask it somehow?"

"Not completely," Elara said, her fingers already tracing runes in the air. "But I can dampen its signature temporarily."

Blue light flowed from Elara's fingertips, weaving around the Stone in Lyra's hand. The glow dimmed, the swirling currents within slowing to a gentle ripple.

"It won't last long," Elara warned, her voice strained from the effort. "A few hours at most."

"Long enough to put some distance between us and them," Kael decided. "Pack quickly. Leave no trace."

They moved with practiced efficiency, dousing the fire, gathering their meager belongings, obscuring signs of their presence. Within minutes, they were moving through the forest, Kael taking point with Rowan close behind, consulting his compass to guide them northwest toward the Cloudspire Mountains.

The forest grew denser as they traveled, ancient trees crowding together, their massive roots creating natural barriers that forced the group to weave a circuitous path. Moss hung from branches in pale green curtains, and the air grew thick with the scent of damp earth and growing things.

"We're entering the Verdant Deep," Rowan explained quietly as they navigated around a particularly massive trunk. "One of the oldest forests in Sylvanthia. The trees here are said to remember the time before the rifts."

"Trees don't remember anything," Mira pointed out. "They're trees."

"Don't be so certain," Elara countered. "The oldest living things often hold wisdom we can't comprehend."

As if in response to her words, the quality of light around them shifted subtly. The dappled sunlight filtering through the canopy took on a greenish hue, and the shadows between the trees seemed to deepen. The forest sounds—birdsong, rustling leaves, the scurry of small creatures—faded to a hushed murmur.

"Does anyone else feel like we're being watched?" Mira whispered, her usual flippancy replaced by genuine unease.

Lyra nodded, feeling the weight of unseen eyes. The Stone in her pouch had grown cooler against her hip, its pulse slowing as if in response to their surroundings. The sense of presence was overwhelming—not hostile, but ancient and alien, observing them with patient curiosity.

"The forest is aware of us," Elara confirmed softly. "We're walking through its thoughts."

"That's... disturbing," Mira muttered.

"Be respectful," Rowan advised, his expression solemn but his eyes alight with scholarly fascination. "The Verdant Deep doesn't welcome those who harm it, but it has been known to aid travelers who show proper reverence."

"My parents brought me here once," he added, voice dropping to barely above a whisper. "I was very young, but I remember how the trees seemed to bend toward them, as if listening to their words." A faint smile touched his lips. "They were studying how the ancient forests responded to the rifts—whether they had developed natural defenses against the distortions."

"And had they?" Elara asked.

Rowan nodded. "The oldest forests exist in a state of... equilibrium with the rifts. Neither fully accepting nor rejecting them, but accommodating their presence while maintaining their own integrity."

"How exactly does one show reverence to a forest?" Mira asked, returning to the more immediate concern.

"By listening," Elara said simply. "By acknowledging its presence."

Lyra found herself slowing her pace, her awareness expanding to embrace the ancient trees around them. The watching presence grew stronger, pressing against her consciousness like cool water. Without thinking, she reached for the Phoenix Stone, drawing it from its pouch.

The Stone's light had changed again—the blue currents now interwoven with threads of deep green that pulsed in rhythm with the forest's breathing. When she held it up, the light spilled between her fingers, casting emerald shadows across her companions' faces.

"Earth Fragment," Elara breathed, her eyes widening. "It's responding to the forest."

"But we don't have the Earth Fragment yet," Rowan pointed out.

"No, but the Stone remembers what it once was," Elara explained. "The forest's ancient earth-energy is awakening that memory."

The watching presence intensified, focusing on the Stone in Lyra's hand. She felt a gentle pressure in her mind—not invasive, but questioning. Without knowing quite how, she understood what was being asked.

"It wants to know why we're here," she said softly. "What we seek."

"Can you answer it?" Elara asked.

Lyra nodded, closing her eyes and focusing on the Stone's warmth. She pictured their journey—the fragments they sought, the rifts they hoped to mend, the Syndicate's dark purpose. She opened her mind to the watching presence, offering these thoughts freely.

For a long moment, nothing happened. Then a sigh seemed to pass through the entire forest, a whisper of leaves and creaking branches that surrounded them completely. The pressure in Lyra's mind eased, replaced by a sense of... acceptance. Not quite approval, but acknowledgment of their purpose.

"I think it's going to let us pass," she murmured.

As if confirming her words, the path ahead seemed to widen slightly. Branches that had blocked their way bent aside, roots that had created obstacles sank back into the earth, and the quality of light brightened, illuminating a clear route through the densest part of the forest.

"Well," Mira said after a moment of stunned silence, "that's certainly useful. Though still deeply unsettling."

They continued their journey, the forest seeming to guide their steps. The watching presence remained, but it felt protective now rather than merely curious. The trees themselves appeared to shift subtly as they passed, creating natural barriers behind them that would slow any pursuers.

"The forest is hiding our trail," Rowan observed, his compass whirring softly as it registered the unusual energy patterns around them. "But it won't stop the Syndicate completely. They have ways of forcing paths through even the most resistant terrain."

"What do you mean?" Lyra asked, troubled by his qualification.

Rowan's expression darkened. "They use corrupted flows—energies twisted from their natural state. I've seen what happens to forests they pass through. The trees... die, but not cleanly. They become warped, poisoned from within."

"You've witnessed this?" Elara asked.

He nodded grimly. "Near the Shadowpeak Rift. An entire valley of ancient oaks, transformed into something that was neither alive nor dead. The wood itself seemed to... bleed when cut."

The image sent a chill through Lyra. The Stone pulsed against her palm, as if sharing her distress.

"So the forest is buying us time," Kael concluded, ever practical, "but we shouldn't waste it."

They pressed on, the Verdant Deep continuing to ease their passage while subtly hindering any who might follow. By midday, they reached a small clearing where a spring bubbled up from between moss-covered stones, forming a clear pool before continuing on as a narrow stream.

"We should rest here," Kael decided, surveying the clearing with a soldier's eye. "Refill our water, eat something. The forest may be aiding us, but we still have a long journey ahead."

As they settled by the spring, Lyra felt the watching presence recede slightly, giving them privacy while maintaining its protective vigilance at the clearing's edge. She knelt by the pool, dipping her hands into the cool water. It felt extraordinarily refreshing, washing away the fatigue of their hurried flight.

"The water here is special," Elara noted, joining her at the pool's edge. "See how it glimmers?"

Indeed, the water seemed to catch the light in unusual ways, tiny motes of gold and silver dancing beneath its surface. When Lyra cupped some in her palm, it felt somehow more substantial than ordinary water, almost like liquid silk against her skin.

"Earth and water in harmony," Elara explained. "This spring draws from the deepest roots of the forest, carrying nutrients and energies most waters lack."

"Is it safe to drink?" Mira asked, eyeing the glimmering liquid with professional interest.

"More than safe," Elara assured her. "It's restorative."

They filled their waterskins and drank deeply from the spring. The water tasted of minerals and something sweeter—like the essence of growing things distilled into liquid form. Lyra felt its effects immediately, a renewed vitality flowing through her limbs, clearing the fog of fatigue from her mind.

"That's remarkable," Rowan said, examining his compass with fresh clarity. "I feel like I've slept for a full night."

"The forest is providing for us," Elara said. "A gift for those it deems worthy."

They ate a simple meal of dried fruit and hard bread, supplemented by edible mushrooms Elara identified growing at the clearing's edge. The food, combined with the spring water, restored their strength completely.

"We should be able to reach the forest's edge by nightfall," Rowan said, consulting his map. "From there, it's three days to the foothills of the Cloudspire Mountains."

"And the Syndicate?" Kael asked, his practical mind always returning to the threat.

"The forest is hindering them," Elara said with quiet confidence. "I can sense its efforts. Paths that open for us close behind us, roots rise to trip their feet, branches lower to block their way."

"But as Rowan said, they have methods to force their way through," Lyra added, unwilling to underestimate their pursuers. "We should assume they're still following, just... delayed."

"A forest after my own heart," Mira remarked with a grin. "Creative obstruction is an art form. But Lyra's right—the Syndicate is nothing if not persistent. Especially Dravus." She glanced at Kael, whose expression had hardened at the name. "He has a reputation for never abandoning a hunt."

"It's not just reputation," Kael said, his voice low. "I've seen his persistence first-hand. At Blackthorn Pass, he tracked my patrol for three days before the ambush. Never resting, barely eating. Like a man possessed."

"What drives someone to such extremes?" Elara wondered.

"Belief," Rowan answered unexpectedly. "The Syndicate elite truly believe in what they're doing. They see themselves as saviors, not destroyers."

"You've had close encounters with them before," Lyra realized, noting the personal knowledge in his tone.

Rowan nodded, absently adjusting his compass. "I was infiltrating one of their research outposts when they captured me. They didn't immediately recognize me as an enemy—thought I was just another scholar they could recruit." His expression grew distant. "I spent two weeks among them, listening to their plans, their philosophies. They speak of the rifts as 'purifying fires' that will cleanse Sylvanthia of weakness and usher in a new age of power."

"How did you escape?" Mira asked.

A shadow crossed Rowan's face. "I didn't. Not alone. There was another prisoner—an old man who created a diversion. He..." Rowan swallowed hard. "He didn't make it out."

The clearing fell silent, each of them absorbing yet another reminder of the stakes they faced.

They continued their journey through the afternoon, the forest continuing to guide their path. The watching presence remained, occasionally drawing their attention to useful things—patches of edible berries, shortcuts through dense undergrowth, signs of game animals nearby. It felt less like being observed and more like being accompanied by a silent, ancient companion.

As the day waned, the trees began to thin, and the quality of light changed from the green-tinged glow of the deep forest to the warmer gold of approaching sunset. Ahead, they could see the forest's edge, where the ancient trees gave way to rolling hills covered in tall grass that rippled like water in the evening breeze.

"We've reached the boundary," Rowan confirmed, checking his compass. "The Verdant Deep ends here."

Lyra paused at the forest's edge, turning back to face the ancient trees. The watching presence had grown stronger again, pressing against her consciousness with a final message. Without words, she understood its meaning—a warning, a blessing, and a promise all at once.

"It says the path ahead holds danger," she translated for the others. "But it will remember us if we return this way."

"A valuable ally," Kael acknowledged, inclining his head toward the forest with unexpected respect.

"Thank you," Lyra said simply to the watching presence, knowing it would understand.

A final sigh passed through the trees, branches swaying in a wind that touched nothing else. Then the presence receded, returning to its ancient dreaming, though Lyra sensed it would remain vigilant against those who followed their trail.

"Will the Syndicate be able to force their way through?" she asked Rowan as they prepared to leave the forest's shelter.

He considered the question, studying the tree line with a critical eye. "Eventually, yes. But it will cost them. Time, energy, perhaps even lives if they're careless. The Verdant Deep doesn't yield easily to corruption."

"So we have a lead, but not safety," Kael summarized. "All the more reason to move quickly."

They stepped from the forest's shelter into the open grasslands beyond. The sudden exposure felt both liberating and vulnerable after the protective canopy of the Verdant Deep. The hills rolled away before them, golden in the setting sun, offering clear sightlines but little cover.

"We should find a defensible position for the night," Kael suggested, scanning the landscape with practiced eyes. "Somewhere with a water source and natural barriers."

"There," Rowan said, pointing to a rocky outcropping perhaps a mile distant. "My maps show a small lake on the far side, fed by a stream coming down from the mountains. The rocks will provide shelter from the wind and eyes."

They set off across the grasslands, the tall grasses whispering around their legs as they walked. The openness of the landscape made Lyra uneasy after the forest's protection, but the Phoenix Stone remained cool and quiet in its pouch, suggesting no immediate danger.

They reached the outcropping as the last light faded from the sky, revealing a formation of weathered boulders that created a natural windbreak. Beyond, as Rowan had promised, lay a small lake, its surface a perfect mirror reflecting the first stars appearing overhead.

"This will do," Kael decided, already assessing the best positions for watch.

They made camp in the shelter of the rocks, building a small, well-shielded fire that would be invisible from a distance. The night air carried a chill that hadn't been present in the forest, and they huddled gratefully around the flames.

"The concealment spell on the Stone is weakening," Elara noted, studying the pouch at Lyra's hip where blue light was beginning to seep through the leather. "I should renew it before we sleep."

Lyra nodded, removing the Stone and placing it in Elara's outstretched hands. The rune-caster's fingers traced delicate patterns over its surface, blue light flowing from her fingertips to wrap around the Stone like a veil. The Stone's glow dimmed again, its pulsing energy muted beneath Elara's spell.

"That should hold until morning," Elara said, returning the Stone to Lyra. The effort had left her slightly pale, fine lines of fatigue etched around her eyes.

"You should rest," Lyra told her, concerned. "You've used a lot of energy today."

Elara nodded, offering a tired smile. "The forest's gift helped, but rune-casting still takes its toll."

"I'll take first watch," Kael volunteered, as he always did. "Mira second, Rowan third. Lyra and Elara need rest more than we do."

No one argued with his assessment. They arranged their bedrolls in the shelter of the rocks, close enough to the fire for warmth but positioned so that the flames wouldn't ruin their night vision. One by one, they settled into sleep, leaving Kael sitting alert at the camp's edge, his sword across his knees, his scarred face turned toward the grasslands they had crossed.

Lyra found sleep elusive despite her fatigue. The Stone's muted presence against her chest seemed to pulse with a restless energy, and her mind refused to quiet. After tossing for nearly an hour, she finally drifted into uneasy slumber.

Her dreams were vivid and strange—she stood in a vast chamber of smooth stone, its walls inscribed with flowing script that shifted and changed as she watched. At the chamber's center hovered the completed Phoenix Stone, radiant with power, its light containing all the colors she had seen and others beyond naming.

A figure stood opposite her, veiled in shadow despite the Stone's brilliance. Though she couldn't see its face, she sensed it smiling.

"So close now," it said, its voice neither male nor female but something else entirely, resonating not in her ears but in her mind. "You've done well to bring three fragments together."

"Who are you?" Lyra asked, though she suspected she already knew.

"I am what waits beyond," the figure replied. "I am what the Syndicate seeks to unleash, what your precious Stone was created to contain."

"Veyra," Lyra breathed.

The figure inclined its head, the gesture somehow both graceful and terrifying. "A name your kind gave me, yes. One of many."

"What do you want?"

"Want?" The figure seemed amused. "I want what all beings want—to be free. To fulfill my purpose."

"Which is?"

"Change," Veyra said simply. "Transformation. The breaking of old patterns to make way for new ones."

"You mean destruction," Lyra countered.

"Such limited thinking," the figure sighed. "Destruction and creation are the same force viewed from different perspectives. A forest fire destroys, yes, but it also clears the way for new growth. I am that fire."

"The rifts you've created are tearing our world apart," Lyra argued.

"Your world was stagnant," Veyra replied. "Trapped in cycles of suffering and petty power. I offer release from those cycles."

"Through chaos."

"Through transformation," the figure corrected. "Pain is inevitable in any birth."

Lyra felt the dream-Stone pulse in response to her emotions—anger, fear, and underneath it all, a disturbing hint of understanding. "The Syndicate thinks you'll grant them power if they free you."

Veyra's laugh was like glass breaking, beautiful and dangerous. "The Syndicate are children playing with forces beyond their comprehension. They see only what they wish to see."

"And what should I see?" Lyra challenged.

The figure stepped closer, and though its features remained in shadow, Lyra felt its gaze boring into her. "The truth that your Order tried to bury—that containment is not the answer. Control is not the answer. The rifts exist because they must exist. They are pressure valves for a reality that would otherwise shatter completely."

"You're lying," Lyra said, but uncertainty colored her voice.

"Am I?" Veyra asked softly. "Ask your Stone. It knows the truth, even if you do not."

The dream-Stone pulsed in response, its light flickering with conflicting energies—amber, blue, and something darker that swirled at its core.

"The fragments seek reunion," Veyra continued. "But ask yourself this—why was the Stone broken in the first place? What truth was the Aethyr Order hiding?"

Before Lyra could respond, the dream began to dissolve, the chamber fading around her, Veyra's presence receding like mist before the sun.

"We will speak again," the figure promised as it vanished. "When you are ready to hear the truth."

Lyra woke with a violent start, a cry caught in her throat. The dream clung to her like cobwebs, Veyra's words echoing in her mind with disturbing clarity. Her heart hammered against her ribs, and cold sweat dampened her skin despite the night's chill.

The camp was quiet, the fire burned down to embers that cast a faint red glow over her sleeping companions. Mira sat at the watch position now, her back straight, head turning at Lyra's sudden movement.

"Bad dream?" the alchemist asked quietly, concern evident in her usually flippant voice.

Lyra nodded, struggling to calm her racing pulse. "Very."

Mira studied her face in the dim light, then patted the rock beside her. "Come sit. I've got about an hour left on my watch anyway, and you look like you could use the company."

Grateful for the invitation, Lyra joined her, drawing her cloak tighter against the pre-dawn chill. The Stone in its pouch felt unusually heavy against her chest, as if the dream had affected it too.

"Want to talk about it?" Mira asked after a moment of companionable silence.

"I dreamed of Veyra," Lyra said, the name still unsettling on her tongue. "The entity trapped beyond the rifts."

Mira's eyebrows rose. "That's... concerning."

"She—it—said things that I can't stop thinking about," Lyra continued, the dream's details still vivid in her mind. "About the rifts being necessary. About the Stone."

"Well, of course it would say that," Mira pointed out reasonably. "Imprisoned entities generally aren't fans of whatever's keeping them locked up."

"I know," Lyra sighed. "But it made me wonder—why was the Stone broken in the first place? Elara said it was to prevent misuse, but what if there was more to it?"

Mira considered this, her clever face thoughtful in the dying firelight. "You could ask her when she wakes. Or Aelion, when we find him again. He seems to know more about the Stone's history than he's telling."

Lyra nodded, though the dream's unsettling questions continued to circle in her mind. "Veyra said we'd speak again."

"That's definitely concerning," Mira said firmly. "Though perhaps not surprising, given what you're carrying." She nodded toward the Stone. "Three fragments now. Maybe that's enough for it to reach through to you somehow."

"Maybe," Lyra agreed, the thought both disturbing and plausible.

They sat in silence for a while, watching the eastern sky lighten with the first hint of dawn. Finally, Mira spoke again, her voice uncharacteristically serious.

"Whatever Veyra told you—whatever it's trying to make you believe—remember one thing: we've seen what the Syndicate does in its name. Villages destroyed, people enslaved or killed, lands corrupted." Her green eyes were fierce in the growing light. "If that's the 'transformation' it's offering, I'll pass."

Lyra managed a small smile, grateful for Mira's straightforward perspective. "You're right."

"Usually am," Mira agreed, her usual flippancy returning. "One of my many charming qualities. Along with my stunning good looks and talent for making things explode in specifically useful ways."

The sky continued to brighten, stars fading as deep blue gave way to paler shades streaked with pink and gold. Around them, the camp stirred—Kael waking instantly alert as always, Elara rising with quiet grace, Rowan blinking sleepily as he reached for his compass.

"No sign of pursuit during the night," Mira reported as they gathered around the rekindled fire. "Seems your forest friend kept its word."

"The Verdant Deep is not easily traversed by those it deems unwelcome," Elara confirmed, her hands cupped around a steaming mug of herbal tea. "The Syndicate will find their path... complicated."

"Good," Kael said. "That gives us time to reach the Cloudspire Mountains. With luck, we can secure the Air Fragment before they catch up to us."

They broke camp efficiently, eating a quick breakfast of dried fruit and the last of their bread. The lake provided fresh water to refill their skins, and Mira took the opportunity to replenish some of her alchemical supplies, collecting samples of the unusual mineral deposits that ringed the water's edge.

"These will make excellent catalysts," she explained, carefully storing crystalline fragments in labeled vials. "Might even stabilize that temporal displacement compound I've been working on."

"Just try not to turn us all into infants," Kael requested dryly.

"No promises," Mira replied cheerfully. "Though I think you'd make an adorable baby. All scowly and serious."

Kael's only response was a long-suffering sigh that suggested he was well accustomed to Mira's teasing.

With their preparations complete, they set off across the grasslands, heading northwest toward the distant peaks of the Cloudspire Mountains. The morning was clear and cool, the sun warm on their backs as they walked. After the close confines of the forest, the open landscape felt liberating, though Lyra remained alert for signs of pursuit.

By midday, dark clouds had gathered over the mountains ahead, and the wind had taken on a biting edge that cut through their cloaks. Thunder rumbled in the distance, and flashes of lightning illuminated the cloud banks from within.

"That storm looks serious," Mira observed, eyeing the approaching weather with professional interest. "And it's moving fast."

"Too fast," Elara agreed, her expression troubled. "And look at the pattern of the lightning."

Lyra studied the storm more carefully and saw what had caught Elara's attention. The lightning wasn't striking randomly—it was forming distinct patterns, almost like writing scrawled across the sky in brilliant white.

"That's not a natural storm," Rowan concluded, his compass whirring frantically in response to the atmospheric disturbance.

"The Air Fragment," Elara suggested. "It must be responding to our approach, just as the Water Fragment did."

Lyra felt the Stone grow warm against her chest, its concealment spell weakening as it responded to the distant call of its missing piece. Veyra's words from her dream echoed in her mind: "The fragments seek reunion."

"Or someone's using it against us," Kael countered grimly, his hand moving to his sword hilt.

CHAPTER FIVE

Shadows at the Gate

T he air grew colder with each step toward the Shadow Syndicate's domain. A biting chill slipped through the seams of Lyra's cloak, sinking deep into her bones. The land itself seemed to resist their presence, its breath carrying a warning etched in frost.

Lyra and her companions pressed forward through the desolate expanse, their boots crunching against brittle, frost-rimmed earth. Each crack sliced through the stillness—a defiant testament to their presence in a world that seemed to recoil from life itself.

The landscape before them was a grim tableau. Twisted trees stood like sentinels, their leafless branches clawing at a sky perpetually shrouded in gray. The ground stretched barren and forsaken, cracked soil littered with jagged shards of stone. Above, dense clouds swallowed the sun's feeble light, casting an eerie pallor that leached color from the world.

"We're entering their territory now," Kael said quietly, his breath fogging in the frigid air. "Everything changes from here."

Lyra nodded, feeling the Phoenix Stone's warmth pulse against her chest, a fragile tether to hope amidst the suffocating gloom. Its faint golden glow seeped through her worn leather pack, a quiet defiance against the pervasive cold.

Her companions flanked her, their presence a steady reassurance against the tension coiling in her gut. Kael led the way, his broad shoulders squared against the biting wind, his dark eyes scanning the horizon with a warrior's vigilance. Mira followed close behind, her red hair a defiant blaze cutting through the muted landscape. Elara walked with quiet grace, her pale eyes sharp with resolve despite her delicate frame. Rowan studied his tattered map with scholarly focus, muttering bearings under his breath. Alaric brought up the rear, his silver hair catching what little light penetrated the gloom, his ancient gaze missing nothing.

"How much farther?" Lyra asked, pulling her cloak tighter against a sudden gust of wind.

Rowan consulted his map, the parchment crackling in the cold. "Three days, perhaps four, depending on the terrain. The Syndicate's stronghold lies at the heart of this wasteland."

"Wonderful," Mira muttered. "A leisurely stroll through a frozen hellscape. Just how I wanted to spend my week."

Despite her words, Lyra noticed how Mira's fingers kept returning to a small brass pendant half-hidden beneath her collar—a talisman from her mother, the only possession she'd managed to save when the Syndicate destroyed her village. The alchemist only touched it when truly anxious, though she'd deny it if anyone pointed it out.

"And the barriers?" Elara asked, her melodic voice subdued.

"Growing stronger," Alaric replied. "I can feel them—wards built on corruption and fear. They know we're coming."

Kael's hand tightened on his sword hilt. "Let them know. Let them fear."

Lyra studied his profile, noting the muscle that jumped along his jaw. Since crossing into the Syndicate's territory, his nightmares had returned with brutal force. Twice now she'd woken to find him sitting alone by the dying embers of their fire, staring into the darkness with haunted eyes. He never spoke of what he saw in those dreams, but Lyra knew. Blackthorn Pass. His sister. Dravus.

The tension within the group was palpable. This final confrontation with the Shadow Syndicate would test every ounce of their strength, every thread of their bond. Yet their resolve burned bright, forged through months of trials—storms weathered, shadows banished, losses mourned in silent vigils beneath unforgiving skies.

They made camp that night in the shelter of a rocky outcropping, huddled around a small fire that seemed to struggle against the pressing darkness. The flames cast flickering shadows across their weary faces as they shared a meager meal of dried meat and hard bread.

"We should discuss what awaits us," Kael said, breaking the silence. He ran a whetstone along his blade with practiced strokes, the rhythmic scrape a counterpoint to the wind's mournful howl. "The Syndicate's stronghold won't fall easily."

"What do we know of its defenses?" Lyra asked.

"Multiple barriers," Alaric replied, his voice carrying the weight of centuries. "Physical walls reinforced with dark magic. Guards, both human and... otherwise. And at its heart, the Syndicate's inner circle—those who seek to harness the rifts for their own power."

"And Dravus?" Kael's hand stilled on his blade, the name hanging in the air between them like a specter.

"He'll be there," Mira said, her usual flippancy absent. "Waiting for us. For you."

A heavy silence fell over the group. They all knew what Dravus had done to Kael at Blackthorn Pass—the scars he carried, both visible and hidden.

"I've dreamed of him," Kael said suddenly, his voice so low they had to lean forward to hear him. "Every night since we crossed into this wasteland. In the dreams, I'm back at the Pass, watching him cut down my men. Watching him take Lirien." His knuckles whitened around the hilt of his sword. "But in the dreams, I'm frozen. I can't move, can't fight. Can only watch."

The confession hung in the air, raw and unexpected from their stoic warrior. Lyra reached across the fire, placing her hand on his arm.

"They're just dreams, Kael," she said softly. "When you face him again, it will be different."

"Will it?" His dark eyes met hers, haunted by doubt he never allowed himself to show in daylight. "What if I freeze again? What if I fail you all as I failed her?"

"You won't," Lyra said with quiet certainty. "And even if you did—which you won't—you wouldn't be facing him alone this time."

"None of us stands alone anymore," Elara added, her gentle voice carrying surprising strength. "That's what they don't understand, what gives us our advantage. The Syndicate breaks bonds. We forge them."

Kael held Lyra's gaze for a long moment, something shifting behind his eyes—not quite peace, but perhaps the beginning of acceptance. "I'll face him," he said finally. "It's time to end it."

"Not alone," Lyra insisted, her fingers tightening on his arm. "We do this together."

He covered her hand with his own, rough calluses against her skin. "Together," he agreed, the word carrying a weight of promise that warmed her more than the meager fire.

Rowan cleared his throat, breaking the moment. "There's something else we should discuss," he said, unfolding a different section of his map. "Something I've been tracking since we left the Verdant Deep."

They all turned to him, grateful for the shift in focus. Rowan rarely spoke unless he had something important to contribute, his quiet nature masking a mind that constantly analyzed and cataloged the world around him.

"The rift patterns are changing," he explained, pointing to crystalline markers embedded in the parchment. They pulsed with a faint light, forming a constellation of blue-white points across the map. "They're not just growing or spreading anymore. They're... realigning."

"Realigning how?" Alaric asked sharply, leaning forward to study the map.

"They're forming a pattern," Rowan said, tracing lines between the markers. "A configuration I've only seen in ancient texts from before the Sundering. If I'm right, the Syndicate isn't just opening rifts randomly. They're trying to recreate a specific arrangement—one that could amplify their power exponentially."

"Or break the barriers between worlds entirely," Alaric murmured, his ancient eyes troubled.

Lyra felt a chill that had nothing to do with the biting wind. "Is that possible?"

"With the right catalyst, yes," Alaric confirmed. "The Phoenix Stone was created to heal rifts, but in the wrong hands, it could be used to tear them wide open. If the Syndicate has found a way to manipulate the rifts' natural resonance patterns..."

"Then we have even less time than we thought," Kael concluded grimly.

"How does this relate to the stronghold?" Lyra asked, turning back to Rowan. "Is there a connection?"

Rowan nodded, his scholarly reserve giving way to genuine alarm. "The stronghold itself appears to be the focal point of the pattern. Look." He traced the lines between the markers again, and Lyra saw how they converged on a single point at the center of the map—precisely where the Syndicate's fortress stood. "They've built their stronghold at the nexus of natural rift lines. It's not just a fortress—it's a conduit."

"A machine," Elara breathed, her scholarly mind grasping the implications immediately. "They're using the structure itself to channel and amplify the rifts' energy."

"Which explains the timing," Alaric added. "The celestial alignment three days from now—the Convergence—would provide the perfect moment to activate such a nexus."

"Three days?" Lyra echoed, alarm spiking through her. "That's barely enough time to reach the stronghold, let alone breach its defenses."

"Then we move faster," Kael said simply. "We rest in shifts and push through the night if necessary."

They settled into their watch rotation, each taking turns to guard while the others found what rest they could. Lyra took the final watch, sitting wrapped in her cloak as the eastern sky lightened from black to deepest gray. The Phoenix Stone rested in her hands, its blue-amber light spilling between her fingers.

"You're troubled," Alaric observed, joining her silently.

Lyra nodded. "What if we fail? What if the Stone isn't enough?"

The ancient mage considered her question, his silver eyes reflecting the Stone's light. "The Stone is powerful, yes, but it's merely a tool. The true strength lies in those who wield it." He gestured to their sleeping companions. "In the bonds you've forged. In the light you carry even in this darkness."

"That's what frightens me," Lyra admitted. "They're here because of me, following me into danger. If anything happens to them—"

"They chose this path," Alaric interrupted gently. "As did you. Honor their choice by believing in it."

Lyra traced her fingers over the Stone's smooth surface, feeling the fragments pulse in response to her touch. "My parents died protecting this," she said softly. "Sometimes I wonder if they knew what they were asking of me. If they understood what it would cost."

"They knew," Alaric said with quiet certainty. "Just as they knew you would be strong enough to bear it."

"Am I, though?" Lyra looked up at him, allowing her doubt to show plainly on her face. "Strong enough?"

Alaric's weathered hand covered hers, both of them now cradling the Stone. "Strength isn't the absence of fear, Lyra. It's continuing despite it. By that measure, you are the strongest person I have ever known."

His words settled over her like a mantle, heavy but strengthening. As dawn broke—a mere lightening of the perpetual gloom—she woke the others, and they continued their journey.

The days that followed tested them in new ways. The terrain grew increasingly hostile—jagged rocks that sliced through boot leather, sudden sinkholes hidden beneath innocent-looking frost, winds that cut like knives and carried whispers of despair. The Syndicate's influence was palpable here, a malevolence that seeped from the very earth.

On the third day, as they navigated a particularly treacherous ravine, Elara stumbled, crying out as her ankle twisted beneath her. Mira caught her before she could fall, supporting the slender rune-caster with surprising gentleness.

"I'm fine," Elara insisted, though her face had gone pale with pain. "Just give me a moment."

Kael called a halt, and they found shelter in the lee of a rocky outcropping while Elara examined her injury. Her delicate fingers traced runes of healing over the swollen joint, blue light seeping into the damaged tissue.

"It's not broken," she reported, "but I'll need to bind it."

As she worked, Lyra noticed the tension between Elara and Mira—a current that had been building since they entered the wasteland. The two women couldn't have been more different: Elara with her quiet grace and careful control, Mira with her brash confidence and chaotic energy. Yet there was something in the way Mira hovered, in the gentleness of her usually careless hands as she helped bind the injury, that spoke of deeper feelings carefully hidden beneath sharp words.

"You should have been watching where you were going," Mira scolded, though there was no real heat in her voice. "What happened to all that elven grace you're so proud of?"

"I'm not an elf," Elara corrected mildly, a familiar exchange between them. "My ancestors simply interbred with them. And I was watching—the ground gave way."

"Well, watch harder next time," Mira muttered, tightening the bandage with expert precision. "I can't be expected to catch you every time you decide to go tumbling off a cliff."

"Of course not," Elara agreed, a smile tugging at her lips. "That would require consistency, which I know terrifies you."

Mira snorted, but Lyra didn't miss the way her fingers lingered on Elara's ankle, nor the softness in her eyes that vanished the moment she realized Lyra was watching.

"What are you looking at?" Mira demanded, her walls slamming back into place. "Never seen a bandage before?"

Lyra raised her hands in surrender, hiding a smile. "Just admiring your technique."

"Yes, well." Mira stood abruptly, dusting off her hands. "Can't have our rune-caster hobbling into battle. Bad for morale."

As they prepared to move on, Rowan approached Lyra, his compass whirring frantically in his palm.

"Something's wrong," he said quietly, showing her the device. Its needles spun in erratic patterns, occasionally freezing before spinning wildly in the opposite direction. "The energy patterns are destabilizing. It's as if the rifts are... agitated."

"What does that mean for the stronghold?" Lyra asked, unease prickling along her spine.

"If my theory is correct," Rowan replied, his scholarly demeanor giving way to genuine alarm, "it means the Syndicate has already begun the preliminary stages of their ritual. The stronghold—the nexus—is drawing power from the surrounding rifts, pulling them into alignment."

"And when the Convergence happens?" Lyra pressed.

Rowan's expression grew grim. "If they succeed in aligning all the rifts and channeling that power during the Convergence, they won't just control the rifts—they'll tear open the barriers between worlds completely. The damage would be catastrophic and irreversible."

"Then we need to reach the stronghold before the Convergence," Lyra concluded. "Stop them before they can complete their ritual."

"Yes," Rowan agreed, tucking away his compass. "And based on these readings, we have less time than we thought. The process is accelerating."

They pressed on, supporting Elara between them when the terrain grew too difficult for her injured ankle. By nightfall, they had reached the edge of a vast, barren plain. In the distance, barely visible through the perpetual gloom, they could make out the silhouette of a massive structure—angular and forbidding, a shadow darker than the surrounding darkness.

"The Syndicate's stronghold," Kael confirmed grimly. "We'll reach it by midday tomorrow if we push hard."

They made camp in the shelter of the last rocky outcropping before the plain, their fire kept deliberately small to avoid detection. As they ate their meager meal, Lyra noticed Rowan sitting apart from the others, his attention fixed on his compass. The device continued its erratic behavior, occasionally emitting a high-pitched whine that set her teeth on edge.

"Any insight?" she asked, joining him at the edge of their camp.

Rowan shook his head, frustration evident in the tightness around his eyes. "The readings make no sense. It's as if the rifts are both expanding and contracting simultaneously. Theoretically impossible, but..." He gestured helplessly at the whirring device.

"Could it be a defense mechanism?" Lyra suggested. "Something the Syndicate is doing to mask their activities?"

"Possibly," Rowan conceded. "Or it could be a sign that whatever they're attempting is already beginning to destabilize the natural order." He looked up at her, his scholarly reserve cracking to reveal the fear beneath. "Lyra, if they succeed—if they manage to align the rifts in the configuration I suspect they're attempting—it won't just affect Sylvanthia. The consequences could extend to realms we can't even comprehend."

The weight of his words settled heavily on Lyra's shoulders. She had always known their quest was important, but the scope of what they faced seemed to grow with each passing day. No longer were they fighting just for justice, or even for Sylvanthia alone—they were fighting for the integrity of reality itself.

As night deepened around them, the wind rose, carrying with it whispers that seemed almost like voices—distant, indistinct, yet somehow malevolent. The twisted trees around their camp creaked and groaned, their skeletal branches scratching at the air like desperate fingers.

"The land itself is corrupted here," Alaric observed, his silver eyes reflecting the firelight as he gazed out into the darkness. "The Syndicate's influence has seeped into the very soil, poisoning everything it touches."

"Can it be healed?" Elara asked, her melodic voice tinged with sorrow.

Alaric was silent for a long moment. "Perhaps," he said finally. "With time. With the Stone restored to its full power. But some scars may never fade completely."

They settled into an uneasy sleep, each taking their turn at watch. The night passed without incident, though Lyra's dreams were troubled by visions of darkness spreading across Sylvanthia like ink through water, consuming everything in its path.

Dawn brought little change to the perpetual gloom. They broke camp quickly, eager to reach the stronghold before the Syndicate's ritual progressed any further. Elara's ankle had improved somewhat thanks to her healing runes, though she still walked with a slight limp that slowed their pace.

As they crossed the barren plain, the stronghold grew more distinct—a massive structure of obsidian and iron, its towers reaching toward the bruised sky like accusing fingers. No banners flew from its battlements, no guards patrolled its walls. It stood silent and watchful, a void cut into the landscape.

"Where are the sentries?" Kael asked, his soldier's instincts on high alert. "A fortress this important should be heavily guarded."

"They don't need conventional defenses," Alaric explained, his expression grim. "The barriers do their work far more effectively than any guard. Besides, they want to conserve their strength for the ritual."

They approached cautiously, using what little cover the plain provided—scattered boulders, shallow depressions in the earth, the occasional withered tree. As they drew closer, Lyra began to feel a pressure building against her mind—a subtle but persistent force that made her thoughts sluggish and filled her with a creeping dread.

"The outer barrier," Alaric murmured. "It affects the mind first, creating fear, doubt, confusion. Many turn back at this point, convinced they've made a terrible mistake in coming here."

"How do we resist it?" Lyra asked, fighting against the growing urge to flee.

"Focus on what anchors you," Alaric advised. "Your purpose. Your companions. The Stone itself. The barrier cannot touch those connections unless you allow it."

Lyra nodded, her hand finding the Phoenix Stone through the fabric of her pack. Its warmth pulsed against her palm, steady and reassuring. She thought of her parents, of the villages destroyed by the Syndicate, of all that would be lost if they failed. The pressure against her mind eased slightly, though it didn't disappear completely.

They continued their approach, the stronghold looming larger with each step. The plain around them grew increasingly strange—patches of ground that shimmered like heat haze, rocks that seemed to shift position when not directly observed, shadows that moved independently of their sources.

"Reality is thin here," Rowan observed, his compass spinning wildly in his palm. "The rifts' influence is stronger than I've ever recorded."

"We're close to the nexus point," Alaric confirmed. "The place where multiple rift lines intersect. It's where the Syndicate built their ritual chamber."

"So how do we get inside?" Mira asked, eyeing the fortress's seamless walls with professional skepticism. "I don't see a welcoming committee or a convenient entrance."

"There," Alaric said, pointing to a narrow ravine that curved toward the eastern side of the stronghold. "The barrier is weakest there, where a natural rift line intersects with the Syndicate's constructed defenses. It creates a... dissonance that we can exploit."

They changed course, heading toward the ravine. As they drew closer, Lyra could see that it was less a natural formation and more a wound in the earth—as if the ground had been torn open by some tremendous force. Jagged rocks lined its edges, and a faint mist coiled along its depths, glowing with an eerie phosphorescence.

"Charming," Mira muttered, peering into the ravine. "Nothing says 'safe passage' quite like a glowing fog in a creepy crevasse."

"The mist is a manifestation of the barrier's energy," Alaric explained. "It will grow stronger as we descend, but it's still our best point of entry."

They began their descent, the ravine's walls rising steeply on either side. The mist swirled around their ankles, cold and clinging, sending tendrils up their legs like questing fingers. The air grew thick and difficult to breathe, tasting of metal and something sweeter, more cloying—like flowers on the edge of rot.

"Stay close," Alaric warned. "The barrier will try to separate us. It will show you visions, play on your fears. Remember what anchors you."

As if triggered by his words, the mist thickened, rising to their waists, then their chests. Lyra's vision blurred, the ravine walls seeming to waver and shift. Whispers filled her ears—voices too indistinct to understand but somehow deeply familiar. The pressure against her mind intensified, no longer subtle but aggressive, invasive.

Suddenly, she was no longer in the ravine. She stood in her childhood home, the day the Syndicate came. Flames licked at the walls, smoke filling the air. Her mother knelt before her, pressing the Phoenix Stone into her hands.

"Run, Lyra," her mother urged, her face streaked with ash and blood. "Hide. Don't let them find you."

"Mother, please," Lyra begged, though she knew how this memory ended. "Come with me."

Her mother smiled sadly. "I can't. I have to give you time." She touched Lyra's cheek. "Remember who you are. Remember what matters."

The scene shifted. Lyra was older, wandering alone through a devastated landscape. The Phoenix Stone hung cold and lifeless around her neck. In the distance, she could see her companions—Kael, Mira, Elara, Rowan, Alaric—walking away from her, their backs turned.

"They'll leave you," a voice whispered in her ear, smooth and persuasive. "When they understand the true cost of what you're asking them to face. When they see what the Stone demands. They'll abandon you, just as everyone eventually does."

Lyra felt tears sting her eyes, the vision cutting deeper than she wanted to admit. Wasn't this her deepest fear? That in the end, she would face the darkness alone?

"Lyra!" A voice cut through the illusion—Kael's voice, urgent and real. "Don't listen to it. We're right here. Stay with us."

The vision wavered. Lyra blinked, and for a moment she could see the ravine again, her companions struggling through the mist beside her. Kael reached for her, his hand outstretched.

"Take my hand," he called. "Focus on what's real."

She reached for him, but the mist surged between them, and the vision reasserted itself. Now she stood before the Syndicate's inner circle, the Phoenix Stone clutched in her fist. They offered her a choice—surrender the Stone and her friends would be spared. Resist, and she would watch them die, one by one.

"Such a simple choice," the same smooth voice whispered. "Such a small sacrifice to save those you love. The Stone for their lives. Why hesitate?"

Lyra felt her resolve weakening. Wasn't that a fair exchange? Wasn't that what any friend would do?

"No!" This time it was Elara's voice that reached her. "The Stone cannot be surrendered, Lyra. Not even for us. It's the only hope Sylvanthia has."

Again, the vision flickered. Lyra caught a glimpse of Elara's pale face, her blue eyes wide with concern. The rune-caster's hands were tracing patterns in the air, her runes glowing against the encroaching mist.

"Fight it," Elara urged. "The barrier feeds on doubt. Believe in yourself as we believe in you."

The vision changed again. Lyra stood alone atop a high tower, the restored Phoenix Stone blazing in her hands. Below her, Sylvanthia burned, rifts tearing open across the landscape like wounds in the world's flesh. In the sky above, something vast and terrible unfurled—a presence more sensed than seen, ancient and hungry.

"This is what awaits if you continue," the voice whispered. "This is the future you create. Turn back now. Save what can be saved. Some burdens are too great to bear."

Lyra felt her knees weaken, despair washing over her in waves. Was this truly what awaited them? Had their quest been doomed from the start?

"Lyra." This time it was Alaric's voice, calm and steady. "The barrier shows only lies and half-truths. It cannot predict the future, only play on your fears of it. Trust in the Stone. Trust in yourself."

The Phoenix Stone pulsed against her chest, its warmth cutting through the chill of the vision. Lyra closed her eyes, focusing on that warmth, on the steady rhythm that matched her heartbeat. This was real. This was true. Everything else was illusion.

"Enough," she said, her voice strengthening with each word. "I see through your deceptions. You have no power over me."

The vision shattered like glass, fragments of false reality falling away to reveal the ravine once more. Her companions surrounded her, each fighting their own battles against the barrier's influence. Kael stood rigid, his face locked in a rictus of horror as he relived Blackthorn Pass. Mira thrashed as if trying to escape invisible bonds, her face contorted with fury and grief. Elara's runes flared erratically as she struggled to maintain her protective spells. Rowan stared into the distance, tears streaming down his face as he reached for something—or someone—only he could see.

Only Alaric seemed relatively unaffected, though strain showed in the tightness around his eyes. His hands moved in complex patterns, silver light flowing from his fingertips to form a protective web around the group.

"We need to break through together," he called over the rising wail of the mist. "The barrier is stronger than I anticipated. It will take all of us, united in purpose, to shatter it."

Lyra understood what she had to do. She reached for the Phoenix Stone, drawing it from her pack. Its light blazed in the gloom, blue-amber radiance cutting through the mist like a blade. The barrier recoiled from it, the mist swirling in agitated patterns.

"Kael," she called, moving to his side. She placed her free hand on his arm, the Stone's light illuminating his tormented face. "Come back to us. Remember what you told me—we face this together."

For a moment, he gave no sign of hearing her. Then his eyes focused, recognition dawning as he fought his way free of the vision. "Lyra," he gasped, his voice hoarse. "I saw—"

"I know," she said gently. "But it wasn't real. This is real. We are real."

Together, they moved to Mira, the Stone's light enveloping her. The alchemist's struggles slowed, then ceased as she blinked in confusion.

"Well, that was unpleasant," she muttered, though her voice shook slightly. "Remind me to develop a potion that shields against mind-twisting magic. Assuming we survive this, of course."

One by one, they brought each other back from the barrier's visions, the Stone's light creating a sphere of clarity around them. When all were free of the illusions, they gathered in a tight circle, the mist churning angrily at the edges of their protected space.

"Now what?" Mira asked, eyeing the barrier with renewed wariness. "I don't fancy fighting our way through more nightmare fog."

"We break it," Alaric said simply. "Not just push through, but shatter it completely. The Stone has the power, but it needs our combined will to focus it."

"How?" Lyra asked.

"Form a circle," Alaric instructed. "Each of you, focus on what drives you—what brought you to this moment, what you fight for. Let those emotions flow into the Stone through Lyra."

They arranged themselves in a circle at the ravine's end, facing the thickest concentration of mist that marked the barrier's heart. Lyra stood at the center, the Phoenix Stone held before her, its light pulsing in time with her heartbeat.

"Remember why we're here," she said, her voice steady despite the fear that still clawed at the edges of her mind—fear she recognized as the barrier's influence, not her own. "Remember everyone who's counting on us. Everyone we've lost."

Her fingers closed around the locket in her pocket, its metal warm against her skin. "We carry their light with us. Their strength. Their hope."

Kael drew his sword, the blade gleaming in the Stone's light. "For Lirien," he said simply, naming the sister he had failed to save.

Mira uncorked a vial of shimmering liquid that caught the light like captured fire. "For my family," she added, her usual flippancy replaced by fierce determination.

Elara's runes glowed blue against her skin as she raised her hands. "For my village," she whispered.

Rowan unfolded his map, the crystalline markers embedded in it beginning to glow in response to the Stone's light. "For my parents," he said firmly.

Alaric's eyes blazed silver-gold as he completed their circle. "For balance," he finished.

Lyra held the Stone before her, feeling its power surge in response to their unified purpose. "Together," she said, "we are stronger than their darkness."

She reached for the Stone's power, feeling it respond to her call. The familiar warmth spread up her arms, but now it was joined by new sensations—the cool fluidity of the Water Fragment, the sweeping freedom of the Air Fragment, the steady strength of the Earth Fragment's echo. The Stone's light intensified, sending rays of blue-amber radiance spearing through the gloom.

Alaric began to chant in a language Lyra didn't recognize—ancient words that seemed to resonate with the Stone itself. The others joined their powers to hers: Mira's alchemical fire, Elara's protective runes, Rowan's spatial awareness, Alaric's elemental command, Kael's unwavering strength.

The barrier before them became visible as their combined power struck it—a wall of writhing darkness shot through with veins of sickly green. It pulsed like something alive, responding to their assault with increased pressure against their minds.

Doubts flooded Lyra's thoughts—memories of failure, fears of inadequacy, the crushing weight of responsibility. For a moment, she faltered, the Stone's light dimming.

"Hold fast!" Alaric called, his voice cutting through the mental fog. "This is the barrier's defense—it feeds on doubt!"

Kael's hand found hers, his grip steady and warm. "Together," he reminded her, his eyes holding hers with an intensity that burned through the barrier's influence. "We've come too far to fail now."

In that moment, Lyra saw beyond his usual stoic mask to the man beneath—the one who had lost everything at Blackthorn Pass, who had rebuilt himself from the shattered pieces, who now stood beside her not because of duty or vengeance, but because of something deeper, something neither of them had dared to name.

"Together," she echoed, drawing strength from his touch, from the unwavering faith in his eyes.

She drew a deep breath and pushed back against the invasive thoughts. She focused on the Stone, on the faces of her companions, on every person counting on them to succeed. The Stone responded, its light surging back to full brilliance.

The barrier shuddered under their combined assault. Cracks appeared in its surface, thin lines of light splintering the darkness. The air filled with a high-pitched keening, like metal under unbearable stress.

"It's working!" Elara cried, her runes flaring brighter as she poured more power into their effort.

The cracks widened, light pouring through the gaps. The barrier's resistance intensified, lashing out with tendrils of darkness that sought to wrap around their minds and drag them into despair.

Lyra felt the Stone pulse in her hands, its rhythm matching her heartbeat. She thought of the young merchant with his locket, of all the lives cut short by the Syndicate's cruelty. Her determination hardened into something unbreakable.

"For Sylvanthia," she said, her voice ringing with authority that surprised even her. "For everyone they've hurt. For the future they would destroy."

She thrust the Stone forward, channeling every ounce of her will through it. The others followed suit, adding their power to hers in a final, desperate push.

The barrier shattered with a sound like a thousand panes of glass breaking at once. The air itself seemed to tear, the dark energy that had formed the barrier dispersing in waves of emerald and midnight blue light. The shockwave knocked them all backward, a physical force that stole the breath from their lungs. For a moment, the world was nothing but swirling color and disorienting silence.

Then, as suddenly as it had begun, the chaos subsided. Where the barrier had stood, there was now only empty air, shimmering slightly like the aftermath of heat lightning. Beyond it lay an open path to the stronghold's eastern wall, unguarded and vulnerable in the wake of the barrier's collapse.

"We did it," Mira said, disbelief coloring her voice. "We actually broke through."

Lyra stared at the path now open before them, her heart pounding with a mixture of triumph and trepidation. The Stone in her hands pulsed with satisfied warmth, as if pleased with what they had accomplished.

"The Syndicate will know," Alaric warned, already moving toward the breach. "Breaking the barrier will have sent ripples through the entire defensive network. We must move quickly."

They hurried forward, emerging from the ravine onto a narrow strip of barren ground that separated them from the stronghold's outer wall. Up close, the obsidian surface seemed to absorb light rather than reflect it, creating an unsettling void against which they appeared unnaturally vivid and exposed.

"There," Elara said, pointing to a section of wall where faint blue lines crisscrossed the black surface. "Those are maintenance runes. I can use them to create an opening."

She approached the wall cautiously, her fingers tracing the barely visible patterns. Blue light flowed from her touch, illuminating an intricate network of runes embedded within the obsidian. With practiced precision, she began to manipulate them, rearranging their configuration, altering their purpose.

The wall groaned, a deep sound that seemed to come from everywhere at once. A seam appeared in the obsidian, widening slowly to reveal a narrow passage beyond.

One by one, they squeezed through the gap, entering the heart of the Syndicate's domain. The air inside was thick with the stench of corruption and decay, pressing against them like a physical weight.

As Lyra passed through the narrow opening, she felt the Phoenix Stone pulse against her palm—both warning and reassurance. Ahead lay the central chamber where the Syndicate's ritual was already underway, the fate of Sylvanthia hanging in the balance. The stronghold itself seemed to breathe around them, a living entity aware of their intrusion.

Whatever price victory would demand, they would pay it together.

CHAPTER SIX

Forged in Combat

The Whispering Woods exhaled a pearlescent mist as dawn broke over the eastern horizon. Dew trembled on unfurling ferns, capturing the first golden light in perfect miniature suns. Lyra stood at the edge of the ancient forest, the weight of the Phoenix Stone heavy against her hip despite its physical lightness. Her fingers traced its warm surface through the worn leather of her pack, seeking reassurance she wasn't certain it could provide.

Behind her, their hastily abandoned camp lay in disarray—bedrolls half-packed, the remnants of their fire still smoldering. The Syndicate's ambush had come just before midnight, forcing them to flee deeper into the wilderness than they had intended. They had lost precious supplies in the escape, but at least they were all still alive.

For now.

"We need to keep moving," Kael said, materializing at her side with the silent grace that still unnerved her after months of traveling together. His dark eyes scanned the tree line, one hand resting casually on his sword hilt. The burns along his forearm—souvenirs from their last encounter with the Syndicate—had begun to heal, but the skin remained angry and red against his tan.

"I know," Lyra replied, squaring her shoulders. "But we can't just blunder in without direction. The Whispering Woods aren't kind to those who enter without purpose."

Kael's expression tightened almost imperceptibly. "You think I don't know that? My people have been the guardians of these woods for generations." He paused, the muscle in his jaw working. "Or they were, before the Syndicate came."

Lyra winced internally. Of course he knew. Kael had lost his entire village to the Syndicate's purge of the woodland settlements—a methodical elimination of anyone who might guide enemies through the forest's secret paths. The fact that he had been away scouting when the attack came was the only reason he still breathed.

"I'm sorry," she said quietly. "I didn't mean—"

"It doesn't matter." Kael cut her off, his voice clipped. "What matters is that we find the Earth Fragment before the Syndicate realizes where we're headed."

Lyra nodded, swallowing further apologies. Kael didn't want her pity. What he wanted—needed—was her focus on the task at hand. The Phoenix Stone pulsed gently against her hip, as if in agreement.

The others approached, their footsteps soft on the mossy ground. Mira came first, her copper hair braided tightly against her head, her green eyes alert despite the dark shadows beneath them. The alchemist's bandolier of vials clinked softly with each step, a rainbow of deadly and healing concoctions at her fingertips. Behind her walked Elara, the rune-caster's pale features composed despite the strain of maintaining their protective wards through the night's chaos.

Rowan brought up the rear, his cartographer's tools tucked securely in their leather case, his normally cheerful face solemn as he consulted his compass. Unlike the others, whose skills in combat or magic made them natural choices for such a dangerous quest, Rowan's expertise lay in maps and measurements, in understanding the lay of the land. The slight hunch of his shoulders betrayed his awareness of this difference, though none of them would have made it this far without his uncanny ability to navigate the ever-shifting landscape of a world fractured by rifts.

"The magnetic disturbances are getting stronger," Rowan reported, frowning at the trembling needle. His long fingers, stained with ink and graphite, adjusted the delicate brass instrument with practiced precision. "Whatever's affecting the Earth Fragment, it's intensifying. The readings are unlike anything I've documented before."

"Can you still track it?" Lyra asked, apprehension coiling in her stomach.

Rowan nodded, though his expression remained troubled. "Yes, but it's... strange. The signal keeps shifting, like it's being moved or... or like it's trying to hide." He glanced up, pushing his wire-rimmed spectacles higher on his nose. "I've been mapping the fluctuations since midnight. There's a pattern to them—almost like a heartbeat."

"Fragments don't hide," Mira pointed out, adjusting her bandolier with practiced fingers. "They're powerful, yes, but they're not sentient."

"Perhaps not," Elara interjected, her melodic voice soft but carrying. "But the Earth Fragment has always been the most... responsive to its surroundings. The texts speak of it having a particular affinity with the natural world."

"Great," Mira muttered. "So we're chasing a magical rock that's playing hide-and-seek in a forest the size of a small kingdom. Should be done by lunch, then."

Despite everything, Lyra felt a smile tug at her lips. Mira's sardonic humor had been a constant throughout their journey, a touchstone of normalcy in a world that grew stranger and more dangerous by the day.

"We'll find it," Lyra said with more confidence than she felt. "The Stone has led us this far. It won't abandon us now."

Kael made a noncommittal sound, his gaze still fixed on the woods. "We should split up. Cover more ground."

"No," Lyra and Elara said simultaneously, then exchanged a quick glance.

"The woods are too dangerous," Elara continued. "Especially now, with the Syndicate so close behind us. We stay together."

"Elara's right," Lyra affirmed. "Besides, I need all of you if we're going to retrieve the Fragment. Each of you has skills I don't."

Kael's expression darkened, but he didn't argue further. Lyra knew he chafed at the delay, at the methodical pace their group often took. As a scout, he was accustomed to moving fast and alone. The necessity of traveling with others—of considering their safety and limitations—was a constant source of tension for him.

"Then we move now," he said, adjusting his pack with a sharp tug. "The longer we stand here debating, the closer the Syndicate gets."

Without waiting for a response, he turned and strode toward the forest's edge, leaving the others to follow. Lyra exchanged a glance with Mira, who rolled her eyes expressively before falling into step behind him.

"He's right about one thing," Mira murmured as Lyra came alongside her. "The Syndicate is getting closer. I found tracks this morning, less than half a day old."

Lyra felt a chill that had nothing to do with the morning air. "You're sure?"

"Unfortunately." Mira's hand drifted to a vial filled with amber liquid at her belt—her most potent explosive compound. "They're hunting us with those shadow-hounds again. I recognized the paw prints."

Lyra suppressed a shudder. The Syndicate's shadow-hounds were nightmare creatures, bred from wolves corrupted by the rifts' dark energy. They could track prey across any terrain, relentless and nearly impossible to kill by conventional means. Their last encounter with the beasts had cost them two companions and very nearly Kael's life.

"Then we need to be faster and smarter," Lyra said, squaring her shoulders. "The Earth Fragment is our priority. Once we have it, we can deal with the Syndicate."

Mira's lips quirked in a humorless smile. "Simple as that, huh?"

"Never said it would be simple," Lyra replied, her hand instinctively finding the Stone at her hip. "Just necessary."

They passed beneath the first sentinel trees of the Whispering Woods, ancient oaks whose massive trunks were wider than three people standing hand-to-hand. The light changed immediately, filtered through countless leaves into a green-gold dapple that shifted with each breath of wind. The air grew richer, laden with the scent of moss and fungi and growing things.

And something else—something ancient and patient and aware.

Lyra felt it the moment they crossed the threshold, a subtle shift in the quality of the silence. The forest was listening.

"Stay close," Kael murmured, his voice barely audible. "The paths shift if you're not careful."

As if to emphasize his point, Lyra glanced back and saw that the forest's edge was already lost to sight, obscured by a gentle bend in the path that she was certain hadn't been there moments before.

"The woods remember the old ways," Elara whispered, her pale eyes wide as she took in their surroundings. "The rift corruption hasn't reached this far yet."

"Small mercies," Rowan muttered, consulting his compass again. He paused, pulling a small leather-bound journal from his pack. With quick, practiced strokes, he sketched the path behind them, adding notations in a cramped, precise hand. "We need to head northeast, toward the heart of the forest. That's where the signal is strongest."

"You're mapping this?" Mira asked, eyebrow raised. "I thought you said the paths shift."

"They do," Rowan confirmed, not looking up from his work. "But they shift according to patterns—like a language. If I can decode it..." He trailed off, adding another notation. "There. See how the moss grows thicker on the north side of these trees? And how the branches bend toward the east? The forest is giving us directions, if we know how to read them."

Lyra had never considered the woods in such terms before. She glanced at Kael, expecting skepticism, but the scout was studying Rowan's observations with grudging interest.

"My grandmother used to say something similar," Kael admitted. "That the forest speaks to those who listen."

Rowan nodded, a brief smile crossing his face. "Exactly. Most people only see trees. I see... well, a map. Living, breathing, constantly changing—but a map nonetheless."

They moved deeper into the woods, following a path that seemed to materialize just steps ahead of them and vanish behind them just as quickly. The trees grew older and more massive the further they went, their trunks gnarled and twisted into fantastical shapes. Moss hung in thick curtains from the branches, and fungi the size of dinner plates sprouted from fallen logs.

Despite the beauty, tension wound tighter with each step. Lyra found herself straining to hear past the natural sounds of the forest, listening for the telltale growl of shadow-hounds or the whisper of Syndicate agents moving through the underbrush.

After several hours of walking, they came to a small clearing where a stream bubbled over moss-covered rocks. By unspoken agreement, they paused to rest and refill their water skins.

"Something's not right," Kael said abruptly, his hand moving to his sword hilt. "The forest is too quiet."

Lyra stilled, listening. He was right. The birdsong and insect chatter that had accompanied them had fallen silent, leaving only the gentle murmur of the stream.

"Could be a natural predator," Mira suggested, though her hand had already moved to her bandolier. "A bear, maybe."

"No," Kael shook his head, his eyes scanning the treeline. "This is different. This is—"

A low, reverberating growl cut through the silence, raising the hairs on the back of Lyra's neck. It was followed by another, then another, until the clearing seemed surrounded by the sound.

"Shadow-hounds," Rowan whispered, his face draining of color. Unlike the others, he had no weapons beyond his cartographer's tools—a compass, a small knife for sharpening pencils, a measuring chain. Yet he squared his shoulders, gripping the metal chain in one hand. "They're circling us. Using the stream to mask their approach from the east."

"How did they find us so quickly?" Elara's hands were already tracing protective runes in the air, blue light trailing from her fingertips.

"Doesn't matter," Kael said grimly, drawing his sword in a single fluid motion. "They're here now."

The first beast burst from the undergrowth in a blur of midnight fur and gleaming teeth. It was massive, the size of a small pony, its eyes glowing with an unnatural emerald light. Kael met its charge with a sweeping arc of his blade, opening a gash along its flank that should have been debilitating.

The hound barely slowed.

Two more followed, converging on the group from different directions. Mira hurled a vial that shattered against one's shoulder, erupting in a cloud of caustic smoke that made the creature howl in rage. Elara's runes flared to life, creating a shimmering barrier that the third beast slammed into with bone-jarring force.

Lyra reached for the Phoenix Stone, feeling its warmth surge up her arm as she called on its power. The familiar amber light spilled from her hands, coalescing into a spear of pure energy that she drove into the first hound's chest as it circled back for another attack on Kael.

The creature shrieked, a sound no natural wolf could make, as the Stone's light burned through its corrupted flesh. It collapsed, twitching, before dissolving into wisps of dark smoke.

"The Stone kills them!" Lyra called out, already turning to face the next threat. "Bring them to me!"

Kael nodded grimly, adjusting his strategy to herd rather than kill. He drove the second hound toward Lyra with a series of precise strikes, while Mira and Elara worked to contain the third.

For a moment, it seemed they might gain the upper hand. Then five more shadow-hounds burst into the clearing.

"There's too many!" Rowan shouted, wielding his measuring chain like a flail as one of the beasts lunged for him. The metal links caught the creature across the muzzle, drawing a howl of pain. "They're using the stream as a corridor—it's how they tracked us so quickly!"

Lyra's heart hammered against her ribs as she dispatched another hound with the Stone's power. She could feel the energy draining from her with each use, her connection to the Stone growing thinner. They couldn't sustain this fight, not against so many.

"The stream!" Elara called suddenly, her voice cutting through the chaos. "Follow it upstream! Quickly!"

Without questioning, they broke and ran, following the winding course of the stream as it cut through the forest. The hounds pursued, their howls echoing through the trees. Lyra's lungs burned as she pushed herself to keep pace with Kael, who led their desperate flight.

The forest around them became a blur of green and shadow. Branches whipped at their faces, roots threatened to trip them with every step. Behind them, the howls grew closer. Lyra could hear the crashing of heavy bodies through the underbrush, the snap of powerful jaws closing on empty air.

"They're gaining!" Mira gasped, glancing back over her shoulder. Her face was streaked with dirt and sweat, a cut above her eye bleeding freely.

"Keep moving!" Kael called back, his voice tight with exertion. "Don't stop for anything!"

Rowan stumbled suddenly, his foot catching in a tangle of roots. He went down hard, his tools scattering across the forest floor. Lyra skidded to a halt, turning back to help him.

"Go!" Rowan shouted, already scrambling to his feet. "I'll catch up!"

But it was too late. A shadow-hound burst from the trees, its massive form bearing down on the cartographer with terrifying speed. Rowan rolled, narrowly avoiding the first lunge, but the beast was already circling back for another attack.

Lyra raised the Stone, its light flaring in response to her desperation. But before she could strike, Kael was there, his sword slashing in a deadly arc that caught the hound across its throat. Black ichor sprayed from the wound, hissing where it touched the ground.

"Move!" Kael ordered, hauling Rowan to his feet with his free hand. The cartographer snatched up his fallen journal but had to leave the rest of his scattered tools behind.

They ran on, the stream widening as they followed its course. The water moved faster now, frothing white over rocks and fallen logs. The sound of it nearly drowned out the pursuing hounds, but not quite.

"There!" Elara pointed ahead, where the stream disappeared beneath a rocky overhang. "The water goes underground there!"

"And we follow it?" Mira asked incredulously. "Into who knows what?"

"You want to stay here and become hound food?" Kael retorted, already angling toward the overhang.

As they drew closer, Lyra realized it wasn't just an overhang—it was the entrance to a cave, partially concealed by a curtain of water flowing over its mouth. The stream widened into a small pool before disappearing into the darkness beyond.

"Through there!" Elara gasped, pointing. "The water—it's blessed—they can't follow!"

Kael reached the cave first, plunging through the water without hesitation. Rowan followed, then Mira, who paused to hurl one last vial behind them. It exploded in a blinding flash that momentarily disoriented the pursuing hounds.

Elara stumbled as she reached the waterfall, her foot catching on a slick stone. Lyra lunged, catching the rune-caster's arm before she could fall. Together, they half-ran, half-fell through the curtain of water and into the darkness beyond.

A shadow-hound leapt after them, its massive form silhouetted against the light filtering through the waterfall. But as it hit the curtain of water, something remarkable happened. The liquid seemed to solidify, glowing with a blue-white light that repelled the creature with such force that it was thrown backward, yelping in pain and surprise. Its companions circled the cave entrance, growling in frustration but unwilling to approach the glowing water.

The change was immediate and disorienting. The howls of the shadow-hounds muffled as if someone had closed a door, replaced by the echoing drip of water and their own ragged breathing. Lyra blinked, trying to adjust to the dimness after the forest's filtered sunlight.

"Is everyone alright?" she asked, still gripping Elara's arm, her heart pounding so hard she could feel it in her throat.

"Mostly," Mira's voice came from nearby, followed by the scratch of a flint and the flare of a small torch. The alchemist's face appeared in the warm light, wet hair plastered to her forehead and a fresh cut along her cheekbone, but otherwise intact. "Though I think I lost two of my best vials in that mess."

"Better the vials than you," Rowan said, emerging from the shadows. He was soaked and muddy, but appeared unharmed. A gash across his knuckles dripped blood where he had struck one of the hounds with his chain, but his eyes were bright with the exhilaration of survival. "Did you see that last one? I thought cartographers were supposed to die with dignity—mapping new territory from the comfort of a hound's stomach."

Despite the tension, Mira snorted. "Is that what they teach you at the Academy? No wonder you dropped out."

"I didn't drop out," Rowan corrected, a familiar argument that seemed to comfort them both. "I took a sabbatical. An extended, possibly permanent sabbatical."

"Kael?" Lyra called, a note of worry creeping into her voice when the scout didn't immediately appear in the torchlight.

"Here." His voice echoed from deeper in the cave. "You all need to see this."

Something in his tone made Lyra's skin prickle. She helped Elara to her feet, then followed the sound of Kael's voice, the others close behind. The cave opened up as they moved away from the entrance, the ceiling rising until it disappeared into darkness above them.

They found Kael standing before a wall covered in ancient paintings. The flickering torchlight brought the images to life—hunters pursuing deer, gatherers collecting fruits, shamans communing with spirits. But it was the central image that drew Lyra's eye: a massive tree, its roots extending deep into the earth, its branches reaching toward the sky. And embedded in its trunk, rendered in faded ochre and charcoal, was a distinct shape that made her breath catch.

The Earth Fragment.

"This is it," she whispered, stepping closer to the painting. "This is what we've been looking for."

"Not quite," Kael corrected, his expression unreadable in the shifting light. "This is a map to what we're looking for. The Fragment itself is still out there."

Lyra studied the painting more carefully. Now that he mentioned it, she could see that the tree wasn't just symbolic—it was a specific landmark. The artists had included details that distinguished it: a lightning scar down one side, a peculiar split in the trunk that formed what looked like a doorway, roots that curved above ground before plunging back into the earth.

"The Heart Tree," Elara breathed, recognition dawning in her eyes. "It's real. I thought it was just a legend."

"What's the Heart Tree?" Rowan asked, already sketching the image in his notebook. His pencil moved with fluid precision, capturing details Lyra hadn't even noticed.

"The first tree of the Whispering Woods," Elara explained, her voice taking on the cadence it always did when she recited lore. "Said to have been planted by the Aethyr Order at the founding of Sylvanthia. Its roots are supposed to connect to every other tree in the forest, forming a network that the Order used to communicate and to channel their magic."

"And apparently," Kael added, "to hide the Earth Fragment."

Lyra felt the Phoenix Stone warm against her hip, responding to the proximity of information about its missing piece. "Can you find this tree?" she asked Kael.

He hesitated, an unusual moment of uncertainty for the confident scout. "Maybe. The old stories say it stands at the heart of the forest, but no one's seen it in generations. The paths that led to it were lost when the Order fell."

"But this map could lead us there," Rowan said, gesturing to the wall painting. He moved closer, his eyes narrowing as he studied the symbols surrounding the central image. "Look—these aren't just decorative. They're coordinates." His finger traced a series of concentric circles around the tree. "This is a navigation system, using the forest itself as reference points. Brilliant, actually."

"You can read this?" Mira asked skeptically.

"Not all of it," Rowan admitted. "But enough. It's similar to the cartographic cipher the Academy uses for mapping unstable territories. If I can translate these symbols..." He flipped to a new page in his notebook, scribbling calculations with growing excitement. "Yes, I think I can plot a course from here to the Heart Tree."

"Even if we find it, extracting the Fragment won't be simple," Elara cautioned. "The Heart Tree is said to be semi-sentient, with defenses against those who would harm it."

"We don't want to harm it," Lyra said firmly. "We just need the Fragment. The Stone will help us communicate that."

Mira made a skeptical noise. "Talking to trees now, are we? Next you'll be having tea with the shadow-hounds."

"The Aethyr Order communed with the natural world," Elara said, a touch defensively. "It's not as far-fetched as it sounds."

"Regardless," Kael cut in, "we need to move. Those hounds can't cross the blessed water, but their handlers will find another way in. We should be gone before they do."

Lyra nodded, though part of her was reluctant to leave the relative safety of the cave. "How do we get to the Heart Tree from here?"

Kael studied the wall paintings again, his eyes tracing the patterns that Rowan was frantically copying down. "There," he said finally, pointing to a series of symbols along the bottom of the image. "That's an old woodland script. It's giving directions from a sacred spring—which might be the source of this stream."

"Can you read it?" Lyra asked.

"Some of it," Kael admitted. "My grandmother taught me a little before she died. It says something about following the... the whispering path? No, the whispering stones. At dawn."

"Whispering stones," Rowan repeated, looking up from his notebook. "Like those?" He pointed to the back of the cave, where the torchlight revealed a line of smooth, rounded stones leading into a narrow tunnel.

They approached cautiously. The stones were unusual—perfectly round and polished smooth, each about the size of a melon. They were spaced at regular intervals, forming a clear path into the darkness.

"This can't be a coincidence," Lyra said, crouching to examine one of the stones. It was warm to the touch, despite the cave's coolness, and seemed to vibrate faintly beneath her fingers.

"It's not," Elara confirmed, her expression awestruck. "These are waystones. The Order used them to mark safe paths through dangerous territory."

"Safe is relative," Mira pointed out. "They're still leading us deeper into a cave we know nothing about."

"Better than waiting here for the Syndicate to find us," Kael countered, already moving to follow the stone path.

Lyra straightened, making her decision. "We follow the stones. But stay alert. The Order's idea of 'safe' might not match ours."

They proceeded single file into the tunnel, Kael leading with his sword drawn, Mira close behind with a torch, then Lyra, Elara, and Rowan bringing up the rear. The tunnel narrowed in places, forcing them to turn sideways to squeeze through, then opened into small chambers before constricting again. Throughout, the line of waystones continued, guiding them deeper into the earth.

"Fascinating construction," Rowan murmured, pausing to examine the tunnel walls. "These weren't carved—they were grown. The Order must have used earth magic to shape the very stone." He ran his fingers along a series of rippling patterns in the rock. "You can see the flow lines, like liquid stone that solidified mid-motion."

"Less admiring, more moving," Kael called back, his voice echoing slightly. "We're not here for a geology lesson."

"On the contrary," Rowan replied, hurrying to catch up. "Understanding how these tunnels were made might help us understand what we're walking into. Knowledge is survival, especially in places like this."

The air grew warmer as they descended, carrying a mineral scent that reminded Lyra of hot springs. The stone walls began to glisten with moisture, and the sound of running water grew louder.

After what felt like hours of careful progress, the tunnel widened dramatically, opening into a vast underground cavern. Mira's torch couldn't illuminate its full extent, but the light reflected off countless crystal formations that hung from the ceiling and jutted from the floor like the teeth of some enormous beast.

"By the Rifts," Rowan whispered, his voice echoing slightly. "It's beautiful."

It was. The crystals caught and amplified the torchlight, creating a constellation of gleaming points throughout the cavern. A underground river cut through the center, its water so clear that the smooth stones lining its bed were visible despite its depth.

And there, on the far bank, stood a sight that made Lyra's heart leap: a massive tree, its trunk as wide as a small house, its branches extending to brush the cavern ceiling. Unlike the trees above, this one was white—bone white—with leaves of palest green that seemed to glow with their own inner light. A jagged scar ran down one side of the trunk, and at its base, the roots curved above ground before plunging back into the earth, just as depicted in the cave painting.

The Heart Tree.

"We found it," Lyra breathed, the Phoenix Stone pulsing eagerly at her hip. "It's really here."

"But how?" Rowan asked, his scholarly curiosity overcoming his awe. "Trees need sunlight. How can it survive down here?"

"The Order's magic," Elara suggested, her eyes wide as she took in the impossible sight. "Or perhaps it draws energy from the earth itself, through its roots."

"Questions for later," Kael said, though even he seemed affected by the tree's majesty. "Right now, we need to get across that river and find the Fragment."

The river posed a challenge. It was too wide to jump and looked too deep to wade. There was no obvious bridge or crossing point.

"We could swim," Mira suggested, eyeing the clear water dubiously.

"I wouldn't," Elara cautioned. "Underground rivers often harbor… things. Creatures that have adapted to the darkness."

As if in response to her words, something large moved beneath the water's surface, creating a ripple that spread across the otherwise placid flow.

"Right," Mira said dryly. "Swimming's out."

Lyra approached the river's edge, drawn by an instinct she couldn't quite name. The Phoenix Stone grew warmer against her hip, almost eager. She drew it out, its blue-amber light casting new patterns across the crystal-studded cavern.

As the Stone's light touched the water, a remarkable transformation occurred. The river's surface began to freeze, not with ordinary ice but with a crystalline lattice that spread from bank to bank. Within moments, a bridge of light-infused crystal spanned the water, solid and gleaming.

"Well," Mira said after a stunned moment. "That's convenient."

"The Stone recognizes this place," Lyra said, understanding dawning. "It's been here before—or part of it has. It's helping us."

"The Earth Fragment," Elara nodded. "It must be calling to the Stone, guiding us to it."

Kael tested the crystal bridge with one foot, then his full weight. It held firm, not even creaking beneath him. "Seems solid enough. I'll go first."

He crossed cautiously, his hand still on his sword hilt. The others followed one by one, Lyra coming last with the Stone still drawn. She could feel its excitement growing as they approached the Heart Tree, its light pulsing in time with her own quickened heartbeat.

The tree was even more impressive up close. Its bark was smooth and warm to the touch, more like polished marble than wood. The pale leaves rustled gently despite the absence of wind, creating a sound like whispered conversations just beyond the edge of hearing.

"Where's the Fragment?" Rowan asked, circling the massive trunk. He produced a small measuring tool from his pack and began taking dimensions, muttering calculations under his breath. "Based on the painting's proportions and these measurements, it should be... here." He pointed to the lightning scar that ran down the tree's side.

Lyra let the Stone guide her toward the spot Rowan had indicated. As she drew closer, she saw that the scar wasn't damage at all, but a deliberate marking—a seam in the trunk that formed the outline of a door.

"Here," she said, placing her palm against the seam. "It's inside."

The moment her hand touched the tree, the whispering of the leaves intensified, becoming almost comprehensible. She felt a presence brush against her mind—ancient, patient, curious.

Who comes? The question wasn't spoken aloud but resonated directly in her thoughts.

Startled, Lyra nearly pulled away. But the Stone pulsed reassuringly in her other hand, encouraging her to respond.

"I am Lyra," she said aloud, unsure if she needed to speak for the tree to understand her. "Bearer of the Phoenix Stone. We seek the Earth Fragment."

The presence in her mind seemed to consider this, sifting through her surface thoughts and memories with gentle but thorough attention.

The Stone returns, it acknowledged finally. *But why should the Fragment leave its sanctuary? The world above is fractured, dangerous.*

"That's why we need it," Lyra explained, aware of her companions watching her with varying degrees of confusion and concern. "To heal the rifts. To restore balance."

Images flashed through her mind—the Syndicate's corruption spreading across Sylvanthia, the rifts tearing reality apart, the darkness seeping into the land itself. The tree was showing her the consequences of failure.

The Fragment has been safe here, the tree continued. *Protected from those who would misuse its power.*

"I understand," Lyra said, her voice steady despite the weight of the tree's scrutiny. "But hiding won't save it forever. The Syndicate grows stronger every day. Eventually, they'll find a way here too."

The tree's presence withdrew slightly, considering. Lyra felt its ancient wisdom weighing her words, testing her resolve.

You speak truth, it conceded finally. *But the Fragment cannot simply be taken. It must be earned.*

"How?" Lyra asked, willing to do whatever was necessary. "Tell me what I must do."

A trade, the tree proposed. *The Fragment for a memory. Your most precious memory, freely given.*

Lyra hesitated, uncertainty flickering through her. "My memory? You want to take my memory?"

Not take, the tree corrected. *Share. The memory remains yours, but becomes mine as well. This is the price. The Fragment must be anchored to something of equal value.*

Lyra considered the request. Her most precious memory... There were so few that hadn't been tainted by loss and grief. Her childhood had ended abruptly with her parents' deaths, and the years since had been marked by struggle and hardship. But there was one memory she treasured above all others, one perfect moment preserved in amber in her mind.

"Alright," she agreed softly. "I'll share my memory."

The tree's presence enveloped her mind more fully, gentle but inexorable. *Show me,* it requested.

Lyra closed her eyes, letting the memory surface. She was seven years old, sitting between her parents on the banks of a sun-dappled stream. Her father was teaching her to carve a whistle from a reed, his large hands guiding her small ones with infinite patience. Her mother was singing softly, weaving wildflowers into a crown for Lyra's hair. The air was sweet with summer, and for that one perfect afternoon, there were no rifts, no Syndicate, no looming darkness—just love and safety and belonging.

The tree absorbed the memory with something like reverence, its presence in her mind warming with what Lyra could only describe as gratitude.

A worthy exchange, it decided. *The Fragment is yours, Phoenix Bearer.*

The seam in the trunk widened, bark parting like lips to reveal a hollow within. Nestled in a bed of pale roots lay a crystal the size of Lyra's palm, earthy brown shot through with veins of green and gold. The Earth Fragment.

With trembling fingers, Lyra reached in and took it. The moment her skin contacted the Fragment, a surge of energy coursed up her arm. Unlike the Phoenix Stone's familiar warmth, this power felt rooted and steady—ancient, patient, inexorable. Images flashed through her mind: seeds unfurling beneath soil, roots delving through stone, mountains rising in slow majesty. The cycle of seasons, the dance of growth and decay, the endless patience of stone and soil.

The Phoenix Stone responded immediately, its amber light blazing to match the Fragment's earthen glow. The two crystals sang to each other, their energies intertwining in a harmony that vibrated through Lyra's very bones.

"Lyra?" Mira's voice seemed to come from a great distance. "Are you alright?"

With effort, Lyra pulled herself back from the communion of Stone and Fragment. Her companions were watching her with expressions ranging from concern to awe. She realized she was smiling, tears streaming unnoticed down her cheeks.

"I'm fine," she managed, her voice husky with emotion. "Better than fine. It's... it's incredible."

She held out her hands, the Phoenix Stone in one, the Earth Fragment in the other. As the group watched, tendrils of light—amber from the Stone, green-gold from the Fragment—reached across the space between them, intertwining like lovers' fingers.

"They're connecting," Elara breathed, her scholarly reserve forgotten in the face of such wonder. "The fragments recognize each other."

"They want to be whole again," Lyra agreed, feeling the truth of it in the resonance between the two crystals. "They've been separated too long."

With a deep breath, she brought her hands together, allowing the Stone and Fragment to touch. There was a flash of light so intense that everyone flinched away, shielding their eyes. When they could see again, the two crystals had merged seamlessly, the Earth Fragment now embedded within the Phoenix Stone like a heart within a body.

The Stone itself had changed, growing slightly larger and heavier. Where it had once been a smooth, translucent amber crystal with occasional flashes of blue, it was now marbled with earthy browns and vibrant greens. Veins of gold and copper traced through its structure like the roots of a tree spreading through fertile soil. When Lyra held it up to the cavern's dim light, she could see depths within it that hadn't been there before—layers and textures that shifted as she turned it, revealing new patterns with each movement.

Most striking was the sensation of the Stone against her palm. Before, it had always felt warm and vibrant, pulsing with a rhythm like a heartbeat. Now, that warmth was tempered with a steadiness she'd never experienced—as if the Stone had found an anchor, a grounding force to balance its fiery energy. She could feel the Earth Fragment's influence spreading through her, connecting her more deeply to the world around her. The cavern's crystals seemed to shimmer in response to her awareness, the stone beneath her feet humming with ancient melodies previously beyond her perception.

"It worked," Lyra whispered, cradling the transformed Stone. "I can feel both energies now—fire and earth, creation and endurance."

The healing begins, the Heart Tree's voice whispered in her mind, fainter now but still present. *But beware—what can heal can also harm, in the wrong hands. And remember, the Air Fragment will not yield to earth and fire alone. You will need to ascend beyond yourself to claim it.*

"I understand," Lyra replied silently. "Thank you for your trust."

The seam in the trunk closed slowly, the bark flowing together until no trace of the opening remained. The whispering of the leaves quieted, though it didn't cease entirely.

"What happened?" Rowan asked, his cartographer's curiosity evident in his wide eyes. His journal was already open, pencil poised to record this unprecedented event. "What did the tree say to you?"

"It warned me," Lyra said, carefully tucking the Stone back into its pouch at her hip. "The Fragment's power is greater than we realized. It can heal the rifts, yes, but it could also widen them if misused. And it told me something about the Air Fragment—that it will require a different approach than what we've used so far. Something about... ascending beyond ourselves."

"The Cloudspire Mountains," Elara said thoughtfully. "They're known for their treacherous winds and shifting cloud formations. Perhaps the Stone's new earth powers will help us remain grounded while we climb to those heights."

CHAPTER SEVEN

The Huntsman's Gambit

D awn broke over the valley, painting the sky in amber and rose. Lyra stood at its heart, the dew-kissed grass cool beneath her boots. The Phoenix Stone rested in her pack, its familiar warmth pulsing against her back. After their victory at the Whispering Woods, the Stone felt different—heavier with purpose, its power steadier with the Earth Fragment now merged within it.

Her companions gathered around her, each preparing for the day ahead. Kael checked his sword, running a whetstone along its edge with practiced precision. The burns on his forearm had nearly healed, though the scars would remain—a permanent reminder of their narrow escape from the Syndicate. Mira knelt nearby, carefully repacking her vials of alchemical compounds, muttering to herself as she counted her dwindling supplies. Elara sat cross-legged on a flat stone, eyes closed in meditation, pale fingers tracing runes that flickered briefly in the morning light. Rowan hunched over his maps, making final adjustments to their route with ink-stained fingers.

"We should reach the Cloudspire Mountains by nightfall," Rowan said, looking up from his work. He pushed his spectacles higher on his nose. "Assuming the weather holds and we don't run into any more of the Syndicate's patrols."

"Bold assumption," Mira replied, securing the stopper on a vial of amber liquid. "When have things ever gone according to plan?"

"The last intelligence we had placed Taryn's division near the eastern valleys," Kael said, his expression darkening at the mention of the Syndicate commander who had once been Mira's friend. "With luck, they're still occupied there."

Mira's hands stilled momentarily. "Taryn doesn't rely on luck. If he's hunting the Air Fragment too, he'll have resources in place."

"They'll be regrouping after what happened at the Heart Tree," Lyra said, joining the conversation. "We bought ourselves some time, but not much."

She touched the pouch at her hip where the transformed Stone rested. Its power had grown with the addition of the Earth Fragment, but it remained incomplete. The Air Fragment was next—hidden somewhere in the treacherous heights of the Cloudspire Mountains. After that, only the Water Fragment would remain.

"I've been studying the old texts about the Air Fragment," Elara said, opening her eyes and rising gracefully to her feet. "It's said to be guarded by wind spirits who test those who seek it. The challenges will be... different from what we faced in the Whispering Woods."

"Different how?" Kael asked, his expression guarded.

Elara hesitated. "The Earth Fragment tested our connection to the land, our ability to communicate with living things. The Air Fragment will test our ability to let go—to trust in what we cannot see or control."

Mira groaned. "Wonderful. More cryptic magical trials."

"At least they're not shadow-hounds," Rowan offered with a wry smile.

"Or Taryn's rift manipulators," Mira added grimly. "He's been experimenting with new techniques since we last crossed paths. The reports from Westhollow described controlled rifts, smaller than natural ones but more deadly."

"All the more reason to reach the Fragment before he does," Lyra said firmly.

They broke camp efficiently, each person handling their assigned tasks without need for discussion. Months of traveling together had formed them into a cohesive unit, their movements synchronized by shared experience and necessity. Lyra felt a swell of pride as she watched them work. They had started as strangers bound only by a common enemy; now they were something closer to family.

As she shouldered her pack, Lyra removed the Stone and held it up to the morning light. Its surface caught the sun, refracting it in patterns that hadn't been there before the Earth Fragment merged with it. Where once it had been a smooth, translucent amber crystal with occasional flashes of blue, it was now marbled with earthy browns and vibrant greens. Veins of gold and copper traced through its structure like roots spreading through soil.

"It's changing," Elara observed, coming to stand beside her. "Evolving with each Fragment we recover."

"I can feel it," Lyra admitted. "It's like... having a conversation with the world. Before, the Stone spoke with fire—urgent, demanding. Now it also speaks with earth—patient, enduring."

"And soon it will speak with air," Elara said. "The texts say each Fragment adds not just power, but perspective. A different way of seeing and interacting with the world."

Lyra nodded, feeling the Stone's weight in her palm. Since merging with the Earth Fragment, it had developed an uncanny connection to the land itself. She could sense stable ground, feel the strength of stone, detect water flowing beneath the surface. In the treacherous mountain terrain ahead, these abilities would prove invaluable.

"The Earth Fragment's influence should help us in the mountains," she said, tucking the Stone away. "I can feel the stability of rock now, sense which paths are safe and which might give way."

"That could mean the difference between life and death up there," Rowan said, glancing toward the distant peaks. "The Cloudspires are notorious for false ledges and sudden rockslides."

Kael approached, his expression serious. "If we're ready, we should move. The path to the mountains grows steeper from here."

Lyra nodded. "Lead on."

They set out, leaving the sheltered valley behind. The landscape changed as they traveled, transitioning from gentle meadows to rocky foothills. By midday, the Cloudspire Mountains dominated the horizon—a jagged wall of stone that seemed to pierce the sky itself. Clouds clung to their peaks, swirling in patterns that seemed almost deliberate, as if guided by unseen hands.

The air grew cooler as they climbed, carrying the scent of pine and snow. The path narrowed, forcing them to walk single file along ledges that offered spectacular views—and fatal falls for the unwary. Kael led the way, his woodsman's instincts serving them well even in this unfamiliar terrain. Lyra followed, with Elara behind her, then Rowan, and finally Mira bringing up the rear.

As they navigated a particularly narrow section, Lyra felt the Stone pulse against her hip. She paused, placing her hand on the rock face beside her. Through the Stone's influence, she could sense a network of cracks beneath the surface, the stone weakened by years of freeze and thaw.

"Stop," she called to the others. "This section isn't stable."

Kael halted immediately, trusting her judgment without question. "How far does it extend?"

Lyra closed her eyes, focusing on what the Stone was showing her. "About twenty feet ahead. The whole ledge is compromised."

"There's another path below," Rowan said, consulting his map. "It adds an hour to our journey, but it connects back to this trail beyond the unstable section."

"An hour is better than a thousand-foot fall," Mira observed dryly.

They backtracked and found the lower path, which proved to be wider and more secure. As they walked, Rowan fell into step beside Lyra.

"The Stone's earth powers are remarkable," he said, his scholarly curiosity evident. "It's like you've gained a new sense entirely."

"It's strange," Lyra admitted. "I can feel the mountain beneath us—not just the surface, but its bones, its strength and weaknesses. It's like reading a map that no one else can see."

"That's essentially what cartography is," Rowan said with a smile. "Reading the land, understanding its patterns, translating that knowledge for others. Perhaps we're not so different, you and I."

Lyra returned his smile, appreciating the comparison. Rowan had changed since they began their journey—the nervous scholar gradually giving way to a more confident explorer. His maps had saved them countless times, his knowledge of terrain proving as valuable as Kael's combat skills or Mira's alchemy.

"I hate mountains," Mira announced after several hours of climbing. "Give me a nice, sensible forest any day."

"You hated the forest too," Rowan reminded her, carefully navigating a section of loose shale.

"I'm consistent in my complaints," Mira replied. "It's part of my charm."

"Is that what you call it?" Kael muttered from ahead, though Lyra caught the hint of a smile on his face.

Their banter lightened the mood, but Lyra remained alert. The Stone grew warmer against her hip the higher they climbed, responding to... something. The Air Fragment was near, she was certain of it. But so was danger. The wind carried whispers that prickled at the edge of her hearing—not quite voices, but not merely the sound of air through stone either.

During a brief rest at a sheltered outcropping, Mira approached Lyra, her expression unusually serious.

"I should have mentioned this earlier," she said, keeping her voice low, "but I've been noticing signs of Syndicate activity since we entered the foothills. Fresh bootprints, broken branches cut with a blade rather than snapped naturally."

"You think they're ahead of us?" Lyra asked, concern creeping into her voice.

"Or paralleling our route," Mira replied. "And if Taryn's leading them..." She trailed off, her hand unconsciously moving to a thin scar at her collarbone—a parting gift from her former friend. "He knows how we think, how we move. And he has resources we don't."

"Why didn't you say something sooner?" Kael asked, joining them.

"Because I wasn't certain," Mira said. "And because I didn't want to slow us down with paranoia. But the signs are getting fresher. They're close."

Kael's expression hardened. "We'll adjust our route. Take a less obvious approach to the higher peaks."

"And if they're waiting for us?" Rowan asked, worry evident in his voice.

"Then we deal with them," Lyra said firmly. "The Stone grows stronger with each Fragment. We're not as vulnerable as we once were."

Late in the afternoon, they came upon an ancient stone bridge spanning a deep chasm. The bridge arched gracefully over the void, its surface carved from pale granite worn smooth by time. Intricate carvings adorned its edges—spirals of flame, waves of water, roots curling through earth, winds weaving through air. Runes etched into the stone glowed with a faint blue light.

Rowan approached the bridge cautiously, consulting his map. "This isn't marked," he said, frowning. "But these runes... they're old. Very old."

"Aethyr script," Elara confirmed, kneeling to examine the markings. "Similar to what we saw in the Heart Tree's cavern, but more refined. This bridge was built by the Order at the height of their power."

"What does it say?" Lyra asked.

Elara traced the symbols with careful fingers. "It speaks of a temple—the Temple of Echoes, where 'the voices of the past guide the keepers of the future.' It says the temple houses 'the key to the Fragment's song.'"

"The key to the Fragment?" Lyra repeated. "You mean we need something from this temple before we can claim the Air Fragment?"

"So it would seem," Elara said, rising to her feet. "The Order rarely made things simple."

Kael tested the bridge with one foot, then his full weight. The stone held firm, not even creaking beneath him. "Seems solid enough. I'll go first."

"Wait," Mira said, stepping forward. She uncorked a vial containing a fine silver powder and sprinkled it along the bridge's edge. The powder sparkled as it settled, but showed no reaction. "No traps that I can detect. At least, none of the conventional sort."

As she worked, Lyra noticed her scanning the far side of the bridge, her movements casual but her eyes alert. Looking for signs of Taryn, Lyra realized. The history between the alchemist and the Syndicate commander was complex—they had trained together as apprentices before the Syndicate's rise to power, and Taryn's betrayal had cut Mira more deeply than she liked to admit.

"The Order preferred trials of wisdom to mere physical traps," Elara said. "Be vigilant, but not fearful."

They crossed the bridge in silence, the wind growing stronger with each step. Below them, the chasm plunged into darkness, so deep that they couldn't see its bottom. The bridge seemed to hum beneath their feet, a subtle vibration that resonated with the Stone's own pulse.

On the far side, a path led to a sheer cliff face where an archway had been carved from the living rock. Unlike the bridge, which was pale granite, the arch was obsidian black, its surface rippling with faint silver reflections. A thin mist clung to the opening, obscuring what lay beyond.

"The Temple of Echoes," Elara breathed, a note of awe in her voice. "I thought it was just a legend."

"Is it safe?" Kael asked, hand resting on his sword hilt.

"Define 'safe,'" Mira muttered.

Lyra stepped toward the arch, drawn by an instinct she couldn't name. The Stone grew warmer against her hip, almost eager. "There's something here we need," she said. "I can feel it."

"Then we go in," Kael said simply. "Together."

Lyra nodded, grateful for his steady presence. "Together."

They stepped through the archway, the mist parting around them like a curtain drawn back. A wave of energy washed over them—not hostile, but powerful, ancient. The temple's interior unfolded before them: a vast, open space with a high ceiling lost to shadow. Pillars of black stone rose like sentinels, their surfaces etched with the same runes they had seen on the bridge. Crystals hung from above, catching what little light filtered through hidden apertures and scattering it in prismatic patterns across the floor.

"This place feels... alive," Rowan whispered, his voice echoing slightly despite his soft tone.

He was right. There was a presence here, a weight of awareness that pressed against their senses. The air itself seemed to breathe, currents moving through the temple in patterns too deliberate to be natural drafts.

The walls bore murals depicting scenes that seemed to shift when viewed from different angles. Lyra approached one, drawn by a flash of familiar color. It showed figures wielding what could only be the Phoenix Stone—men and women from different eras, facing various threats. As she watched, the images moved subtly, telling a story without words.

"The Stone's history," she murmured.

"Not just history," Elara said, joining her. "Legacy. These are the previous bearers—the ones who carried the Stone before you."

Lyra studied the figures more closely. They were diverse in appearance and approach—some wielded the Stone as a weapon, others as a tool of healing or creation. But all shared a certain quality in their stance, a determination that transcended time and circumstance.

"Look at this one," Rowan called from further along the wall. He pointed to a mural showing a woman with dark hair and green eyes startlingly similar to Lyra's own. She stood on a battlefield, the Stone blazing in her hands as she faced a tide of shadow.

"That's... unsettling," Lyra said, staring at what could have been her own face painted centuries ago.

"The Stone chooses its bearers for a reason," Elara said quietly. "Perhaps certain bloodlines carry an affinity for its power."

"Or perhaps it's just a coincidence," Mira offered, though she sounded unconvinced by her own suggestion.

Kael, who had been scouting ahead, called back to them. "There's something here you should see."

They followed his voice to the center of the temple, where a circular dais rose from the floor. On it stood a pedestal of the same black stone as the walls, but inlaid with veins of silver that pulsed with a subtle light. Atop the pedestal rested a crystal unlike any Lyra had seen before—clear as water but shifting with inner light, neither solid nor liquid but somewhere in between.

"What is it?" she asked, approaching cautiously.

"I believe it's what we came for," Elara replied. "The key mentioned in the bridge inscription."

Lyra reached for the crystal, but Kael caught her wrist.

"Wait," he said. "It's too easy. The Order wouldn't leave something this valuable unprotected."

As if in response to his words, the air around the pedestal shimmered, and a figure materialized before them—translucent, glowing with a soft silver light. It had the form of a person, but its features were indistinct, its edges blurring into the air around it.

"Keepers of the Stone," the figure spoke, its voice neither male nor female but a harmony of tones that resonated through the chamber. "You seek the key to the Air Fragment."

"We do," Lyra confirmed, stepping forward. The Stone pulsed against her hip, responding to the spectral guardian's presence.

"The key is not freely given," the guardian continued. "It must be earned through trials that test not just strength, but wisdom, unity, and sacrifice."

"Of course it does," Mira sighed. "Nothing's ever simple with ancient magical artifacts, is it?"

The guardian seemed to study her for a moment, its featureless face tilted slightly. "Simplicity is rarely the path to power, alchemist."

Mira blinked, surprised at being addressed directly. "Fair point."

"What are these trials?" Kael asked, his voice practical and to the point.

"Three challenges you shall face," the guardian replied. "One of mind, one of heart, one of soul. Succeed, and the key is yours. Fail, and you shall join the echoes that dwell within these walls—memories only, never to leave."

A chill ran through the group at these words. Lyra glanced at her companions, reading the determination in their faces despite the threat. They had come too far to turn back now.

"We accept your trials," she said firmly.

The guardian inclined its head. "Then let the first challenge begin."

The temple floor shifted beneath them, sections of stone sliding away to reveal a complex pattern of tiles—some solid, others clearly unstable. The pattern extended from the dais where they stood to a far doorway that hadn't been visible before. Between them and the door, mechanisms whirred to life—blades that swung in rhythmic arcs, jets of flame that burst from hidden apertures, sections of floor that dropped away into darkness only to rise again moments later.

"A challenge of mind," the guardian announced. "Find the true path through chaos."

Rowan stepped forward immediately, his cartographer's eye already analyzing the pattern. "It's a puzzle," he said, excitement overcoming caution. "The tiles form a map—see how they echo the constellations?"

He pointed to sections of the floor where the tiles formed familiar star patterns. Lyra hadn't noticed it at first, but now she could see it—the Great Bear, the Hunter, the Phoenix itself.

"The safe path follows the seasonal progression," Rowan continued, pulling out his journal and sketching rapidly. "Winter to spring to summer to fall. See? The winter constellations are here, near us. Then spring, there. Summer beyond, and fall just before the door."

"Brilliant," Elara breathed. "But the obstacles—"

"They follow patterns too," Rowan said, still sketching. "The blades swing in a six-count rhythm. The flame jets follow a four-count. The dropping tiles are on an eight-count. We need to time our movements to the intersections of these patterns."

"And how exactly do we do that without getting sliced, burned, or dropped into whatever's below?" Mira asked skeptically.

Rowan looked up from his journal, a rare confidence in his expression. "Trust me. I can guide us through."

And he did. With Rowan calling directions and counting rhythms, they navigated the deadly obstacle course one by one. It was terrifying work—Lyra felt the heat of flames as she darted between jets, the whisper of blades passing inches from her face, the stomach-dropping lurch as tiles shifted beneath her feet. But Rowan's calculations were flawless. They reached the far door without a single injury, breathless but triumphant.

"Well done, cartographer," the guardian's voice echoed around them. "Few have mapped the chaos so precisely."

Rowan flushed with pride, accepting the rare clap on the shoulder from Kael with a startled smile.

The door before them opened onto a new chamber, smaller than the first but no less impressive. Here, the walls were mirrors—perfect reflections that created an infinite regression of their own images stretching in all directions. In the center stood another pedestal, this one bearing a small silver bowl filled with clear liquid.

"The second challenge," the guardian announced, materializing beside the pedestal. "A challenge of heart. Face your deepest fears, your darkest truths."

"How?" Lyra asked, approaching cautiously.

"The Waters of Truth," the guardian gestured to the bowl. "Look into them, and you will see what you most fear to face. Acknowledge it, accept it, and you may pass. Deny it, and be lost to the mirrors."

Kael stepped forward without hesitation. "I'll go first."

Before anyone could object, he leaned over the bowl and gazed into the water. Immediately, his body tensed, his knuckles white as he gripped the pedestal's edge. Lyra couldn't see what he saw, but the pain in his expression was unmistakable.

"Lirien," he whispered, the name of his lost sister escaping like a prayer.

For long moments he stood frozen, tears streaming unnoticed down his face. Then, with visible effort, he straightened.

"I couldn't save you," he said to whatever image he saw in the water. "I wasn't there when the Syndicate came. I've carried that guilt for years." He took a shuddering breath. "But I know now—it wasn't my fault. And I honor your memory by protecting those I can, by fighting for a world where no one else loses what I lost."

The water in the bowl rippled, then stilled. Kael stepped back, his expression raw but somehow lighter, as if a burden had been partially lifted.

One by one, they faced the Waters of Truth. Mira confronted her fear of betrayal, stemming from her brother's death and deepened by Taryn's defection to the Syndicate. "You showed me that trust can be broken," she whispered to the water, "but that doesn't mean I should stop trusting altogether. My strength comes from knowing who deserves that trust—and these people do."

Elara faced her secret belief that her gentle nature made her a liability to the group. Rowan confronted his fear that his knowledge would never be enough to make a real difference.

"Maps can't change the world," he admitted, his voice steady despite the pain in his eyes. "But they can guide those who will. My strength isn't in fighting or magic—it's in understanding paths, in seeing patterns others miss. That's how I contribute, how I make a difference."

Finally, it was Lyra's turn. She approached the pedestal, heart pounding. The water showed her not her past, as she had expected, but a possible future—herself wielding the completed Stone, its power corrupting her as it had corrupted others before her. In the vision, she stood triumphant over a ruined landscape, the very rifts she sought to heal torn wider by her misuse of the Stone's power.

"This isn't me," she whispered, horrified.

"But it could be," her reflection seemed to answer. "Power changes people. How can you be sure you're different?"

Lyra stared into her own eyes, seeing the doubt there, the fear. And she realized—this was her deepest fear. Not failure, but success followed by corruption. The possibility that in seeking to heal the world, she might become its destroyer.

"I can't be certain," she admitted finally, both to the vision and to herself. "Power does change people. But I'm not alone." She glanced at her companions. "They keep me grounded. They would stop me if I strayed from our purpose. And I trust them to do so, even if it meant standing against me."

The water stilled, and the guardian nodded in approval.

"Truth acknowledged," it said. "The second trial is passed."

The mirrors around them shimmered and dissolved, revealing a passage to a third chamber. This one was open to the sky, a circular space with a floor of polished stone and walls that rose only waist-high. Beyond them, the mountains stretched in all directions, clouds swirling between peaks in complex patterns. The wind was stronger here, carrying whispers that almost formed words.

In the center of this open space stood a final pedestal. Unlike the others, this one held nothing.

"The third challenge," the guardian said, appearing beside them. "A challenge of soul. To gain, you must give. A sacrifice freely made opens the way forward."

"What kind of sacrifice?" Lyra asked warily.

"That is for you to determine," the guardian replied. "But know this—it must be meaningful, personal, and given without reservation."

The companions exchanged glances, uncertainty in their expressions. What could they offer that would satisfy such a requirement?

Mira stepped forward first, reaching for a vial at her belt—one with a distinctive blue glow. "This is the last of my family's legacy," she said, her voice unusually solemn. "The formula my father perfected before he died. I've been saving it, telling myself I was preserving his memory." She placed the vial on the pedestal. "But he didn't create this to be hoarded. He made it to help people."

The vial glowed brighter for a moment, then vanished. The pedestal remained empty.

"A worthy offering," the guardian acknowledged. "But not what is needed here."

Rowan approached next, laying his most precious possession on the stone—a journal filled with maps and observations collected over years of travel. "My life's work," he said simply. "Knowledge meant to be shared, not kept for myself alone."

The journal, like the vial, glowed and vanished. Still, the pedestal remained empty.

Elara offered a silver pendant that had belonged to her mother. Kael laid down a knife that had been his father's. Each gift was accepted and vanished, but none fulfilled the requirement.

Finally, Lyra stepped forward, the Stone warm in her hands. Surely this wasn't what the guardian wanted—the very object they were trying to complete? And yet, what else did she have that held true value?

Then she understood. It wasn't about material offerings at all.

"I offer my certainty," she said quietly. "My belief that I know what the Stone's power is meant for, how it should be used." She placed her empty hands on the pedestal. "I acknowledge that its purpose may be greater than my understanding, that I am its keeper but not its master."

The pedestal began to glow, a soft light that spread outward in concentric circles.

"A true sacrifice," the guardian said, approval in its voice. "To relinquish control is often harder than surrendering possessions."

The light from the pedestal intensified, coalescing into a crystal identical to the one they had seen in the first chamber. It floated above the stone, rotating slowly, catching the light in hypnotic patterns.

"The key is yours, Bearer of the Stone," the guardian said. "Use it wisely."

Lyra reached out and took the crystal. It was cool to the touch despite its glow, and surprisingly heavy for its size. As her fingers closed around it, visions flashed through her mind—swift impressions of soaring heights, rushing winds, freedom and perspective beyond anything she had known. The Air Fragment's essence, calling to her through the key.

"Thank you," she said to the guardian, her voice steady despite the power coursing through her.

The guardian inclined its head. "Remember what you have learned here. The Temple of Echoes preserves not just knowledge, but wisdom. The trials you faced reflect the challenges that await in claiming the Air Fragment itself."

"Where exactly is the Fragment?" Kael asked. "We know it's somewhere in these mountains, but—"

"The key will guide you," the guardian interrupted. "Follow its call when dawn touches the highest peak. But be warned—the Syndicate also seeks what you seek. They approach even now, drawn by the Stone's growing power."

"How much time do we have?" Lyra asked urgently.

"Hours, not days," the guardian replied. "Rest here if you must, but do not delay overlong."

With those words, the spectral figure faded, leaving them alone in the open chamber as twilight deepened around them.

"We should stay the night," Kael said, ever practical. "Attempting those peaks in darkness would be suicide, Syndicate or no Syndicate."

Lyra nodded, though anxiety gnawed at her. The Syndicate was coming. Had they tracked the group directly, or were they simply following the same clues about the Fragment's location? Either way, the race was tightening.

They made camp in the temple's main chamber, the vast space offering protection from the mountain winds while the guardian's lingering presence kept other threats at bay. As the others prepared a small meal from their supplies, Lyra sat apart, studying the crystal key.

Elara joined her after a while, settling gracefully beside her. "The trials changed you," she observed. "All of us, really."

Lyra nodded. "I feel... less certain than before. Is that strange? I thought finding the key would bring clarity, but instead..."

"Instead you have questions you didn't have before," Elara finished for her. "That's wisdom beginning to take root. Certainty is often the enemy of truth."

"That's not very comforting," Lyra said with a small smile.

"Comfort and growth rarely walk hand in hand," Elara replied, returning the smile. "But you're stronger for the questions. We all are."

Across the chamber, Mira had engaged Rowan in what appeared to be a heated debate about the temple's construction, while Kael listened with the patient expression of someone who had heard such arguments many times before. Despite the danger ahead, there was a moment of peace in their circle—a family forged through hardship, bound by purpose and growing affection.

Lyra tucked the crystal key safely away and joined them, accepting a bowl of simple stew with gratitude. Tomorrow would bring new challenges—the Air Fragment itself, the Syndicate's pursuit, the continuing quest to heal the rifts that threatened their world. But tonight, in this ancient place of echoes and wisdom, they had earned a moment of respite.

As night deepened, Kael organized a watch rotation. "I'll take first watch," he said, already moving toward the temple entrance. "Mira second, then Rowan, then Elara. Lyra, you need to rest—the Stone draws on your energy, and tomorrow will demand all you have."

Lyra wanted to protest but knew he was right. The trials had taken more from her than she wanted to admit. She settled into her bedroll, the Stone and the crystal key both secure against her body, their combined warmth lulling her toward sleep.

Her dreams were vivid—images of soaring through clouds, of winds that spoke in voices both strange and familiar, of a peak that gleamed like polished metal beneath the morning sun. The Air Fragment called to her, its song weaving through her unconscious mind, preparing her for what was to come.

Lyra woke before dawn, the crystal key pulsing with soft light beside her bedroll. She sat up, instantly alert. The key was active, responding to something. Outside, the sky was just beginning to lighten, the stars fading as night surrendered to day.

"Everyone up," she called, her voice cutting through the silence of the temple. "It's time."

The others stirred, transitioning from sleep to wakefulness with the efficiency of those accustomed to danger. Within minutes, they had packed their meager camp and stood ready, watching as Lyra held the key aloft.

The crystal's glow intensified as she turned toward the eastern wall of the open chamber. Through the waist-high barrier, they could see the mountains stretching before them, their peaks catching the first hint of dawn's light.

"There," Lyra said, pointing to the tallest peak visible from their position. Unlike the others, which were dark stone, this one gleamed with a silvery sheen, as if made of metal rather than rock. "That's where we need to go."

"The Spire of Winds," Elara said, recognition in her voice. "It's mentioned in the ancient texts—a place where the boundary between our world and the realm of air grows thin."

"How far?" Kael asked, already assessing the terrain between them and their destination.

"A few hours' climb," Rowan estimated, consulting his maps. "If we take that ridge path and then cross the saddle between those two lesser peaks, we can reach the base of the Spire by mid-morning."

"And the Syndicate?" Mira asked, scanning the landscape below for signs of pursuit.

"No sign yet," Kael replied, his keen eyes searching the mountain paths. "But they're coming. We should move now, while we still have the advantage."

They left the Temple of Echoes through a narrow staircase carved into the cliff face, descending to a path that wound along the mountainside. The key guided them, its glow brightening when they chose the correct fork in the trail, dimming when they strayed. The morning air was crisp and cold, carrying the scent of snow from the higher elevations.

The climb was challenging but not impossible. The Earth Fragment's influence on the Stone proved invaluable, allowing Lyra to sense stable footholds and warn of loose rocks before they gave way. At one point, she pressed her palm against a seemingly solid ledge and felt the weakness beneath—a network of fissures that would have collapsed under their weight. They detoured around it, adding time to their journey but avoiding what could have been a fatal fall.

"The Stone's connection to the earth is saving our lives," Rowan observed as they navigated a particularly treacherous section. "It's as if you can read the mountain itself."

"In a way, I can," Lyra replied. "It's like the Stone is translating the mountain's language for me—its strengths, its weaknesses, its history written in layers of rock."

"A living map," Rowan said with appreciation. "No wonder cartographers spend years studying a single mountain range. There's so much we can't see with our eyes alone."

"Something's not right," Kael said suddenly, pausing on a narrow ledge. They had been climbing for nearly two hours, and the Spire of Winds now loomed closer, its metallic surface catching the morning sun in blinding flashes.

"What is it?" Lyra asked, coming to stand beside him.

Kael pointed to a thin column of smoke rising from a valley to their left. "Campfire. Too controlled to be natural. Someone's up here with us."

"The Syndicate?" Mira asked, her hand moving to her bandolier.

"Maybe," Kael replied, his expression grim. "But they wouldn't be so careless as to let their fire smoke unless—"

"Unless they want us to see it," Lyra finished for him. "A distraction."

As if in confirmation of her words, a sound reached them—the faint but unmistakable crack of stone breaking under pressure, coming from the path ahead.

"Ambush," Kael said, drawing his sword in a single fluid motion. "They're trying to funnel us."

"Positions," Lyra ordered, the Stone already warming in her hand. "Kael, front. Mira, cover our flanks. Elara, shields ready. Rowan, watch our backs."

They moved with practiced coordination, forming a defensive formation on the narrow path. Kael took point, his sword held at the ready. Mira positioned herself where she could deploy her vials in multiple directions. Elara's fingers traced protective runes in the air, preparing barriers. Rowan drew his dagger, his other hand reaching for the measuring chain at his belt—a simple tool that he had learned to use as an improvised weapon, the weighted end capable of striking with surprising force at a distance.

No sooner had they settled into position than figures appeared on the path before them—three men in the distinctive black and silver of the Syndicate, their faces obscured by masks that covered all but their eyes. Each carried a curved blade that gleamed with an unnatural purple light.

"Rift-steel," Elara whispered, her face paling. "Be careful—those blades are forged in the heart of rifts. They can cut through magical defenses and leave wounds that resist healing. Even a scratch can be dangerous."

More figures appeared behind them, blocking their retreat. They were trapped on the narrow mountain path, with sheer cliffs above and a fatal drop below.

"Well, well," one of the masked figures called, his voice carrying a mocking lilt. "The Stone-bearer and her little band of heroes. How convenient that you've done all the hard work of finding the Fragment's location for us."

The man removed his mask, revealing a face Lyra had seen only in Mira's descriptions—handsome but for a jagged scar that ran from temple to jaw, with cold eyes that assessed them like a predator sizing up prey.

"Taryn," Mira spat, recognition and hatred mingling in her voice. "I should have known you'd slither your way into this."

Taryn laughed, the sound sharp as breaking glass. "Mira, my dear. Still holding a grudge? It was just business, you know."

"You sold us out to the Syndicate," Mira replied, her voice cold with fury. "You got people killed. That's not business—that's betrayal."

"Semantics," Taryn shrugged. "But enough reminiscing. Hand over the Stone and the key, and we might let you live. Fight, and, well..." He gestured to the steep drop beside the path.

Lyra stepped forward, the Stone warming in her hand. "You know we won't surrender it. The Stone is our only hope of healing the rifts."

"Healing the rifts?" Taryn laughed again. "Is that what you think it's for? How charmingly naive. The Stone isn't meant to heal—it's meant to control. To harness the rifts' power, not close them."

"You're wrong," Lyra said, though a flicker of doubt crossed her mind. Was this what the Waters of Truth had shown her—the possibility that the Stone's purpose wasn't what she believed?

"Am I?" Taryn's smile was cold. "Ask your rune-caster. The Aethyr Order didn't create the Stone to mend the world—they created it to rule it."

Lyra glanced at Elara, whose expression had grown troubled.

"There are... competing theories about the Stone's original purpose," Elara admitted reluctantly. "But what matters is how we choose to use it now."

"How touching," Taryn sneered. "But I'm tired of talking. Last chance—surrender, or die here on this mountain."

Lyra met Kael's eyes, then Mira's, then Rowan's. Each nodded slightly, ready for what came next.

"Now!" she shouted.

Their response was immediate and coordinated. Kael lunged forward, his sword arcing toward Taryn. Mira hurled two vials simultaneously—one at the rift itself, another at the agents behind them. Elara's runes flared to life, creating a shield that deflected the first surge of rift energy.

Rowan's response surprised even his companions. With practiced precision, he swung his measuring chain in a wide arc, the weighted end striking a Syndicate agent's wrist with enough force to crack bone. The agent's rift-steel blade clattered to the ground, and Rowan kicked it over the edge of the path before the man could recover. In the same fluid motion, he ducked beneath another agent's swing, using his smaller size and quickness to his advantage.

"The cartographer has teeth!" Taryn called, genuine surprise in his voice as he parried Kael's attack.

CHAPTER EIGHT

Veiled Blades

T he first light of dawn spilled across the horizon, painting the sky in hues of
amber and rose. Lyra stood at the edge of a still lake, its surface a perfect
mirror reflecting the silhouettes of twisted pines and distant mountains. A soft
mist clung to the water's edge, curling around her boots as she watched her
companions prepare for the day ahead.

Kael knelt by the remains of their campfire, methodically checking his sword
for any signs of damage from yesterday's skirmish. The burns on his forearm—a
reminder of their narrow escape from the Syndicate's trap in the Cloudspire
Mountains—had begun to heal, but the scars would remain. Mira sat cross-legged
nearby, carefully sorting her remaining alchemical supplies, her brow furrowed
in concentration. Elara moved through a series of graceful stretches, her morning
ritual to prepare her body for the channeling of magic. Rowan hunched over his
maps, making notes in the margins with a stub of charcoal.

Lyra touched the Phoenix Stone where it rested against her chest, its warmth
pulsing beneath her tunic like a second heartbeat. With the Air Fragment now

merged with it, the Stone had changed again—lighter somehow, as if it might float away if not secured. Veins of silver now threaded through its amber and green depths, shifting like captured wind when the light struck it.

"You're up early," Kael said, coming to stand beside her. His voice was low, meant only for her ears.

"Couldn't sleep," Lyra admitted. "Too much on my mind."

He nodded, understanding without needing further explanation. The Air Fragment had been secured, but not without cost. The battle with Taryn and his Syndicate forces had left them all shaken, and the Fragment's integration with the Stone had been more violent than the Earth Fragment's gentle merging. For hours afterward, Lyra had felt as though her body might simply dissipate into the air, her consciousness scattered to the winds.

"How does it feel now?" Kael asked, nodding toward the Stone.

Lyra considered the question. "Different. When we added the Earth Fragment, everything felt more... solid. Grounded. Now it's like there's a storm contained within it, waiting to be released." She paused. "And I can hear whispers sometimes, just at the edge of hearing. As if the wind is trying to tell me something."

Concern flickered across Kael's face. "Is it dangerous?"

"I don't think so. Just unfamiliar." She managed a small smile. "I'll adjust, like I did before."

"The Air Fragment should prove useful where we're headed," Kael said, gesturing toward the southern horizon. "The marshlands are known for sudden fogs and treacherous winds. Having some influence over the air itself could mean the difference between finding our path and becoming hopelessly lost."

Lyra nodded, having had similar thoughts. Already she'd noticed that she could sense shifts in the wind before they occurred, could feel the subtle patterns of air currents against her skin. In the marshlands, where visibility could drop to arm's length in moments, such awareness might prove invaluable.

"We should reach Rivermeet by midday," Rowan called, looking up from his maps. "If we follow the eastern trail."

Lyra turned toward him, grateful for the practical interruption. "Rivermeet is still free of Syndicate control?"

"Last we heard," Rowan confirmed, pushing his spectacles higher on his nose. "It's one of the few trading posts they haven't seized. The river makes it defensible, and they've had strong leadership."

He traced a path on his map with an ink-stained finger. "The real challenge will come after Rivermeet. The southern marshlands are treacherous even in the best of times. Shifting channels, carnivorous flora, not to mention the fever-flies that swarm during the warm season." He frowned. "And there are old stories about the marshes—places where the water itself seems alive. Hungry."

"Folklore," Mira said dismissively, though Lyra noticed she added an extra vial of purification salts to her pack.

"Perhaps," Rowan replied, not looking up from his map. "But I've learned that most folklore has roots in truth. Especially in places touched by the rifts."

"Good," Lyra said, bringing the conversation back to their immediate plans. "We need supplies, and information about what's happening in the lowlands."

They broke camp efficiently, each person handling their assigned tasks without need for discussion. Months of traveling together had formed them into a cohesive unit, their movements synchronized by shared experience and necessity. Within half an hour, they were on the trail, following a winding path that dipped into a shallow vale before climbing toward the distant hills.

The morning was cool, the air fresh with the scent of pine and loam. Birds called from the forest canopy, and once, a deer bounded across their path, startling Mira into nearly dropping a vial. Despite the beauty around them, Lyra couldn't shake a growing sense of unease. The Stone seemed to pulse more insistently against her chest, as if warning her of something ahead.

"Do you feel that?" she asked Elara, who walked beside her.

The rune-caster nodded, her pale eyes scanning the horizon. "There's a disturbance in the flow of energy. Something has happened nearby."

They crested a small rise, and the source of the disturbance became immediately apparent. Below them lay what had once been a village—now a collection of charred ruins. Blackened timbers jutted from collapsed walls like broken bones. Gardens had been trampled, wells fouled. The few structures still standing bore the scorch marks of deliberate burning.

"Syndicate," Kael growled, his hand moving to his sword hilt.

Lyra's stomach clenched at the sight. This was why they fought—to prevent scenes like this from repeating across Sylvanthia. She scanned the devastation, looking for any sign of survivors.

"There," Mira said, pointing to a small cluster of people gathered near what might have been the village square. "Some of them made it."

They approached cautiously, aware that their armed group might appear threatening to people who had just suffered an attack. As they drew closer, Lyra could see that the survivors—perhaps twenty in all—were in desperate condition. A woman cradled a crying toddler whose face was smudged with soot. An old man clutched a pitchfork, his knuckles white with tension. Others sat in numb silence, staring at nothing.

Lyra stepped forward, hands open to show she carried no weapon. "We mean you no harm," she called. "We're enemies of the Syndicate."

The old man with the pitchfork stepped forward, his weathered face a mask of suspicion. "Prove it," he demanded, his voice hoarse from smoke or shouting.

Lyra hesitated, then slowly reached for the Phoenix Stone. As her fingers touched it, its light flared visibly even through her clothing, a warm glow that illuminated her face from below.

The old man's eyes widened, and he lowered his pitchfork. "The Stone of Light," he whispered. "The legends speak of it—a power to heal the land."

"We're trying to do just that," Lyra said gently. "What happened here?"

A middle-aged woman stepped forward, her arm in a crude sling. "Syndicate raiding party came three days ago. Said we hadn't paid our 'protection' tribute." Her mouth twisted on the word. "When our headman said we had nothing left to give, they made an example of him. Then they burned everything they couldn't carry away."

"We hid in the root cellars," the old man added. "Those of us who could. The rest..." He gestured vaguely toward a row of fresh mounds at the edge of the village. Graves.

Lyra felt a familiar anger rising within her—the same fury that had driven her since her parents' death at Syndicate hands. She turned to her companions. "We can't leave them like this."

Kael nodded, already removing his pack. "We have supplies to share."

"And I can treat the wounded," Elara added, her hands already reaching for her healer's kit.

They spent the next two hours helping the villagers as best they could. Mira and Rowan distributed food and helped patch shelters from salvaged materials. Kael organized a perimeter watch, teaching a few of the stronger villagers basic defensive formations in case the raiders returned. Elara moved from person to person, treating burns and cuts with gentle efficiency.

Lyra found herself sitting with the woman who held the toddler, now sleeping fitfully against her shoulder.

"He's not mine," the woman said, noticing Lyra's gaze. "His mother was killed in the attack. I found him hiding under a cart."

"What will you do now?" Lyra asked.

The woman looked around at the ruined village. "Rebuild, I suppose. What choice do we have? This is our home."

"You could come with us to Rivermeet," Lyra suggested. "It's safer there."

The woman shook her head. "And then what? Become refugees, dependent on others' charity? No. We'll rebuild. We always do." She met Lyra's eyes. "But we need more than just food and medicine. We need to know this won't happen again. We need hope."

Lyra felt the weight of the woman's words. This was the reality across Sylvanthia—ordinary people caught in a conflict they hadn't chosen, trying to survive from one day to the next. The Phoenix Stone might be powerful, but what good was it if they couldn't protect villages like this?

"We're going to stop them," Lyra promised. "The Syndicate. We're gathering allies, and when we're strong enough, we'll take the fight to them."

"Pretty words," the woman said, not unkindly. "But we've heard promises before."

Before Lyra could respond, Kael approached, his expression tense. "We need to move," he said quietly. "Scout spotted dust on the northern road. Could be more Syndicate forces."

Lyra nodded, rising to her feet. "We've done what we can here. We should reach Rivermeet before dark."

As they prepared to leave, the old man who had first challenged them approached. "Thank you," he said gruffly. "For the food and medicine. And..." he hesitated, "for giving us a reason to believe again. Word of your coming will spread. Others will know the Stone of Light has returned."

"Keep your people safe," Lyra replied. "And if you can, spread the word. We're gathering forces at Rivermeet. Anyone who wants to fight back against the Syndicate is welcome."

They departed with the villagers' gratitude following them like a physical presence. Lyra felt both heartened by their appreciation and burdened by the responsibility it represented. So many people were counting on them, on her. The Stone seemed heavier against her chest.

"You did what you could," Kael said as they walked, reading her expression with the ease of long familiarity. "We can't save everyone."

"Not yet," Lyra agreed. "But we will."

The trail to Rivermeet wound through increasingly populated countryside. They passed small farms where farmers paused in their work to watch them pass, and twice they encountered merchant caravans heading toward the trading post. The merchants eyed their weapons warily but offered respectful nods when they saw Rowan's cartographer insignia.

By mid-afternoon, they crested a hill and saw Rivermeet spread below them. The town straddled a wide river, with sturdy stone bridges connecting the two halves. Walls of timber and earth surrounded it—not the formidable fortifications of a true city, but enough to deter casual raiders. Smoke rose from dozens of chimneys, and even from this distance, they could hear the bustle of commerce.

"It's grown since I was last here," Rowan observed. "More buildings on the eastern bank."

"Refugees," Kael guessed. "People fleeing Syndicate territory."

They approached the main gate, where a pair of guards in leather armor watched their approach with professional interest.

"State your business," one called as they drew near.

"Travelers seeking supplies and lodging," Lyra replied. "And perhaps information."

The guard studied them, taking in their weapons and travel-worn appearance. "You've come from the north?"

"Yes," Kael answered. "Through the Cloudspire Mountains."

The guard's eyebrows rose slightly. "Not many make that journey these days. The mountain passes are dangerous."

"We had our reasons," Mira said with a tight smile.

After a moment's consideration, the guard nodded. "You'll find the Rivermeet Inn on the main square. Tell Hilda that Dorn sent you—she might have rooms available. As for supplies, the market runs until sundown."

They passed through the gate into a town humming with activity. The main street was lined with shops and stalls, merchants calling their wares to passing customers. The air was rich with the scents of cooking food, tanned leather, and the earthy smell of the river itself. After weeks in the wilderness, the press of humanity felt both overwhelming and comforting.

"We should split up," Kael suggested. "Cover more ground. Mira, you handle the alchemical supplies. Rowan, see if you can find any maps of the southern territories. Elara and I will secure lodging."

"And I'll see what information I can gather," Lyra added. "Meet at the inn by sundown."

They separated, each heading toward their assigned tasks. Lyra wandered through the market, listening to conversations, gauging the mood of the town. Most people seemed cautiously optimistic—trade was good, the harvest had been bountiful, and the Syndicate had not yet turned its full attention to Rivermeet. But underneath ran a current of tension. Merchants spoke of disrupted trade routes, of villages that no longer sent goods to market, of friends and relatives who had fled Syndicate territory with nothing but the clothes on their backs.

Near the central square, Lyra noticed a crowd gathered around a woman standing on a wooden crate. She was tall and lean, with short-cropped gray hair and the bearing of someone accustomed to command. A jagged scar ran from her left temple to her jaw, pulling her mouth into a slight permanent grimace.

"The Syndicate grows bolder by the day," the woman was saying, her voice carrying across the square. "Last week they raided Oakhollow. Before that, Westcreek. They take our food, our goods, our children. They claim to offer protection, but they're nothing but thieves and murderers in fine cloaks."

Murmurs of agreement rippled through the crowd. Lyra edged closer, intrigued.

"And what does Lord Merrin do?" the woman continued, her voice rising. "He sits in his fine keep and sends 'diplomatic envoys.' He tells us to be patient, to avoid provocation. While our neighbors burn!"

This brought louder agreement, a few shouts of anger.

"I say we've been patient long enough. I say it's time to fight back. The Rivermeet Militia has held this town safe for generations. Now we must do more—we must take the fight to them, before they come for us too!"

The crowd cheered, and the woman acknowledged them with a raised fist. As she stepped down from her makeshift platform, people pressed forward to speak with her. Lyra waited, watching the interactions. The woman listened to each person with focused attention, offering nods or brief responses. There was something compelling about her—a natural authority that drew people in.

As the crowd began to disperse, Lyra noticed a young man standing slightly apart, watching the woman with obvious admiration. He was perhaps a few years older than Lyra, with dark hair tied back from a face that seemed designed for smiling. Though he wore simple clothes—a woodsman's leather jerkin over a homespun shirt—there was something in his bearing that suggested more than a common laborer. A sword hung at his hip, its hilt worn smooth from use, and a bow was slung across his back. The way he scanned the crowd, alert yet relaxed, marked him as someone accustomed to assessing threats.

When the crowd finally dispersed, Lyra approached the scarred woman. "That was quite a speech," she said.

The woman turned, assessing Lyra with sharp eyes. "Not a speech. Just the truth." She extended a calloused hand. "Saria, Captain of the Rivermeet Militia."

"Lyra," she replied, clasping the offered hand. "I'm... a traveler."

"No ordinary traveler comes through the Cloudspire Mountains in these times," Saria observed. "Especially not one who listens to rabble-rousing speeches with such interest."

Lyra smiled slightly. "You're observant."

"I'm alive," Saria countered. "Which means I notice things. Like the fact that you carry no visible weapon, yet you move like someone who knows how to fight. Or that your companions have spread through my town with very specific purposes."

Lyra felt a flash of alarm. "You've been watching us."

"Since you entered the gate," Saria confirmed unapologetically. "New arrivals get attention, especially these days."

The young man Lyra had noticed earlier approached, his stride confident but not aggressive. Up close, she could see a thin scar that traced his jawline, and his eyes—a striking amber color—held a sharp intelligence that belied his easy smile.

"Captain," he said, nodding respectfully to Saria. "The western patrol has returned. No sign of Syndicate activity along the river."

"Good," Saria replied. "Gavrin, this is Lyra. One of our... visitors from the north."

Gavrin's gaze swept over Lyra, assessing and curious. "Welcome to Rivermeet," he said, his voice carrying a slight accent Lyra couldn't place. "Though I wonder what brings anyone through the Cloudspires willingly."

"Necessity," Lyra replied simply.

A smile tugged at the corner of his mouth. "The best reason for most difficult journeys." He turned to Saria. "I'll check on the eastern patrol. They should have reported by now."

"Do that," Saria agreed. "And Gavrin—" she added as he turned to go, "stay sharp. I don't like how quiet things have been."

He nodded, his expression sobering. "Always, Captain." With a last curious glance at Lyra, he moved away, his stride purposeful.

"My second-in-command," Saria explained once he was out of earshot. "Best scout I've ever trained. He has a knack for finding paths others miss and sensing trouble before it arrives."

"He seems young for such responsibility," Lyra observed.

Something flickered across Saria's scarred face—pride, perhaps, or concern. "Age isn't always the best measure of capability. Gavrin's seen more of the Syndicate's cruelty than most veterans twice his age. His village was one of the first to fall when they began their expansion." She paused. "But we're not here to discuss my militia. Lyra the traveler, why don't you tell me why you're really here?"

Lyra hesitated, weighing her options. They needed allies, and Saria clearly had influence in Rivermeet. But caution had kept them alive this long.

"Perhaps somewhere more private," she suggested.

Saria studied her for a moment, then nodded. "The militia headquarters is nearby. We can speak there."

She led Lyra to a sturdy building near the town wall. Inside, a dozen men and women in leather armor similar to the gate guards' moved about with purpose. Maps covered one wall, marked with pins and notations. Weapons racks held an assortment of swords, spears, and bows.

Saria directed Lyra to a small side room furnished with a simple table and chairs. "Now," she said, closing the door behind them, "let's have the truth."

Lyra took a deep breath. "We're gathering allies against the Syndicate. Not just to defend, but to strike back—to end their control once and for all."

"Bold words," Saria said, leaning against the table. "What makes you think you can succeed where others have failed?"

In answer, Lyra reached for the Phoenix Stone. As her fingers touched it, its light bloomed, filling the small room with a warm glow that pulsed with the colors of fire, earth, and air.

Saria's eyes widened, the scar on her face standing out starkly in the Stone's light. "The Stone of Light," she breathed. "It's real."

"It is," Lyra confirmed, letting the light fade. "And with it, we have a chance to heal the rifts that give the Syndicate its power."

"The rifts," Saria repeated. "Those tears in reality that bleed dark energy. The source of their unnatural magic."

Lyra nodded. "The Stone was created to counter that energy, to mend the rifts. We've recovered two of the four Fragments that power it. Once we have all four, we can close the rifts permanently—and without them, the Syndicate loses its advantage."

Saria was silent for a long moment, her expression thoughtful. "There are stories," she said finally. "Old tales passed down through my family. About a time before the rifts, when magic flowed naturally through the land. About the Aethyr Order that created artifacts of great power, including a stone that could heal the world."

"Those stories are true," Lyra said. "The Stone was lost for generations, but my parents rediscovered it. They... died protecting it from the Syndicate."

"And now you carry their burden," Saria observed.

"Their legacy," Lyra corrected gently. "And I'm not alone. My companions and I have faced the Syndicate before and survived. But we need more than just the five of us to take the fight to their stronghold."

"And you want the Rivermeet Militia to join you," Saria concluded.

"We need fighters who know the land, who understand what's at stake. From what I saw in the square, you have the people's trust. They'll follow you."

Saria pushed away from the table and paced the small room. "I've been trying to convince Lord Merrin to take action for months. He prefers caution, diplomacy." She spat the last word like a curse. "Meanwhile, the Syndicate grows stronger, and more villages burn."

"Then help us," Lyra urged. "With your militia and our knowledge of the Syndicate's weaknesses, we have a real chance."

"It's not that simple," Saria said, though Lyra could see the idea had taken root. "I answer to the town council. I can't commit my fighters without their approval."

"Then let me speak to the council," Lyra suggested. "Let me show them the Stone, tell them our plan."

Saria considered this, then nodded slowly. "They meet tomorrow at midday. I can arrange for you to address them." She fixed Lyra with an intense gaze. "But be prepared for skepticism. They're cautious people, merchants and landowners. They'll want more than just legends and promises."

"I understand," Lyra said. "Thank you for the opportunity."

As she turned to leave, Saria added, "One more thing, Lyra. If you're planning what I think you're planning, you should know that the Syndicate has spies everywhere. Even in Rivermeet. Be careful who you trust."

Lyra nodded, the warning settling like a cold weight in her stomach. "Always."

The Rivermeet Inn was a three-story building of weathered stone and dark timber, its common room warm with firelight and the murmur of conversation. Lyra found her companions at a corner table, tankards of ale before them and the remains of a hearty meal.

"There you are," Mira said as Lyra slid onto the bench beside her. "We were starting to worry."

"I made a potentially valuable contact," Lyra replied, keeping her voice low. "Saria, Captain of the Rivermeet Militia. She's arranged for us to address the town council tomorrow."

Kael raised an eyebrow. "You told her about the Stone?"

"I showed her," Lyra admitted. "We need allies, Kael. Real fighters, not just villagers with pitchforks."

"She's right," Elara said, her fingers tracing patterns in the condensation on her tankard. "The Syndicate grows stronger by the day. We can't face them alone."

"And Rivermeet is strategically positioned," Rowan added, spreading a small map on the table. "It controls the river crossing, and it's a natural gathering point for the surrounding villages. If we're going to build a resistance, this is the place to start."

Kael still looked troubled. "I don't like revealing our hand so quickly. We don't know who we can trust here."

"Saria warned me about the same thing," Lyra said. "The Syndicate has spies in town. But we can't hide forever. At some point, we have to take a stand."

Before Kael could respond, the innkeeper approached their table—a plump, middle-aged woman with a no-nonsense expression.

"You'll be the travelers Dorn sent," she said, wiping her hands on her apron. "I'm Hilda. Got two rooms available, if you don't mind sharing."

"That will be fine," Elara assured her. "Thank you."

"Food's extra, but worth it," Hilda continued, eyeing Lyra. "You look like you could use a hot meal, girl."

Despite her concerns, Lyra found herself smiling. "That obvious, is it?"

"Been running this inn twenty years," Hilda replied. "I know a hungry traveler when I see one. Stew and bread coming up." She turned to go, then paused. "Word of advice—whatever business brought you to Rivermeet, keep it quiet. Walls have ears these days."

With that cryptic warning, she bustled away toward the kitchen.

"Charming," Mira muttered. "Another warning about spies."

"Which we should heed," Kael said firmly. "No more talk of our plans tonight. We'll save it for the council meeting tomorrow."

The stew, when it arrived, was as good as promised—thick with chunks of meat and vegetables, served with crusty bread still warm from the oven. Lyra hadn't realized how hungry she was until the first bite, and for a while, they ate in appreciative silence.

As the common room grew more crowded, a fiddler in the corner struck up a lively tune. Soon people were clearing space for dancing, the mood growing festive despite the undercurrent of tension Lyra had sensed throughout the town.

"People need moments like this," Elara observed, following Lyra's gaze. "A chance to forget their troubles, even briefly."

"I'm going to get some air," Lyra said, suddenly feeling the press of bodies and the heat of the fire too intensely. "I won't go far."

Outside, the night was cool and clear, stars pricking the velvet darkness above. Lyra leaned against the inn's outer wall, breathing deeply. The Stone seemed to pulse more strongly at night, its energy resonating with the quiet darkness.

"Heavy thoughts for such a fine evening," a voice said from nearby.

Lyra turned to see Gavrin, Saria's second-in-command, leaning against a hitching post. In the soft light spilling from the inn's windows, his amber eyes seemed to glow with an inner fire.

"Just needed some air," Lyra replied cautiously.

"As did I," Gavrin said, pushing away from the post to approach. "Taverns grow stuffy, especially when filled with so many... interesting visitors."

Lyra tensed slightly. "Are we particularly interesting?"

"A group of armed travelers coming through the Cloudspire Mountains? Certainly more interesting than another merchant caravan." He smiled, the expression genuine despite the probing words. "Saria mentioned she spoke with you earlier. She doesn't often take such immediate interest in strangers."

"We have common concerns," Lyra said carefully.

Gavrin nodded, his expression growing more serious. "The Syndicate. They cast a long shadow these days." He glanced toward the inn, then back to Lyra. "I lost my family to them when I was sixteen. My entire village, wiped out because our headman refused to pay their 'tribute.' I was away hunting when they came. Returned to find nothing but ashes and bodies."

The raw pain in his voice resonated with Lyra's own loss. "I'm sorry," she said quietly. "I understand. They killed my parents seven years ago."

Something passed between them then—a recognition of shared grief, of wounds that never fully healed.

"Saria found me half-starved in the woods a week later," Gavrin continued after a moment. "Took me in, trained me. Gave me purpose beyond mere survival." His hand rested briefly on his sword hilt. "Now I help her keep Rivermeet safe. But it's not enough, is it? Not when villages keep burning."

"No," Lyra agreed. "It's not enough."

Gavrin studied her face in the dim light. "There's something different about you and your companions. A purpose. A mission." He held up a hand as Lyra began to respond. "Don't worry, I'm not asking for details. Not yet. But know this—when the time comes to truly fight back against the Syndicate, many in Rivermeet will stand with you. Myself included."

Before Lyra could respond, the inn door opened, spilling light and noise into the street. Kael stood framed in the doorway, his hand resting casually on his sword hilt.

"Everything alright out here?" he asked, his eyes fixed on Gavrin.

"Just getting some air," Lyra repeated. "And meeting Saria's second-in-command properly."

Kael nodded, his posture relaxing slightly but his gaze still wary. "The council meeting is set for midday tomorrow. We should get some rest."

Gavrin took the hint. "Until tomorrow, then," he said with a slight bow to Lyra. "May the stars guide your dreams."

As he walked away, Kael moved to stand beside Lyra. "Friendly, isn't he?"

"He lost his family to the Syndicate," Lyra said quietly. "Like us."

Kael's expression softened slightly. "A common enough story these days. Still, caution costs nothing."

"Agreed," Lyra said, though she found herself watching Gavrin's retreating figure with interest. There was something about him—a quiet intensity beneath the easy smile—that intrigued her. "Let's get some sleep. Tomorrow will be a long day."

The night passed without incident, though Lyra's dreams were troubled by images of burning villages and shadowy figures pursuing her through marshlands that seemed to reach up and grasp at her ankles. She woke before dawn, the Stone warm against her chest, its energy restless as if responding to her own unease.

Their group gathered in the inn's common room for a simple breakfast of porridge and dried fruit. Elara looked rested, her pale face serene as she sipped herbal tea. The rune-caster rarely showed anxiety, but Lyra noticed the way her fingers moved in small patterns against her cup—a nervous habit she'd developed over their months together.

"How are you feeling about the council meeting?" Lyra asked her quietly.

Elara considered the question. "Hopeful, but cautious. I've studied the histories of places like Rivermeet—trading towns that try to remain neutral in conflicts. They rarely succeed." She met Lyra's eyes. "They need us as much as we need them, whether they realize it yet or not."

Rowan, by contrast, was visibly nervous, repeatedly adjusting his maps and notes. "I've been working on our presentation," he said, pushing his spectacles higher on his nose. "I've charted all Syndicate movements in the region for the past three months. The pattern is unmistakable—they're isolating Rivermeet, cutting off its trade routes one by one."

"Good," Lyra said. "The council will need concrete evidence, not just our word."

As midday approached, they made their way to the town hall, a solid structure of stone and timber that stood near the central square. Saria met them at the entrance, her scarred face set in determined lines.

"They're all assembled," she said without preamble. "Lord Merrin, the merchant guild representatives, the town elders. Be direct but respectful. Merrin appreciates forthrightness, but the merchants startle easily at any threat to trade."

"Understood," Lyra said, feeling her heartbeat quicken. So much depended on this meeting.

The council chamber was a circular room in the town hall, dominated by a large round table of polished oak. Tall windows admitted the pale light of early morning, supplemented by oil lamps hanging from iron brackets. Ten chairs surrounded the table, nine of them occupied when Lyra and her companions were escorted in.

Saria stood as they entered, making introductions. "Honored councilors, these are the travelers I spoke of. Lyra, Kael, Mira, Elara, and Rowan."

Lyra took in the council members quickly—a mix of ages and backgrounds, from the richly dressed man who could only be Lord Merrin to a weather-beaten woman with the callused hands of a farmer. Their expressions ranged from open curiosity to barely concealed skepticism.

"Welcome to Rivermeet," Lord Merrin said, his voice cultured and measured. He was younger than Lyra had expected, perhaps in his early thirties, with the bearing of someone born to privilege but not made soft by it. "Captain Saria tells us you bring important news regarding the Syndicate."

"We do," Lyra confirmed. "And a proposal for action."

"Bold words," said an older man with a merchant's guild pin on his lapel. "Especially from outsiders who know nothing of our situation."

"With respect, councilor," Kael replied evenly, "we know more about the Syndicate than most. We've fought them directly and survived. We've seen their strongholds and their methods firsthand."

This caused a stir among the council members.

"You've been inside Syndicate territory?" the farmer woman asked, leaning forward.

"Multiple times," Lyra said. "Most recently through the Cloudspire Mountains, where we confronted one of their commanders."

"Taryn the Cruel," Mira added, her voice tight with remembered anger. "He leads their northern division."

Lord Merrin's eyebrows rose. "You faced Taryn and lived? Impressive, if true."

"It's true," Lyra assured him. "But we didn't come to boast of past victories. We came because the Syndicate threatens all of Sylvanthia, and it's time to take the fight to them."

"With what army?" the merchant scoffed. "Rivermeet's militia is brave, but small. The Syndicate has hundreds, perhaps thousands of fighters, not to mention their rift magic."

"We have something that can counter their magic," Lyra said. She reached for the Phoenix Stone, drawing it out from beneath her tunic. As it emerged, its light filled the chamber, pulsing with the combined energies of fire, earth, and air.

Gasps and murmurs filled the room. One councilor, an elderly woman in the robes of a scholar, rose to her feet.

"The Phoenix Stone," she breathed. "After all these years..."

"You recognize it?" Lyra asked, surprised.

"I am Archivist Thea," the woman replied. "Keeper of Rivermeet's historical records. And yes, I recognize the Stone of Light from ancient texts. It was created by the Aethyr Order to heal the rifts in our world."

"That's right," Lyra confirmed. "My parents rediscovered it years ago. The Syndicate killed them trying to claim it, but I escaped with the Stone. Since then, my companions and I have been working to restore its full power by recovering the four Fragments that were separated from it."

"We've secured two Fragments so far," Elara added, stepping forward. Her quiet voice carried a surprising authority that drew all eyes to her. "Earth and Air. Once we have Water and Fire as well, the Stone will be capable of closing the rifts permanently."

Elara's fingers traced subtle patterns in the air as she spoke, small runes that shimmered briefly before fading. "I've studied the ancient texts that speak of the Stone's creation. The Aethyr Order designed it as a counter to the chaos that the rifts unleash. Each Fragment we recover not only increases its power but changes the nature of that power—allowing it to address different aspects of the rifts' corruption."

Rowan nodded, adding his own expertise. "The texts also speak of the Water Fragment's location—hidden somewhere in the southern marshlands. My cartographic research suggests it's likely in the region known as the Deepmire, where the water flows in strange patterns that defy normal geography."

"And without the rifts," Kael continued, "the Syndicate loses its greatest advantage. Their rift-magic, their shadow-beasts, their ability to move unseen through the darkness—all gone."

The council members exchanged glances, their skepticism giving way to cautious hope.

"This is... extraordinary," Lord Merrin said finally. "But what does it have to do with Rivermeet?"

"We need allies," Lyra said simply. "Fighters who know the land and understand what's at stake. The next Fragment—Water—is hidden somewhere in the southern marshlands. The Syndicate knows this too, and they're already moving forces in that direction."

"You're asking us to commit our militia to your quest," Saria stated, making it clear she supported the idea.

"Yes," Lyra confirmed. "And to help us gather more allies from the surrounding villages. Together, we can secure the Water Fragment before the Syndicate does, and then take the fight to their main stronghold to claim the final Fragment."

CHAPTER NINE

Secrets Unearthed

Dawn broke over the horizon, painting the sky in hues of amber and rose as Lyra and her companions prepared for another day of travel. The Phoenix Stone rested against her chest, pulsing with warmth that seemed to synchronize with her heartbeat. She traced her fingers along its smooth surface, feeling the power coiled within—not just magical energy, but something alive and responsive.

"The Stone's been restless all night," she said, her voice low enough that only Kael, who was kneeling nearby to roll his bedding, could hear. "It's never felt quite like this before."

Kael glanced up, concern etched in the lines around his eyes. "Restless how?"

"Like it's searching for something." Lyra struggled to find the right words. "Or responding to something nearby."

Aelion approached, his weathered staff tapping softly against the ground with each step. The ancient mage's silver hair caught the early light, giving him an ethereal appearance.

"We're nearing places of old power," he said, his deep voice carrying the weight of centuries. "The Stone responds to such things—like recognizing like."

Lyra noticed how his eyes darted toward the distant treeline that marked their destination. Something in his manner suggested knowledge withheld, secrets kept close. Not for the first time, she wondered exactly how much Aelion knew about the Phoenix Stone that he hadn't shared.

"We should reach the forest by midday," Rowan announced, carefully folding his maps and tucking them into a leather case. His fingers, stained with ink from countless hours of cartography, moved with practiced precision. "If we maintain our pace, that is."

Kael nodded, rising to his feet and brushing dirt from his knees. His hand rested habitually on the hilt of his sword, the metal gleaming in the early morning light. "The sooner we cross the open plains, the better. We're too exposed here."

His eyes scanned the horizon with practiced vigilance, searching for threats that experience had taught him could materialize without warning. "The Syndicate has scouts everywhere these days."

Lyra observed the warrior's tension, the way his shoulders never fully relaxed. Since losing his sister Lirien to the Syndicate, Kael had transformed into their unofficial guardian, taking upon himself the burden of everyone's safety.

"You can't protect everyone all the time, Kael," Lyra said, coming to stand beside him.

"I can try," he replied, his voice a low rumble of determination. He didn't look at her, his gaze still fixed on the horizon. "I won't lose anyone else."

The unspoken words hung between them: *Not like I lost Lirien.*

Mira approached, her collection of vials clinking against one another as she walked. The alchemist moved with the careful precision of someone accustomed to handling volatile substances. "I've prepared some healing potions," she announced, distributing small bottles filled with amber liquid. "One for each of us. They're stronger than my usual mixture."

Lyra accepted the vial, holding it up to the light. The liquid was thicker than Mira's standard healing potions, with flecks of something iridescent suspended within. "What did you change?"

"Added crushed moonflower petals," Mira explained, a hint of pride in her voice. "They accelerate the body's natural healing processes. Tricky to work with—too much and they cause fever dreams, too little and they're useless." She tucked a stray lock of hair behind her ear, a rare gesture of uncertainty. "I haven't had a chance to test this batch properly, but the theory is sound."

"So we're your test subjects," Rowan said, eyeing his vial with newfound wariness.

Mira rolled her eyes. "Would you prefer I wait until you're bleeding out to try something new? Besides, I tested it on myself first. Gave myself a small cut yesterday."

"And?" Elara prompted.

"The cut healed," Mira said with a shrug. "And I had the most fascinating dream about flying fish playing musical instruments. But I adjusted the dosage after that."

Rowan carefully tucked the vial into his belt pouch. "Remind me to only use this if I'm at death's door."

"You'll be begging for it the next time you get a splinter," Mira retorted, but her smile took any sting from her words.

Within the hour, they had broken camp and were moving across the rolling plains that separated them from the Forest of Whispers. The grass was tall, reaching past their knees in places, rippling like water in the morning breeze. Small wildflowers dotted the landscape, adding splashes of purple and yellow to the sea of green.

Elara walked beside Lyra, her delicate features contemplative. The rune-caster had been unusually quiet since their last encounter with the Syndicate's forces, where her protective sigils had faltered under sustained attack.

"Something troubles you," Lyra observed, not a question but a statement.

Elara sighed, her breath forming a small cloud in the cool morning air. "I worry that my magic won't be enough when we truly need it," she confessed, her voice barely above a whisper. "The runes... they require such precision, such focus. In the chaos of battle..." She left the thought unfinished.

She traced a symbol in the air between them, a curved line intersecting with three straight ones. It shimmered momentarily before fading. "Each rune draws power from specific elements—earth, air, fire, water, spirit. The combinations are nearly infinite, but the execution must be flawless. One line out of place, one hesitation in the casting, and the entire spell can collapse." Her fingers trembled slightly. "Or worse."

"Worse?" Lyra prompted.

"Magic seeks balance," Elara explained. "A miscast rune doesn't simply fail—it can invert, drawing power from the caster instead of the elements. The last time we faced the Syndicate, my barrier almost turned inward. I felt it... feeding on me."

"But you held it," Lyra reminded her. "Your magic has saved us more than once. Strength isn't always about raw power. Sometimes it's about knowing exactly where to apply the force you have."

A small smile tugged at Elara's lips. "When did you become so wise?"

"I'm not wise," Lyra replied, her hand unconsciously reaching for the Phoenix Stone. "I'm just learning, like all of us."

The Stone warmed beneath her touch, a gentle pulse that seemed to affirm her words. Yet Lyra couldn't shake the feeling that it was responding to something else—something ahead.

The conversation faded as they continued their journey, each lost in their own thoughts. The landscape gradually transformed around them—the open plains giving way to scattered trees that grew more numerous as they approached the forest's edge. The wind carried new scents: moss, decay, growth, secrets.

By midday, they stood at the threshold of the ancient woodland. Massive trees towered above them, their trunks wider than a person could encircle with their arms, their canopies creating a dappled mosaic of light and shadow on the forest floor. The air was different here—richer, heavier with the scent of earth and growing things, yet also charged with something that raised the fine hairs on Lyra's arms.

"The Forest of Whispers," Aelion murmured, his ancient eyes taking in the sylvan expanse with a mixture of reverence and caution. "It has stood since before my time, and it holds many secrets."

"Friendly secrets, or the kind that might try to kill us?" Mira asked, only half-joking as she eyed the shadows between the trees.

"That depends," Aelion replied cryptically, "on whether it deems us friend or foe."

"Oh, wonderful," Mira muttered. "A judgmental forest. Just what we needed."

A sudden gust of wind rushed past them, bending the grass at their feet and stirring the leaves of the nearest trees. It carried a sound—not quite a voice, but something that resembled words just beyond comprehension. Lyra felt the Phoenix Stone grow warmer against her skin, responding to the forest's greeting.

Rowan consulted his maps once more. "According to this, there's an old trail that cuts through the heart of the forest. It should lead us to the valley beyond." He traced a faded line on the parchment. "But these markings suggest the path isn't... entirely physical."

"What does that mean?" Kael asked, skepticism evident in his tone.

"It means," Rowan said carefully, "that the trail may respond to intention as much as direction. The notes here mention something about 'walking with purpose' and 'the path revealing itself to those who seek with honest hearts.'"

"Sounds like mystical nonsense," Kael muttered.

"Perhaps," Rowan acknowledged. "But these maps haven't led us astray yet."

"Because they've dealt with normal geography," Kael countered. "Not forests that apparently judge your character."

"You fear being found wanting?" Mira asked, her tone light but her eyes sharp.

Kael's expression darkened. "I fear wasting time on riddles when the Syndicate grows stronger by the day."

"The forest is not a riddle," Aelion interjected, his voice cutting through the tension. "It is alive in ways you cannot yet comprehend. And it is our fastest route to the valley—unless you prefer to spend an extra week circling around."

Kael's jaw worked, but he nodded curtly. "Lead on, then."

As they ventured deeper into the forest, the light grew dimmer, filtered through layers of leaves and branches. The canopy above was so dense in places that it seemed more like twilight than midday. Conversation dwindled, replaced by the natural sounds of the woodland—the rustle of leaves, the occasional call of a bird, the soft padding of their own footsteps on the moss-covered ground.

Yet beneath these familiar noises ran an undercurrent of something else—a whispering that seemed to follow them, always just beyond clear hearing. It wasn't threatening, exactly, but it raised the hairs on the back of Lyra's neck nonetheless.

The path they followed was barely visible, more suggestion than trail, marked by subtle differences in the undergrowth. Twice they lost it entirely, only to have Lyra inexplicably drawn in the correct direction, the Phoenix Stone growing warmer as she turned the right way.

"The Stone guides you," Aelion observed after the second occurrence. "It recognizes the forest's power."

"But what is it recognizing?" Lyra asked. "I feel like we're being watched, assessed."

"We are," Aelion confirmed. "The forest is aware of us—not like human awareness, but something wilder, more primal."

"Is it dangerous?" Lyra asked, brushing aside a low-hanging branch.

"All magic can be dangerous," Aelion replied. "But I don't sense hostility. Curiosity, perhaps. Caution, certainly."

A branch snapped somewhere to their left, the sound sharp in the hushed atmosphere. Kael's sword was in his hand before the echo faded, his body tensed for combat. Mira had a vial ready between her fingers, and Elara's hands were already tracing the beginnings of a protective rune.

"Wait," Lyra said, placing a hand on Kael's arm. The Phoenix Stone pulsed against her chest, not in warning but in... recognition?

From between the trees emerged a creature unlike any Lyra had seen before. It resembled a deer in basic form, but its coat shimmered with colors that shifted as it moved, like sunlight through leaves or moonlight on water. Small luminescent fungi grew along its flanks and antlers, giving it an ethereal glow in the forest dimness. Its eyes, large and liquid, held an intelligence that was unmistakably sentient.

It regarded them for a long moment, unafraid, before turning and walking unhurriedly deeper into the forest. After a few paces, it stopped and looked back at them, expectation clear in its posture.

"It wants us to follow," Elara whispered.

"Or it's leading us into a trap," Kael countered, though he had lowered his sword slightly.

The creature made a sound—not quite a deer's call, but something more melodic, almost like laughter.

"I don't think it means us harm," Lyra said, feeling the Stone's warmth spread through her chest. "The Stone... it recognizes this being somehow."

"The forest has many guardians," Aelion said. "This one appears to have been sent to guide us."

"And if it's guiding us somewhere we don't want to go?" Mira asked pragmatically.

"Then we exercise caution," Rowan replied, studying the creature with fascination. "But we're already lost, more or less. At least this way we're moving with purpose."

"I vote we follow the magical glowing deer," Mira said, already stepping forward. "It's not the strangest thing we've done this week."

The creature led them along a path that seemed to materialize before their eyes, winding between massive trees whose trunks were wider than Lyra was tall. The forest grew denser around them, yet somehow more navigable, as if the very undergrowth was shifting to accommodate their passage.

As they walked, Lyra noticed patterns carved into some of the trees—symbols that resembled Elara's runes, yet older somehow, more primal. Elara noticed them too, her fingers tracing the air in front of one particularly elaborate marking.

"These are ancient forms," she murmured. "The foundation of modern runic language. I recognize elements, but the combinations..." She shook her head in wonder. "There's power here I've never encountered in any text."

"Can you decipher them?" Rowan asked, already pulling out his notebook.

"Not fully," Elara admitted. "But this one"—she indicated a spiral pattern intersected by three straight lines—"seems to relate to pathways. Physical and... otherwise."

"Otherwise?" Kael questioned.

"Between realms," Elara clarified. "The texts speak of thin places where the veil between worlds grows permeable."

Kael's expression darkened. "Like the rifts the Syndicate is trying to widen."

"Similar in concept, perhaps, but different in execution," Aelion said. "The rifts are tears, forced openings that damage the fabric between worlds. What Elara describes are natural convergences, places where different realms touch gently, like overlapping circles."

Their guide continued on, seemingly unperturbed by their conversation. As they followed, the quality of light changed subtly, taking on a golden hue that didn't match the time of day. Sounds became more muffled, as if they were walking through layers of soft fabric, and the air grew thick with the scent of moss and honey.

"We're entering a thin place now," Aelion said quietly. "Stay close together. It would be... unfortunate to become separated here."

The warning sent a chill down Lyra's spine. The Phoenix Stone grew warmer still, almost hot against her skin, but not painfully so—more like it was awakening, stretching after a long sleep.

The deer-like creature led them to a clearing where the trees formed a perfect circle around a small pond fed by a bubbling spring. The water was crystal clear, reflecting the golden light that seemed to have no source. At the edge of the clearing stood what appeared to be ruins—stone pillars carved with the same symbols they had seen on the trees, arranged in a semicircle facing the pond.

Their guide stopped at the edge of the water, dipped its head as if in reverence, then turned and melted back into the forest, its coat shimmering into invisibility among the dappled light.

"What is this place?" Lyra asked, her voice hushed.

"A sanctuary," Aelion replied. "A place of power and protection." He approached one of the stone pillars, running his hand along the carvings. "These are older than I am—much older."

"That's saying something," Mira muttered, but her usual irreverence was tempered by obvious awe.

"We should make camp here," Rowan suggested. "Water, shelter, and I suspect this clearing is safer than anywhere else in the forest."

No one argued with his assessment. They set about establishing their camp with the efficiency born of practice—Kael gathering firewood, Mira preparing their meager rations, Elara setting protective runes around the perimeter, and Rowan documenting their day's journey in his ever-present notebook.

Lyra found herself drawn to the pond. She knelt beside it, gazing into its depths. The surface was perfectly still, like a mirror reflecting the golden light that suffused the clearing. As she watched, however, the reflection began to change—the light blurring, the water's surface rippling though there was no breeze.

"Aelion," she called softly, not taking her eyes from the water. "Something's happening."

The ancient mage joined her by the pond's edge, his weathered face reflected alongside hers in the mysterious waters. "Ah," he breathed, recognition in his voice. "A Seeing Pool. Rare, even in places of old magic like this."

"What does it show?" Lyra asked, transfixed by the shifting patterns in the water.

"That depends on the viewer," Aelion replied. "And on what the forest believes they need to see."

The ripples in the water stilled, and new images formed—not reflections of the clearing, but scenes Lyra didn't recognize. A village in flames. People fleeing in terror. And at the center of the destruction, a figure wreathed in shadows, wielding power that seemed to devour the light around it.

The figure turned, as if sensing observation, and Lyra gasped. Though the face was mostly obscured by swirling darkness, she caught a glimpse of features that seemed hauntingly familiar—high cheekbones, a sharp jaw, eyes that burned with an intensity she recognized. The figure raised a hand, and the shadows parted briefly, revealing a pendant around their neck—a black stone shot through with veins of crimson, the inverted mirror of her own Phoenix Stone.

"Veyra," she whispered, the name coming to her lips unbidden.

The figure in the vision seemed to hear her, their head tilting slightly as if in acknowledgment. A cold smile spread across what was visible of their face, and then the shadows closed in again, obscuring them completely.

"You know that name?" Aelion asked sharply, his gaze suddenly intense.

"I... I don't know," Lyra said, confused by her own reaction. "It just came to me. Who is Veyra?"

Aelion's expression grew guarded. "A name from the past. From the time when the rifts first appeared."

Before Lyra could press him further, the vision shifted again, showing the same village—but rebuilt, flourishing, its people living in peace. And standing among them, Lyra saw herself and her companions, the Phoenix Stone glowing with a warm, golden light that seemed to infuse the very air.

But even in this vision of hope, shadows lurked at the edges, as if the darkness was waiting, patient and inevitable. And in the deepest shadow, barely visible, stood the figure again—Veyra—watching with those burning eyes.

"What does it mean?" she asked, turning to Aelion.

The ancient mage's eyes were distant, as if he too was seeing visions in the pool. "It shows both possibility and choice," he said finally. "The destruction that may come if the Syndicate succeeds... and the renewal that may follow if they are stopped."

He hesitated, then added, "But note the shadows that remain even in the vision of peace. The pool speaks truth—darkness is never fully vanquished, only held at bay for a time."

The water rippled once more, then settled back into a normal reflection of the clearing. Lyra sat back on her heels, her mind filled with the images she had seen—particularly the shadowed figure with the black stone pendant.

"Do you think it's true?" she asked. "That we can really make that kind of difference?"

Aelion's gaze was steady. "The pool shows possibilities, not certainties. But yes, I believe the potential is there—in the Stone, and in all of you."

"And the figure in the shadows?" Lyra pressed. "Veyra? Why did I know that name?"

Aelion's expression grew more guarded still. "The Stone holds memories beyond your own. It has existed for centuries, passed from keeper to keeper. Perhaps it remembers what you cannot."

Lyra sensed evasion in his answer, but before she could push further, their conversation was interrupted by Kael's return with an armload of firewood.

"Everything alright?" he asked, noting their serious expressions.

"Yes," Lyra replied, rising to her feet. "Just... learning what we're fighting for."

As Kael arranged the firewood, Lyra noticed how his movements were slightly stiff, favoring his right side. "You're hurt," she observed.

"It's nothing," he dismissed. "Caught my side on a branch."

"Let me see," Mira insisted, already reaching for her pack of medical supplies.

Reluctantly, Kael lifted his tunic to reveal a shallow gash along his ribs—not from any branch, but clearly made by a blade.

"When did this happen?" Lyra demanded, alarm rising in her throat.

"While gathering wood," Kael admitted. "I sensed movement, investigated. Found a scout—Syndicate, by his markings."

"And you didn't think to mention this?" Mira asked incredulously as she cleaned the wound.

"I handled it," Kael said flatly. "He won't be reporting back."

A chill settled over the group. The Syndicate's presence, so close, shattered the sanctuary's illusion of safety.

"We should move on," Rowan suggested, glancing nervously at the surrounding trees.

"No," Aelion countered. "The scout was likely alone, and this clearing offers protection beyond what you can see. The forest itself guards this place."

"The forest didn't stop that scout from getting close enough to cut Kael," Mira pointed out.

"Perhaps because it wanted us to know of the danger," Aelion suggested. "The forest doesn't think as we do, but it is not indifferent to our safety."

Kael winced as Mira applied one of her healing mixtures to his wound. "Whether we stay or go, we should be prepared. The Syndicate rarely sends scouts alone, no matter what Aelion believes about the forest's protection."

"We'll set watches," Lyra decided. "Two at a time, rotating through the night."

Mira finished bandaging Kael's side, her movements gentle despite her sharp words. "There," she said, securing the bandage. "Try not to get stabbed again before morning. I'm running low on supplies."

"I'll do my best," Kael replied dryly, but Lyra noticed how his posture had already improved, the pain easing from his features. Whatever Mira had put in that healing mixture, it worked quickly.

"That should hold until morning," Mira said, packing away her supplies. "The cut wasn't deep, thankfully. More of a warning than a serious attempt to kill."

"A warning?" Elara asked, looking up from where she was setting the last of her protective runes.

"If a Syndicate scout wanted Kael dead, he'd have aimed for something more vital than a glancing blow to the ribs," Mira explained. "This feels more like a message: 'We know where you are.'"

The fire crackled in the silence that followed Mira's words, shadows dancing across the ancient stones. The warmth of the flames couldn't quite dispel the chill that had settled over the group with the knowledge that they were being hunted, even here in the heart of the whispering forest.

"Well," Rowan said finally, attempting to lighten the mood, "since we're staying, we might as well make the best of it. I found some wild onions while gathering kindling. They'll improve the stew, at least."

"And I've still got that flask of Tarrin brandy," Mira added, reaching into her pack. "Medicinal purposes only, of course."

"Of course," Kael echoed, the ghost of a smile touching his lips.

"We should share stories," Mira suggested unexpectedly, distributing portions of their evening meal—a stew made from dried meat, wild onions, and the last of their preserved vegetables. "Something to take our minds off... well, everything."

"What kind of stories?" Elara asked, accepting her share with a grateful nod.

"Good ones," Mira replied with a shrug. "Happy memories. Things worth fighting for." Her gaze slid to Kael, who stared into the fire with brooding intensity. "We all have those, don't we?"

Kael looked up, his expression unreadable in the flickering light. For a moment, Lyra thought he might refuse, retreat further into the shell of grief and guilt he wore like armor. But then, surprisingly, he nodded.

"I'll start," he said, his voice rough. "Since you're so eager for stories."

The others fell silent, attentive. Kael rarely spoke of his past.

"Before the Syndicate came to our village," he began, his eyes fixed on the dancing flames, "Lirien and I used to sneak out at dawn to fish in the river. Our father had taught us where the best spots were—quiet pools where the current slowed and the fish gathered." A ghost of a smile touched his lips. "Lirien was always better at it than I was. More patient. She could stand perfectly still, waiting for just the right moment..."

His voice trailed off, the memory clearly both sweet and painful. After a moment, he continued, "One morning, she caught a fish so big that it nearly pulled her into the river. I had to grab her around the waist to keep her from falling in. We both ended up soaked anyway, laughing so hard we could barely stand."

The smile on his face became more genuine, if tinged with sadness. "We brought that fish home like a trophy. Our mother pretended to be angry that we'd gone out alone, but she cooked it for dinner that night, and it fed the whole family."

He fell silent, the story complete. In the quiet that followed, Lyra could almost see it—two children by a river at dawn, their lives still whole, the future still bright with possibility.

"Thank you," she said softly, meeting Kael's gaze across the fire. "For sharing that."

He nodded once, then looked away, but Lyra thought his shoulders seemed a little less burdened, as if the act of remembering the good along with the bad had lightened his load, if only momentarily.

"My turn," Mira announced, breaking the emotional tension with her usual practicality. "Though I warn you, my childhood was decidedly less idyllic."

She launched into a tale of growing up in the bustling port city of Tarrin, where she'd learned her trade from an irascible old alchemist who'd caught her trying to steal from his shop. "He said I had nimble fingers and a quick mind," she recalled with a grin. "And that he'd rather put those qualities to use than see them wasted in a thief's life."

Her story was punctuated with colorful descriptions of explosive experiments gone wrong and the various unusual ailments she'd helped treat. By the end, even Kael was smiling at her animated retelling.

"Rowan?" Mira prompted, turning to the cartographer. "Surely a man who loves maps has a story about getting spectacularly lost."

Rowan adjusted his spectacles, a slight flush coloring his cheeks. "Well, there was the time I tried to map the Cave of Echoes..."

His story, involving a mishap with a colony of bats and an accidental discovery of an underground river, drew genuine laughter from the group. Lyra noticed how the tension in his shoulders eased as he spoke, as if the sharing of this lighthearted tale was a release for him as well.

When he finished, all eyes turned to Elara, who had been quietly listening, her delicate features illuminated by the firelight.

"I don't have many happy memories from my early years," she admitted, her voice soft. "My gift for runes manifested when I was very young, and it... frightened people."

The group waited patiently as she gathered her thoughts.

"But there was one day," she continued, a small smile forming, "when I was about twelve. I'd wandered away from the village, tired of the whispers and stares. I found a meadow filled with wildflowers, more colors than I'd ever seen in one place." Her eyes grew distant with the memory. "I spent hours there, just watching bees move from blossom to blossom. And I realized that magic was like that—moving through the world, connecting things, creating beauty."

She traced a small rune in the air, a simple symbol that glowed briefly with a soft blue light. "That was the first time I created a rune of my own choosing, not out of fear or necessity, but simply because I wanted to capture the feeling of that moment. It was small magic—just a tiny light, like a firefly—but it was mine. And it was beautiful, not frightening."

The silence that followed was comfortable, respectful of the vulnerability she had shared.

"Aelion?" Lyra prompted gently. "Do you have a story to share?"

The ancient mage had been so quiet during the others' tales that Lyra had almost forgotten he was there. He looked up now, his weathered face thoughtful.

"When you have lived as long as I have," he said slowly, "memories begin to blur together. But there are moments that remain clear, like stones standing above the tide."

He stared into the fire, its light reflecting in his ancient eyes. "I remember a summer festival, long ago in a city whose name has been forgotten by all but me. There was music unlike anything you've heard—instruments crafted from materials no longer found in this world. The whole city danced from dusk until dawn, and for that one night, all divisions were forgotten. Nobles danced with beggars, scholars with warriors, the old with the young."

His voice took on a wistful quality. "I danced with a woman whose laughter was like silver bells. Her name was Thera, and she wore flowers in her hair." He fell silent for a moment. "That was before the rifts, before the darkness came. Before I understood the price of power."

The cryptic ending to his story hung in the air, raising more questions than it answered. But something in Aelion's expression discouraged further inquiry, at least for now.

"And you, Lyra?" Elara asked gently. "What memory sustains you?"

Lyra hadn't expected the question to turn back to her. She gazed into the fire, searching for a memory that wasn't shadowed by loss.

"I remember the day my father first showed me the Phoenix Stone," she said finally. "I was nine, and he'd just returned from a long journey. He called me into his study, closed the door like we were sharing a great secret."

She smiled at the memory. "He unwrapped it from layers of silk, and it glowed in the dim room, so beautiful it took my breath away. He let me hold it, and it was warm in my hands, like it was alive."

The Stone pulsed gently against her chest as she spoke, as if responding to her memory.

"He told me it was special, that it had chosen our family as its guardians. I didn't understand what that meant then. I just knew it was the most wonderful thing I'd ever seen." She paused, swallowing past the sudden tightness in her throat. "He said that someday it would be my responsibility, but not to worry—that day was far in the future."

The unspoken truth—that "someday" had come much sooner than anyone expected—hung in the air between them.

"He would be proud," Kael said quietly, unexpectedly. "Of what you're doing now. Of who you've become."

Lyra met his gaze across the fire, surprised and touched by the rare direct comfort. "Thank you," she whispered.

As they shared their stories, Lyra noticed that the forest around them had grown quieter, as if listening. The whispering that had followed them throughout the day had ceased, replaced by an attentive silence. The Phoenix Stone pulsed gently against her chest, its rhythm somehow in harmony with the crackling fire and the soft breathing of her companions.

When all had shared their tales and the night grew deeper, they established a watch rotation and settled down to rest. Lyra took the first watch with Kael, sitting with her back against one of the ancient stone pillars, the Stone a comforting presence against her skin.

The forest was alive with night sounds—the soft hooting of owls, the rustle of small creatures in the undergrowth, the whisper of leaves stirred by the gentle breeze. Yet beneath these familiar noises, Lyra sensed something else—a presence, ancient and watchful, neither hostile nor entirely benign.

"Do you think the Syndicate scout was alone?" she asked Kael, who sat a few feet away, his sword across his knees.

"No," he replied honestly. "But they might not know exactly where we are. The forest is vast, and we've left little trail to follow."

"What do you make of this place?" Lyra gestured to the clearing, the stone pillars, the Seeing Pool.

Kael considered the question. "I'm not comfortable with things I can't fight," he admitted. "Magic, ancient forests, visions in pools of water—they're beyond my understanding. But..." He paused, choosing his words carefully. "I've learned to trust your instincts. And the Stone's. If you feel this place is important, then it is."

It was as close to an endorsement of the mystical as Lyra had ever heard from him. She smiled slightly, touched by his trust.

"The vision I saw in the pool," she said, her voice low so as not to wake the others. "It showed destruction, but also renewal. As if we have a real chance to change things."

"We do," Kael said with quiet certainty. "That's why we're here. That's why we keep fighting."

"There was a figure in the vision," Lyra continued, drawn to share what had disturbed her. "Someone wielding dark power, leading the Syndicate forces. I couldn't see their face clearly, but there was something... familiar about them. And they wore a pendant—a black stone with red veins, like a dark mirror of the Phoenix Stone."

Kael frowned. "Did Aelion recognize them?"

"He seemed to," Lyra admitted. "When I said the name Veyra—which came to me without thinking—he reacted strongly. But then he evaded my questions."

"Veyra," Kael repeated, testing the name. "I've never heard it before."

"Nor had I, until the vision. Yet it felt... known somehow." Lyra shook her head, frustrated by the fragments of understanding that danced just beyond her grasp. "Aelion knows more than he's telling us. About the Stone, about these Veyra, about everything."

"He's lived for centuries," Kael said. "He'd have to be more forthcoming than most to share everything he knows."

"But if it affects our mission—"

"Then he should tell us," Kael agreed. "But perhaps he has his reasons for keeping certain things to himself. Knowledge can be a burden as much as a weapon."

They lapsed into comfortable silence, each alert to the sounds of the forest around them. After a time, Lyra found herself thinking of the stories they had shared—each unique, each revealing something essential about the teller. They were more than just a group thrown together by circumstance now. They were becoming something greater than the sum of their parts—a fellowship bound by shared purpose and growing friendship.

Her gaze traveled around the sleeping forms of her companions, each unique, each carrying their own wounds and strengths. Mira, the pragmatic alchemist whose sharp tongue hid a generous heart. Elara, the gentle rune-caster whose quiet strength was so easy to overlook. Rowan, the meticulous cartographer whose knowledge had guided them through so many perils. Aelion, the ancient mage whose wisdom was matched only by his secrets.

And Kael, the warrior whose grief had forged him into a protector, whose determination to prevent further loss drove him forward despite his own pain.

Together, they formed a circle of protection around the Phoenix Stone and its purpose. Whatever lay ahead, they would face it united.

As if in response to her thoughts, the Phoenix Stone pulsed once, warmly, against her heart. Lyra smiled, placing her hand over it in silent acknowledgment. The path forward might be fraught with danger, but in this moment, surrounded by allies in the heart of the whispering forest, she found herself filled with a tentative hope.

The night deepened around her, stars peeking through gaps in the forest canopy. Lyra remained vigilant, guarding her sleeping companions, the Stone's gentle warmth a reminder of what they fought to protect—not just their own lives, but the possibility of a world renewed, where villages could flourish in peace and children could laugh by riversides without fear.

It was a future worth fighting for. And as the night slowly gave way to the first hints of dawn, Lyra renewed her silent pledge to see that future realized, whatever the cost might be.

Morning came with a pearlescent light filtering through the forest canopy, dappling the clearing with shifting patterns. Lyra, who had finally gotten a few hours of sleep after her watch, woke to find Elara already up, kneeling by the Seeing Pool with an expression of intense concentration.

"What are you doing?" Lyra asked, coming to sit beside her.

"Studying the runes around the pool," Elara replied without looking up. "They're connected to the ones on the stone pillars and the trees we passed yesterday. It's a network, a system of protection and... communication, I think."

"Communication with what?"

"The forest itself, perhaps." Elara traced a symbol in the air, mirroring one carved into the stone at the pool's edge. "These runes are old, but they're not static. They've been renewed over time, maintained."

"By whom?" Lyra asked, glancing around the seemingly deserted clearing.

"That's what I've been wondering." Elara finally looked up, her pale eyes troubled. "Someone—or something—has been tending this place for centuries. The question is: are they still here?"

Before Lyra could respond, there was movement from the other side of the clearing. Kael was up, his hand already on his sword hilt as he scanned the treeline. "We're not alone," he said quietly.

CHAPTER TEN

The Phoenix Bearers

T he first light of dawn crept over the horizon, painting the sky in vibrant hues of amber and gold. Lyra stood at the edge of the cliff, the Phoenix Stone warm against her chest as she gazed across the awakening landscape. Behind her, the others were breaking camp, their movements efficient after weeks of traveling together.

The journey from the Forest of Whispers had taken them through valleys and highlands, each day bringing them closer to the heart of the Shadow Syndicate's territory. Though they hadn't spoken of it openly, Lyra knew they all felt the growing tension—a sense that they were approaching a crucial turning point in their quest.

"Beautiful, isn't it?" Kael's voice came from beside her as he joined her at the cliff's edge. "Hard to believe there's so much darkness in a world that can create something so magnificent."

Lyra nodded, studying his profile in the dawn light. The warrior's face was etched with determination, but she could see the weariness in his eyes—the toll that fighting the Syndicate had taken on him.

"That's why we fight," she said softly. "To protect this beauty. To ensure everyone has the chance to witness mornings like this without fear."

Kael's expression softened slightly. "You sound like my sister used to. Lirien always saw the light, even in the darkest places."

The mention of his sister—lost to the Syndicate years ago—was rare. Lyra remained silent, giving him space to continue if he wished.

After a moment, he turned away from the view. "We should move. According to Rowan's maps, there's a village in the valley below. We can resupply there before continuing east."

The descent from the highlands was steep but manageable. By midday, they had reached the valley floor, where a well-worn path led them toward the village of Easthollow. As they approached, Lyra was struck by the unexpected signs of prosperity. Fields of grain swayed in the gentle breeze, and the distant sounds of hammers and saws suggested construction was underway.

"This doesn't look like a place suffering under the Syndicate's shadow," Mira observed, her alchemist's eyes scanning the surroundings with curiosity.

"Perhaps the Syndicate's influence hasn't reached this far west," Elara suggested, though her tone betrayed her doubt.

Aelion shook his ancient head. "No place is truly beyond their reach. But resistance takes many forms."

Their questions were answered as they entered the village proper. What from a distance had appeared to be ordinary construction revealed itself as rebuilding. Many structures showed signs of recent damage—charred beams hastily reinforced, walls partially collapsed and being rebuilt. Yet despite this, the villagers moved with purpose and energy that spoke of resilience rather than defeat.

A group of children playing near the village well spotted them first. Instead of the wariness Lyra had come to expect in Syndicate-controlled territories, these children's faces lit up with recognition.

"It's them!" one boy shouted, abandoning his game and running toward the village center. "The Phoenix bearers are here!"

The phrase caught Lyra off guard. She exchanged puzzled glances with her companions as more villagers gathered, excitement rippling through the crowd.

An older woman with silver-streaked hair stepped forward, her weathered face breaking into a warm smile. "Welcome to Easthollow," she said, bowing her head slightly. "I am Elder Marisa. We've been hoping you would pass this way."

"You know who we are?" Lyra asked, surprised.

"Word travels, even in these troubled times," Marisa replied. "Especially news of hope. Stories have reached us of a group led by a woman with the Phoenix Stone, breaking the Syndicate's hold wherever they go." Her eyes moved to the stone visible at Lyra's throat. "The descriptions match you and your companions."

Kael stepped forward, his posture cautious despite the warm reception. "The Syndicate has been here."

It wasn't a question, but Marisa nodded, her expression darkening. "Three weeks ago. They demanded tribute—food, supplies, and young people to serve in their ranks." Her voice hardened. "We refused."

"And they attacked," Rowan concluded, gesturing to the damaged buildings.

"Yes. But we were prepared." Pride entered Marisa's voice. "After hearing of your victories in the northern villages, we decided to stand against them. We had hidden stores of food, evacuation plans for the children and elderly. When they came with fire and shadow, we were ready."

"You drove them off?" Mira asked, clearly impressed.

"Not without cost," Marisa admitted. "But yes. And now we rebuild, stronger than before." She gestured to the bustling activity around them. "Your example gave us courage. And now you're here in person—a sign that we chose rightly."

Lyra felt a strange mixture of pride and unease at the elder's words. They had indeed helped villages resist the Syndicate, but never had she imagined their actions would inspire others to take such risks.

"You're welcome to stay with us," Marisa continued. "Rest, resupply. We have little enough to share, but what we have is yours."

"We're grateful for your hospitality," Lyra replied, "but we can't stay long. The Syndicate—"

"Will return," Marisa finished for her. "We know. But not today, and not tomorrow. Tonight, at least, you will have warm beds and a proper meal."

As the sun began to set, the village square transformed. Tables were brought out, laden with food—simple fare but plentiful. Lanterns hung from posts cast a warm glow over the gathering, and someone produced instruments: a fiddle, a hand drum, a wooden flute. The music began softly, then grew in confidence as more villagers joined the celebration.

Seated at the central table with her companions, Lyra watched the scene with a mixture of joy and melancholy. This was what they were fighting for—moments of community and happiness in a world threatened by darkness. Yet she couldn't shake the knowledge that their presence had likely placed these people in greater danger.

Kael seemed to sense her thoughts. "You're worried about them."

"The Syndicate will hear that they sheltered us," Lyra said quietly. "When they return—"

"They'll find a village better prepared than before," Kael interrupted. "Look around you, Lyra. These aren't people living in fear. They've chosen to stand and fight."

"Because of us," she countered. "Because of stories they've heard—stories that might be exaggerated, that might give them false hope."

"Is it false hope if it inspires them to action?" Elara asked, joining their conversation. "Hope is a powerful force, Lyra. The Phoenix Stone isn't just a weapon against darkness—it's a symbol that reminds people they have the power to resist."

Before Lyra could respond, Elder Marisa approached their table, accompanied by a young woman whose arm was in a sling—an injury from the recent attack, Lyra guessed.

"This is my daughter, Sera," Marisa introduced her. "She has something she wishes to tell you."

Sera stepped forward, her good hand clutching something tightly. "When the Syndicate came," she began, her voice soft but steady, "I was helping defend the eastern gate. One of their shadow-mages struck me with a spell that should have killed me." She opened her hand, revealing a small wooden pendant carved in the shape of a phoenix. "But this protected me. My grandfather carved it after hearing stories of your Phoenix Stone. He said it would keep the darkness at bay."

Lyra stared at the pendant, feeling the Phoenix Stone at her throat grow warmer in response. "I don't understand. It's just wood—"

"But it's not just wood, is it?" Aelion interjected, his ancient eyes studying the pendant with interest. "It's a symbol of belief. Of resistance against darkness. In its own way, it carries a fragment of the same power as the Stone itself."

Sera nodded eagerly. "That's what Grandfather said. That the Phoenix's power isn't just in the Stone, but in what it represents—the light that pushes back the shadows."

Mira leaned forward, her scientific curiosity piqued. "May I?" she asked, holding out her hand for the pendant.

Sera passed it to her. Mira examined it closely, then gasped softly. "There are runes carved into it—tiny ones, almost invisible unless you know what to look for." She glanced at Elara. "Do you recognize them?"

Elara took the pendant, her brow furrowing as she studied the markings. "These are ancient protection symbols," she confirmed. "Similar to ones I've used, but older. Much older." She looked up at Sera. "Your grandfather—is he here tonight?"

Sera shook her head, sadness crossing her features. "He died in the attack. He used his knowledge of the old ways to help us fight, but the effort was too much for him."

A moment of respectful silence followed this revelation. Then Elara carefully handed the pendant back to Sera. "Your grandfather was a wise man. He understood something fundamental about magic—that intention and belief are as important as technique."

The conversation might have continued, but it was interrupted by a sudden commotion at the edge of the square. A man burst through the crowd, his clothes torn and dirty, his face streaked with soot. "Riders!" he gasped, stumbling toward Elder Marisa. "Syndicate riders, coming from the east!"

The festive atmosphere shattered instantly. Villagers began gathering children, dousing lanterns, moving with the practiced efficiency of those who had prepared for this moment. Marisa turned to Lyra and her companions, her expression grave.

"You should go," she said. "If they find you here—"

"We're not leaving you to face them alone," Kael interrupted, already reaching for his sword.

"This is our fight too," Lyra agreed, feeling the Phoenix Stone pulse against her skin, responding to her rising determination. "How many riders?"

"A dozen, maybe more," the messenger reported. "Led by a shadow-mage in a black cloak."

Aelion's expression darkened at this news. "A punitive force, sent to make an example of the village that dared resist."

"Then we'll give them a different kind of example," Lyra said, her voice steady despite the fear churning in her stomach. She turned to the villagers who had gathered around them. "We stand with you, but we need to be smart about this. Kael, what's our strategy?"

The warrior assessed the situation quickly, his military training evident in his decisive tone. "We need to meet them before they reach the village proper. Funnel them into a position where their numbers don't give them as much advantage." He looked to Marisa. "Is there a narrow approach to the village? A bridge or a pass?"

"The eastern road crosses a stream via a stone bridge," Marisa confirmed. "It's the only crossing point for a mile in either direction."

"Perfect," Kael nodded. "Elara, can you set up protective wards around the village itself? In case any get past us?"

The rune-caster nodded, already mentally cataloging the symbols she would need.

"Mira, we'll need your light potions—anything that can counteract shadow magic."

The alchemist patted her satchel. "Already prepared. I've been experimenting with some new formulations since our last encounter."

"Rowan, you know the terrain better than any of us. Where should we position ourselves for maximum advantage?"

The cartographer unfolded his map, quickly identifying the bridge Marisa had mentioned. "Here," he pointed. "The road narrows as it approaches the bridge, with dense woods on either side. If we position archers in the trees..."

"We have skilled hunters who can shoot," Sera offered. "Not many, but they know how to hit their targets."

"Good," Kael approved. "Aelion, can you use the stream itself as a weapon? Water against shadow?"

The ancient mage nodded thoughtfully. "Water reflects light and disrupts darkness. Yes, I can work with that."

"And me?" Lyra asked, the Phoenix Stone warm against her skin, ready to be called upon.

Kael met her eyes, his expression solemn. "You're our beacon, Lyra. The shadow-mage will be drawn to you—to the Stone. We use that. Let them think you're vulnerable, and when they commit to attacking you..."

"We spring the trap," Lyra finished, understanding his plan.

They moved quickly after that, positioning themselves along the eastern road. The village hunters took their places in the trees flanking the approach to the bridge, arrows nocked and ready. Elara remained in the village, setting protective wards around its perimeter, while Mira distributed her potions to those who would be in the direct line of attack.

Aelion stood by the stream, his ancient hands moving in slow, deliberate patterns as he communed with the water. Under his guidance, the gentle flow became more purposeful, the current strengthening as it responded to his will.

Rowan positioned himself on a small rise overlooking the bridge, where he could observe the entire battlefield and relay signals if needed. And Kael...Kael stood at Lyra's side on the bridge itself, his sword drawn, its blade gleaming in the moonlight.

"Are you ready?" he asked quietly.

Lyra took a deep breath, feeling the Phoenix Stone's warmth spread through her body. "Yes," she answered, and was surprised to find it was true. The fear was still there, but it was overshadowed by something stronger—a determination to protect these people who had found the courage to stand against darkness.

They didn't have to wait long. The sound of hoofbeats broke the night's silence, growing louder as the Syndicate force approached. Torches appeared in the distance, bobbing points of light that illuminated the riders—dark figures on darker horses, moving with unnatural synchronicity.

At their head rode a figure in a black cloak, face hidden by a deep hood. Even at a distance, Lyra could feel the malevolent energy radiating from the shadow-mage—a cold that went beyond the physical, reaching for the soul itself.

Kael squeezed her hand briefly, then stepped back, melting into the shadows at the edge of the bridge as planned. Lyra stood alone, the Phoenix Stone visible at her throat, its glow intensifying as the dark riders drew nearer.

The riders slowed as they approached the bridge, clearly surprised to find a solitary figure blocking their path. The hooded leader raised a hand, and the procession halted.

"So," a voice emerged from beneath the hood, feminine but distorted, as if multiple voices spoke in unison. "The rumors are true. The Phoenix Stone has found a new bearer."

Lyra stood her ground, forcing herself to meet the shadow-mage's hidden gaze. "And you are?"

A cold laugh answered her. "I am Veyra's Voice, child. Her will made manifest in this world." The figure pushed back her hood, revealing a face that might once have been beautiful but was now a canvas of shadow and light, constantly shifting, never settling on a single form. "The question is, who are you to stand against the inevitable darkness?"

At the mention of Veyra's name, Lyra sensed a sudden tension in the air—not from the approaching enemies, but from somewhere behind her. Though she couldn't see him from her position, she felt Aelion's shock and dismay ripple through the night like a stone dropped in still water. The ancient mage's magic faltered momentarily, the stream's flow stuttering before he regained control.

"I am Lyra," she answered simply, filing away Aelion's reaction for later consideration. "And darkness is never inevitable while light remains."

The Voice laughed again, the sound like breaking glass. "Pretty words. But words won't save this village—or you." She gestured to her riders. "Kill her. Bring me the Stone."

The riders surged forward, but as they reached the narrowest point of the road, Kael's signal—a sharp whistle—cut through the night. Arrows rained down from the trees, finding gaps in the riders' armor with unerring accuracy. Simultaneously, Mira's potions arced through the air, shattering against the ground in front of the advancing force. Brilliant light erupted, causing the shadow-infused horses to rear and scream in panic.

Kael emerged from his hiding place, sword flashing as he engaged the nearest rider. The battle was joined in earnest, chaos erupting as the carefully laid trap was sprung.

Lyra focused on the Voice, who remained mounted at the edge of the fray, her shifting face contorted with fury. "You think your petty ambush can stop what's coming?" the shadow-mage snarled, raising her hands. Darkness gathered between her palms, coalescing into a sphere of pure negative energy. "Let me show you the true meaning of power!"

She hurled the sphere toward Lyra, who instinctively raised her hand, calling on the Phoenix Stone's power. Light erupted from the Stone, meeting the darkness midair. The two forces collided with a sound like thunder, sending shockwaves across the battlefield.

For a moment, they seemed evenly matched—light and darkness pushing against each other in perfect opposition. Then the Voice made a twisting gesture with her hand, and the darkness began to envelop the light, slowly consuming it.

Lyra felt the Stone's power draining, her connection to it weakening as the Voice's dark magic overpowered her. Panic threatened to overwhelm her—she wasn't strong enough, wasn't skilled enough to counter this level of shadow magic.

Then, just as the darkness seemed about to triumph, the stream beneath the bridge surged upward in a great wall of water. Aelion's voice rang out, ancient words of power that caused the water to shimmer with inner light. The liquid wall crashed into the sphere of darkness, and where they met, steam hissed and roiled.

"Now, Lyra!" Aelion called. "While the elements war, strike at the source!"

Understanding flashed through her mind. The Voice's power was formidable, but it required concentration—concentration now divided between maintaining the sphere of darkness and protecting herself from Aelion's water magic.

Lyra gathered her will, focusing not on the clashing energies but on the Voice herself. The Phoenix Stone blazed at her throat, its light lancing out in a focused beam that pierced through the chaos of battle, striking the shadow-mage directly.

The Voice screamed, a sound of rage and pain that cut through the night. The sphere of darkness dissipated as her concentration shattered, and the water from Aelion's spell crashed down, soaking friend and foe alike.

For a moment, the Voice seemed to flicker, her shifting features stabilizing into a single form—a woman's face, gaunt and pale, with eyes that burned with hatred. Then the shadows gathered around her once more, and she yanked her horse's reins, wheeling the beast around.

"Retreat!" she commanded, her voice cracking with fury. "This isn't over, Phoenix-bearer. The darkness always returns!"

The surviving riders disengaged, following their leader as she galloped back the way they had come. Several lay unmoving on the ground, while others limped away, wounded by arrow or sword.

Silence fell over the battlefield, broken only by the sound of heavy breathing and the gentle gurgle of the stream returning to its normal flow. Lyra swayed on her feet, the effort of channeling the Stone's power leaving her drained. Kael was at her side in an instant, supporting her with a strong arm around her waist.

"Are you hurt?" he asked, his eyes scanning her for injuries.

She shook her head. "Just tired. That was..." She trailed off, unable to find words for what had just happened.

"Impressive," Kael finished for her, a rare smile touching his lips. "You stood against a shadow-mage and forced her to retreat. Not many can claim such a victory."

"It wasn't just me," Lyra protested. "Aelion's intervention was crucial, and your plan—"

"Worked because you had the courage to stand your ground," Kael interrupted. "Don't diminish what you accomplished here tonight."

Before Lyra could respond, villagers began emerging from the trees and from behind the protective wards Elara had set. They approached cautiously at first, then with increasing confidence as they realized the Syndicate forces had truly retreated.

Elder Marisa made her way to Lyra, her face alight with wonder. "You did it," she breathed. "You drove them away."

"For now," Lyra cautioned, unwilling to give false hope. "They'll return, possibly with greater numbers."

"And we'll be ready," Marisa replied, her voice firm. "Tonight has shown us what's possible when we stand together against the darkness." She turned to address the gathered villagers. "Tonight, we've witnessed the power of the Phoenix Stone—not just its magic, but the courage it inspires in all of us. The Syndicate thought to find us cowering in fear. Instead, they found us standing tall, shoulder to shoulder with the Phoenix-bearers themselves!"

A cheer went up from the crowd, their faces transformed by newfound determination. Lyra watched them, feeling a complex mixture of pride, hope, and trepidation. They had won tonight, yes—but at what cost? The Voice would report back to her superiors. The Syndicate would now know exactly where Lyra and her companions were, and they would come in force.

As if reading her thoughts, Aelion appeared at her side, his ancient face weary but his eyes bright with an inner fire she hadn't seen before.

"You're worried about what comes next," he observed.

"We've painted a target on this village," Lyra said quietly. "When the Syndicate returns—"

"They will find a people prepared to resist," Aelion finished. "Look around you, Lyra. What do you see?"

She followed his gaze, taking in the scene. Villagers were tending to the wounded, gathering dropped weapons, already planning improvements to their defenses. There was fear, yes—but it was overshadowed by a sense of purpose, of community united by a common cause.

"I see hope," she admitted.

"Exactly." Aelion nodded. "And that is more powerful than any magic, dark or light. The Syndicate rules through fear. When people lose their fear..."

"They lose their power," Lyra finished, understanding dawning.

"The Phoenix Stone is not just a weapon," Aelion continued. "It is a catalyst. It awakens something that already exists within people—the courage to stand against darkness, to believe in a better world."

Lyra touched the Stone at her throat, feeling its warmth. "But what about Veyra? The Voice said she was Veyra's will made manifest. Who is Veyra?"

A shadow passed over Aelion's ancient features, and he seemed to age before her eyes. His shoulders slumped slightly, and his gaze became distant, fixed on memories only he could see.

"Aelion?" Lyra pressed gently. "You know that name, don't you? I felt your reaction when the Voice spoke it."

The ancient mage was silent for so long that Lyra thought he might not answer. When he finally spoke, his voice was barely above a whisper.

"Yes, I know that name. All too well." He glanced around at the celebrating villagers. "But this is neither the time nor the place for such dark histories. Enjoy this victory, Lyra. Tomorrow is soon enough for old sorrows."

There was such pain in his voice that Lyra didn't have the heart to press further. Instead, she nodded, respecting his reluctance. "Tomorrow, then. But I need to know what we're facing, Aelion. All of it."

"Yes," he agreed, his eyes meeting hers with sudden intensity. "You do. And you will." With that, he turned and walked away, his tall figure moving through the crowd like a ghost from another time.

Despite her curiosity about Veyra, Lyra recognized the wisdom in Aelion's words. They had fought hard tonight, and there would be more battles to come. She rejoined her companions, who had been drawn into the village's impromptu celebration.

Mira was deep in conversation with a local herbalist, comparing notes on medicinal plants and potion ingredients. Elara sat with a group of children, showing them simple protective runes they could draw on their homes. Rowan had spread his maps on a table, discussing the terrain with village hunters who knew the area intimately.

And Kael... Kael stood slightly apart, watching it all with a guarded expression. Lyra moved to his side.

"Not in a celebratory mood?" she asked gently.

He glanced at her, then back at the villagers. "They don't understand what they're up against."

"Maybe not fully," Lyra agreed. "But they've chosen to fight anyway. That counts for something, doesn't it?"

Kael was silent for a long moment. "When the Syndicate came to my village," he finally said, his voice low, "we weren't prepared. We had no warning, no defenses, no Phoenix Stone." His hand tightened on his sword hilt. "What happened here tonight... it's what I wish had happened there."

The admission cost him, Lyra could tell. Kael rarely spoke of his past, of the village and family he had lost to the Syndicate. She placed her hand over his, feeling the tension in his grip.

"Then we make sure their story ends differently," she said. "We help them prepare. We teach them what we know. And when the Syndicate returns—because they will return—these people will be ready."

Kael met her gaze, something shifting in his eyes. "You've changed," he observed. "When we first met, you were uncertain of your path, of your ability to wield the Stone's power."

"I still am, sometimes," Lyra admitted. "But I'm learning. We all are."

A hint of a smile touched Kael's lips. "Yes. We are."

The celebration continued late into the night, but eventually, exhaustion claimed them all. The villagers had prepared accommodations—simple but comfortable beds in homes that had been spared the worst of the Syndicate's attack. Lyra found herself sharing a small room with Elara, while the others were housed nearby.

As she lay in the darkness, the events of the day replaying in her mind, Lyra found herself thinking of the Voice's words. *Veyra's will made manifest.* Who was Veyra? And why did Aelion seem so deeply affected by the mere mention of her name?

Sleep claimed her before she could puzzle it out further, but her dreams were troubled—filled with shifting shadows and a woman's face, gaunt and pale, with eyes that burned with hatred.

Morning came too soon, the first light of dawn filtering through the simple curtains at the window. Lyra rose, finding Elara already awake and preparing for the day ahead.

"Did you sleep well?" the rune-caster asked, noting Lyra's drawn expression.

"Strange dreams," Lyra replied, rubbing her eyes. "Nothing clear, just... unsettling."

Elara nodded in understanding. "The Phoenix Stone responds to your emotions, your experiences. After a battle like last night's, it's not surprising your dreams would be affected."

They joined the others in the village square, where Elder Marisa and several other villagers had prepared a hearty breakfast. The mood was subdued compared to the previous night's celebration, but there was a quiet determination in the air—a sense of purpose that hadn't been there when they first arrived.

As they ate, Kael outlined his recommendations for the village's defenses. "The bridge is your strongest point," he explained, sketching in the dirt with a stick. "It creates a natural bottleneck. Strengthen it, but also prepare to destroy it if necessary. Better to lose a bridge than a village."

Marisa nodded, absorbing his advice. "And if they come from another direction?"

"They'll have to cross the stream somewhere," Rowan pointed out. "Water is your ally against shadow magic. Aelion showed us that last night."

The ancient mage nodded. "Water reflects light, disrupts darkness. Keep buckets of it ready, not just for fires but for direct use against shadow-infused attackers."

The planning continued through breakfast, with Mira explaining how to create simple light potions using locally available ingredients, and Elara teaching basic protective runes that even non-mages could activate.

As the sun climbed higher, Lyra knew it was time to move on. The Syndicate would be regrouping, possibly already planning their next move. Standing still made them an easy target.

"We need to continue east," she said during a lull in the conversation. "The Voice will report back to her superiors. They'll know where we are now."

Elder Marisa nodded, though sadness touched her eyes. "We understand. You have your own path to follow." She gestured to the village around them. "But know that you have friends here now. Easthollow stands with the Phoenix-bearers."

"And we stand with Easthollow," Lyra promised. "This isn't goodbye. It's just until we meet again."

The villagers gathered to see them off, offering supplies for their journey and heartfelt thanks for their help. Sera approached Lyra just before they departed, pressing something into her hand.

"Take this," she said. "For luck."

Lyra opened her palm to find the wooden phoenix pendant. "But this is yours. Your grandfather made it for you."

Sera smiled. "He made it to protect me, and it did. Now you carry the real Phoenix Stone into greater danger than I'll ever face. Maybe this can offer you a little extra protection too."

Touched by the gesture, Lyra carefully tucked the pendant into a pocket close to her heart. "Thank you. I'll treasure it."

With final farewells exchanged, they set out on the eastern road, leaving East-hollow behind. The path ahead would lead them deeper into Syndicate territory, closer to the heart of the darkness they sought to defeat.

As they walked, Mira fell into step beside Lyra. "So," the alchemist said, her tone casual but her eyes sharp with curiosity, "are we going to talk about what the Voice said last night? About Veyra?"

Lyra glanced ahead to where Aelion walked with Rowan, deep in conversation about the terrain ahead. "I tried to ask him about it," she admitted. "He said it was 'a conversation for another time.'"

Mira snorted. "Typical. The old man loves his secrets."

"But you've heard the name before?" Lyra pressed.

"Rumors, mostly," Mira replied, lowering her voice. "In Tarrin, where I trained as an alchemist, there were stories about the origins of the Syndicate. About a powerful sorceress who discovered a way to harness shadow magic, to bend it to her will. Some said she became one with the shadows, neither living nor dead, but something in between." She shrugged. "I always thought it was just a story to frighten apprentices into being careful with their experiments."

"But you don't think so now?"

Mira's expression grew serious. "After what I've seen these past months? The Syndicate's power, the Phoenix Stone, the ancient magic Aelion and Elara wield? I'm starting to think there's truth in a lot of old stories."

The conversation fell silent as they continued their journey, but Lyra's mind was racing. If Veyra was real—if she was the power behind the Syndicate—then their mission was even more daunting than she had imagined. They weren't just fighting an organization; they were fighting a legacy of darkness that stretched back generations.

The eastern road led them through rolling hills and scattered woodlands, the landscape growing wilder as they moved farther from settled lands. By midday, they had left the last of the cultivated fields behind, entering a region where nature had reclaimed what humans had once built. Crumbling stone walls and the occasional collapsed foundation were all that remained of villages long abandoned.

"What happened here?" Lyra asked as they passed through what must once have been a sizable settlement, now reduced to overgrown ruins.

"The First Shadow War," Aelion replied, his voice heavy with memory. "Three generations ago, when the Syndicate first rose to power. These eastern lands were the first to fall."

"And no one has returned?" Elara asked, tracing her fingers along a moss-covered stone that might once have been part of a home.

"Some tried," Aelion said. "But the shadow magic lingered in the soil, in the water. Crops withered, children sickened. Eventually, they gave up."

The revelation cast a pall over their journey. They walked in silence for a time, each lost in their own thoughts about the devastation the Syndicate had wrought and what it would take to heal such deep wounds.

As afternoon faded toward evening, they began to look for a suitable place to make camp. Rowan, scouting ahead, returned with news of a sheltered hollow near a small stream—defensible and with access to fresh water.

They had just begun to set up camp when Kael suddenly tensed, his hand going to his sword. A subtle change came over his posture—the relaxed vigilance of a seasoned warrior shifting to heightened alertness.

"What is it?" Lyra asked, her voice barely above a whisper.

Kael raised a finger to his lips, then pointed to his ear. *Listen.*

At first, Lyra heard nothing unusual—just the normal sounds of the wilderness at dusk: the rustling of leaves in the gentle breeze, the distant call of birds settling for the night, the soft gurgle of the nearby stream. Then, gradually, she became aware of something else—a subtle disturbance in the natural rhythm of the forest. The birds had gone silent in one particular direction, and there was a faint, almost imperceptible sound of movement through the underbrush.

"Someone's coming," Kael murmured, positioning himself between the sound and the others. "From the east. Moving slowly."

Mira silently reached for her satchel, fingers closing around one of her defensive potions. Elara began tracing protective runes in the air, her movements subtle and precise. Aelion and Rowan spread out, forming a loose semicircle with Kael at its center.

The sounds grew closer, more distinct—the soft crunch of footsteps on fallen leaves, the occasional snap of a twig. Whoever was approaching made no attempt to mask their presence, which Lyra found oddly reassuring. An enemy would likely try for stealth.

"Just one person," Kael assessed, his voice low but no longer a whisper. "Moving deliberately. Not trying to hide."

Moments later, a figure emerged from the trees—a woman, tall and lean, with close-cropped silver hair and the weathered look of someone who had spent years in the wilderness. She carried a simple wooden staff but no other visible weapons. Most striking were her eyes—a vibrant, unnatural green that seemed to glow in the fading light.

She stopped at the edge of their camp, studying them with those unsettling eyes. "The Phoenix Stone," she said, her voice rough as if from disuse. "I felt its power. Didn't expect to find it in the hands of one so young."

Lyra stepped forward, her hand instinctively going to the Stone at her throat. "Who are you?"

The woman's gaze shifted to her, those green eyes seeming to look through her rather than at her. "My name is Thorn. I was once a Keeper of the Green Path, before the Syndicate corrupted the eastern forests." She gestured to the wilderness around them. "Now I watch over what remains, trying to heal what can be healed."

"A druid," Aelion said, recognition in his voice. "I thought your order was lost decades ago."

Thorn's mouth twisted in a grim smile. "Not lost. Just scattered. Reduced. Like much else in these lands." She returned her attention to Lyra. "You're heading east. Toward the heart of the Syndicate's power."

It wasn't a question, but Lyra nodded anyway. "We are."

"Then you're either very brave or very foolish." Thorn planted her staff in the ground, leaning on it slightly. "Probably both. But you won't get far without help. The paths ahead are treacherous, guarded by more than just the Syndicate's soldiers."

"What do you mean?" Kael asked, his posture still wary despite the woman's apparent lack of hostility.

"The land itself has been twisted by shadow magic," Thorn explained. "Ordinary maps won't help you navigate it. Ordinary weapons won't protect you from what lurks in the darkness." She straightened, decision made. "I'll guide you. As far as the Whispering Vale, at least. Beyond that..." She shrugged. "We'll see if you live that long."

The blunt assessment might have been offensive coming from anyone else, but there was something about Thorn's manner—a hard-earned pragmatism born of survival in hostile territory—that made it difficult to take offense.

"Why would you help us?" Mira asked, voicing the question on everyone's mind.

Thorn's gaze shifted to Mira, those eerie green eyes narrowing slightly. "Because the Phoenix Stone represents the last real hope of cleansing these lands. And because I'm tired of watching the shadows spread." She tapped her staff against the ground, and tiny green shoots immediately sprouted around it. "The Green Path teaches balance. The Syndicate has tilted the world too far toward darkness for too long."

A silence fell over the camp as they considered her offer. Lyra exchanged glances with her companions, reading the mixture of caution and curiosity in their expressions. Finally, she nodded.

"We welcome your guidance, Thorn. The path ahead is unknown to us, and we need all the allies we can find."

The druid nodded once, her expression unchanging. "We'll leave at first light. The shadows are too active after dark to travel safely." Without another word, she moved to the edge of their camp and sat cross-legged on the ground, her back against a tree, her staff across her knees.

As night fell fully, they finished setting up camp, each occasionally casting curious glances at their new companion. Thorn remained motionless, her eyes closed, seemingly oblivious to their scrutiny.

Later, as they sat around the small fire, keeping their voices low, Mira leaned toward Lyra. "Do you think we can trust her?"

"Aelion seems to recognize her order," Lyra replied. "And the Phoenix Stone... it doesn't react to her the way it does to the Syndicate's shadows."

"Still," Kael interjected, "we should remain cautious. The eastern territories are dangerous for more reasons than just the Syndicate."

Lyra nodded, her hand unconsciously touching the wooden phoenix pendant Sera had given her. The day's events had reinforced what she was beginning to understand about their quest—that the Phoenix Stone's power extended far beyond its ability to combat shadow magic. It was a symbol that inspired courage and resistance, a beacon of hope in a world where darkness had held sway for too long.

They were venturing into the unknown, guided by a stranger with mysterious powers. But wasn't that the nature of their entire journey? Step by step into darkness, holding fast to the light they carried within—not just the Phoenix Stone, but the bonds between them, the determination to create a better world.

As she prepared for sleep, Lyra gazed up at the stars visible through the trees. Tomorrow would bring new challenges, new dangers. But also, perhaps, new hope. The rising dawn would reveal the path ahead, and together, they would face whatever it held.

CHAPTER ELEVEN

Corrupted Passage

The morning after meeting Thorn brought a dawn shrouded in mist. Lyra woke to find the druid already awake—or perhaps she hadn't slept at all—sitting cross-legged at the edge of their camp, her strange green eyes fixed on the eastern horizon. The rest of the companions were still asleep, exhausted from the previous day's journey and the battle at Easthollow.

Lyra approached quietly, careful not to disturb the others. "Good morning," she said, keeping her voice low.

Thorn didn't look at her. "Is it? The mist speaks of shadow magic. It clings to these lands like a disease."

Lyra glanced at the swirling tendrils of fog that wound between the trees. In the dim light of dawn, they did seem unnatural—too purposeful in their movements, too deliberate in the way they avoided certain patches of ground.

"Can you tell if we're being watched?" she asked.

Thorn finally turned to her, those eerie green eyes assessing. "Always. The Syndicate has eyes everywhere in these eastern territories. But they're not close. Not yet." She rose in one fluid motion, staff in hand. "Wake the others. We should move while the shadows are still thin."

By the time the sun had fully risen, they were already deep into territory that none of them, save Thorn, had ever traversed. The landscape had changed subtly but unmistakably. Trees grew at odd angles, their trunks twisted as if they had writhed in pain while growing. The underbrush was sparse, the ground covered instead with a carpet of pale, colorless moss that seemed to absorb sound, making their footsteps eerily silent.

"Cheerful place," Mira muttered, eyeing a particularly contorted tree whose branches seemed to reach for them like grasping hands. "Reminds me of my aunt Hester's parlor. She had a thing for decorating with dead animals."

Kael shot her a look. "Keep your voice down."

"Why?" Mira challenged. "Thorn said the Syndicate isn't close."

"I said they're not close yet," the druid corrected without turning around. "But sound carries strangely in the corrupted woods. What's whispered here might be heard leagues away—by ears you wouldn't want listening."

That sobered them all, and they continued in silence for a time, following Thorn's sure steps through terrain that seemed to shift and change when viewed from the corner of one's eye.

Around midday, they came to a stream that cut across their path—or what had once been a stream. The channel was still there, carved into the earth, but no water flowed. Instead, a viscous black substance oozed slowly along the streambed, giving off a faint, acrid smell.

"What is that?" Elara asked, her nose wrinkling in disgust.

"Shadow ichor," Aelion replied before Thorn could answer. The ancient mage's face was grim. "I've seen it before, but never in such quantities. It's the physical manifestation of corrupted magic—what happens when natural flows of power are twisted and tainted."

Thorn nodded in agreement. "The Syndicate has been drawing power from the land for generations, taking but never giving back. This is the result."

Rowan knelt at the edge of the dry bank, careful not to touch the black substance. The cartographer's normally reserved expression had given way to open concern as he studied the corruption. His fingers hovered over his map case, as if he wished to document this blight but knew no ink could properly capture its wrongness.

"Can it be cleansed?" he asked, looking up at Thorn. "The land, I mean."

"Perhaps," Thorn said, but her tone suggested skepticism. "If the source of corruption is eliminated. If those with power care enough to try." She looked pointedly at the Phoenix Stone at Lyra's throat. "That's why your quest matters. The Stone has the power to heal as well as destroy."

They skirted the corrupted stream, following its course for a time before Thorn led them away from it, deeper into the twisted woods. As the day wore on, Lyra noticed that the wildlife had all but disappeared. No birds sang, no small creatures rustled in the underbrush. The silence was oppressive, broken only by their own movements and the occasional creak of warped wood straining against itself.

"I don't like this," Kael murmured, his hand never far from his sword hilt. "It feels like we're being herded."

"We are," Thorn confirmed, surprising them with her bluntness. "The safe paths through these woods are few and growing fewer. The Syndicate knows this. They don't need to follow us when they can predict our route."

"That's... not reassuring," Mira said. "At all. You know, most guides try to make their clients feel safe, not terrified."

Thorn's mouth quirked in what might have been the ghost of a smile. "Safety is an illusion in the eastern territories. Better you understand the danger than walk blindly into it."

"So we're walking into danger with our eyes wide open instead," Mira replied. "Fantastic. Much better."

"Actually, it is," Rowan interjected, his normally quiet voice firm. "Knowledge is power, especially in unfamiliar territory." He patted the leather case that held his maps. "The difference between a successful journey and a fatal one often comes down to what you know before you set out."

Mira rolled her eyes but didn't argue further. The cartographer's logic was sound, even if it didn't make their situation any less perilous.

As afternoon faded toward evening, the twisted woods began to thin, giving way to a landscape that was somehow even more unsettling. The trees here were not merely warped but dead—skeletal forms reaching toward a sky that had grown increasingly overcast. The ground was bare, the soil a pale, ashy gray that stirred with their every step, releasing puffs of dust that tasted of decay.

"We're nearing the Whispering Vale," Thorn announced, stopping at the edge of what appeared to be a vast depression in the land. "We'll make camp here for the night. Going further in darkness would be... unwise."

They set up camp in the shelter of the dead trees, no one questioning Thorn's decision. Whatever lay ahead in the Vale, none of them were eager to face it without rest and preparation.

As they ate a cold meal—Thorn had vetoed a fire, warning that light would attract unwanted attention—Lyra found herself studying their guide. The druid sat slightly apart from the group, her staff laid across her knees, her strange eyes constantly scanning the darkening landscape.

"You said you were a Keeper of the Green Path," Lyra said, breaking the silence. "What exactly does that mean?"

Thorn's gaze shifted to her, assessing. "The Green Path is—was—an order dedicated to maintaining the balance of natural magic in these lands. We tended the flows of power, ensured they remained clean and uncorrupted." Her mouth twisted in a bitter smile. "Obviously, we failed."

"Against the Syndicate?" Elara asked, joining the conversation.

"Against Veyra," Thorn corrected, her voice hardening at the name.

Lyra felt a chill that had nothing to do with the evening air. "The Voice mentioned that name. She called herself 'Veyra's Voice.'"

Thorn's eyes narrowed. "You've encountered one of the Voices? And lived?" She looked at Lyra with new respect. "Perhaps there is hope after all."

"Who is Veyra?" Kael demanded, his patience clearly wearing thin with the cryptic responses. "Aelion refuses to speak of her, and now you're being just as evasive."

Thorn's gaze shifted to Aelion, who sat stiffly, his ancient face impassive. "You haven't told them? After all this time, after bringing them into the heart of danger, you've kept them ignorant?"

"They know what they need to know," Aelion replied, his voice unusually defensive. "The full history would only burden them with—"

"With the truth?" Thorn interrupted, anger flashing in her eyes. "They deserve to know what they're really fighting, old man. Or have you forgotten the cost of secrets?"

A tense silence fell over the camp. Lyra looked between Thorn and Aelion, sensing a history between them that went beyond their respective orders.

"Tell us," she said finally, addressing both of them. "We need to know."

Aelion sighed heavily, the weight of centuries seeming to press down on him. "Veyra was... is... the founder of the Shadow Syndicate. A sorceress of immense power who discovered how to harness shadow magic—how to draw power from the very fabric of reality by creating imbalance and discord."

"She was also his student," Thorn added, her voice sharp with accusation. "Aren't you going to tell them that part, Aelion?"

The ancient mage's face crumpled with grief and shame. "Yes," he admitted. "Veyra was my most gifted pupil, centuries ago. I taught her the old magics, the ways of harmony and balance. I never imagined she would twist that knowledge into something so... corrupted."

"You couldn't have known," Lyra said gently, seeing the genuine remorse in Aelion's eyes.

"Couldn't he?" Thorn challenged. "The signs were there. Her ambition, her disregard for the natural order, her obsession with power. The Keepers warned him, but he wouldn't listen."

"That's enough, Thorn," Elara interjected, her normally calm voice sharp with anger. "Whatever happened in the past, Aelion has dedicated centuries to fighting the Syndicate. His guidance brought us this far."

"And yet here we are," Thorn replied, gesturing to the blighted landscape around them. "In lands so corrupted they may never recover, facing an enemy that grows stronger with each passing year."

"What happened to Veyra?" Rowan asked, his quiet voice cutting through the tension. He had been listening intently, his cartographer's mind clearly mapping not just physical terrain but historical connections as well. "Is she still alive after all this time?"

Aelion and Thorn exchanged glances, their mutual animosity momentarily set aside.

"No one knows for certain," Aelion answered. "She disappeared during the First Shadow War, after unleashing a ritual that tore rifts in the fabric of reality. Some believe she was consumed by her own magic. Others..."

"Others believe she transcended," Thorn finished. "That she became something beyond human, neither living nor dead, but existing in a state between worlds."

"The Voices," Lyra realized. "They're not just speaking for her—they're channeling her, aren't they? That's why their faces shift and change."

Thorn nodded, impressed by Lyra's insight. "That's the theory. Each Voice is a conduit for a fragment of Veyra's consciousness, allowing her to extend her influence across the realm even in her... altered state."

"So we're not just fighting an organization," Kael concluded, his expression grim. "We're fighting a person—or whatever Veyra has become."

"Yes," Aelion confirmed. "And that is why the Phoenix Stone is so crucial. It's one of the few artifacts with the power to counter Veyra's shadow magic—to heal the rifts she created and restore balance to the flows of power."

A heavy silence fell over the camp as they all absorbed this information. Lyra touched the Stone at her throat, feeling its warmth pulse in response to her troubled thoughts. The scope of their mission had just expanded dramatically. They weren't merely fighting to free villages from the Syndicate's control; they were battling a force that had corrupted the very land itself.

"Well," Mira said finally, breaking the silence. "That explains why they keep trying to kill us. Here I thought it was my sparkling personality they objected to."

The unexpected humor broke the tension, drawing surprised laughter from several of the companions. Even Thorn's mouth quirked in what might have been a smile.

"Your... sparkling personality probably doesn't help," Kael replied, a rare teasing note in his voice.

Mira clutched her chest in mock offense. "I'll have you know I'm delightful. Just ask anyone who hasn't tried to murder me."

"That's a rather short list," Elara observed dryly.

"Quality over quantity," Mira retorted with a grin.

Lyra found herself smiling despite the gravity of their situation. This was what had gotten them through every challenge so far—not just their individual strengths or the power of the Phoenix Stone, but the bonds between them. The way they could find moments of lightness even in the darkest circumstances.

As night fully descended, they arranged watches, with Thorn insisting on taking the first shift. "Sleep while you can," the druid advised. "The Vale will test you in ways you cannot imagine."

Lyra settled into her bedroll, exhaustion tugging at her limbs, but her mind was too active for sleep to come easily. She lay awake, staring up at stars partially obscured by the skeletal branches of dead trees, thinking about Veyra and Aelion, about the history that had led them to this moment.

Eventually, she drifted into a restless sleep, her dreams filled with shifting faces and whispered voices that seemed to come from everywhere and nowhere at once.

She woke to Kael's hand on her shoulder, his touch gentle but urgent. "Lyra," he whispered. "Something's wrong."

Instantly alert, she sat up, taking in the predawn darkness and the tense postures of her companions. Thorn stood at the edge of their camp, her staff held defensively before her, those strange green eyes fixed on something in the distance.

"What is it?" Lyra asked, keeping her voice low as she moved to join them.

"Listen," Thorn replied simply.

Lyra strained her ears and soon caught what had alarmed the others—whispers, countless overlapping whispers, too faint to make out words but unmistakably human in cadence. They seemed to be coming from the Vale below them, rising and falling like the tide.

"The Vale earns its name," Thorn said grimly. "Those are the voices of the lost—those who wandered in without protection or guidance and never found their way out again."

"Are they... ghosts?" Mira asked, her usual bravado notably absent.

"Not exactly," Aelion answered, his ancient face lined with concern. "More like echoes—impressions left on the fabric of reality by strong emotions. Fear, desperation, hope... they all leave traces in places where the veil between worlds is thin."

"And the veil is very thin in the Vale," Thorn added. "It's one of the places where Veyra's ritual tore a rift. The whispers are strongest at dawn and dusk, when the world is between states."

As if to confirm her words, the whispers began to fade as the first light of true dawn touched the eastern horizon. Soon they were gone entirely, leaving behind an eerie silence that was somehow even more unsettling.

"We need to cross the Vale today," Thorn announced, her tone brooking no argument. "Stay close to me, do exactly as I say, and whatever you do, don't listen to the whispers. They'll try to lure you off the path."

They broke camp quickly, no one particularly eager to linger after what they'd heard. As the sun rose fully, they got their first clear look at the Whispering Vale—and Lyra felt her heart sink at the sight.

The Vale was vast, stretching for miles in either direction, a great wound carved into the land. What might once have been a lush valley was now a desolate wasteland. The ground was cracked and barren, with occasional pools of the same black ichor they'd seen in the corrupted stream. Skeletal trees dotted the landscape, their bare branches reaching up like the hands of the drowning. And hanging over everything was a thin, shimmering haze that distorted vision, making distances difficult to judge.

"Lovely," Mira muttered. "Absolutely charming. Remind me to book my next vacation here."

"This way," Thorn said, ignoring the alchemist's sarcasm. She set off down a barely visible path that wound between the larger cracks in the ground, her staff leaving small glowing marks with each tap against the earth.

They followed in single file, with Kael directly behind Thorn, then Lyra, Mira, Elara, Rowan, and finally Aelion bringing up the rear. The descent into the Vale was steep in places, the path crumbling beneath their feet, forcing them to catch themselves on the skeletal trees—which, Lyra noticed with disgust, felt warm to the touch, as if they still contained life despite their dead appearance.

As they reached the bottom of the Vale and began to cross its expanse, the air grew noticeably heavier, pressing against them like an invisible weight. The shimmering haze thickened, making it difficult to see more than a few yards ahead or behind. Lyra found herself focusing intently on Kael's back, afraid that if she looked away even for a moment, he might disappear into the haze.

They had been walking for perhaps an hour when the whispers returned—faint at first, barely perceptible, but growing steadily louder. They seemed to come from all around, sometimes sounding as if they were right next to Lyra's ear, causing her to turn sharply only to find nothing there.

"Don't listen," Thorn called back, her voice sounding strangely distant despite being only a few paces ahead. "Focus on the path, on each other. The whispers will try to separate us."

Lyra tried to follow this advice, fixing her gaze on Kael's broad shoulders, counting her steps to give her mind something to focus on besides the increasingly insistent whispers. But it was hard, so hard, especially when the voices began to sound familiar.

Lyra, they seemed to say. *Lyra, come to us. We've been waiting for you.*

She shook her head, trying to clear it. Just tricks, she told herself firmly. Just the echoes Aelion mentioned, playing on her fears and hopes.

But then a voice rose above the others—a voice she would have recognized anywhere.

Lyra, my darling. It's Mother. I'm here, just a little way off the path. Come to me.

Her step faltered. It couldn't be. Her mother was dead, had been for years. And yet... the voice was so clear, so familiar. What if, somehow, her mother's spirit had been trapped here? What if she needed help?

"Lyra." This voice was real, accompanied by a firm hand on her arm. Kael had stopped and turned, his eyes concerned as they searched her face. "Stay with us. Whatever you're hearing, it's not real."

She blinked, realizing with a shock that she had begun to drift off the path, drawn by the whispers. "I... I heard my mother," she admitted, her voice small.

Kael's expression softened with understanding. "I know. I hear Lirien sometimes. But it's not them. It's the Vale, using our memories against us."

Lyra nodded, grateful for his steadying presence. "Thank you."

They continued on, the whispers growing louder and more insistent with each step. Lyra noticed that the others were struggling too. Mira muttered angrily to herself, clearly arguing with voices only she could hear. Elara's hands moved constantly, tracing protective runes in the air that flared briefly before being absorbed by the haze.

Behind her, Rowan's footsteps had become uneven, hesitant. Lyra glanced back to see the cartographer's normally composed face twisted with emotion, his eyes darting to the side of the path as if following something only he could see.

"Rowan?" she called softly. "Are you alright?"

He startled, as if her voice had broken a trance. "I—yes. It's just..." He trailed off, swallowing hard. "The whispers. They sound like my family. From Highcliff, before the Syndicate came." His voice dropped to a barely audible murmur. "I hear my sister calling me a coward for running while she stayed to fight."

The raw pain in his voice made Lyra's heart ache. She hadn't known Rowan had lost a sister too. He spoke so rarely of his past.

"It's not her," she reminded him gently, echoing Kael's words. "It's the Vale, using your guilt against you."

Rowan nodded stiffly, his jaw tight. "I know. But knowing doesn't make it easier to ignore." He straightened his shoulders with visible effort. "I'll be alright. Keep moving."

Only Thorn seemed relatively unaffected, moving forward with purpose, her staff leaving those faint glowing marks that helped them stay on the path. And Aelion... Lyra couldn't see the ancient mage behind her, but she could feel his presence, a steady pulse of power that helped anchor her against the pull of the whispers.

They had reached what seemed to be the center of the Vale when Thorn suddenly stopped, raising her staff in warning. "Something's wrong," she said, her voice tight. "The path ahead has changed."

Lyra peered past Kael but could see nothing through the haze except more of the same blighted landscape. "Changed how?"

"It's gone," Thorn replied grimly. "Or hidden. This isn't natural—even the Vale's corruption follows patterns. This is deliberate interference."

"The Syndicate?" Kael asked, his hand moving to his sword hilt.

"Most likely," Thorn confirmed. "They must have sensed our presence."

As if summoned by her words, the haze before them thickened and darkened, coalescing into a form that made Lyra's heart race with dread. It was another Voice—similar to the one they had faced at Easthollow, but not identical. Where that Voice had been female, this one appeared male, though its features shifted and changed just as unnervingly.

"Trespassers," the Voice intoned, its words echoing strangely, as if multiple people were speaking in imperfect unison. "You walk where you are not welcome."

Thorn stepped forward, her staff held before her. "We walk the Green Path, as is our right. Your corruption has no claim here."

The Voice laughed, a sound like breaking glass. "The Green Path is dead, druid. As dead as your order. As dead as you soon will be." Its shifting gaze moved past Thorn, fixing on Lyra. "The Stone-bearer. Veyra will be pleased when I bring her your head—and the Stone."

"You're welcome to try," Kael growled, drawing his sword. The blade gleamed oddly in the hazy light, seeming to cut through the distortion around it.

"Oh, I will," the Voice promised. "But not alone."

It raised its hands, and the whispers that had been a constant background noise suddenly intensified, becoming a roar that made Lyra clap her hands over her ears. The haze around them churned and twisted, forming into humanoid shapes—dozens of them, surrounding their small group on all sides.

"The lost," Thorn spat, her voice tight with anger. "You're using the echoes of the dead against us."

"They serve Veyra now," the Voice replied, its shifting face settling momentarily into a smile that was somehow worse than its usual fluid state. "As all things eventually will."

The haze-figures began to close in, their movements jerky and unnatural. They had no distinct features, just vaguely human shapes made of the same shimmering haze that filled the Vale, but their intent was clear.

"Form a circle!" Kael commanded, his military training taking over. "Backs together!"

They moved quickly, forming a defensive ring with Lyra at its center. She reached for the Phoenix Stone, feeling its warmth against her palm, drawing on its power. Light began to gather around her, pushing back against the haze.

The Voice hissed in displeasure. "Kill them all. Bring me the Stone."

The haze-figures surged forward. Kael met them with his sword, which sliced through the first few as if they were made of smoke—but where it cut, the haze reformed almost immediately. Mira threw her potions, which exploded in bursts of brilliant light that momentarily dispersed larger sections of haze, but again, the figures simply reformed.

"Physical attacks won't work!" Aelion called out, his ancient voice rising above the chaos. "They're not truly corporeal!"

"Then what will work?" Mira demanded, frustration evident as she reached for more potions.

"Light and will," Aelion replied. "Elara, your runes! Thorn, the Green Path draws power from life—use it!"

The rune-caster and the druid nodded in unison, understanding what Aelion meant. Elara began to trace complex patterns in the air, her fingers leaving glowing trails that coalesced into protective symbols. Where the haze-figures touched these runes, they recoiled as if burned.

Thorn planted her staff firmly in the ground and began to chant in a language Lyra didn't recognize. Green light spiraled up from the earth, twining around the staff and then spreading outward in a web-like pattern. Where it touched the cracked ground, tiny shoots of green pushed through—actual living plants, growing in soil that had been dead for generations.

The Voice shrieked in rage. "Stop them!"

More haze-figures formed, pressing in from all sides. Kael and Rowan fought desperately to keep them back, their weapons passing through the figures but at least disrupting them momentarily. Mira continued to throw her potions, creating brief openings in the seemingly endless assault.

Lyra felt the Phoenix Stone grow warmer against her skin, responding to the danger. She closed her eyes, focusing on the power within it, drawing it forth. The light around her intensified, becoming a radiant aura that pushed back against the encroaching haze.

"Lyra," Aelion's voice came from just behind her, strained but steady. "The Stone responds to your will. Direct it at the Voice—it's controlling the haze-figures. Cut off the head, and the body will fall."

She opened her eyes, searching through the chaos for the Voice. It stood back from the battle, its shifting features contorted with malicious glee as it directed the haze-figures with sweeping gestures of its arms.

Focusing her will, Lyra channeled the Stone's power, shaping it into a concentrated beam of light that lanced out toward the Voice. The Voice saw it coming and tried to dodge, but the light followed it, striking it squarely in the chest.

The effect was immediate and dramatic. The Voice screamed, a sound of pure agony that cut through the roar of whispers. Its form began to flicker and distort even more wildly than usual, as if it was having trouble maintaining its cohesion.

"Again!" Aelion urged. "Don't let up!"

Lyra pushed more power through the Stone, the beam of light intensifying. The Voice's screams rose in pitch, becoming almost unbearable. Around them, the haze-figures began to falter, their movements becoming erratic.

Seeing their advantage, Thorn redoubled her efforts, the green light from her staff spreading farther, touching more of the blighted ground. Elara's runes grew more complex, forming a web of protection around their group that the haze-figures couldn't penetrate.

The Voice made one last, desperate attempt to flee, its form dissolving into pure haze that tried to seep away through the cracks in the ground. But Lyra's light followed it, relentless, burning away the haze until nothing remained but a faint, acrid smell like scorched air.

With the Voice destroyed, the haze-figures lost their cohesion, dissipating back into the general miasma that filled the Vale. The whispers faded to their previous level—still present, but no longer the overwhelming roar they had become during the attack.

Lyra swayed on her feet, the effort of channeling so much of the Stone's power leaving her drained. Kael was at her side in an instant, supporting her with a strong arm around her waist.

"Are you alright?" he asked, concern evident in his voice.

She nodded, too exhausted for words. The Stone at her throat had cooled, its power temporarily spent.

"That was... impressive," Thorn said, studying Lyra with new respect. "I've never seen anyone destroy a Voice so completely."

"Will it stay destroyed?" Rowan asked, his practical nature asserting itself even in the aftermath of such an otherworldly battle.

"For a time," Aelion answered. "The Voices are manifestations of Veyra's will, not truly independent beings. She can create another, but it requires considerable effort and power on her part."

"So we've bought ourselves some breathing room," Mira concluded, brushing haze-residue from her clothes with a look of disgust. "Fantastic. Can we please get out of this nightmare valley now?"

Thorn nodded, her attention returning to the path ahead. "The interference is gone. I can see the way forward again." She frowned, studying the ground. "But the Voice's attack has changed things. The path is... different."

"Different how?" Elara asked, her voice still strained from the effort of maintaining so many protective runes.

"Shorter," Thorn replied, surprise evident in her tone. "The attack was meant to stop us, but in destroying the Voice, we've actually cleared a more direct route through the Vale."

"Finally, some good luck," Mira muttered. "About time."

With Thorn once again leading the way, they resumed their journey across the Vale. The path did indeed seem clearer now, the haze less oppressive. The whispers continued, but they were easier to ignore, as if the destruction of the Voice had weakened their pull.

Lyra leaned on Kael as they walked, gradually recovering her strength. The Phoenix Stone slowly warmed against her skin again, its power returning.

"Thank you," she said quietly. "For keeping me grounded when I heard... when I thought I heard my mother."

Kael's expression softened. "We all have ghosts that haunt us. It helps to have someone to pull us back when they threaten to drag us away."

The simple honesty in his words touched her deeply. They had come so far together, from wary allies to... something more. Something she wasn't quite ready to name, but that gave her strength nonetheless.

They walked for several more hours, the landscape gradually changing as they neared the far side of the Vale. The ground became less cracked, with occasional patches of the same pale moss they had seen in the twisted woods. The skeletal trees gave way to ones that, while still twisted and unhealthy, at least had some leaves clinging to their branches.

By late afternoon, they had reached the beginning of the ascent out of the Vale. The path steepened, winding up through rocky terrain that was challenging but not treacherous. The haze thinned with each step they took upward, and the whispers faded until they were barely audible.

As they neared the top of the rise, Lyra felt a weight lifting from her shoulders—a pressure she hadn't fully registered until it was gone. She took a deep breath, the air cleaner and fresher than it had been in the depths of the Vale.

"We're almost through," Thorn announced, her voice reflecting a rare note of relief. "Just a little further."

But as they crested the rise, the druid suddenly stopped, her staff raised in warning. Ahead of them, blocking the path out of the Vale, stood a line of figures in dark robes, their faces hidden by deep hoods.

"Syndicate," Kael hissed, his hand going to his sword.

"Not just any Syndicate," Thorn replied, her voice tight. "Shadow-binders. Elite agents."

Lyra studied the figures with growing dread. There were seven of them, standing perfectly still, as if they had been waiting for some time. Unlike the Voice and its haze-figures, these were clearly corporeal—solid beings of flesh and blood, though the dark magic that surrounded them was palpable even at a distance.

These were no ordinary Syndicate agents. Each shadow-binder wore robes of a fabric so black it seemed to absorb light, with intricate silver embroidery along the hems that shifted and moved like liquid metal. Their hands, pale and marked with dark veins that pulsed beneath the skin, emerged from wide sleeves. Most disturbing were the silver masks they wore beneath their hoods—featureless except for narrow eye slits from which an unnatural violet light emanated.

"How did they know we'd be here?" Mira whispered.

"The Voice," Aelion replied grimly. "It must have sent a message before we destroyed it."

The central figure in the line stepped forward, lowering its hood to reveal not a silver mask but a face that was unnervingly normal—a middle-aged man with neatly trimmed hair and a scholar's features, save for the eyes, which were solid black, without iris or pupil.

"Stone-bearer," he called, his voice carrying clearly across the distance between them. "I am Corvus, Hand of the Shadow. Surrender the Phoenix Stone, and you and your companions will be allowed to leave with your lives."

"That's generous of you," Mira called back, her sarcasm returning in full force. "Considering how many of your friends we've already sent to whatever dark hole you call an afterlife."

Corvus's expression didn't change. "You misunderstand. This is not a negotiation. It is mercy—something Veyra rarely offers. The Stone for your lives. A simple exchange."

"And if we refuse?" Kael challenged.

"Then you die here," Corvus replied, as calmly as if discussing the weather. "And we take the Stone from your corpse." He looked directly at Lyra. "You have destroyed a Voice—an impressive feat. But do not mistake that victory for true power. You are outnumbered, exhausted from your crossing of the Vale, and far from any allies who might come to your aid."

He was right, Lyra realized with a sinking feeling. They were in no condition for another battle, especially against what appeared to be highly trained Syndicate agents. The Phoenix Stone had regained some of its power, but not enough for another display like the one that had destroyed the Voice.

"We need a plan," she murmured to the others. "Any ideas?"

"I might have one," Thorn replied, her voice equally low. "But it's risky, and you'll have to trust me completely."

"What choice do we have?" Kael asked grimly.

Thorn nodded, then raised her voice to address Corvus. "The Stone-bearer will speak with you alone. A parley, under the ancient laws of the Green Path."

Corvus's black eyes narrowed slightly. "The Green Path has no authority here, druid."

"Perhaps not," Thorn conceded. "But even the Syndicate once respected the rules of parley. Or has Veyra forgotten all the old ways in her pursuit of power?"

A flash of something—anger? respect?—crossed Corvus's face before his expression returned to its neutral state. "Very well. A parley. The Stone-bearer may approach. Alone and unarmed."

"No," Kael protested immediately, his voice a harsh whisper. "It's too dangerous."

"It's our only chance," Thorn insisted. "Trust me. I have a plan."

Lyra looked between them, then at the line of shadow-binders waiting on the path. Every instinct told her not to walk into what was almost certainly a trap. But Thorn had guided them safely through the Vale, and they were out of options.

"I'll do it," she decided. "But be ready... for whatever happens."

Kael's face was a mask of barely contained fury and fear. "Lyra—"

"I know," she cut him off, meeting his gaze steadily. "But Thorn's right. We don't have a choice."

Before he could argue further, she turned to Thorn. "What's the plan?"

The druid leaned close, speaking so softly that only Lyra could hear. "The Vale's corruption runs deep, but there are still living roots beneath the surface, dormant but not dead. My magic can awaken them, but I need your help. I'll need to plant the seeds of power deep within the earth. When they rise, they'll create a diversion that should give us a chance to escape."

Lyra nodded, her hand instinctively going to the Phoenix Stone. "What's the signal?"

"You'll know it," Thorn assured her. "Just be ready."

Taking a deep breath to steady herself, Lyra stepped forward, walking slowly toward Corvus while the others remained behind. Each step felt heavier than the last, as if the very air was thickening around her. The shadow-binders watched her approach with those unsettling violet eyes glowing behind their silver masks, their stillness unnatural and predatory.

Corvus watched her approach with those unsettling black eyes, his face still unnervingly calm. "A wise decision," he said as she drew near. "There's no need for further bloodshed."

"I want your word," Lyra replied, trying to keep her voice steady. "If I give you the Stone, my friends go free."

"Of course," Corvus agreed smoothly. "Veyra is not unreasonable. The Stone is all that matters."

He extended his hand, palm up, waiting. Lyra hesitated, her fingers touching the warm surface of the Phoenix Stone at her throat. Behind her, she could feel the tension radiating from her companions, especially Kael, who was likely one heartbeat away from charging forward despite the odds.

"Now, Stone-bearer," Corvus prompted, a hint of impatience finally cracking his composed facade. "My patience is not limitless."

Just as Lyra was beginning to wonder if Thorn's plan had failed, she heard it—a low, thrumming note that seemed to vibrate through the very ground beneath her feet. The signal.

Without hesitation, she gripped the Phoenix Stone and channeled its power downward, directing a surge of energy into the earth where Corvus stood. At the same moment, Thorn slammed her staff into the ground, sending a wave of green magic racing across the surface of the Vale.

The effect was instantaneous and dramatic. The ground erupted as ancient roots, awakened by the combined power of the Phoenix Stone and Thorn's druidic magic, burst upward in a tangled mass of writhing vegetation. The shadow-binders were caught completely by surprise, several of them ensnared immediately by the rapidly growing plants.

"Run!" Thorn shouted. "Now!"

Lyra didn't need to be told twice. She turned and sprinted back toward her companions as chaos erupted behind her. The shadow-binders were fighting back, dark energy slicing through the animated roots, but the plants continued to grow and multiply, creating a living barrier between the two groups.

"This way!" Thorn called, veering off the path and leading them along a narrow ridge that skirted the edge of the Vale. "The eastern pass! Quickly!"

They ran, adrenaline overriding their exhaustion. Behind them, shouts and the crackle of dark magic indicated that the shadow-binders were beginning to break free of the vegetative trap. But the head start was enough—they reached a narrow cleft in the rocks that Lyra would never have noticed without Thorn's guidance, slipping through just as the first shadow-binder crested the ridge behind them.

The passage twisted sharply, then opened onto a steep downward slope. They half-ran, half-slid down it, emerging into a thick forest of ancient pines whose heavy boughs created a canopy so dense that little light penetrated to the forest floor.

"They won't follow us in here," Thorn panted, finally slowing her pace. "Not immediately, at least. The old growth resists their corruption. We'll have time to rest and plan our next move."

Lyra collapsed against the trunk of a massive pine, her heart racing from the narrow escape. "That was... too close."

"But effective," Rowan noted, his observant eyes scanning their surroundings. "Where are we?"

"The Eastern Wilds," Thorn replied. "One of the few places in these territories still relatively untouched by the Syndicate's influence. The trees here are ancient, their roots deep. They remember a time before Veyra, before the corruption. That memory gives them strength."

As they caught their breath in the sheltering darkness of the ancient forest, Lyra felt the Phoenix Stone warm against her skin, its power resonating with the natural magic of their surroundings. They had survived the Whispering Vale and escaped the shadow-binders, but she knew their journey was far from over. Somewhere ahead lay the heart of the Syndicate's power—and Veyra herself, or whatever she had become.

But for now, they were safe. And in this world of shadow and corruption, that was no small victory.

CHAPTER TWELVE

The Teacher's Burden

Dawn broke with reluctance over the Eastern Wilds, pale light filtering through the ancient pines that had sheltered the companions through the night. The forest floor remained dark, dappled with only occasional shafts of sunlight that penetrated the dense canopy. After their narrow escape from the shadow-binders at the edge of the Whispering Vale, everyone moved with the quiet caution of those who know they're being hunted.

Thorn led them deeper into the forest, following paths invisible to untrained eyes. The druid moved with fluid grace, her silver-cropped hair catching the sparse light, her strange green eyes constantly scanning their surroundings. Behind her walked Kael, then Lyra, Mira, Elara, and Rowan, with Alaric bringing up the rear.

The ancient mage moved with deliberate steps, his weathered face composed despite the exhaustion that pulled at his ancient frame. Three centuries of life had taught him to conserve energy, to pace himself through crises that would burn out younger companions. As he walked, his eyes tracked not just their surroundings but the subtle flows of energy that permeated the forest—currents invisible to ordinary sight but clear as rivers to his trained perception.

These flows troubled him deeply, though he kept his concern from showing on his face. The corruption he sensed was familiar—a signature he hadn't encountered in its pure form for over a century. Veyra's touch was unmistakable, like a melody played in a distinctive key, recognizable even when the specific notes changed.

"How far until we reach somewhere safe?" Mira asked, breaking the silence that had stretched since dawn. The alchemist's usual sarcasm had given way to practical concerns after their confrontation with Corvus and his shadow-binders.

"Nowhere in these lands is truly safe," Thorn replied without turning. "But there's a place ahead where we can rest without constant vigilance. The trees there remember the old ways. Their roots run deep, untouched by the Syndicate's corruption."

"That sounds suspiciously like 'several more hours of walking,'" Mira muttered.

"At least," Thorn confirmed, the ghost of a smile touching her lips.

Alaric allowed himself a small smile at the exchange. Mira's irreverence reminded him of another alchemist he had known long ago—a bright-eyed woman named Serafina who had challenged conventional wisdom with similar sardonic wit. The memory carried both warmth and pain; Serafina had been among the first casualties when Veyra's corruption began spreading through the ancient academies.

So many lost over the centuries. So many bright flames extinguished before their time.

The thought sobered him, drawing his attention back to their current predicament. The younger companions viewed their quest through the lens of immediate concerns—survival, the defeat of the Syndicate, the healing of rifts. They couldn't grasp the true scale of what they faced, the cycles of conflict that had repeated across centuries.

Perhaps that was for the best. Hope flourished more easily in those who hadn't witnessed repeated failures.

They walked in silence again, each lost in their own thoughts. Lyra's mind kept returning to the revelations of the previous day—Veyra, once Alaric's student, now transformed into something beyond human. The founder of the Shadow Syndicate. The source of the corruption that had blighted these lands for generations.

The Phoenix Stone rested warm against her chest, its power replenished after the night's rest. Lyra touched it through her shirt, drawing comfort from its steady heat. The Stone had destroyed a Voice—one of Veyra's direct conduits. What else might it be capable of?

Alaric observed this gesture, noting how naturally Lyra had adapted to the Stone's presence. In three centuries of watching various artifacts pass from bearer to bearer, he had rarely seen such intuitive harmony develop so quickly. The Stone responded to her in ways it hadn't to previous bearers—even her parents, skilled as they had been.

It troubled him more than he cared to admit. The Phoenix Stone's awakening coincided too neatly with other signs he had observed—subtle shifts in the world's energetic patterns, the increased activity of the Syndicate, the weakening of boundaries between realities that had remained stable for decades. A convergence was approaching, one he had hoped would not arrive during his lifetime.

"The flows here are... different," Elara said softly to Lyra, her voice carrying back to Alaric's sensitive hearing. "Purer than in the Vale, but still not what they should be. It's like listening to music where some notes are slightly off-key."

"You can sense the magical flows that clearly?" Lyra asked.

"It's how my rune-casting works," Elara explained. "I don't create power; I redirect what already exists, shaping it through patterns."

Alaric listened with approval. The young rune-caster's understanding, while still developing, showed remarkable intuition. In another era, she might have been his student, her talents nurtured in the academies that had once dotted Sylvanthia before Veyra's corruption forced their closure.

Another path lost to time and shadow.

Thorn raised a hand, signaling for silence. The druid stood motionless, head tilted as if listening to something beyond human hearing. After a long moment, she relaxed slightly.

"There's a stream ahead," she said. "We should refill our water supplies. The lands beyond the forest are... dry."

The understated warning sent a chill through the group. They had all heard Thorn's descriptions of the Blighted Plains that lay between them and their destination. A wasteland corrupted by shadow magic, where reality itself became unreliable.

Alaric moved forward, closing the gap between himself and the others. "I should examine the water before we drink," he said quietly. "Corruption often manifests first in flowing water, where energy naturally gathers."

Thorn nodded, accepting his expertise without question. Though the druid was naturally protective of her domain, she recognized Alaric's greater experience with the specific corruption they faced.

When they reached the stream, Alaric knelt at its edge, his weathered hands hovering just above the clear water. To ordinary eyes, the stream appeared pristine—crystal water flowing over smooth stones, small fish darting in the shallows. But Alaric's perception revealed more.

Threads of darkness, too subtle for even Thorn or Elara to detect, wove through the water's energy pattern. Not enough to cause immediate harm, but present nonetheless—the first tendrils of corruption reaching into this protected space.

"It is safe to drink," he announced after completing his examination, "but we should purify it first." From within his robes, he withdrew a small pouch of crystalline powder—an alchemical compound he had prepared decades ago for exactly this purpose. As he sprinkled it into their water containers, the powder dissolved with a brief flash of blue light.

"What is that?" Mira asked, her alchemist's curiosity piqued despite her exhaustion.

"Crystallized moonlight," Alaric replied, a hint of amusement touching his ancient eyes at her skeptical expression. "Or more accurately, a compound of minerals exposed to specific lunar phases and treated with essences that respond to corruption."

"That's... not a standard alchemical approach," Mira noted, studying the now-settled water with professional interest.

"No," Alaric agreed. "The formula predates modern alchemical classifications. I learned it from my third master, nearly two centuries ago."

The casual reference to his age silenced further questions, as it often did. The younger companions frequently forgot the true span of his existence—the accumulation of knowledge and experience that centuries of life had provided. Sometimes this amnesia was convenient, allowing him to observe without the burden of constant deference. Other times, like now, it created distance he did not desire.

They continued their journey after the brief rest, the character of the forest changing subtly as they progressed. The trees stood taller, their trunks straighter, the undergrowth healthier. Even the quality of light shifted, the dappled shadows taking on a greenish hue that spoke of ancient, undisturbed growth.

Around midday, the forest began to change more dramatically. The trees stood straighter, their bark less gnarled, their leaves a deeper, healthier green. The undergrowth thickened with ferns and flowering plants that Lyra didn't recognize. The air itself felt different—cleaner, somehow, with a subtle sweetness that hinted at growing things.

"We're entering the heart of the Eastern Wilds," Thorn explained, noting their curious glances. "One of the last places where the old magic still flows uncorrupted."

"I can feel it," Elara said, her fingers tracing patterns in the air as if following invisible currents. "The flows here are... pure. Balanced."

Alaric felt it too, more profoundly than the others could comprehend. The balanced flows here were like a half-remembered melody suddenly heard clearly after years of distortion—achingly familiar yet startling in its clarity. This was how all of Sylvanthia had once felt, before Veyra's ritual tore the first rifts in reality.

The memory transported him momentarily to another time—walking these same forests with Veyra at his side, both of them young (or in his case, younger), exploring the natural flows of energy that permeated the world. Her brilliant mind had grasped concepts in days that took others years to master. Her questions had challenged him, pushed him to articulate understandings he had previously held only intuitively.

Where had it gone wrong? When had her curiosity curdled into hunger, her wonder transformed to ambition? He had asked himself these questions a thousand times over the centuries, and still had no satisfying answer.

"The Keepers of the Green Path maintained this sanctuary for centuries," Thorn was saying, pulling Alaric from his reverie. "Even after our order was scattered, the protections remained."

"And the Syndicate never tried to corrupt it?" Rowan asked, the cartographer's eyes taking in every detail of their surroundings, mentally mapping this hidden refuge.

"They tried," Thorn replied, her voice hardening. "Many times. But the forest defends itself. The deeper you go, the stronger its resistance."

As if to confirm her words, a sudden wind rustled through the trees, stirring leaves and branches in a pattern too coordinated to be natural. The companions felt the hairs rise on the backs of their necks—not from fear, but from a strange sense of recognition. The forest was aware of them.

"It's... watching us," Lyra said.

Thorn nodded. "The old growth has its own consciousness, of a sort. Not like ours, but aware nonetheless. It recognizes the Phoenix Stone." She pointed to Lyra's chest. "Fire and growth—seemingly opposed, yet part of the same cycle of renewal."

Alaric watched the interplay between Lyra and the forest energies with careful attention. The Phoenix Stone's resonance with the uncorrupted flows confirmed what he had suspected—its power was growing, awakening to its full potential after decades of dormancy. This was both promising and concerning. Greater power meant greater capacity to heal the rifts, but also greater risk if that power was misdirected or corrupted.

The druid led them onward, the path widening as they went deeper. By mid-afternoon, they emerged into a clearing unlike anything most of them had seen before. Massive trees ringed the space, their trunks wider than a house, their canopies reaching hundreds of feet into the sky. At the center stood a single tree that dwarfed even these giants—an ancient colossus with bark the color of burnished copper and leaves that shimmered with an inner light.

"The Heart Tree," Thorn said, her voice dropping to a reverent whisper. "The oldest living thing in Sylvanthia."

They approached the massive tree with instinctive caution, feeling the weight of age and power that emanated from it. The ground beneath their feet had transformed from forest soil to a carpet of soft moss interspersed with tiny white flowers that released a subtle fragrance when crushed.

For Alaric, the moment carried a profound sense of homecoming. He had stood in this very clearing over two centuries ago, when the Heart Tree had been merely enormous rather than colossal. He had sat beneath its branches with the Keepers of the Green Path, sharing knowledge and insights across their different traditions. He had watched young druids take their oaths, had participated in rituals of renewal during the darkest days after Veyra's first rise to power.

And before that—long before—he had brought Veyra herself here, when she was still his most promising student. The memory struck him with unexpected force. They had spent three days in contemplation beneath the Heart Tree's younger canopy, discussing the nature of balance and the responsibility that came with power.

"The greater your capacity," he had told her, "the greater your obligation to maintain harmony rather than dominance."

She had seemed to understand then, her brilliant eyes alight with genuine insight. What had changed in the decades that followed? What seed of corruption had taken root in her understanding, transforming wisdom into the twisted philosophy that now animated the Syndicate?

"We can make camp here," Thorn said, pulling Alaric from his painful reminiscence. "No harm will come to us within sight of the Heart Tree."

As they set up camp, Alaric moved to the massive trunk, placing his palm against the ancient bark. To the others, it might have appeared a simple gesture of reverence, but he was actually initiating a form of communication—one of the oldest magics he knew, predating even the formal schools and traditions that had arisen in later eras.

Old friend, he projected into the living consciousness of the tree, *it has been many seasons since I stood beneath your branches.*

The response came not as words but as impressions—a sense of recognition, of cycles completing and beginning anew. The Heart Tree remembered him, as it remembered all who had communed with it over the millennia of its existence.

We face the shadow once more, Alaric continued, allowing his concerns to flow through the connection. *The one who broke faith. The one who tears the fabric of reality for power.*

The Tree's response carried complex emotions—sorrow for what had been lost, determination to preserve what remained, and something else that surprised Alaric: hope. Not blind optimism, but a deeper certainty born from witnessing countless cycles of destruction and renewal.

You see something I do not, Alaric realized. *Some pattern beyond my perception.*

The impression that flowed back contained no specific information, merely a sense of convergence—many streams flowing toward a single point, a moment of potential transformation. The Heart Tree, with its perspective spanning millennia, perceived the current crisis not as an endpoint but as a transition—painful, perhaps even catastrophic, but ultimately part of a larger pattern.

I wish I shared your certainty, Alaric admitted. *Too many cycles have I witnessed, too many promising beginnings that ended in shadow.*

The Tree's final communication before their connection faded was simple but profound—an impression of a seedling breaking through scorched earth, finding life where none seemed possible. Not a guarantee, but a reminder that possibility persisted even in the darkest circumstances.

Alaric withdrew his hand from the bark, feeling both comforted and disquieted by the exchange. The Heart Tree's perspective transcended human understanding, its patience born from a lifespan measured in millennia rather than decades. What might appear as catastrophe to him could be merely transition from the Tree's vantage point—cold comfort to those who would not survive to see what emerged from the ashes.

As evening approached, the companions gathered around a small fire, the first they had risked since entering the Eastern Wilds. The Heart Tree's protection made such ordinary comforts possible, a brief respite from the vigilance their journey required.

Alaric observed his companions with quiet assessment. They had grown since their journey began—not just in skill but in understanding, in their connections to one another. Lyra had progressed from reluctant bearer to purposeful leader. Kael had tempered his protective instincts with strategic thinking. Elara had begun integrating her academic knowledge with practical application. Mira's defensive sarcasm had softened, revealing glimpses of genuine care beneath. Rowan's quiet competence had expanded to include occasional insights that surprised even himself.

They were becoming what they needed to be, these young ones. The question that troubled Alaric was whether their growth would come quickly enough, whether the lessons they still needed to learn could be absorbed before they faced Veyra's full power.

Some lessons could only be taught through experience, through failure and recovery. But time was a luxury they increasingly lacked.

As the meal concluded and night settled fully over the clearing, Alaric rose from his place by the fire. The burden of knowledge he had carried for centuries pressed upon him with renewed urgency. The time for partial truths and protected ignorance had passed.

"I owe you all an explanation," he said, his voice carrying the gravity of centuries. "About Veyra. About my part in what she became."

A hush fell over the camp. Even the forest seemed to still, as if listening.

"You don't have to do this, Alaric," Elara said softly, concern in her eyes.

"I do," he contradicted gently. "These secrets have remained buried too long. And you—all of you—deserve to know the truth of what we face."

He settled back down, his ancient eyes reflecting the dancing flames. The story he was about to tell had been rehearsed countless times in the privacy of his thoughts, yet speaking it aloud still felt like tearing open a wound that had never properly healed.

"Veyra came to me as a student over three centuries ago. A young woman of extraordinary talent and boundless curiosity." The memories flowed more easily than he had expected, vivid despite the centuries that separated present from past.

"I had never encountered a mind like hers—so quick to grasp the most complex magical principles, so eager to push beyond established boundaries."

His gaze grew distant, seeing across the centuries to the bright-eyed young woman who had appeared at his woodland dwelling one autumn morning, requesting tutelage with a confidence that bordered on arrogance. He had nearly turned her away—he had taken no new students for decades at that point, preferring solitude to the responsibility of shaping young minds. But something in her determination had reminded him of himself in younger days, and against his better judgment, he had agreed to test her aptitude.

"I was... flattered by her interest in my teachings. Proud of her progress. I ignored the warning signs—her fascination with power for its own sake, her disregard for the balance that underlies all true magic."

"You were her teacher, not her keeper," Elara interjected. "Her choices were her own."

Alaric shook his head, a sad smile touching his ancient features. "A teacher bears responsibility for what their student becomes. I saw the path she was taking, but I convinced myself I could guide her back to balance. I was wrong."

The admission cost him, even after centuries of private acknowledgment. He had failed Veyra—or perhaps more accurately, had failed to recognize that she was beyond his guidance long before their final confrontation.

"What happened?" Lyra asked, drawn into the ancient mage's tale despite the darkness it evoked.

"She discovered texts I had hidden away—dangerous knowledge from the early days of magic, before we understood the cost of certain powers." Alaric's voice dropped lower, forcing them to lean forward to hear. "Spells that drew power not from the natural flows of energy, but by creating imbalance. By tearing the fabric between worlds."

He remembered the day with perfect clarity—returning to his dwelling after a week's absence to find his most secure wards bypassed, the hidden chamber beneath his library opened. Veyra had not even attempted to conceal her transgression, meeting him with eyes fever-bright with discovery and a dozen ancient texts spread before her.

"Shadow magic," Thorn said, her voice hard.

Alaric nodded. "When I confronted her, she claimed she sought only knowledge, not power. I believed her—or wanted to believe her. By the time I realized the extent of her experiments, she had gathered followers, created the first iteration of what would become the Shadow Syndicate."

He did not share the full truth of that confrontation—how Veyra had tried to recruit him, offering him partnership in her "great work" of transcending the limitations of natural magic. How she had looked at him with genuine confusion when he recoiled from her offer, unable to comprehend why he would reject power freely available for the taking.

"The First Shadow War," Rowan said, connecting the historical dots.

"Yes." Alaric's face shadowed with pain. "I led the coalition against her—mages, druids, warriors from across Sylvanthia. We thought we had won when we cornered her in her stronghold. But instead of surrendering, she enacted a ritual none of us had foreseen."

The memory of that day haunted him still—the twisted tower of black stone, the unnatural storm gathering above it, the sense of fundamental wrongness that permeated the air as Veyra channeled power through rifts torn in the fabric of reality itself.

"The ritual that tore the rifts," Lyra concluded, remembering their conversation in the Vale.

"She channeled all her accumulated power into a single spell—one designed to transform her into something beyond mortality. The backlash created rifts in reality itself, wounds in the world that bled shadow magic." Alaric's hands trembled slightly as he spoke, the weight of centuries-old failure pressing upon him. "We thought she had destroyed herself in the process. For decades, there was peace. The rifts remained, but they were contained. Then, gradually, the Syndicate reemerged. The Voices appeared, speaking with Veyra's authority, if not her actual presence."

What he did not say—could not bring himself to share even now—was how close he had come to stopping her before the ritual reached completion. How he had fought his way to the central chamber, had seen Veyra suspended in a maelstrom of shadow energy, her form already beginning to transform. How he had raised his staff, summoning power to strike her down—and had hesitated, remembering the bright-eyed student who had once sat at his feet, asking questions that challenged and delighted him.

That moment of hesitation had cost the world centuries of corruption and suffering. A burden he had carried alone through the long years that followed.

A heavy silence fell as they absorbed the weight of this history. The fire crackled, sending sparks spiraling up toward the star-filled sky visible through the opening in the Heart Tree's canopy.

"There's something I don't understand," Elara said finally, her analytical mind probing for clarity. "If Veyra sought to transcend mortality, why would she risk everything on a ritual that might destroy her? There must have been a specific catalyst—something that pushed her to act when she did."

Alaric looked at her sharply, surprise flickering across his ancient features. The rune-caster's insight was keen, cutting to a truth he had not intended to reveal. Yet having committed to honesty, he could not now withhold this crucial detail.

"You have keen insight, rune-caster. Yes, there was a catalyst." He hesitated, then continued with evident reluctance. "Veyra was dying. A wasting disease that even her considerable power couldn't cure. The ritual was her desperate attempt to escape death."

What he did not add was that the disease had been his final attempt to stop her—a last resort after reasoning, confrontation, and even magical binding had failed. He had introduced a subtle corruption into her personal magical workings, one designed to gradually weaken her connection to the power sources she had come to rely upon. He had intended it as a temporary measure, a way to diminish her abilities until she could be contained by more conventional means.

But Veyra's brilliance had turned even this against him. She had recognized the corruption not as an attack but as an opportunity—studying its properties, its method of disrupting natural energy flows, and incorporating those principles into her final ritual. What he had meant as containment became instead the template for her transcendence.

Another failure. Another burden carried through centuries.

"So all of this—the corruption, the Syndicate, the suffering of countless people—began because one woman feared her own mortality?" Kael's voice held controlled anger.

"Fear is the root of much evil," Alaric replied quietly. "And Veyra's fear was... magnified by her power, her belief that she was meant for something greater than a mortal span of years."

He understood Kael's anger. The young warrior saw the situation in clear moral terms—Veyra's selfishness against the greater good, her personal fear weighed against centuries of suffering. A perspective untainted by the complex emotions that clouded Alaric's own judgment even after so many years.

"So what exactly are we facing?" Kael asked, ever the strategist. "Is Veyra alive? Dead? Something in between?"

"I don't know," Alaric admitted, the uncertainty still troubling him after centuries of speculation. "The ritual she attempted was theoretical, never before implemented. My belief is that she exists in a state between worlds—neither fully here nor entirely gone. The Voices are her anchors to our reality, allowing her to extend her will without fully manifesting."

"And the Phoenix Stone?" Lyra touched the warm gem at her throat. "How does it fit into all this?"

Alaric considered his answer carefully. The Stone's true nature and origins remained one of the few secrets he had not yet decided to share—not from any desire to deceive, but from genuine uncertainty about how such knowledge might affect their path forward.

"The Stone is ancient, predating even my understanding," he said, offering a partial truth. "But its essential nature is one of balance and renewal. Fire that destroys, yet makes way for new growth. It's anathema to shadow magic, which exists by creating imbalance and discord."

"That's why it could destroy the Voice," Lyra realized.

"Yes. And potentially, it could heal the rifts Veyra created—restore the balance to the flows of magic throughout Sylvanthia."

What he did not say was that the Stone was awakening to capabilities beyond what even he had witnessed in previous cycles—responding to Lyra in ways that suggested possibilities both wondrous and terrifying. The Phoenix Stone had always been a catalyst for transformation, but the specific form that transformation took depended greatly on the bearer's understanding and intent.

"Could it destroy Veyra herself?" Kael pressed.

Alaric and Thorn exchanged glances, a silent communication passing between the two oldest members of their group. "Perhaps," the ancient mage said. "If we could reach her true form, whatever that may be now. But finding her won't be simple. She exists beyond normal perception."

"The Voices are our key," Thorn said. "They're connected to her. If we could capture one instead of destroying it..."

"We might trace the connection back to its source," Elara finished, her mind racing with the magical implications. "It would be dangerous—following such a link would expose us to Veyra's direct awareness."

"We've already got her attention," Mira pointed out. "Corvus and his shadow-binders weren't tracking us for the exercise."

"True," Thorn conceded. "But there's a difference between being hunted and deliberately placing ourselves within her power."

The conversation continued late into the night, strategies proposed and discarded, the full complexity of their mission becoming clearer with each passing hour. Alaric contributed where needed, but increasingly found himself observing rather than directing—watching these younger minds grapple with problems he had contemplated for centuries without resolution.

Perhaps that was the true hope in this cycle—not that he would finally discover the solution that had eluded him for so long, but that these new perspectives might see possibilities his experience-weighted mind had overlooked.

Eventually, exhaustion claimed them one by one, until only Lyra and Kael remained awake, taking the first watch together. Alaric retreated to his bedroll, though sleep would be long in coming. The day's revelations had stirred memories and emotions long suppressed, bringing the past into sharper focus than he had allowed in decades.

As he lay beneath the Heart Tree's protective canopy, he found himself remembering not the final confrontation with Veyra, nor her transformation into the entity they now faced, but earlier days—the bright beginning before shadow fell.

Veyra sitting cross-legged beside a mountain stream, eyes closed in concentration as she learned to perceive the subtle energy flows in moving water. Her triumphant smile when she successfully redirected a tiny rivulet without physically touching it.

Veyra debating magical theory with scholars twice her age, her arguments so incisive and well-constructed that even those who disagreed could not help but admire her intellect.

Veyra beneath this very Heart Tree, two centuries ago, lying on her back watching sunlight filter through the leaves, asking questions about the nature of consciousness and whether trees dreamed.

Before ambition. Before corruption. Before fear of death transformed wonder into hunger.

Had there been a moment when intervention might have changed her course? A word he could have spoken, an insight he might have shared, that would have led her toward balance rather than dominance? Or had her path been set from the beginning, her brilliance inevitably drawing her toward the power that ultimately consumed her?

Questions without answers, regrets without resolution. The burden of centuries.

Sleep finally claimed him as the night deepened, bringing dreams of what might have been—and what might yet be, if the cycle of shadow and renewal finally found its completion.

Morning arrived with gentle insistence, sunlight filtering through the Heart Tree's vast canopy to dapple the clearing with gold. Alaric woke with the dawn, as had been his habit for centuries. The younger companions still slept, their forms huddled in bedrolls around the cold remnants of the previous night's fire.

He rose silently, moving to the edge of the clearing where a small stream emerged from between massive roots before winding away into the forest. Kneeling beside it, he performed the ritual of renewal that had anchored his days since before any of his current companions were born—a series of movements and focused breaths that realigned his energy with the natural flows around him.

The ritual complete, he remained kneeling, allowing his awareness to expand beyond physical limitations. The Heart Tree's protective influence created a sanctuary where such meditation could safely reach beyond ordinary perception, touching aspects of reality normally obscured by corruption.

What he sensed troubled him deeply. The balanced flows within the clearing remained strong, but the corruption beyond had intensified since their arrival. Something was responding to their presence—or more specifically, to the Phoenix Stone's awakening power. The shadow was gathering, preparing.

"You feel it too."

The voice startled him from his meditation. Thorn stood nearby, her strange green eyes focused on the forest beyond the clearing's edge. The druid's connection to the natural world gave her a perception almost as acute as his own, though filtered through a different tradition.

"Yes," Alaric acknowledged, rising to his feet with the careful movements his ancient body required. "The corruption is responding to our presence. Organizing."

"The shadow-binders will be hunting us more actively now," Thorn said, her voice matter-of-fact rather than fearful. "After what happened in the Vale, they know the Phoenix Stone represents a genuine threat."

"More than they realize," Alaric murmured, almost to himself.

Thorn's keen gaze shifted to him, assessing. "You know more about the Stone than you shared last night."

It wasn't a question, and Alaric didn't treat it as one. The druid had lived long enough, had witnessed enough, to recognize when knowledge was being parceled out selectively.

"Some truths reveal themselves only when the time is right," he said after a moment's consideration. "The Stone's full nature is one such truth."

"And you believe you know when that time will be?" There was no challenge in Thorn's tone, merely curiosity.

"I believe the Stone itself will make that determination," Alaric replied. "It has its own... awareness. Its own purpose that transcends any single bearer."

Thorn accepted this with a nod, her expression suggesting she had suspected as much. "The Heart Tree communicated with you yesterday."

Again, not a question. The druid's perception was unsettlingly acute.

"Yes," Alaric confirmed. "It sees patterns beyond my perception—cycles completing and beginning anew. It views our current crisis as transformation rather than ending."

"A perspective earned through millennia of witnessing the forest's cycles of destruction and renewal," Thorn observed. "Death and rebirth are not opposites to the ancient growth, merely phases of the same process."

"A comfort to those who survive to see what emerges from the ashes," Alaric said, echoing his thoughts from the previous day. "Less so to those consumed in the fire."

Thorn's mouth curved in a small, sad smile. "The burden of shorter-lived species—we experience as catastrophe what the ancient ones perceive as transition." She gestured toward their sleeping companions. "They carry hope untainted by centuries of witnessed failure. Perhaps that is their greatest strength."

"And our greatest responsibility," Alaric added quietly. "To guide without extinguishing that hope through the weight of our experience."

They stood in companionable silence then, two ancient souls who understood one another in ways the younger companions could not yet comprehend. Both had witnessed cycles of struggle against corruption, had seen promising beginnings end in shadow. Both carried the weight of failed attempts and lost companions.

Yet both continued to fight, to seek new paths forward, to guide those who might succeed where previous generations had failed.

As the others began to stir, Alaric moved to help prepare for the day ahead. The revelations of the previous night had shifted something within him—not removing the burden of centuries, but perhaps distributing its weight more evenly. Sharing the truth of Veyra, of his own failures, had been painful but necessary.

The companions would face the days ahead with clearer understanding of what they confronted. And he would face those days with something he had not fully allowed himself in decades: not blind optimism, but the tentative possibility that this cycle might end differently than those that came before.

The Heart Tree had shown him a seedling breaking through scorched earth. Not a guarantee, but a reminder that possibility persisted even in the darkest circumstances.

As they prepared to continue their journey, Alaric watched Lyra check the Phoenix Stone, her fingers brushing the gem with instinctive familiarity. The Stone pulsed in response, its light briefly visible even through the fabric of her shirt—growing stronger, more responsive, awakening to possibilities long dormant.

Yes, this cycle might indeed be different. Not because of his ancient wisdom, but because of what these younger souls brought to the eternal struggle—perspectives unclouded by centuries of witnessed failure, determination untainted by resignation, and a capacity for growth he had forgotten was possible in such a short span of years.

For the first time in longer than he could remember, Alaric allowed himself to feel something beyond duty, beyond responsibility.

Hope.

CHAPTER THIRTEEN

Capturing Shadows

The Temple of Echoes loomed against the jagged backdrop of the Razorback Mountains, its ancient stone façade seeming to absorb the morning light rather than reflect it. From their vantage point in the druids' sanctuary, Lyra studied the distant structure through a gap in the cliff face that served as a natural window. Three towers of uneven height rose from the main temple body, their surfaces etched with symbols that even at this distance radiated wrongness.

"How long has the Syndicate controlled the temple?" she asked, not taking her eyes from the distant structure.

Sylva, the First Keeper of the Green Path, stood beside her, silver-streaked hair bound in intricate braids that marked her rank among the druids. "They claimed it during the Second Shadow War, nearly a century ago. Before that, it stood abandoned since Veyra's transformation."

"And it was built over one of the original rifts," Lyra said, recalling what Thorn had told them.

"The first and largest," Sylva confirmed. "The temple predates Veyra by centuries. Our histories suggest it was constructed to contain the rift, which existed naturally before she tore open others."

This new information sent Lyra's thoughts spinning. "A natural rift? I thought they were all created by Veyra's ritual."

"That's the common belief," Aelion said, joining them at the window. The ancient mage moved stiffly after the previous day's battle on the Blighted Plains, but his eyes remained sharp and alert. "The truth, as always, is more complex. Veyra didn't create the rifts from nothing—she expanded existing weak points in the fabric between worlds."

"And the Temple of Echoes was built over the weakest point," Sylva added. "By an order that predates even the Green Path. They called themselves the Wardens of the Veil."

Lyra felt the Phoenix Stone warm against her skin, responding to the conversation—or perhaps to the proximity of the temple itself. "What happened to these Wardens?"

"They disappeared long before my time," Aelion said. "But their work remained. The temple contained the rift successfully for centuries, until Veyra's ritual destabilized it along with the others."

A silence fell between them as they contemplated the temple. Even from this distance, Lyra could sense the corruption that emanated from it—a subtle wrongness that made her skin prickle.

"We should gather the others," she said finally. "We need to plan our approach."

They found their companions in the central chamber of the sanctuary, where the druids had provided food and fresh supplies. Kael and Rowan sat together, deep in conversation over a rough map that the cartographer had been sketching. Mira sorted through her alchemical supplies, replenishing her stocks with ingredients the druids had provided. Elara sat cross-legged on a stone bench, her eyes closed in meditation, faint traces of runic light dancing around her fingertips.

The rune-caster had recovered somewhat from her ordeal on the Plains, but her face remained drawn, dark circles shadowing her eyes. The corrupted magic had affected her more deeply than the others, her sensitivity to magical flows making her both more powerful and more vulnerable in such environments.

Thorn stood apart from the others, conversing quietly with a group of druids. The reunion with her order had stirred complex emotions in the solitary woman. Lyra had noticed both joy and tension in Thorn's interactions with her fellow Green Path members—particularly with Sylva, whose relationship with Thorn seemed fraught with unspoken history.

As Lyra, Aelion, and Sylva entered, conversations quieted. All eyes turned to them, expectant.

"We've been studying the temple," Lyra began without preamble. "And learning its history. It's older and potentially more dangerous than we realized."

She outlined what they'd learned about the natural rift and the Wardens who had built the temple to contain it. As she spoke, she noticed Rowan's expression change from interest to something more intense.

"The Wardens of the Veil," the cartographer repeated when she finished. "My grandfather mentioned them in his stories. He said they were keepers of ancient artifacts that could sense disturbances in reality."

"Like the compass you mentioned," Lyra recalled their conversation in the Eastern Wilds.

Rowan nodded, excitement breaking through his usual reserve. "If the Temple of Echoes was their headquarters, there might be records there—or even the compass itself."

"Assuming the Syndicate hasn't found and destroyed everything of value," Kael cautioned, ever practical.

"The Syndicate seeks power, not knowledge for its own sake," Aelion said. "They may have overlooked artifacts they couldn't immediately use."

"This compass," Sylva interjected, her keen eyes fixed on Rowan. "What exactly would it do?"

"According to my grandfather, it could locate rifts in the fabric of reality—even ones that weren't visible to the naked eye." Rowan's voice gained confidence as he spoke of his family's lore. "It was called the Wayfinder."

A murmur ran through the gathered druids. Sylva and Thorn exchanged significant glances.

"The Wayfinder is not merely legend," Sylva said. "Our oldest records mention it. If it still exists, and if we could recover it..."

"It could lead us to Veyra," Thorn finished. "To her true form, wherever it exists between worlds."

The implications hung in the air. Finding Veyra would mean confronting the source of the corruption directly—a prospect both terrifying and necessary.

"So we have two objectives," Kael said, the strategist in him already mapping out possibilities. "Capture a Voice to trace its connection back to Veyra, and search for this Wayfinder compass."

"Both extremely dangerous," Mira pointed out, though her tone held excitement rather than fear. The alchemist thrived on challenges. "Breaking into a Syndicate stronghold, snatching one of Veyra's direct conduits, and hunting for an artifact that might not even exist."

"We've faced worse odds," Lyra reminded her with a smile that belied her own apprehension.

"Have we, though?" Mira countered, but she was grinning as she said it.

Elara, who had remained silent during the discussion, finally spoke. "If we do capture a Voice, I believe I can devise a ritual to trace its connection back to Veyra." The rune-caster's voice was soft but certain. "The patterns I observed in the Blighted Plains suggest that all shadow magic maintains a link to its source. A Voice, being a direct manifestation of Veyra's will, would have the strongest connection."

"What would this ritual entail?" Aelion asked, his ancient eyes sharp with interest.

"A combination of runic magic and the Phoenix Stone's power," Elara explained. "The Stone can illuminate the connection, while my runes can stabilize and trace it. Essentially, we would be creating a magical tether that we could follow back to its origin point."

"Back to Veyra," Lyra said, understanding dawning.

Elara nodded. "Precisely. But we would need to maintain the Voice in a contained state long enough to complete the ritual. And the Voice will fight us every moment."

They spent the remainder of the day planning their approach to the temple. The druids provided valuable intelligence—the Green Path had been observing the Syndicate's activities for years, mapping patrol routes and noting changes in security.

"They've doubled their forces in the past month," Sylva told them as they gathered around a detailed model of the temple that the druids had constructed. "Ever since you destroyed the Voice in the Whispering Vale. Veyra knows you're coming for her."

"How many shadow-binders?" Kael asked, studying the model with narrowed eyes.

"At least a dozen, including Corvus," Thorn replied. "Plus regular Syndicate soldiers—perhaps fifty."

"And a Voice?" Lyra asked.

Sylva nodded grimly. "One has been in residence since the Vale incident. It rarely leaves the central chamber, where the rift is located."

Kael traced a finger along the model, following what appeared to be a narrow path up the mountainside to the temple's rear. "What about this approach? It seems less guarded."

"For good reason," Thorn said. "That path is treacherous—narrow ledges over sheer drops, prone to rockslides. The Syndicate doesn't bother guarding it because few would attempt it, and fewer would survive."

"Which makes it perfect for us," Kael concluded.

"If by 'perfect' you mean 'likely to kill us before the Syndicate gets a chance to,' then sure," Mira muttered, but there was no real objection in her tone.

As night fell, they finalized their plan. They would approach the temple before dawn, using the treacherous mountain path to avoid the main patrols. Sylva and a small contingent of druids would create a diversion at the main entrance once they were in position, drawing attention away from their actual point of entry—a forgotten maintenance passage that Thorn remembered from her earlier visits to the temple.

"Rest well," Sylva advised as they concluded their planning. "Tomorrow will test all your strengths."

Lyra tried to follow this advice, retiring to the small alcove the druids had provided for her. But sleep proved elusive. Her mind raced with thoughts of what awaited them at the temple—the Voice, the rift, possibly the Wayfinder. And beyond all that, Veyra herself, the architect of the corruption that had spread across Sylvanthia.

After an hour of restless tossing, she gave up and rose, wrapping a borrowed cloak around her shoulders against the night's chill. Perhaps some fresh air would clear her mind.

She found her way to a small balcony carved into the cliff face, overlooking the valley below. The night was clear, stars burning with cold fire in the black vault of the sky. In the distance, the Temple of Echoes was a darker shadow against the mountainside, no lights visible in its windows.

"Can't sleep either?"

Lyra turned to find Kael standing in the entrance to the balcony, his broad shoulders filling the narrow space. Despite the late hour, he looked alert, his eyes reflecting the starlight.

"Too much on my mind," she admitted.

He joined her at the balcony's edge, his presence solid and reassuring beside her. They stood in companionable silence for a time, gazing out at the night-shrouded landscape.

"Are you afraid?" she asked finally, voicing the question that had been circling in her thoughts.

Kael considered this with his usual thoroughness. "Yes," he said simply. "I'd be a fool not to be. But fear can be useful if you don't let it control you. It sharpens the senses, heightens awareness."

"And if it does control you?" The question emerged softer than she intended, revealing more vulnerability than she'd meant to show.

Kael turned to face her, his expression serious in the dim light. "That's when you rely on the people around you. No one can be strong all the time, Lyra. That's why we travel together, fight together."

The simple truth of his words settled something within her. Since finding the Phoenix Stone, she had carried the weight of its power and responsibility—sometimes forgetting that she didn't carry it alone.

"Thank you," she said, meeting his gaze. "For reminding me of that."

He smiled, the expression softening the hard planes of his face. "That's what I'm here for. That, and hitting things with my sword when diplomacy fails."

His unexpected humor startled a laugh from her, releasing some of the tension she'd been holding. They talked a while longer, sharing memories of simpler times and hopes for what might come after their current mission. When Lyra finally returned to her alcove, sleep came more easily, her mind calmed by the reminder of the bonds she shared with her companions.

Dawn arrived with mist curling through the valleys, obscuring the lower slopes of the mountains. They gathered in the sanctuary's main chamber for a final review of their plan, checking weapons and supplies with the focused efficiency of those accustomed to danger.

Mira distributed small vials to each of them. "Restorative elixir," she explained. "The druids helped me refine the formula. It should provide a temporary boost of energy in a crisis."

Elara handed out strips of cloth inscribed with protective runes. "Wear these against your skin," she instructed. "They'll provide some defense against shadow magic."

Rowan had been working through the night as well, Lyra realized, as he unrolled a detailed map of the temple's interior, more precise than the druids' model. "I compiled this from Thorn's memories and the Green Path's observations," he explained. "The archives should be here, in the eastern wing, assuming the Syndicate hasn't repurposed the space."

Kael inspected his sword, recently sharpened and polished. The blade caught the morning light, seeming to hold it for a moment before releasing it in a flash. "Remember," he said, looking at each of them in turn, "our primary objective is to capture the Voice, not destroy it. Everything else is secondary."

"Including the Wayfinder," Rowan acknowledged, though disappointment flickered across his face.

"We'll search for it if the opportunity arises," Lyra assured him. "But Kael's right—the Voice is our priority."

Sylva approached, accompanied by the druids who would create the diversion. "It's time," she said simply. "The mist will provide additional cover, but it won't last long once the sun rises higher."

They followed her to the sanctuary's hidden exit, a narrow tunnel that wound through the living rock of the mountain. The passage was tight in places, forcing them to proceed single-file, their way lit by glowing crystals embedded in the walls.

"A gift from the earth," Sylva explained when Lyra commented on the crystals. "They respond to the Green Path's magic, storing and releasing light as needed."

After what felt like an hour of walking, the tunnel began to slope upward. The air grew cooler, carrying the scent of pine and stone. Finally, they emerged onto a narrow ledge halfway up the mountainside, the valley spread below them, still shrouded in mist.

"This is where we part ways," Sylva said. "My group will circle around to approach the main entrance. Wait for our signal before you proceed to your entry point."

"What's the signal?" Mira asked.

Sylva's mouth curved in a rare smile. "You'll know it when you see it."

With that cryptic response, she and her druids departed, moving along the ledge with the sure-footed confidence of those who knew the mountain intimately.

Thorn took the lead as they continued their own journey, following a path so narrow in places that they had to press their backs against the cliff face and edge sideways. The drop beside them was sheer and dizzying, disappearing into the mist hundreds of feet below.

"I'm developing a new appreciation for solid ground," Mira muttered as they navigated a particularly treacherous stretch.

"Focus on the path, not the fall," Thorn advised from ahead. "The mountain will support you if you respect its nature."

"The mountain is a pile of rocks that doesn't care if I live or die," Mira retorted, but she followed the druid's advice nonetheless, keeping her eyes on the path rather than the abyss beside it.

They had been climbing for nearly an hour when Thorn raised a hand, signaling a halt. The temple was visible now, its dark stone walls rising just ahead, merging with the natural rock of the mountainside in places. No windows broke the smooth surface on this side, only a small door almost invisible against the surrounding stone.

"The maintenance passage," Thorn whispered. "Used by the temple's original caretakers to access the exterior for repairs. The Syndicate likely doesn't even know it exists."

"How do we get in?" Kael asked, eyeing the door. "I don't see a handle."

"The Green Path remembers what others forget," Thorn replied enigmatically. She approached the door and placed her palm against its center, murmuring words in the ancient language of the druids. For a moment, nothing happened. Then, faint lines of green light spread from her hand, tracing the outline of the door and seeping into the stone.

With a sound like a sigh, the door swung inward, revealing a dark passage beyond.

"Wait for the signal," Thorn reminded them as she pulled her hand back.

They didn't have to wait long. Just as the sun broke fully over the eastern horizon, dispelling the last of the mist, a sound like thunder rolled across the valley. They turned to see a spectacular sight at the temple's main entrance far below: trees—full-sized, mature oaks—were erupting from the bare rock of the temple approach, their roots cracking stone as they grew with unnatural speed. Syndicate guards scattered in panic as the sudden forest engulfed their positions.

"That," Mira said with feeling, "is a signal."

"Sylva always did have a flair for the dramatic," Thorn remarked dryly. "Come. While they're distracted."

They slipped through the door into a narrow, dusty passage that smelled of age and disuse. Thorn led the way, her staff providing a dim green light that illuminated just enough of the path ahead to navigate by. The passage sloped downward, taking them deeper into the temple's heart.

After several minutes of cautious progress, they reached a junction where their passage intersected with a wider corridor. Thorn extinguished her light and peered carefully around the corner.

"Clear," she whispered. "But we need to move quickly. The main hall is two levels down, and the archives Rowan seeks are on this level, in the eastern wing."

"We split up," Kael decided. "Rowan, Mira, and Elara search for the Wayfinder. Lyra, Thorn, Aelion, and I will head for the main hall to locate the Voice."

It was the plan they had discussed, but saying it aloud made it real—and dangerous. Splitting their forces in enemy territory was a risk, but it maximized their chances of accomplishing both objectives.

"Be careful," Lyra told the archive team. "If you're discovered, abort the search and head for the rendezvous point. Don't try to reach us."

"Same goes for you," Mira replied. "No heroics."

They parted at the junction, Rowan's team heading east while Lyra's group took a staircase leading downward. The temple's interior was austere, its stone walls bare of decoration save for occasional carved symbols similar to those they had seen on the exterior. The air grew heavier as they descended, carrying a metallic tang that made Lyra's tongue tingle unpleasantly.

"Shadow magic," Aelion murmured, noticing her grimace. "We're getting closer to the rift."

They encountered their first Syndicate guards at the bottom of the staircase—two robed figures standing watch outside a large set of double doors. Before the guards could raise an alarm, Kael and Thorn moved in perfect synchronization, neutralizing them with swift, silent efficiency. They dragged the unconscious bodies into an alcove, out of sight of casual passersby.

"The main hall lies beyond those doors," Thorn whispered, nodding toward the entrance the guards had been protecting. "But we can't just walk in. There will be others inside, including shadow-binders."

"We need a distraction," Kael said, thinking aloud. "Something to draw most of them out, leaving the Voice with minimal protection."

Lyra touched the Phoenix Stone, feeling its warmth pulse against her fingers. "The Stone responds to the rift," she said. "I can feel it pulling, like it wants to be closer. Maybe we can use that connection."

Aelion's ancient eyes sharpened with interest. "What are you suggesting?"

"If I channel a small amount of the Stone's power—not enough to be immediately threatening, but enough to be noticed—it might draw attention away from the main hall. The shadow-binders would be sent to investigate."

"Risky," Kael said, frowning. "It would reveal your presence."

"But not my location," Lyra countered. "Not if I release the energy and then move quickly to a different position."

They debated briefly, weighing options, before agreeing that Lyra's plan offered the best chance of success. They found a small side chamber that would serve their purpose—close enough to be felt by those sensitive to the Stone's power, but with multiple exit routes.

Lyra stood in the center of the chamber, the others positioned near different doorways, ready to move once she had released the Stone's energy. She closed her eyes, focusing on the connection between the Phoenix Stone and the rift that lay somewhere below them. The Stone responded eagerly, almost too eagerly, its power rising to meet her call with an intensity that surprised her.

Careful, she cautioned it silently. *Just enough to be noticed.*

She released a measured pulse of energy, directing it downward toward where she sensed the rift to be. The Stone flared briefly against her skin, a flash of warmth that subsided almost immediately. For a moment, nothing happened.

Then, faintly at first but growing louder, they heard the sound of running feet and shouted orders. Shadow-binders and Syndicate soldiers rushed past their hiding place, heading toward the area where Lyra had released the Stone's energy.

"It worked," Kael whispered as the sounds receded. "Let's move."

They slipped from the chamber and made their way quickly to the double doors, now unguarded. Pressing his ear against the wood, Kael listened intently before nodding. "Fewer voices inside now. This is our best chance."

Thorn and Aelion positioned themselves on either side of the doors while Kael and Lyra prepared to enter first. On Kael's signal, they pushed the doors open and moved swiftly into the main hall beyond.

The space that greeted them stole Lyra's breath. The hall was vast, its ceiling lost in shadow far above. Pillars of dark stone rose like ancient trees, carved with symbols that seemed to writhe at the edge of vision. The air shimmered with an unsettling distortion, as if reality itself was thin here.

And at the center of it all, a pit. Not large—perhaps twenty feet across—but profound in its wrongness. No light escaped its depths. It was not merely dark; it was an absence, a void that rejected illumination. The rift.

Near the pit's edge stood three figures. Two were shadow-binders, their silver masks gleaming in the dim light. The third was unmistakably a Voice—its form humanoid but constantly shifting, features flowing like wax in heat, never settling into a fixed appearance.

The Voice turned as they entered, its fluid face rippling with surprise that quickly transformed into malicious delight.

"The Stone-bearer comes at last," it said, its voice a discordant symphony of overlapping tones, higher and more melodic than the Voice they had encountered in the Vale. "How delightful. Veyra has spoken of you often in our communion."

This Voice was different from the one in the Vale—more articulate, almost theatrical in its mannerisms. Its fluid form moved with an unsettling grace, like a dancer performing for an audience only it could see.

"We're not here for conversation," Lyra replied, the Phoenix Stone warming against her skin in response to the Voice's presence.

"No? Pity." The Voice's features briefly coalesced into a semblance of a pout before dissolving again. "The others of my kind are so dreadfully serious. All doom and gloom and 'the darkness shall consume you.' No appreciation for the artistry of what we do." It gestured toward the rift with a flourish. "This is the first and greatest of Veyra's masterpieces—the doorway between what is and what could be. Doesn't it inspire a certain... awe?"

While the Voice spoke, Kael had been subtly shifting his position, moving to flank the shadow-binders. Thorn and Aelion spread out as well, creating a loose semicircle around their adversaries.

"The only thing it inspires is revulsion," Lyra said, keeping the Voice's attention fixed on her. "The rift is a wound in reality, and the Phoenix Stone exists to heal such wounds."

The Voice's form rippled with what might have been laughter. "Oh, such conviction! Such charming naivety!" It drifted closer to the edge of the rift, trailing wisps of shadow like a torn cloak. "The Stone is merely one expression of power, child. Veyra has tapped into something far greater—the power to reshape reality itself. Why heal a wound when you can use it as a doorway to transformation?"

"Because some doors should remain closed," Aelion said, speaking for the first time since entering the hall. "As the Wardens of the Veil understood."

The Voice's shifting features momentarily stabilized, focusing on Aelion with sudden intensity. "The teacher speaks," it said, its tone shifting from playful to cold. "The one who failed his most brilliant student. How does it feel, ancient one, to know that your greatest pupil has surpassed you in every way? That while you cling to the fading remnants of your power, she has transcended the very limitations of mortality?"

"If transcendence means becoming a parasite that feeds on suffering, then I'll gladly accept my limitations," Aelion replied, unmoved by the Voice's taunts.

The Voice's form rippled with apparent anger. "Enough pleasantries," it hissed, all pretense of charm vanishing. "Veyra will have the Stone, and you will all feed the rift's hunger." It gestured sharply to the shadow-binders. "Kill the others. Bring the Stone-bearer to me."

The shadow-binders moved with unnatural speed, darkness gathering around their hands like living smoke. Kael met the first with his sword, the blade slicing through the shadow magic but encountering solid resistance when it reached the robed figure beneath. Thorn engaged the second, her staff whirling in complex patterns that left trails of green light in the air.

Aelion raised his hands, ancient words of power flowing from his lips as he wove a protective spell around Lyra. The air around her shimmered with a subtle barrier, deflecting the tendrils of darkness that the Voice sent lancing toward her.

Lyra reached for the Phoenix Stone, channeling its power into a focused beam of light that she directed at the Voice. Unlike in the Vale, she wasn't trying to destroy it—not yet. They needed to capture it, to use its connection to Veyra.

The Voice screamed as the light struck it, its form rippling more violently. But it didn't flee or disintegrate. Instead, it seemed to draw power from the rift behind it, darkness swirling up from the void to reinforce its shifting body.

"You cannot defeat me here," it hissed, voice distorted by pain and rage. "Not at the source of Veyra's power. Here, I am more than just a Voice—I am an Echo, a perfect reflection of her will!"

It counterattacked, sending a wave of shadow magic that broke against Aelion's barrier but forced Lyra back several steps from its sheer force. The ancient mage staggered, the strain of maintaining the protection evident in his lined face.

Meanwhile, Kael and Thorn fought a desperate battle against the shadow-binders. These were no ordinary Syndicate agents; they moved with the fluid grace of those who had given themselves fully to shadow magic, their physical forms enhanced by the dark power they channeled.

Lyra realized with growing dread that they were outmatched. The Voice—or Echo, as it called itself—was too powerful here, drawing strength from the rift, and the shadow-binders were keeping Kael and Thorn too occupied to help capture it. They needed something to change the balance of the confrontation.

As if in answer to her unspoken need, a thunderous explosion rocked the temple, the shock wave powerful enough to make dust rain from the distant ceiling. The Voice and shadow-binders faltered momentarily, distracted by this unexpected development.

"What was that?" Kael shouted, taking advantage of his opponent's distraction to land a solid blow that sent the shadow-binder stumbling back.

"Mira," Lyra guessed, a smile tugging at her lips despite the dire situation. "Has to be."

The momentary distraction gave them an opening. Lyra channeled more power through the Stone, not in a direct attack this time but in a wide-dispersal pattern that Elara had helped her develop. Light bloomed throughout the chamber, temporarily banishing the shadows that the Voice and its servants wielded.

In that moment of illumination, Aelion struck. The ancient mage had been conserving his strength, waiting for precisely this opportunity. He cast a binding spell of tremendous power, ancient words echoing in the vast space as bands of golden light encircled the Voice, constricting its fluid form into a more solid shape.

"Now, Lyra!" he called, strain evident in his voice. "I cannot hold it for long!"

Lyra drew deeply on the Phoenix Stone's power, shaping it not into a destructive force but into a containing vessel—a cage of pure light that enclosed the Voice, cutting it off from the rift's power. The Voice shrieked, its many-layered voice rising to a pitch that made Lyra's ears ring.

"This is temporary!" it spat, its form writhing within the containment. "You cannot hold what is not fully in your reality! I am beyond your comprehension, beyond your pitiful magics!"

With the Voice contained and their master's power diminished, the shadow-binders lost their advantage. Kael and Thorn pressed forward, forcing them back step by step toward the edge of the rift.

"Surrender," Kael demanded, his sword at one shadow-binder's throat.

The masked figure laughed, the sound hollow behind the silver face covering. "There is no surrender in Veyra's service. Only victory or dissolution."

Before anyone could stop them, both shadow-binders stepped backward into the rift. There was no sound as they fell—the void swallowed them in complete silence. But the rift itself pulsed in response, a ripple of darker-than-black that spread outward from the point of their disappearance. The air in the chamber grew suddenly colder, and Lyra felt the Phoenix Stone flare hot against her skin in warning.

"The rift feeds," the Voice said from within its cage, its tone almost reverent. "Each sacrifice strengthens the connection between worlds. Those loyal servants have not died—they have been transformed, absorbed into Veyra's greater purpose."

Kael stared at the spot where the shadow-binders had vanished, his face grim. "They chose oblivion over capture."

"Not oblivion," Aelion corrected, his ancient eyes troubled as he studied the rift. "Something worse. Their essence, their very being, has been consumed by whatever lies beyond—fuel for Veyra's continued existence between worlds."

The implications sent a chill through Lyra. How many others had fed the rift over the centuries? How many had been consumed to maintain Veyra's unnatural state?

"We need to move," Thorn said urgently, breaking into these dark thoughts. "That explosion will have alerted every Syndicate agent in the temple. And they'll have felt the Voice's capture."

As if to confirm her words, alarms began to sound throughout the temple—a high, keening wail that set Lyra's teeth on edge.

"The rendezvous point," Kael decided. "Let's hope the others made it there as well."

Maintaining the cage of light around the Voice required constant focus from Lyra, making their retreat more difficult. They moved as quickly as they could through the temple's corridors, encountering surprisingly little resistance—most of the Syndicate forces seemed to be responding to Mira's explosion in another part of the complex.

They reached the rendezvous point—a small courtyard near the temple's western edge—and found it empty. Kael positioned himself at the entrance, sword ready, while Thorn scouted the perimeter and Aelion helped Lyra maintain the Voice's containment.

"How long can you hold it?" the ancient mage asked quietly, noting the sheen of sweat on Lyra's forehead.

"As long as necessary," she replied, though in truth she could feel her strength waning. The Voice fought continuously against its prison, testing every facet of the light cage for weaknesses.

"Your determination is admirable," the Voice said, its tone conversational despite its captivity. "But futile. Even now, Veyra feels my distress. She will not abandon one of her Echoes."

"Good," Lyra replied, meeting its shifting gaze steadily. "That's exactly what we're counting on."

The Voice's fluid features momentarily froze in what might have been surprise. "Ah," it said after a moment, understanding dawning. "Clever. You intend to use me as a tether—to follow my connection back to Veyra herself." It laughed, the sound like shattering glass. "Bold. Possibly even brilliant. And utterly, irrevocably fatal for all of you."

Minutes stretched into what felt like hours as they waited, tension mounting with each passing moment. The alarms continued to wail, and distant shouts suggested the Syndicate was organizing a more thorough search of the temple.

Just as Lyra was beginning to fear the worst, Mira burst into the courtyard, her face smudged with soot but wearing a triumphant grin. Elara and Rowan followed close behind, the cartographer clutching something to his chest.

"Sorry we're late," Mira announced. "Had to take a scenic route after I accidentally blew up half the eastern wing."

"Accidentally?" Kael echoed, one eyebrow raised.

"Well, more or less," Mira hedged. "Those alchemical supplies the druids gave me were more potent than I expected. But it created an excellent diversion."

"Did you find it?" Lyra asked Rowan, nodding toward whatever he held.

The cartographer's normally reserved face split into a rare, wide smile as he opened his hands to reveal a small, intricate device. It resembled a compass, but instead of a simple needle, it contained a complex arrangement of gears and crystals surrounding a central spinning element.

"The Wayfinder," he confirmed. "Just where the records said it would be, in a hidden compartment in the archives."

"A pretty ba uble," the Voice commented, its fluid features shifting to peer at the artifact. "A trinket from a bygone age. Do you truly believe that primitive device can lead you through the spaces between worlds?"

"I believe in my family's legacy," Rowan replied firmly, closing his hand protectively around the Wayfinder.

"Can you make it work?" Thorn asked, returning from her perimeter check.

"I think so," Rowan said, studying the device. "The mechanism is intact, and there were partial instructions in the archives. It needs to be activated with a specific type of energy..."

"Later," Kael interrupted. "We need to move now. The Syndicate is sweeping the temple systematically, and they'll reach this section soon."

They exited the courtyard through a small door that Thorn indicated, finding themselves on a narrow ledge similar to the one they had used to enter the temple. But instead of following the treacherous path back the way they had come, Thorn led them downward, using a series of switchbacks that zigzagged down the mountainside.

The descent was harrowing, made more difficult by the need to move quickly while Lyra maintained her focus on containing the Voice. The captured entity had grown quieter, perhaps conserving its energy, but Lyra could feel it testing her control, probing for weaknesses in its prison of light.

"We need to reach the designated point," Thorn urged as they navigated a particularly narrow section. "Sylva and the others will be waiting with the pathway ready."

As they rounded the final bend, Lyra saw Sylva standing on a flat outcropping below, surrounded by a circle of druids. The First Keeper looked up, relief visible on her face as she spotted them.

"Quickly," she called. "The pathway won't hold for long!"

With that cryptic encouragement, she left them to their preparations. Kael immediately began checking his weapons and armor, his methodical movements a ritual that centered him before conflict. Elara sat cross-legged on her pallet, eyes closed, fingers tracing practice runes in the air as she prepared the patterns she might need. Mira inventoried her alchemical supplies, muttering formulations under her breath, while Rowan studied his family maps with renewed interest after the revelations about his lineage.

Lyra found herself too restless for such preparations. Her thoughts circled around Aelion's unfinished revelations and the mysterious connection he shared with the Temple they would soon infiltrate. She stepped outside, seeking air and space to process all they had learned.

The sanctuary hummed with quiet activity as druids went about their work among the living structures. Above, the canopy had begun to darken with approaching evening, dappled light shifting to deeper shadows. Lyra wandered a short distance, following a path that led to a small clearing where a spring bubbled up from among moss-covered stones.

She was contemplating the clear water when Aelion appeared beside her, moving with the silent grace that belied his apparent age. His face was drawn, his ancient eyes troubled.

"Sylva has confirmed what I feared," he said without preamble. "The Temple's power recognizes those who approach it. When we enter, it will know me—not as Aelion, but as Alaric, last of the Seven Wardens who built it."

"Alaric," Lyra repeated, testing the unfamiliar name. "That's your true name?"

"It was, long ago." He gazed into the spring as if seeing reflections of distant memories. "When we enter the Temple, its magic will strip away the identity I've worn for centuries. The name Aelion will fade from memory—even yours—replaced by Alaric."

"Why would you hide your true name all this time?"

"Because names have power, especially in places of old magic. Because the Syndicate has sought the last Warden for generations, knowing he alone holds knowledge they desperately desire." He turned to face her fully. "And because some burdens are easier to bear when separated from the identity that acquired them."

As the sanctuary darkened around them, Lyra felt the weight of centuries in his gaze—the loneliness of outliving everyone who had known his true self, the vigilance of maintaining a secret for longer than nations had existed.

"Then we'll call you Alaric," she said simply, accepting this revelation as she had accepted so many others on their journey. "And whatever awaits us at the Temple, we'll face it together."

CHAPTER FOURTEEN

The Child Who Sees

The Voice's containment had become increasingly difficult in the days following their escape from the Temple of Echoes. What had begun as a triumphant capture—the ethereal entity bound by Aelion's magic and Lyra's light cage—had transformed into a burden that drained their resources and resolve.

"It's growing stronger," Lyra observed, her voice tight with strain as she reinforced the light cage for the third time since dawn. The Phoenix Stone burned hot against her skin, responding to the Voice's constant attempts to break free. "Or I'm growing weaker."

They had made camp in a secluded clearing, far from the main roads that might bring them unwanted attention from Syndicate patrols. The Voice—or Echo, as it called itself—hovered within its magical prison, a shimmering distortion that occasionally coalesced into almost-human features before dissolving back into formlessness.

Elara knelt beside the cage, carefully etching reinforcement runes into the earth surrounding it. "The connection to Veyra remains intact," she reported, her fingers moving with practiced precision despite her evident fatigue. "I can trace the energy flow, but severing it would require more power than we currently possess."

"Then this entire effort has been for nothing," Kael said, frustration evident in his voice. He stood guard at the edge of the clearing, sword drawn, eyes constantly scanning the tree line. The Voice's presence made him particularly uneasy—as if it might summon Syndicate forces through its link to Veyra.

"Not nothing," Rowan countered, looking up from the Wayfinder compass they had recovered alongside the Voice. The ancient artifact lay partially disassembled before him as he studied its intricate mechanisms. "We've learned the Voices aren't merely messengers but conduits—direct extensions of Veyra's consciousness. And the compass, once I decipher its workings, should lead us to the rifts she created."

Mira approached, carrying a steaming cup of her latest alchemical concoction. "This might help," she offered to Lyra. "It won't restore your energy completely, but it should take the edge off the drain."

Lyra accepted the cup gratefully, wincing at the bitter taste but feeling a welcome warmth spread through her limbs as she drank. The constant effort of maintaining the Voice's containment had left her hollow-eyed and pale, the Phoenix Stone's demands on her strength growing more taxing with each passing hour.

As the others continued their preparations for the day ahead, Lyra found herself staring at the captured Voice. Its formless features occasionally solidified into a cruel smile, as if it understood something she did not. The burden of leadership weighed heavily on her shoulders—each decision potentially risking her companions' lives, each delay allowing the Syndicate to strengthen its position across Sylvanthia.

She withdrew a small leather pouch from inside her tunic, carefully emptying its contents into her palm while ensuring the others weren't watching. The silver pendant caught the morning light, its surface worn smooth from years of handling. It had been her mother's—a simple thing, unadorned except for the small constellation etched on one side.

"What would you do?" she whispered to the pendant, running her thumb over the familiar pattern. "You always seemed so certain, even when facing impossible odds."

The memory surfaced unbidden—her mother standing before the village council, voice unwavering as she argued against surrender to the Syndicate's demands. *"Some prices are too high, even for safety,"* she had said. Lyra had been only twelve, watching from the shadows, marveling at her mother's courage while simultaneously terrified of its consequences.

Now, years later, she understood that courage differently. It wasn't fearlessness—it was action despite fear, conviction despite doubt. Her mother had been afraid that day; Lyra could see it now in the memory, the slight tremor in her hands that only a daughter would notice.

The Phoenix Stone pulsed warmly against her skin, responding to her thoughts as it increasingly did these days. Its connection to her seemed to be deepening, becoming more intuitive, more... personal. Sometimes she felt as though it was trying to tell her something, if only she knew how to listen properly.

"I'm not her," Lyra murmured, closing her fingers around the pendant. "I'm not either of them. They knew their purpose, their path. I'm still... finding mine."

Yet even as she spoke the words, she recognized their diminishing truth. The path that had seemed so unclear weeks ago was gradually revealing itself, not as a straight line but as a series of connections—between her, the Stone, her companions, and something larger that she could sense but not yet fully comprehend.

Thorn emerged from the forest, her druidic senses having alerted her to approaching danger. "Syndicate scouts," she reported tersely. "A dozen, maybe more, moving in a search pattern. They'll reach this position by nightfall."

"We need to make a decision," Aelion stated, his ancient eyes fixed on the captured Voice. "We cannot maintain this containment indefinitely, nor can we risk the Voice leading our enemies directly to us."

The Echo pulsed within its cage, its formless features briefly resolving into a cruel smile. When it spoke, its voice seemed to come from everywhere and nowhere at once, a discordant chorus of whispers.

"He comes for you," it said, the words slithering through their minds like ice. "The Silver-Eyed One. Lord Ravenna. He has seen your faces through my eyes. Felt your presence through my essence. There is nowhere you can hide that he will not find you."

Lyra straightened, forcing strength into her voice despite her exhaustion. "We didn't capture you to hide. We captured you to learn."

"And what have you learned, Bearer of Light?" the Echo mocked. "That your strength wanes while ours grows? That for every Voice you silence, three more speak? That the rifts multiply and the barriers between worlds thin?"

"We've learned enough," Lyra replied, meeting the Echo's gaze unflinchingly. She turned to Aelion. "Can we extract what we need without maintaining the containment?"

The ancient mage considered this. "Perhaps. The Wayfinder compass has absorbed some of the Echo's essence through proximity. It should function without the Voice's continued presence."

"And Sera?" Elara asked, glancing toward the young girl who sat quietly at the edge of their camp. They had found her hiding in the temple archives during their infiltration, an orphan who had survived by scavenging and avoiding the Syndicate's notice. "Will she be safe if we release it?"

"I can mask her presence," Thorn offered. "My connection to the Green Path can shield one as young and innocent as she."

Lyra nodded, decision made. "Then we end this now. We've learned what we can, and maintaining the containment only weakens us for the confrontations to come."

"You would release me?" the Echo asked, its whispers suddenly uncertain. "Knowing I will return to my master? Knowing I will tell him everything I have seen?"

"You've already told him," Kael stated flatly. "We've felt your connection to him pulsing since we captured you. This changes nothing except freeing us from the burden of containing you."

Aelion stepped forward, ancient words of power forming on his lips. "There is one final piece of knowledge we require," he said, his voice resonating with authority that made even the Echo quiver. "Where does Ravenna go next? What target has he set his silver eyes upon?"

The Echo writhed within its cage, caught between its nature as Veyra's extension and the compelling force of Aelion's magic. "The village," it finally hissed. "The one that sent for you. Eastward, where the river forks. He leaves a message written in blood. A reminder of unfinished business."

Lyra's heart sank. The village of Riverfork had sent a messenger weeks ago, seeking help against Syndicate raids. They had promised to come after securing the Voice and the Wayfinder.

"We're too late," she whispered.

"Not if we move now," Kael countered, already gathering his gear. "Ravenna's forces may still be there."

Aelion raised his staff, the ancient wood thrumming with power. "Stand back," he commanded. "I will dissolve the containment in a way that will temporarily sever its connection to Veyra. It will buy us perhaps a day before it can report our exact location and intentions."

They formed a circle around the captured Echo, each contributing to the ritual in their own way. Elara's runes flared with protective light. Thorn murmured words of binding that called upon the ancient forests. Mira prepared a catalyst that would amplify Aelion's spell. Rowan quickly reassembled the Wayfinder compass, its needle spinning wildly as it absorbed the ambient energy.

Lyra stood at the center, the Phoenix Stone blazing against her skin as she channeled its power through Aelion's ritual. With a final surge of energy that left her gasping, the containment shattered—not in the catastrophic release they had feared, but in a controlled dissolution that sent the Echo spiraling upward like smoke from a doused fire.

"You have made a grave error," the Voice's whispers lingered as its form dispersed. "He will find you. He will remind you of what was taken. He will claim what remains."

Then it was gone, leaving behind only a fading chill in the air and the ominous spinning of the Wayfinder's needle as it settled toward the east—toward River-fork.

"We move now," Lyra ordered, swaying slightly as the Stone's energy receded. Kael was immediately at her side, his steady hand supporting her elbow. "Thorn, you and Sera should remain here. The village may not be safe."

The druid nodded, placing a protective hand on the girl's shoulder. "We will seek sanctuary with my order. The Green Path has hidden groves even the Syndicate cannot find."

"Will we see you again?" Lyra asked, realizing this might be a permanent parting.

"When the paths align," Thorn replied with the cryptic certainty of her kind. "The forest remembers its friends."

They gathered their essentials quickly, leaving behind anything that would slow their urgent journey. Within the hour, they were moving eastward at a pace that bordered on reckless, driven by the Echo's warning and the fear of what they might find.

The Wayfinder compass led them unerringly toward Riverfork, its needle glowing with an inner light that intensified as they drew closer to their destination. By the time the village should have come into view beyond the next rise, the compass was vibrating in Rowan's hands, its mechanisms humming with an almost anxious energy.

Lyra crested the hill first, then stopped so abruptly that Kael nearly collided with her. Her sharp intake of breath told him what they would see before his eyes confirmed it.

Where Riverfork should have stood with its neat cottages and bustling marketplace, only smoldering ruins remained. The destruction was complete and deliberate—not the chaotic aftermath of a raid but the methodical erasure of a community.

"We're too late," Mira whispered, coming to stand beside them. "They're all gone."

"Not all," Kael corrected grimly, pointing toward a lone figure moving among the ruins. "Someone survived."

The sun breached the horizon reluctantly, as if hesitant to illuminate what remained of the scorched village. Lyra stood motionless at the forest's edge, watching amber light crawl across blackened timbers and collapsed roofs. The morning air carried the lingering scent of ash mixed with something more sinister—a metallic tang that whispered of violence still fresh.

Behind her, her companions emerged from the trees in silence. Kael moved to stand beside her, his hand resting on his sword hilt, ready as always for whatever shadows might lurk in the ruins. Mira's usual animated features had settled into grim lines, while Elara's pale face seemed to reflect the ashen landscape before them. Rowan studied the ground with the focused intensity that made him such an effective cartographer, reading stories in soil that others couldn't see. Aelion stood slightly apart, his ancient eyes taking in the devastation with the weary recognition of one who had witnessed too many similar scenes across too many years.

"Three days," Lyra said finally, her voice barely audible. "Just three days since their messenger reached us."

The boy had arrived at their camp near dusk, his horse lathered and trembling from hard riding. He'd spoken of strange figures seen at the village perimeter, of folk gone missing from outlying farms. The village elder, recognizing the patterns from rumors of other settlements, had sent him to find the group that traveled with the Phoenix Bearer.

Now the village was gone, and with it, any hope of arriving in time.

"This wasn't a random attack," Kael observed, his trained eye picking out details others might miss. "Look at the burn patterns—controlled, systematic. They started at the north end and worked south, building by building."

"How terribly considerate of them to be so organized about their atrocities," Mira muttered, her sarcasm failing to mask her horror.

Rowan knelt to examine the churned earth of what had been the village square. The cartographer's fingers traced patterns in the soil with practiced precision.

"Multiple groups moved through here. Some on horseback, others on foot. Disciplined formations, not a chaotic mob."

"Syndicate forces," Aelion confirmed, his voice heavy with certainty. "But not their usual approach. This was... deliberate. Unhurried."

"Because they wanted to leave a signature," Elara said quietly. "Like artists signing their masterpiece of destruction."

Mira pushed forward, her usual vibrant demeanor subdued by the scene before them. "There might be survivors. Some villagers could have fled to the hills or hidden in root cellars."

"If there's anyone left to find, we'll find them," Kael agreed, his jaw set with determination.

They separated to move through the ruins, calling out periodically into the eerie silence. The devastation proved more complete the further they ventured into what had been a thriving community just days before. Homes had been systematically burned, the village hall collapsed, the small temple to local gods desecrated with symbols that made Elara turn away, her face pale.

Lyra found herself drawn to what remained of the village center, where a stone well still stood amid the destruction, its rim cracked but intact. The Phoenix Stone pulsed warmly against her chest as she approached—a gentle rhythm that had become so familiar over their months of travel that she sometimes forgot to notice it. Now, however, the pulsing intensified, almost urgent.

She paused, placing her palm against the Stone through her tunic. Its warmth spread through her fingers, and with it came a certainty that couldn't be explained by logic alone.

Lyra leaned over the well's edge, peering into the darkness below. "Hello?" she called, her voice echoing against damp stone. "Is anyone down there?"

For a moment, silence answered her. Then, so faint she might have imagined it, came a sound—a small, muffled whimper.

"Here!" she shouted, straightening abruptly. "Someone's alive!"

The others converged quickly. Kael and Rowan worked to rig a makeshift pulley using rope from their packs and a broken beam as a lever. Elara prepared healing spells, her slender fingers tracing patterns in the air that left faint luminous trails. Mira readied bandages and healing salves from her seemingly bottomless satchel of supplies.

"I don't suppose anyone thought to pack a proper well bucket?" Mira asked, eyeing their improvised contraption with skepticism. "No? Just checking. I do so love testing experimental rope mechanics over fifty-foot drops."

When they finally raised the wooden bucket from the well's depths, a child no more than six years old huddled inside, eyes wide with terror. A girl, her dark hair matted with soot, her simple dress torn and stained. She shrank back as the bucket settled on the ground, pressing herself against its wooden slats as if trying to disappear.

"It's all right," Lyra soothed, kneeling slowly to appear less threatening. "We're friends. You're safe now."

The child made no response, her gaze darting from face to face with the wariness of a cornered animal. Lyra removed her cloak and held it out, moving with deliberate gentleness.

"You must be cold. And hungry too, I imagine. We have food, and clean water."

Slowly, hesitantly, the girl reached for the offered cloak. Her small fingers closed around the fabric, but she made no move to take it fully or to leave the relative security of the bucket.

"Perhaps she doesn't understand our language," Elara suggested quietly.

"Or she's too frightened to speak," Mira added. "After what she's witnessed…"

The child's gaze suddenly fixed on something beyond Lyra's shoulder. Following her line of sight, Lyra discovered a symbol burned into the remnants of what must have been the village hall—a spiraling glyph that seemed to absorb the morning light rather than reflect it.

"What is that?" she asked, though something in her already knew the answer would bring no comfort.

Elara moved closer to examine the mark, careful not to touch it. "Lord Ravenna's personal sigil," she said, her voice tight with recognition. "The Syndicate's High Inquisitor."

"Well, isn't that special," Mira said, her flippant tone belied by the tension in her shoulders. "Of all the evil overlords who could have destroyed this village, we get the one with his own personalized brand."

Aelion's weathered face darkened at the name. "This changes matters considerably."

"You know of him?" Kael asked, though the question seemed almost rhetorical. Aelion's long life had intersected with most of the significant figures in Sylvanthia's troubled history.

"I know enough," the ancient mage replied. "Ravenna is not like other Syndicate leaders. Where they seek power through conquest or wealth, he pursues knowledge—particularly forbidden knowledge. The kind that corrupts as it illuminates."

"And he was here personally," Rowan added, his tone making it clear how unusual—and troubling—this fact was. "The High Inquisitor doesn't typically involve himself in village raids."

"Which means this wasn't just another village," Aelion concluded. "They were targeted specifically."

The child suddenly moved, scrambling from the bucket with unexpected speed. Before anyone could react, she had pressed herself against Lyra, small arms wrapping around her waist with desperate strength. Surprised, Lyra gently returned the embrace, feeling the girl's body trembling against her.

"It's all right," she murmured, stroking the tangled hair. "You're safe now. We won't let anyone hurt you."

Over the child's head, she met Kael's gaze. A silent understanding passed between them—whatever had brought Ravenna to this village, it couldn't be coincidence. The High Inquisitor's presence, so soon after they had received the village's call for help, suggested a deliberate trap.

A trap they had narrowly avoided by arriving too late.

They made camp that evening in a protected glade nearly a league from the ruined village, close enough to a small stream to provide fresh water but far enough from the main trails to avoid casual discovery. As darkness fell, Mira coaxed a fire to life while Elara set subtle wards around their perimeter—not strong enough to repel a determined attack, but sufficient to warn of approaching danger.

The child—who still hadn't spoken—sat close to Lyra, refusing to move more than an arm's length away from her. Mira had cleaned the worst of the soot from the girl's face and hands, revealing skin pale from shock and hunger. The alchemist had also managed to coax her to eat a little stew and drink some water sweetened with honey, but any attempt at conversation had been met with wide-eyed silence.

"Give her time," Aelion advised as they gathered around the fire after the simple meal. "The mind protects itself from trauma in different ways. Speech will return when she feels truly safe."

"Which may not be anytime soon," Kael observed grimly. "Not if Ravenna is hunting us personally."

"We don't know that he is," Elara pointed out, though her tone suggested she was trying to convince herself as much as the others. "The village might have been targeted for other reasons."

"Three days after they sent for us?" Rowan shook his head. "That's not coincidence."

"No," Lyra agreed quietly. "It's a message. A demonstration of what happens to those who seek our help."

"Wonderful," Mira sighed. "I've always wanted to be the reason innocent villages get razed to the ground. It's been a lifelong ambition."

A heavy silence fell over the group, broken only by the crackling of the fire and the soft sounds of the forest around them. Each face reflected the same grim understanding: their presence had become as much a danger to others as a protection.

The child stirred against Lyra's side, her small body tensing. Looking down, Lyra found the girl's eyes open and alert, fixed on her face with an intensity that seemed beyond her years.

"He watched it all burn," she whispered, her voice emerging as fragile as new ice on a winter pond.

The sudden speech startled everyone into stillness. Lyra kept her own reaction carefully measured, afraid that any strong response might silence the child again.

"Who did?" she asked gently.

"The man with the silver eyes." The girl's voice remained soft but gained strength with each word, as if breaking through a barrier. "He stood in the square and watched. Didn't shout or smile. Just watched."

"Ravenna," Aelion murmured, confirming what they already suspected.

"Did he speak to you?" Kael asked, keeping his tone gentle despite the urgency of the question.

The child nodded, her gaze dropping to her small hands, which had twisted together in her lap. "He said we were a lesson. That anyone who helped the Phoenix Bearer would suffer the same." Her lower lip trembled. "He knew your name. Called you the daughter of traitors."

The words struck Lyra like a physical blow. Few knew of her parentage, and fewer still knew how they had died—executed for opposing the Syndicate's early rise to power. She had been just a child herself then, hidden away with distant relatives while her parents' names were systematically erased from official records, their contributions to Sylvanthia's scholarly traditions attributed to others.

"Did he say anything else?" Kael asked, his eyes fixed on Lyra's face, clearly noting her shock.

The child nodded again, reluctance evident in her posture. "He left a message. Said to tell you he keeps your parents' bones on his desk to remind him of unfinished business."

Silence fell over the camp, heavy and suffocating. Lyra felt a roaring in her ears, as if she stood too close to a waterfall. The Phoenix Stone flared hot against her skin, responding to the surge of emotion that threatened to overwhelm her.

Without a word, she rose and walked away from the firelight, needing distance, needing air that wasn't thick with implications and the weight of horrified gazes.

The forest embraced her with its familiar sounds and scents—the rustle of night creatures, the sharp tang of pine, the petrichor rising from soil still damp from recent rain.

Footsteps followed—Aelion's measured tread, unmistakable after months of travel together. The ancient mage didn't speak immediately, allowing her the space to process what she'd heard. When he finally broke the silence, his voice carried no judgment, only a deep sadness.

"You knew," Lyra said without turning. "You knew who Ravenna was to me."

"I suspected," Aelion admitted. "Your parents were prominent in the early resistance—scholars whose research undermined the Syndicate's claims to ancient authority. Ravenna was an ambitious young commander then, rising quickly through the ranks. Their defiance humiliated him publicly when they exposed his manipulation of historical texts."

"And now he hunts their daughter." Lyra's voice sounded hollow even to her own ears.

"It has become personal for him, yes." Aelion moved to stand beside her, his ancient eyes reflecting starlight. "But that makes him vulnerable. Hatred narrows vision. Creates blind spots."

"Or it makes him more dangerous."

"Both, perhaps." The old mage sighed, a sound weighted with centuries of witnessing human folly. "Ravenna has always been dangerous—brilliant and ruthless in equal measure. But his fixation on your family suggests an emotional component to his calculations that wasn't present before."

"Emotional?" Lyra turned to face him fully. "He keeps my parents' bones as trophies. That's not emotion—that's madness."

"The line between the two is often thinner than we care to admit," Aelion replied. "Especially in those who have touched shadow magic as deeply as Ravenna has."

They stood in silence for a time, the night deepening around them. Finally, Lyra asked the question that pressed most heavily on her heart.

"Did you know them well? My parents?"

Aelion's expression softened with memory. "I did. Your father was perhaps the finest linguistic scholar of his generation—able to decipher texts others had abandoned as indecipherable. Your mother specialized in magical artifacts, particularly those from the First Age. They were... luminous together. Their minds sparked off each other in ways that produced insights neither might have reached alone."

"I barely remember them," Lyra admitted, the words painful to voice. "Just fragments—my father's laugh, my mother's hands turning the pages of a book. The smell of her hair when she hugged me."

"They would be proud of who you've become," Aelion said with quiet certainty. "And of what you carry forward in their name."

The Phoenix Stone pulsed gently against her skin, as if in agreement. Lyra touched it through her tunic, drawing comfort from its steady warmth.

"Come," Aelion said after another moment of silence. "We should rejoin the others. There are decisions to be made about our path forward."

As they walked back toward the campfire, Lyra found herself reflecting on the journey that had brought her to this moment. When the Phoenix Stone had first come to her, she had seen it as a burden—a responsibility thrust upon her by circumstance rather than choice. She had accepted it out of necessity, not conviction.

But somewhere along the way, something had changed. The Stone had become more than an artifact she carried; it had become part of her identity, her purpose. And her companions had transformed from fellow travelers into something closer to family—each with their own strengths and flaws, each essential in ways she couldn't have anticipated.

Now, facing an enemy who had made his hatred for her family a cornerstone of his ambition, she felt a clarity she hadn't experienced before. This wasn't just about the rifts, or Veyra's return, or even the Syndicate's growing power. This was about legacy—what her parents had stood for, what they had died protecting, and what she would now carry forward.

The realization didn't banish her doubts or fears. If anything, it made them more acute, more personal. But it also gave her something her earlier resolve had lacked—a sense of continuity, of purpose that extended beyond immediate threats to something deeper and more enduring.

As they reached the edge of the firelight, Lyra paused, looking at the faces turned expectantly toward her. These people had chosen to follow her, to risk their lives for a cause that had become shared through months of hardship and occasional triumph. They deserved honesty, not just about their situation but about her own evolving understanding of it.

"Ravenna's involvement changes things," she said, her voice steady despite the emotions churning beneath. "This isn't just about the Syndicate anymore, or even about the rifts. It's become personal—for him, and now for me."

"How so?" Elara asked, though her expression suggested she already understood.

"My parents were scholars who opposed the Syndicate's rise," Lyra explained, deciding that full disclosure was necessary. "They discovered evidence that the organization's claims to ancient authority were fabricated—texts altered, histories rewritten to support their agenda. They published their findings, turning public opinion against the Syndicate in key regions."

"And Ravenna never forgave them for it," Aelion added. "He was the architect of those falsified histories—a young officer then, but already ambitious and ruthless."

"They were executed for treason," Lyra continued, the words still difficult to speak aloud even after so many years. "I was hidden away with distant relatives, my connection to them obscured to protect me."

"And now Ravenna knows who you are," Kael concluded, his expression darkening. "The daughter of the scholars who humiliated him."

"Not just knows," Lyra corrected. "He's been hunting me specifically. The village wasn't random—it was a message meant for me. A demonstration of what happens to those who stand with me against him."

The child, who had remained silent during this exchange, suddenly spoke again. "He said the Stone should have been his. That it was stolen from him before you were born."

This revelation brought a fresh wave of stunned silence. Aelion's brow furrowed deeply, his ancient eyes troubled.

"That's impossible," the mage said finally. "The Phoenix Stone has been passed down through your mother's bloodline for generations. It was never Ravenna's to claim."

"Unless he believes he has some connection to that bloodline," Elara suggested, her scholarly mind immediately seeking logical explanations. "Perhaps a distant relation?"

"Or he simply covets what he cannot have," Mira offered pragmatically. "Powerful men often convince themselves they're entitled to things that were never theirs."

Lyra found herself staring into the fire, watching the flames dance and shift. The Phoenix Stone seemed to respond to her contemplation, its warmth pulsing in a rhythm that matched her heartbeat.

"Whatever his claim," she said finally, "the Stone chose me, not him. And I choose to use it as my parents would have wanted—to protect, not to dominate. To heal, not to destroy."

She looked up, meeting each of her companions' gazes in turn. "But I need to be honest with all of you. Ravenna's involvement makes our path more dangerous. He won't stop hunting us—hunting me—until either he has the Stone or he's defeated. Anyone who stands with me becomes a target for his vengeance."

"As if we weren't already," Mira remarked dryly. "I think we passed the point of plausible deniability when we started sealing rifts and capturing Voices."

"What Mira means," Elara translated with a gentle smile, "is that we've made our choices, just as you've made yours. We stand together, regardless of the risks."

"The question isn't whether we continue," Kael added, his voice carrying the quiet authority that had made him their de facto tactical leader. "It's how we proceed knowing what we now know."

Rowan nodded agreement, unfolding one of his meticulously drawn maps. "Ravenna's personal involvement changes our strategic considerations. We need to be more cautious about which communities we approach, more selective about who we trust with information."

"And we need to understand more about Ravenna himself," Aelion added. "His methods, his weaknesses, the extent of his power. If he's made this personal, we must respond accordingly."

As they began discussing specific plans—routes to avoid, potential allies to contact, information sources to pursue—Lyra felt a small hand slip into hers. The child looked up at her with solemn eyes that had witnessed too much for their years.

"My name is Sera," she whispered, the words clearly requiring great courage to speak. "I want to help you stop the silver-eyed man."

Lyra knelt to meet the girl at eye level. "That's very brave, Sera. But you've been through so much already. We'll find somewhere safe for you, somewhere Ravenna can't reach."

Sera shook her head with surprising determination. "There's nowhere safe. Not while he lives." Her small face hardened with a resolve that seemed out of place on such young features. "I can help. I see things others don't."

Before Lyra could respond, Aelion moved closer, studying the child with new-found interest. "What kind of things do you see, child?"

Sera hesitated, then pointed toward the Phoenix Stone concealed beneath Lyra's tunic. "I see how it connects to you. Like golden threads that go from it to your heart. And I saw the voice-thing before you caught it. I could feel where it was hiding."

The companions exchanged significant glances. Children with natural magical sensitivity were rare but not unknown—often manifesting abilities that trained mages spent decades developing.

"A Seer-child," Aelion murmured. "No wonder Ravenna left her alive. He would have recognized her potential and wanted to use it."

"Or study it," Elara added grimly. "The Syndicate has been collecting individuals with unusual abilities for years."

Sera's small hand tightened around Lyra's. "Please don't send me away. The silver-eyed man will find me if I'm alone."

The request placed Lyra in an impossible position. Taking a child with them would complicate their already dangerous journey, yet abandoning her to an uncertain fate seemed equally unconscionable. She looked to her companions, seeking guidance.

"The Green Path might still be an option," Kael suggested. "Thorn's people have protected children before."

"Or the scholars at Highkeep," Elara offered. "Their wards are among the strongest in Sylvanthia."

"Both reasonable options," Aelion acknowledged. "Though neither is without risk, especially if Ravenna is specifically hunting for her."

Sera watched this exchange with the wary attention of a child accustomed to adults making decisions about her fate. When she spoke again, her voice carried a certainty beyond her years.

"I dreamed about you," she said to Lyra. "Before the silver-eyed man came. I saw you holding a light that pushed back shadows. That's how I knew to hide in the well. That's how I knew you'd come."

The simplicity of her declaration silenced their deliberations. If the child truly possessed the Sight, her dreams might carry genuine prophecy—glimpses of possible futures that could guide their path.

"Perhaps," Aelion said carefully, "the child's place is with us, at least for now. Until we better understand the nature of her abilities and Ravenna's interest in her."

Lyra looked into Sera's eyes—young yet old, frightened yet determined—and saw something of herself reflected there. Another orphan of the Syndicate's cruelty, another life disrupted by powers beyond her control.

"You can stay with us for now," she decided, squeezing the child's hand gently. "But you must promise to obey immediately when any of us gives you an instruction. Our journey is dangerous, and there may be times when you'll need to hide or run without question."

Sera nodded solemnly. "I promise."

"Then it's settled," Lyra said, rising to her feet. "We'll need to adjust our plans to accommodate Sera's presence, but her abilities might prove valuable, especially if she can sense Voices or other Syndicate agents before we encounter them."

"We should test the extent of her sensitivity," Elara suggested. "Carefully, of course. If she truly has the Sight, it manifests differently in each individual."

"Tomorrow," Kael said firmly. "The child needs rest, as do we all. I'll take first watch."

As the others prepared for sleep, arranging their bedrolls around the fire, Lyra found herself drawn again to the edge of their camp. The night sky stretched above, stars scattered like distant beacons across the darkness. She withdrew her mother's pendant once more, tracing the constellation etched into its surface—the same pattern that now shone overhead.

"I understand better now," she whispered to the stars, to her parents' memory. "Why you stood against them, even knowing the risk. Some prices are too high, even for safety."

The Phoenix Stone pulsed warmly in response, as if acknowledging her growing conviction. Ravenna's personal vendetta had clarified something within her—transformed what had been obligation into purpose. The burden remained heavy, but she no longer carried it reluctantly.

She was her parents' daughter, bearer of their legacy as surely as she bore the Phoenix Stone. And in Sera, she recognized a responsibility that transcended their immediate mission—a chance to protect a child as she herself had once been protected, to ensure that another generation might grow up to challenge darkness rather than succumb to it.

With this new clarity, Lyra returned to the fire's warmth, to her companions who had become family, and to the path that now stretched before them—more dangerous than before, but also more meaningful.

CHAPTER FIFTEEN

After the Fall

Silver moonlight sliced through the narrow opening of the cave, illuminating the haggard faces of Lyra's companions. Three days had passed since the mountain's collapse—three days of cautious travel through unfamiliar valleys, evading Syndicate patrols that seemed bewilderingly numerous for an organization supposedly decapitated by Ravenna's presumed death.

"This doesn't make sense," Kael muttered, keeping his voice low despite their isolation. He traced lines on the crude map Rowan had sketched in the dirt. "These patrol patterns suggest coordination, not chaos."

Mira passed around a flask of herbal tea, its bitter aroma cutting through the cave's damp air. "Perhaps Ravenna had lieutenants ready to assume command," she offered, though her tone betrayed her doubt. "Or perhaps bureaucracy survives even when its architects don't."

"How reassuring," Elara replied, accepting the flask with a wry smile. "Immortal paperwork—truly mankind's most terrifying creation."

Lyra sat slightly apart from the others, her hand absently tracing the hollow at her throat where the Phoenix Stone had rested for so long. Its absence felt like a phantom limb—something missing that her body still expected to find. The loss of its constant warmth left her feeling strangely vulnerable, as if she'd surrendered armor she hadn't realized she was wearing.

"You should rest," Alaric advised, settling beside her with the careful movements of one whose joints protested each new position. "Your body is still adjusting to the Stone's absence."

"Is that what this is?" Lyra asked, keeping her voice low. "This... emptiness?"

The ancient mage nodded. "The Stone's energy became intertwined with your own. Its loss creates an imbalance that time will eventually correct." His weathered face softened with sympathy. "Though some connections leave permanent marks upon us."

Lyra glanced toward her companions, now engaged in quiet debate over their next destination. "Like them," she murmured.

"Indeed." Alaric's gaze followed hers. "Though I was thinking of your parents."

The mention sent a familiar pang through Lyra's chest—grief mingled with something harder to define. "Ravenna said he kept their bones. Do you think that was true, or merely calculated cruelty?"

"With Ravenna, often both." Alaric sighed. "He understood that truth makes the sharpest weapon—particularly when wielded at precisely the right moment."

"You speak of him as if he's still alive."

Alaric's silence stretched uncomfortably before he finally replied. "I have lived long enough to develop a healthy skepticism about the deaths of particularly determined individuals. Especially when no body is recovered."

The pain in Lyra's chest hadn't subsided in the three days since the mountain's collapse. Each time she reached for the Phoenix Stone's familiar warmth, her fingers closed around empty air, leaving a hollow ache where its presence had once filled her.

She closed her eyes, the memories of that fateful day at the monastery temple washing over her unbidden.

The ancient halls of the Order of the Veiled Sky's monastery had trembled as Ravenna—Lord Ravenna, the Syndicate's High Inquisitor—activated the Midnight Stone. His silver eyes had gleamed with triumph as the dark artifact pulsed with malevolent energy, sending fractures through the stone floor beneath their feet.

"You're too late," he had said, his voice carrying despite the rumbling. "The resonance trap is already in motion. When the Midnight Stone and Phoenix Stone occupy the same sacred space, their opposing energies create... interesting effects."

Lyra had felt the Phoenix Stone growing hot against her skin, responding to the proximity of its dark counterpart. Beside her, Kael had drawn his sword while Thorn used her druidic magic to stabilize the crumbling archway, buying them precious seconds.

"Get Sera and the others out!" Aelion had shouted to Elara, who quickly ushered the young girl and the wounded Rowan toward the exit. The ancient mage then turned to Lyra with grave intensity. "From this moment forward, call me Alaric. If we survive this, the name Aelion must be forgotten—it draws too much of the Syndicate's attention."

The Phoenix Stone had pulsed erratically as the temple's central chamber began to collapse. Ravenna had raised the Midnight Stone high, its obsidian surface absorbing light rather than reflecting it.

"The trap requires both Stones," he had explained with the calm of a scholar rather than a madman. "Either both are destroyed, or one consumes the other. I'm willing to take that gamble."

Mira had called out a warning as the ceiling began to give way. "Lyra, the resonance is building! The Stones are creating some kind of feedback loop!"

Time seemed to slow as Lyra made her decision. With a silent apology to her parents' memory, she had removed the Phoenix Stone from around her neck and hurled it toward Ravenna—not as an offering, but as a weapon. The two Stones had collided in midair, creating a blinding flash and a shockwave that had thrown everyone backward.

The last thing Lyra remembered was Kael's arms around her, dragging her toward the exit as the mountain itself seemed to fold inward, burying the temple chamber and, presumably, both Stones within it.

Lyra opened her eyes, her hand instinctively moving to her throat where the Phoenix Stone had hung for so long. The physical weight was gone, but the responsibility remained. Somehow, she would need to find strength without it.

"You did what you had to do," came Kael's voice from beside her. He had an uncanny ability to sense when she was reliving that moment. "Mira and Elara got Sera safely to that village we passed. Rowan's hands are healing. We survived."

"But without the Stone—" Lyra began.

"You are more than the Stone," Kael said firmly. "You always have been."

She nodded, though the conviction didn't quite reach her heart. The cave that sheltered them felt colder without the Stone's warmth, but they couldn't linger here. Syndicate patrols were still searching the area, and without the Phoenix Stone's protection, they needed to keep moving.

"Do you think Ravenna really died in there?" she asked quietly.

Kael's expression darkened. "I've learned not to underestimate the Syndicate. Or him."

Alaric—she was still getting used to calling him that—approached from the cave entrance. "The path to the River Lys should be clear by midday. Meridian lies three days' journey beyond that."

"Meridian?" Lyra questioned.

"A market town," Rowan explained, joining their conversation. "Small enough to avoid Syndicate attention, large enough for trade caravans. We need supplies and information."

Lyra rose to her feet, determination replacing the hollow feeling in her chest. The Phoenix Stone might be gone, but their mission remained. And somehow, she would find a way to continue without it.

Dawn found them already moving, following game trails through dense forest to avoid the main roads where Syndicate patrols concentrated. Rowan led the way, his connection to the natural world guiding them through passages that seemed invisible until he pointed them out. The cartographer had grown more confident in wilderness settings since they'd begun their journey months ago, his scholarly demeanor now balanced with practical skills honed through necessity.

"Your recovery from the Nightshade's poison has been remarkable," Lyra commented as she fell into step beside him. "No lingering effects?"

Rowan flexed his fingers reflexively—a habit he'd developed since the poisoning. "Occasional numbness in my hands, especially in the morning. The monks said it might persist for months." A wry smile crossed his face. "A small price to pay for surviving something that should have killed me."

By midday, they reached the River Lys, a broad, lazy waterway that would guide them to Meridian. After debate about which bank offered the safer route, they chose the eastern path despite its exposure, preferring that risk to the treacherous marshlands of the western shore.

The journey passed without incident, though they maintained vigilant watches during their overnight camps. On the third day, Meridian's impressive sandstone walls appeared on the horizon, glowing amber in the morning light.

As they approached the town gates, Alaric briefed them on what to expect. "Meridian maintains strict neutrality through force. The Arbiters who patrol the streets tolerate no violence or obvious magic use. Weapons must be checked at the gate."

"I don't like surrendering our weapons," Kael stated flatly.

"Nor I," Rowan agreed, absently flexing his still-recovering fingers. "After the Nightshades, I prefer keeping something sharp within reach."

"If Meridian's neutrality is as strictly enforced as rumored, it may be the safest place we've encountered in months," Lyra decided. "We stay together and follow their rules—for now."

The inspection at the gate proceeded efficiently. Each traveler presented themselves to a guard who recorded their name and purpose in a ledger. Weapons were checked at a separate station, tagged with identifying markers, and stored in a secure armory.

When their turn came, the guard—a woman with a practical braid and impassive expression—regarded them with practiced assessment.

"Names and purpose," she requested, quill poised above her ledger.

"Lyra," she replied, deciding that honesty would serve better than transparent lies. "With companions Kael, Mira, Elara, Rowan, and Alaric. We seek supplies and perhaps lodging for a night or two."

The guard's eyebrow raised slightly as she recorded their names. "Interesting company you keep," she remarked without looking up. "Purpose of visit?"

"As I said, supplies and—"

"Your actual purpose," the guard interrupted, finally meeting Lyra's gaze directly. "Meridian values honesty above most virtues."

Lyra hesitated, weighing her options. Behind her, she felt her companions tense slightly.

"We seek information," she finally admitted. "About Syndicate movements in the region. We've had... encounters with them recently and wish to avoid further confrontation."

The guard studied her for a long moment before nodding once. "Acceptable. Proceed to weapons check, then through the main gate. The Arbiters maintain an information exchange at the central square. For the right price, you'll find what you seek." She lowered her voice slightly. "And a word of advice—the Sleeping Serpent Inn on the east side offers private rooms with no questions asked. Better than the larger establishments for those avoiding attention."

Surprised by this unexpected assistance, Lyra thanked her. The guard merely nodded and turned her attention to the next traveler in line.

After surrendering their weapons—Kael and Rowan with visible reluctance—they passed through the imposing gates into Meridian proper. The contrast with the world outside its walls struck Lyra immediately. Clean cobblestone streets branched from the main thoroughfare, lined with shops displaying wares from across the known world. Citizens moved about their business with purpose but without the fearful hurry that characterized so many settlements in these troubled times.

"It's like stepping into another world," Mira murmured, her eyes wide as she took in the colorful market stalls and well-maintained buildings.

"One that exists at considerable cost," Alaric observed, nodding toward a group of Arbiters patrolling nearby. Unlike the gate guards, these figures wore distinctive black armor trimmed with silver, their faces partially concealed by fitted helmets. Each carried a short staff marked with glowing runes.

They secured two adjoining rooms at the Sleeping Serpent Inn, a modest three-story building on a quiet side street. The innkeeper—a broad-shouldered woman with a scar bisecting one eyebrow—asked no questions beyond how many rooms they required and for how long.

"We should divide tasks," Kael suggested once they had settled in. "Some of us gather supplies while others seek information. We'll attract less attention in smaller groups."

"Agreed," Lyra nodded. "Mira, you and Elara handle supplies. Rowan, you accompany Alaric to the information exchange. Kael and I will explore the town, get a feel for the place."

No one challenged this division, though Mira's barely suppressed smile suggested future teasing would be inevitable. They agreed to reconvene at the inn by sunset, then separated to their assigned tasks.

The central square of Meridian bustled with activity as Lyra and Kael approached. A vast expanse of polished stone surrounded an elaborate fountain, with imposing buildings housing the town's governance along the perimeter. People from all walks of life mingled freely—merchants, scholars, laborers, and children—all under the watchful eye of the black-armored Arbiters.

"Peace maintained by force," Lyra observed, nodding toward an incident where two arguing men were swiftly approached by Arbiters. No words were exchanged—the Arbiters simply positioned themselves between the disputants, their runed staffs glowing slightly. Within moments, the argument dissipated, the participants moving away in opposite directions.

"Effective, if somewhat chilling," Kael acknowledged.

They continued their circuit of the square, eventually approaching a circular building with open sides that housed what must be the information exchange the gate guard had mentioned. Inside, dozens of small tables were staffed by individuals of varying appearance, each engaged in quiet conversation with clients. Money and documents changed hands with subtle efficiency.

"Information as commodity," Lyra mused. "Buying and selling knowledge like grain or cloth."

After observing the exchange from a respectful distance, they found a small teahouse overlooking the square where they could rest and watch the rhythms of Meridian life. The proprietor served them fragrant tea and honey-drizzled pastries.

"What do you make of this place?" Lyra asked after they had settled at a table near the window.

Kael considered the question while watching the flow of people below. "It's built on contradiction," he finally said. "Freedom through rigid control. Peace through implicit threat. Neutrality maintained by force of arms."

"Yet it works," Lyra observed. "Look at them—they're not afraid. Not like people everywhere else we've traveled."

"Fear takes different forms," Kael replied. "The absence of one type doesn't preclude the presence of others."

Their philosophical discussion continued as afternoon light slanted golden through the teahouse windows. For a brief interlude, they were not fighters or leaders or bearers of ancient artifacts—just two people sharing thoughts and observations, finding connection in the exchange of ideas rather than the crucible of danger.

The illusion of normalcy shattered when a commotion erupted in the square below. People scattered as a group of Arbiters surrounded someone near the fountain. Lyra and Kael moved to the window for a better view, tensing as they recognized the figure at the center of the disturbance.

"Rowan," Lyra breathed, alarm spiking through her. "What happened?"

They abandoned their tea and hurried downstairs, pushing through gathering onlookers to reach the edge of the confrontation. Rowan stood rigidly as Arbiters formed a tight circle around him, their runed staffs glowing with obvious magical energy. The cartographer's face was pale but composed, his scholarly dignity somehow intact despite the circumstances. His hands—those precise instruments that had mapped their journey through wilderness and danger—were bound before him with glowing restraints.

Alaric stood nearby, his expression grave but controlled.

"What's the meaning of this?" Kael demanded, addressing the nearest Arbiter.

The black-armored figure turned slightly, revealing a face partially concealed by a fitted helmet. "This individual attempted unauthorized access to restricted information. He will be escorted to holding for assessment."

"There must be some mistake," Lyra interjected, stepping forward. "He's with us, and we were explicitly directed to the information exchange by your own gate guards."

"The exchange provides approved information only," the Arbiter replied impassively. "Your companion attempted to bribe a broker for classified intelligence regarding Syndicate leadership structure—information Meridian has deemed sensitive and restricted."

Lyra glanced at Alaric, who gave an almost imperceptible nod confirming the accusation. She turned back to the Arbiter, mind racing for a diplomatic solution.

"He meant no harm," she began, but the Arbiter raised a hand to silence her.

"Intent is irrelevant. Actions determine consequences. He will be held for assessment, then likely expelled from Meridian." The Arbiter's tone remained professionally neutral. "You may retrieve him at the eastern gate at dawn tomorrow."

Rowan caught Lyra's eye over the Arbiter's shoulder. "It's all right," he called, his voice steady despite the circumstances. "Just a misunderstanding. I'll be fine until morning." His gaze conveyed more than his words—a warning not to escalate the situation, not to risk the others for his sake.

Further protest seemed futile as the Arbiters began moving Rowan toward their headquarters. The crowd parted before them, conversations resuming with the incident already becoming gossip rather than concern.

Alaric approached them, his expression troubled. "I apologize. The situation... escalated unexpectedly."

"What happened?" Kael asked quietly as they moved away from lingering on-lookers.

"We discovered something disturbing," Alaric replied, keeping his voice low. "Syndicate communications have continued uninterrupted since the mountain collapse. Orders still flow from central command, bearing Ravenna's seal."

"That's impossible," Lyra protested. "Unless..."

"Unless he survived," Kael finished grimly. "Which means everything we sacri-ficed at the temple—"

"Was for nothing," Alaric confirmed. "When Rowan learned this, he attempted to acquire more specific information about Ravenna's whereabouts. The broker refused, and when Rowan became insistent..."

"The Arbiters intervened," Lyra concluded, understanding dawning. "They monitor the exchange constantly."

"With both visible and invisible means," Alaric nodded. "I sensed magical sur-veillance but couldn't warn Rowan in time."

The holding cells beneath Meridian's Arbiter headquarters were surprisingly clean, if spartan. Rowan sat on a narrow stone bench, his bound hands resting in his lap. The magical restraints emitted a soft blue glow that illuminated the otherwise dim cell.

Unlike the dungeons he'd seen during their travels, this space seemed designed for temporary detention rather than punishment or interrogation. A small window near the ceiling admitted a shaft of late afternoon sunlight. The door was solid oak reinforced with iron bands, but without the menacing spikes or barred openings common in more sinister facilities.

Rowan flexed his fingers against the restraints, feeling the lingering effects of the Nightshade poison that had nearly taken his life weeks earlier. The numbness in his fingertips came and went unpredictably, a constant reminder of his mortality. As a cartographer, his hands were his most precious tools—the thought of losing their dexterity had terrified him more than death.

He closed his eyes, methodically organizing his observations as he always did when mapping unfamiliar territory. The Arbiters who had arrested him moved with practiced efficiency but without unnecessary roughness. They had recited his infraction and consequences in formulaic language that suggested a system built on consistency rather than cruelty. Even their restraints, while effective, were calibrated to restrict without causing pain.

Meridian operated by rules—strict, unyielding rules, but rules nonetheless. And where rules existed, patterns could be discerned. Patterns were Rowan's specialty.

The sound of approaching footsteps interrupted his thoughts. The door opened to admit an Arbiter carrying a tray with bread, cheese, and water. Unlike those who had arrested him, this one wore no helmet, revealing the face of a middle-aged woman with close-cropped gray hair and eyes that assessed him with clinical detachment.

"Meal service," she announced, placing the tray on a small shelf near the door. "Standard provision for all detainees."

Rowan raised his bound hands. "These make eating somewhat challenging."

The Arbiter considered this practical problem without changing expression. She removed a small crystal from her belt and touched it to the restraints. The glowing bands loosened slightly, allowing greater movement while still preventing escape.

"You have fifteen minutes," she stated. "The restraints will retighten automatically."

"Thank you," Rowan replied, genuinely appreciative of this small concession. "May I ask a question?"

The Arbiter paused at the door. "You may ask. I may not answer."

"Why is information about Syndicate leadership classified? Neutrality would suggest making all intelligence equally available—or equally restricted."

A flicker of something—surprise, perhaps—crossed the Arbiter's face before her professional mask returned. "Meridian's neutrality is maintained through carefully negotiated agreements with all major powers. The specific terms of these agreements are not public knowledge."

"So Meridian has an arrangement with the Syndicate," Rowan concluded. "Protection in exchange for discretion?"

"Enjoy your meal," the Arbiter replied, neither confirming nor denying his assessment. "A magistrate will review your case in the morning."

As the door closed behind her, Rowan allowed himself a small smile. Even in detention, he was gathering information—mapping the political landscape as surely as he had mapped physical territories. The Syndicate's influence extended further than they had realized, reaching even into supposedly neutral havens like Meridian.

He ate methodically, savoring the simple but fresh food. As he chewed, he contemplated what he had learned at the information exchange before his arrest. The broker had been surprisingly forthcoming about general Syndicate movements—patrol routes, supply chains, regional commanders—until Rowan had inquired specifically about Ravenna.

The broker's sudden reticence had been telling in itself. Not the caution of someone protecting valuable information, but the fear of someone avoiding a forbidden topic. When pressed, she had glanced nervously toward the ceiling—toward the magical surveillance Rowan hadn't noticed until too late.

That reaction confirmed what the continued communications suggested: Ravenna was alive, his influence intact, and his name inspired fear even in Meridian's supposedly secure confines.

As the magical restraints tightened again around his wrists, Rowan leaned back against the cell wall. He would be released at dawn, carrying with him intelligence that might prove crucial to their next steps. His detention was not a failure but an unexpected opportunity to observe Meridian's inner workings from a perspective few outsiders ever witnessed.

Sometimes, he reflected, the most valuable maps were those drawn from within the fortress walls.

Back at the Sleeping Serpent Inn, Lyra and her companions gathered to assess their options. Mira and Elara had returned from their supply run with practical goods and useful gossip gleaned from local merchants.

"Syndicate patrols have increased along the northern roads," Elara reported. "The herbalist mentioned caravans being searched more thoroughly than usual."

"Looking for us, perhaps," Kael suggested. "Or for anyone connected to the Order of the Veiled Sky."

"We need to confirm whether Ravenna truly survived," Lyra said, the hollow feeling in her chest intensifying with this new knowledge. "Rumors and sealed communications aren't definitive proof."

"Rowan might have learned more if the Arbiters hadn't intervened," Kael pointed out. "Their reaction suggests Meridian has some arrangement with the Syndicate—perhaps part of their vaunted neutrality."

"Or they fear retaliation if they allow anti-Syndicate activities within their walls," Alaric suggested. "Pragmatism often masquerades as principle."

The discussion continued as evening shadows lengthened across the room. They debated retrieving Rowan and departing immediately versus waiting until morning as instructed. The potential consequences of defying Meridian's authorities had to be weighed against the risk of remaining in a place that might not be as neutral as it claimed.

"I don't like leaving him there overnight," Mira said, her usual flippancy absent. "Rowan's not like the rest of us—he observes battles, he doesn't fight them."

"He's stronger than he appears," Kael reminded her. "And sometimes observation is its own form of strength. He'll learn things in their custody that might prove valuable."

A knock at their door silenced the debate instantly. Kael moved to answer it, positioning himself to block any immediate threat. He opened the door cautiously to reveal the innkeeper, her scarred face impassive as ever.

"Message for you," she stated without preamble, extending a sealed parchment. "Delivered by a broker from the exchange. No name given."

Kael accepted the message with murmured thanks. The innkeeper lingered a moment longer, then added in a lower voice, "Whatever trouble your friend found, best not to compound it. Meridian forgives first offenses. Second chances are considerably rarer."

With that cryptic warning, she departed, heavy footsteps receding down the corridor.

Kael brought the message to Lyra, who broke the plain wax seal and unfolded the parchment. The group gathered around as she read the flowing script aloud:

"The answers you seek lie not in Meridian but three days north in the ruins of Aetherhall. What was broken can be mended. What was lost can be reclaimed. The Silver-Eyed One gathers strength for purposes that threaten more than your small company. If you would learn truth rather than rumor, seek the Lady of Whispers at the new moon. She keeps watch over what remains."

The message bore no signature, only a small symbol inked at the bottom—a crescent moon bisected by a vertical line. The same symbol Caius had drawn in the dirt before they departed for the temple.

"The Order of the Veiled Sky," Alaric breathed, recognition evident in his voice. "They've found us."

"Or set a trap," Kael countered, his natural caution reasserting itself. "This could be Syndicate manipulation."

"The symbol is correct," Alaric insisted. "And Aetherhall was once a sanctuary of the Order before it fell during the Mage Wars. This knowledge isn't widely available."

"The new moon is four days hence," Elara calculated. "If we depart after retrieving Rowan tomorrow, we'd reach these ruins just in time."

"Convenient timing," Mira observed skeptically. "Almost suspiciously so."

Lyra studied the message again, something about the phrasing tugging at her memory. "What was broken can be mended," she repeated softly. "What was lost can be reclaimed." Her hand rose unconsciously to her throat where the Phoenix Stone had rested. "They're talking about the Stone."

As her fingers touched the empty space where the Phoenix Stone had hung, Lyra felt something—a whisper of warmth, so faint she might have imagined it. A fleeting sensation like the echo of a familiar voice calling from a great distance. Her breath caught, heart quickening at the unexpected feeling.

"Impossible," Alaric shook his head, not noticing her reaction. "The resonance trap would have destroyed both artifacts completely. The energy released was catastrophic."

"Yet Ravenna apparently survived," Kael pointed out. "Perhaps the Stones did as well."

Lyra remained silent, uncertain whether to mention the phantom warmth she'd felt. Was it merely wishful thinking, her mind creating what her heart desperately wanted to believe? Or had something of the Stone's essence truly reached out to her, confirming what the message suggested?

She moved to the window, needing space to process this new information. The Phoenix Stone had been more than a tool or weapon to her—it had become part of her identity, its constant presence both burden and comfort. Its loss had left her adrift, questioning her purpose and value to their cause. The possibility of its recovery stirred conflicting emotions: hope and doubt, longing and fear.

Was she drawn to this possibility because it would help their mission, or because it would restore her sense of self? Was she willing to risk her companions for the chance to feel whole again? The questions circled in her mind like birds of prey, seeking vulnerable thoughts to seize upon.

"Lyra?" Elara's gentle voice broke through her thoughts. "What are you thinking?"

She turned back to face her companions, these people who had become her family through shared danger and purpose. "I'm thinking that if there's even a chance the Stone survived, we need to know. Not just for what it might mean for our fight against the Syndicate, but for what it might reveal about Ravenna's survival."

"It could be exactly what he wants," Kael cautioned. "Drawing us into another trap."

"I know," Lyra acknowledged. "But we can't ignore this. If Ravenna lives and is gathering strength, as this message suggests, we need to understand what we're facing."

"And Rowan?" Mira asked. "We can't leave without him."

"Of course not," Lyra agreed immediately. "We'll retrieve him at dawn as instructed, then make our decision."

The discussion continued late into the night, weighing risks against potential rewards, examining the message for hidden meanings or inconsistencies. Alaric shared what he knew of Aetherhall—once a great center of learning before its destruction in the Mage Wars centuries ago. Its ruins were said to contain knowledge that had been lost elsewhere, preserved in chambers deep beneath the surface.

"If any place might hold answers about the Stones, it would be Aetherhall," the ancient mage concluded. "The Order of the Veiled Sky maintained a significant presence there before its fall."

As the others debated the practicalities of the journey—supplies needed, routes to take, potential dangers—Lyra found herself returning to the window, drawn to the quiet streets below. Somewhere in the city, Rowan sat in detention, perhaps gleaning information even in his captivity. And somewhere beyond Meridian's walls, answers awaited—about the Stone, about Ravenna, about the path forward.

The weight of decision pressed upon her. As leader, her choices affected not just herself but those who trusted her judgment. Without the Stone's guidance, she felt the responsibility more keenly than ever before. Was she worthy of their faith? Could she lead them without the artifact that had marked her as chosen?

Kael joined her at the window, his quiet presence a comfort she'd come to rely on. "You're troubled," he observed.

"I'm weighing what's right against what I want," she admitted. "And finding it difficult to separate the two."

"Tell me."

She sighed, organizing her thoughts. "Part of me desperately wants to believe the Stone can be recovered—not just for our cause, but for myself. I feel... diminished without it. Yet I can't let that desire cloud my judgment or put all of you at risk."

"And what does your judgment tell you, setting aside desire?" Kael asked, his voice free of pressure or expectation.

Lyra considered the question carefully. "That we need answers, regardless of what they might be. If Ravenna survived, we need to know how and what he plans. If the Stones survived, we need to understand what that means for the balance of power." She met his gaze directly. "My judgment tells me that hiding from truth never serves us, even when that truth might be painful."

Kael nodded, a small smile touching his lips. "That sounds like the Lyra I follow. Stone or no Stone."

His simple faith in her loosened something tight in her chest. Before she could respond, Mira called them back to the ongoing planning.

"So we're agreed," the alchemist summarized. "We retrieve Rowan at dawn, gather our weapons, and depart immediately for Aetherhall. We'll need provisions for at least a week's journey."

"And a contingency plan if we're separated," Elara added. "The road north passes through territories known to harbor Syndicate sympathizers."

They continued refining details until exhaustion finally drove them to seek rest. As the others settled into sleep, Lyra found herself lying awake, her mind too active for slumber. The absence of the Phoenix Stone felt particularly acute tonight, its phantom warmth a reminder of all they had lost—and might yet regain.

She pressed her fingers against the hollow of her throat, seeking any trace of that fleeting warmth she'd felt earlier. Nothing came, leaving her uncertain whether it had been real or merely her desperate hope manifesting as sensation. Either way, the memory of it strengthened her resolve. Tomorrow they would begin a new journey—toward answers, toward truth, perhaps even toward restoration.

Dawn arrived with thin gray light filtering through the window. They gathered their few possessions and made their way to the eastern gate where Rowan would be released. A small group of travelers already waited there, some clearly being expelled for various infractions, others simply departing with the morning caravan.

The Arbiters appeared precisely as the sun breached the horizon, escorting several detainees to the gate. Rowan walked among them, his bearing dignified despite obvious fatigue. When he spotted his companions, relief washed across his face.

"Right on time," he greeted them with forced lightness as the Arbiters removed his restraints. "I was beginning to think you might have found more pleasant company."

"And miss your charming morning disposition?" Mira quipped, though her relief was evident in her quick assessment of his condition. "You look terrible, by the way."

"Meridian's hospitality leaves something to be desired," he replied, rubbing his wrists where the restraints had been. "Though I did learn some interesting things about their relationship with the Syndicate."

"Save it for when we're beyond the walls," Kael advised quietly, nodding toward the watching Arbiters.

They reclaimed their weapons at the armory, then passed through the gates into the countryside beyond. Only when Meridian's walls had receded in the distance did they pause to properly welcome Rowan back and share the mysterious message that had arrived in his absence.

"Aetherhall," he murmured, studying the parchment with scholarly interest. "I've read accounts of its libraries. If even half the stories are true, it would be a repository of knowledge unmatched in the modern world."

"And potentially our best chance to learn the truth about Ravenna and the Stones," Lyra added.

"My detention confirmed what we suspected," Rowan said, his voice taking on the precise tone he used when reporting observations. "Meridian has a formal arrangement with the Syndicate—protection in exchange for information control. The Arbiters monitor communications meticulously, particularly regarding Syndicate leadership."

"Did you learn anything specific about Ravenna?" Kael asked.

"Not directly," Rowan admitted. "But the reaction to his name was telling. Even within Meridian's supposedly secure walls, people fear mentioning him." He flexed his fingers absently. "The most valuable information came from what wasn't said, what questions weren't answered. The silence around certain topics speaks volumes."

"So we head north," Lyra concluded. "To Aetherhall and this Lady of Whispers. If there's even a chance the Stone survived..."

Rowan nodded, his eyes bright despite his exhaustion. "Then we have a new destination. And perhaps, a new hope."

As they set off northward, Lyra felt something stir within her that had nothing to do with the absent Phoenix Stone. A sense of purpose—not bestowed by an external artifact but arising from within. From the choices she made and the companions who stood beside her.

The path ahead remained uncertain, fraught with danger and unanswered questions. Ravenna might still live. The Stones might be lost forever or waiting to be reclaimed. The Order of the Veiled Sky might offer salvation or betrayal.

But for the first time since the mountain's collapse, Lyra felt something fill the hollow space where the Stone had rested. Not the Stone's warmth, but something equally powerful. Something entirely her own.

They walked in companionable silence as the morning sun climbed higher, casting long shadows across the rolling landscape. Meridian's walls diminished behind them, a fading reminder of the rigid order they were leaving behind.

Ahead lay the wild unknown—forests and hills, rivers and valleys, and eventually the ancient ruins of Aetherhall with whatever secrets they might contain. Lyra's hand rose unconsciously to her throat once more, fingers brushing the empty space where the Phoenix Stone had hung.

For just a moment—so brief she might have imagined it—she felt that whisper of warmth again. A distant echo, like the faintest pulse of a heart beating in synchrony with her own. Then it was gone, leaving only questions and possibilities.

Lyra dropped her hand and quickened her pace, leading her companions northward toward whatever awaited them. The dawn of a new era had begun.

Chapter Sixteen

Reclamation's Choice

D awn crept reluctantly over Meridian's eastern wall, pale light washing the sandstone battlements in shades of amber and gold. Lyra stood waiting at the designated gate, her companions arrayed behind her in various states of preparedness for the journey ahead. The air hung heavy with morning mist, obscuring the distant hills they would soon traverse.

"They're late," Kael murmured, his restless energy evident in the way he shifted his weight from foot to foot. Without his sword—still secured in Meridian's armory—he seemed somehow diminished, though no less vigilant.

"Arbiters are never late," Elara replied softly. "They operate on their own precise schedule, which rarely aligns with the convenience of others."

As if summoned by her observation, the gate's smaller inset door swung open. Two black-armored Arbiters emerged, flanking Rowan whose expression remained carefully neutral despite the circumstances. He carried his belongings in a simple pack, apparently unharmed but visibly fatigued.

"Your companion is released as promised," the lead Arbiter announced without preamble. "His infraction has been recorded. Should he return to Meridian, he will do so with this mark against him."

"We understand," Lyra replied with matching formality. "Thank you for your... consideration."

The Arbiter's helmeted head tilted slightly, suggesting an unspoken assessment. "Your weapons await retrieval at the checkpoint. Once collected, you are expected to depart Meridian territory by midday."

"Generous timeframe," Mira muttered under her breath. "They could at least pretend we're not being expelled."

The Arbiters showed no reaction to her comment, though Lyra suspected their helmets concealed enhanced hearing along with their identities. With a synchronized bow that somehow conveyed both respect and dismissal, they retreated through the gate, leaving Rowan standing alone before his companions.

"Well," he said after a moment, attempting lightness despite the shadows beneath his eyes, "that was an educational experience I'd prefer not to repeat."

Kael clasped his shoulder in wordless support as Alaric asked, "How were you treated?"

"Professionally," Rowan answered, falling into step as they moved toward the weapons checkpoint. "No cruelty, no comfort. They asked the same questions repeatedly through the night—who I was, why I sought restricted information, who sent me." A humorless smile crossed his face. "I got the distinct impression they already knew the answers and were merely confirming their intelligence."

"Did they mention the message?" Lyra asked quietly. "About Aetherhall?"

Rowan's eyebrows rose in surprise. "No. What message?"

They brought him up to speed as they retrieved their weapons, a process conducted with the same efficient impersonality that characterized all of Meridian's official interactions. Kael visibly relaxed once his sword was strapped to his back again, completing some essential circuit of his identity.

The group departed through Meridian's northern gate without ceremony, following a well-maintained road that wound through cultivated fields before ascending into more rugged terrain. Only when the city's walls had diminished to a distant smudge on the horizon did they pause to properly assess their situation and plan their approach to Aetherhall.

"Three days north, the message said," Elara mused, consulting a weathered map she'd purchased in Meridian's market. "That would place it here, in the foothills of the Sentinel Range."

"Assuming the message is trustworthy," Kael reminded them, his natural caution reasserting itself now that they'd left Meridian's protection. "We should proceed as if entering hostile territory."

"The Order of the Veiled Sky isn't hostile," Alaric countered, though without heat. "Secretive, yes. Selective about their alliances, certainly. But not enemies."

"Unless they've been compromised," Mira pointed out. "Like Caius."

The reminder sobered them all. They continued their journey in thoughtful silence, each contemplating the implications of the mysterious message and the path it had set them upon. The landscape gradually shifted from farmland to wild meadows, then to scattered copses of silver birch that rustled in the afternoon breeze.

They made camp that night in a sheltered hollow, establishing watches and keeping their fire small to avoid drawing attention. During her shift, Lyra found herself studying her companions' sleeping forms, struck by how vulnerable they appeared in repose. Kael's perpetual vigilance softened in sleep, the furrow between his brows smoothing out. Mira curled like a child, one hand tucked beneath her cheek. Elara slept with perfect stillness, as if conserving energy even in unconsciousness. Rowan twitched occasionally, perhaps still processing his confinement in Meridian.

Only Alaric remained awake, sitting cross-legged at the edge of their camp with his staff laid across his knees. His eyes reflected the dying embers of their fire, giving him an otherworldly appearance.

"You should rest," Lyra said softly, approaching him. "I can watch alone."

"Sleep becomes less necessary with age," he replied with a slight smile. "One of the few compensations for the indignities of time."

She settled beside him, drawing her cloak tighter against the night's chill. "You're worried about Aetherhall."

It wasn't a question, but he nodded anyway. "The ruins hold memories. Not all of them pleasant."

"You've been there before."

"Long ago." His gaze turned distant. "Before the Mage Wars, Aetherhall was the Order's greatest sanctuary. A place of learning and contemplation, where knowledge was preserved and wisdom cultivated." A shadow crossed his features. "Its fall marked the beginning of the Order's decline from prominence to secrecy."

"What happened?"

Alaric sighed, the sound carrying centuries of regret. "What always happens when power is involved. Fear. Betrayal. Those who once protected knowledge began to hoard it instead. Those who should have stood united turned against each other." He gestured vaguely northward. "Aetherhall burned for seven days. The sky was black with ash for a month afterward."

"And now someone from the Order wants us to go there," Lyra mused. "Why? What could remain in ruins centuries old?"

"That," Alaric said with sudden weariness, "is the question that has kept me from sleep."

Morning brought low clouds and the promise of rain, hastening their preparations to continue northward. They traveled efficiently, Rowan's wilderness skills guiding them along game trails and forgotten paths that shaved hours from their journey. By nightfall, they had covered more ground than expected, bringing them into the first gentle rises of the foothills.

They made camp beneath a rocky overhang that offered protection from the drizzle that had begun mid-afternoon. As they settled around a small fire, Mira produced a flask from her pack with a flourish.

"I liberated this from the Sleeping Serpent before we left," she announced, un-stoppering it to release the aroma of spiced spirits. "Seemed appropriate for a cold, wet evening."

"Liberated?" Elara raised an eyebrow. "An interesting euphemism for theft."

"I left payment," Mira protested, passing the flask to Kael. "Just... not in an ob-vious location. The innkeeper struck me as someone who appreciates initiative."

"Or someone who will add you to a very specific list of problematic guests," Rowan suggested with a wry smile.

The flask made its way around their circle, bringing warmth and loosening the tension that had accumulated during the day's journey. Conversation flowed more easily, drifting from practical concerns to more personal reflections.

"I've been thinking about Meridian," Elara said after a comfortable lull. "About the price they pay for their security."

"Seems reasonable to me," Mira shrugged. "No violence, no obvious magic, follow the rules—get peace and prosperity in return."

"But at what cost?" Elara persisted. "Freedom of expression. The right to disagree openly. The natural friction that drives growth and change."

"Some would say those are luxuries," Kael observed. "When survival is uncertain, philosophical ideals become secondary."

"Yet without those ideals, what are we surviving for?" Alaric interjected quietly. "A life without friction is a life without growth."

The discussion continued, touching on governance, freedom, and the compro-mises communities make for security. Lyra listened more than she spoke, struck by the passion with which her companions engaged with these abstract concepts even amid their own precarious circumstances. It reminded her of late-night discussions with her parents before their deaths—the way they'd instilled in her the importance of questioning, of never accepting comfort at the expense of conscience.

Eventually the conversation circled back to their immediate concerns: the journey to Aetherhall, the mysterious Lady of Whispers mentioned in the message, the possibility that the Phoenix Stone might somehow have survived the temple's destruction.

"Even if it did survive," Rowan said, his expression troubled, "would recovering it be wise? The resonance trap that destroyed the temple was triggered by bringing the Stones into proximity. What's to prevent the same catastrophe from recurring?"

"The circumstances would be different," Alaric replied, though his tone suggested he shared Rowan's concern. "The trap was specifically designed and placed. A natural encounter between the Stones might produce different results."

"'Might' being the operative word," Mira pointed out. "Not exactly reassuring when discussing powers that can level mountains."

"We're getting ahead of ourselves," Lyra interjected. "We don't know that the Stone survived. We don't know what awaits us at Aetherhall. Until we do, speculation only feeds anxiety."

Her practical assessment brought nods of agreement. They established watches for the night and settled into their bedrolls as the fire burned down to embers. Despite her own advice against speculation, Lyra found sleep elusive, her mind turning over possibilities both hopeful and dire.

What if the Phoenix Stone had survived? Would its recovery restore the sense of purpose she'd lost with its destruction? Or had that loss forced her to confront a deeper truth about herself—that she was more than merely the Stone's bearer?

And what of Ravenna? If he too had survived, what new threats might he pose? The thought of facing him again, this time without the Stone's protection, sent a chill through her that had nothing to do with the night air.

Dawn brought clearing skies and renewed determination. They broke camp efficiently and continued their journey northward, the terrain growing steadily more challenging as they ascended into the foothills. By midday, they could see the first true mountains of the Sentinel Range, their peaks wreathed in clouds.

"Aetherhall lies in that valley," Alaric said, pointing toward a narrow gap between two rugged slopes. "We should reach it by nightfall if we maintain our pace."

The afternoon's travel proved more arduous than expected. What appeared to be a direct route on their map revealed itself as a series of steep ridges and sudden ravines, forcing them to backtrack several times. The sun had begun its descent toward the western horizon when they crested a final rise and beheld their destination spread before them.

Aetherhall's ruins occupied a natural bowl in the landscape, nestled between protective slopes like a cupped hand. Even in decay, the scale of the former sanctuary impressed itself upon the eye. Tumbled walls of white stone traced the outlines of what must have been dozens of buildings—dormitories, libraries, observatories, meditation halls. At the center rose the remains of a massive domed structure, half-collapsed but still reaching skyward with surprising grace.

"The Hall of Echoes," Alaric murmured, a catch in his voice betraying emotion he rarely displayed. "The heart of Aetherhall, where the Order's greatest minds gathered to share discoveries and debate philosophies."

They descended carefully into the valley as lengthening shadows pooled between the ruins. The silence felt expectant rather than empty, as if the very stones watched their approach with ancient curiosity. No birds called in the twilight; no small creatures rustled in the underbrush that had reclaimed portions of the sanctuary. The only sound was the whisper of wind through broken archways and roofless chambers.

"We're being observed," Kael said quietly, his hand resting on his sword hilt. "Since we entered the valley."

Lyra nodded, having sensed the same presence—not threatening, but unmistakably attentive. "They know we're here."

"The Lady of Whispers," Elara suggested. "The message said to seek her at the new moon. That's tonight."

They made their way toward the central dome, picking a path through rubble and occasional patches of wild roses that had somehow taken root among the stones. As they drew closer, Lyra noticed curious patterns etched into the fallen blocks—symbols similar to those she'd seen in the Order's monastery, but more elaborate, more ancient in their design.

The dome's interior opened to the sky where its ceiling had partially collapsed, creating a natural amphitheater. The floor remained largely intact—a vast mosaic depicting celestial bodies in their courses, rendered in tiles of lapis, silver, and gold that somehow retained their luster despite centuries of exposure to the elements.

"It's beautiful," Mira breathed, her usual irreverence temporarily suspended by genuine awe.

"And functional," Alaric added, gesturing toward the mosaic. "A map of the heavens as they appeared when Aetherhall was built. The Order believed the stars influenced the flow of magic through our world—that certain alignments strengthened or weakened the barriers between realms."

"Is that true?" Rowan asked, studying the intricate patterns with newfound interest.

"All beliefs contain elements of truth," a new voice answered from the shadows beneath the intact portion of the dome. "Even those long discarded by so-called rational minds."

They turned as one toward the source of the voice. A figure emerged from the darkness—a woman of indeterminate age, her silver-streaked black hair falling in a single braid to her waist. She wore simple robes of midnight blue that seemed to absorb rather than reflect the fading light, cinched at her waist with a belt of intricately woven silver threads. Her features held a striking harmony—high cheekbones balanced by a strong jaw, a straight nose above full lips that curved slightly at one corner, as if perpetually on the verge of sharing a secret.

But it was her eyes that commanded attention—large and almond-shaped, a color that shifted between deep violet and midnight blue depending on how the light struck them. They held the depth of experience that suggested great age, yet her skin remained largely unlined save for fine creases at the corners of those remarkable eyes, as if she had spent centuries smiling at private jokes.

Around her neck hung a pendant that caught the fading light: a crescent moon bisected by a vertical line, the symbol of the Order. Her hands, when she raised them in formal greeting, were long-fingered and elegant, adorned only with a single silver ring on her right index finger, its surface etched with symbols too small to decipher at a distance.

"The Lady of Whispers," Lyra said, certainty in her voice.

The woman inclined her head slightly, the movement graceful as flowing water. "One of my titles, yes. Though I answer to many names in many places." Her voice carried a musical quality, as if each word were carefully selected for both meaning and melody.

Alaric had gone utterly still beside Lyra, his usual composed demeanor giving way to naked shock. The color drained from his face as he stared at the Lady, his knuckles white where they gripped his staff.

"Seraphine," he whispered, the name emerging as if pulled from the depths of long-buried memory.

The Lady's gaze shifted to him, those remarkable eyes softening with recognition. "Alaric. It has been... a very long time."

"I thought you perished in the fall," he said, his voice uncharacteristically unsteady. "I searched the ruins for days."

"And I thought you had abandoned the Order," she replied, something complex passing between them—old pain, perhaps, or unresolved questions. "We have both carried misconceptions, it seems."

"You know each other," Kael observed, glancing between them with heightened alertness, clearly assessing whether this unexpected connection represented threat or advantage.

"We did," Alaric replied, composure gradually returning to his features though tension remained evident in the set of his shoulders. "In another life."

The Lady of Whispers—Seraphine—regarded him for a moment longer before her gaze moved deliberately to each of the others in turn, lingering longest on Alaric. "The Ancient. The Cartographer. The Alchemist. The Runeweaver." Her eyes finally settled on Lyra. "And the Bearer Without a Burden. You've come seeking what was lost."

"You know why we're here," Kael stated rather than asked, his posture subtly shifting to place himself between the woman and Lyra.

"I know many things, Protector," she replied with a faint smile that deepened the mystery in her eyes. "Including your instinct to shield her from perceived threats. Admirable, if unnecessary in this instance."

"The message said you keep watch over what remains," Lyra said, stepping forward to stand beside Kael rather than behind him. "What exactly does that mean?"

The Lady of Whispers gestured toward the night sky visible through the broken dome. Stars had begun to appear as twilight deepened toward true darkness. "The new moon rises unseen. The time between is liminal—neither one state nor another. Appropriate for discussions of things both destroyed and preserved."

"With respect," Elara interjected with barely concealed impatience, "we've traveled far based on your cryptic invitation. Clarity would be appreciated."

"Clarity is rarely kind," the woman replied, though without offense. Her lips curved into that almost-smile again, a expression that suggested she had witnessed this same human impatience countless times before. "But you've earned directness through your sacrifices." She turned and moved toward a section of wall that appeared more intact than the rest, her movements fluid and unhurried, robes whispering against the ancient stone floor. "Come. What I must show you cannot be seen in darkness."

As they followed, Alaric fell into step beside Lyra, his expression troubled. "Be wary," he murmured, too softly for the others to hear. "Seraphine was—is—a master of subtle manipulation. She reveals only what serves her purposes."

"You don't trust her," Lyra observed, surprised by his reaction. "Yet you said the Order weren't enemies."

"The Order, no. But individuals within it..." He left the thought unfinished as they approached the concealed doorway where the Lady waited.

They followed her through the hidden entrance into a passage that sloped gently downward. Lyra expected darkness but was surprised to find the tunnel illuminated by globes of soft blue light set into niches along the walls. These weren't torches or lanterns but something magical—light without flame, steady and unwavering.

The passage opened into a chamber that immediately struck Lyra as incongruous with the ruins above. Where Aetherhall lay in picturesque decay, this underground space appeared perfectly preserved—its walls smooth white stone inlaid with silver filigree, its ceiling a dome of what looked like actual stars suspended in midnight blue.

At the chamber's center stood a pedestal of the same white stone, upon which rested a crystalline container. Inside, floating in a medium that seemed neither liquid nor gas, hung a familiar object that caused Lyra's heart to skip a beat.

The Phoenix Stone.

Not as she remembered it—the vibrant golden-red had dimmed to a muted amber, and hairline fractures marred its previously flawless surface—but unmistakably the same artifact she had carried for so long.

"How?" she whispered, moving toward the pedestal as if drawn by an invisible thread. "The resonance trap destroyed it. I felt it shatter."

"What you felt was transformation, not destruction," the Lady of Whispers explained, her voice taking on a deeper resonance in the chamber's perfect acoustics. She moved to stand opposite Lyra across the pedestal, the blue light casting ethereal shadows across her remarkable features. "The trap was designed to release the Stones' energy while preserving their physical forms—rendered dormant but not annihilated."

"You recovered it from the temple ruins," Alaric said, his tone suggesting he was fitting pieces together in his mind. His earlier shock had been replaced by cautious analysis, though his gaze still returned frequently to the Lady's face, as if searching for answers to unspoken questions. "How? The entire mountain collapsed."

"The Order maintains certain... capabilities that survived Aetherhall's fall," the woman replied with deliberate vagueness, her fingers tracing patterns in the air above the crystalline container. Where they passed, the medium inside rippled slightly, as if responding to her touch even through the barrier. "When we sensed the resonance trap's activation, we dispatched recovery teams immediately."

"Teams," Kael repeated, focusing on the plural. "You found both Stones."

The Lady of Whispers inclined her head in acknowledgment, the silver in her braid catching the light. "The Midnight Stone was also recovered, yes. It resides elsewhere, under different guardianship."

"And Ravenna?" Lyra asked, the question that had haunted her since receiving the message. "Did he survive as well?"

A shadow passed over the woman's features, darkening those shifting eyes to near-black. "The Silver-Eyed One lives, though not unscathed. The energies released by the trap exacted a toll on all present. He was... changed by the experience."

"Changed how?" Mira pressed.

"His connection to the Midnight Stone was altered. Where once he merely sought its power, now he carries a fragment of it within himself—a splinter embedded in his essence during the cataclysm." The Lady's expression grew grave, the angles of her face sharpening with concern. "It grants him capabilities he previously lacked while gradually consuming what remains of his humanity."

The implications settled over the group like a physical weight. Ravenna—already dangerous, already obsessed with power—now enhanced by the very artifact they had sacrificed to keep from him.

"So our efforts accomplished nothing," Lyra said bitterly. "Worse than nothing. We've created a more formidable enemy."

"Not nothing," the Lady of Whispers countered gently, her hand reaching across the pedestal though she stopped short of touching Lyra. "You prevented the full power of the Midnight Stone from falling into his hands. You bought time—precious time that we now must use wisely."

"To do what, exactly?" Rowan asked. "If the Stones are dormant as you say, what purpose does preserving them serve?"

"Dormant does not mean dead," the woman replied, her gaze returning to the Phoenix Stone floating in its crystalline prison. "The Stones can be awakened, their power restored through proper ritual." Her eyes, now decidedly violet in the chamber's blue light, fixed on Lyra. "But only by one who has carried them before. Only by one whose essence they recognize."

Understanding dawned in Lyra's eyes. "You want me to reactivate the Phoenix Stone."

"I present the possibility," the Lady corrected carefully, her long fingers splaying in a gesture of openness. "The choice must be yours, freely made with full knowledge of the consequences."

"Which are?" Kael asked, suspicion evident in his tone.

"Reawakening the Stone creates a renewed bond between artifact and bearer. The connection you felt before would be reestablished, but deeper, more complete." She addressed Lyra directly now. "It would grant you access to greater power than you wielded previously, but at correspondingly greater cost to your own life force. Each use would draw more deeply from your essence."

"Shortening her life," Alaric translated bluntly. His earlier wariness toward the Lady had hardened into something closer to hostility. "This is convenient, isn't it? The Stone requiring a sacrifice you need not make yourself."

"I have made my sacrifices, Alaric," the Lady replied, a flash of genuine emotion breaking through her composed exterior. "As you well know." She turned back to Lyra. "But yes, eventually the Stone's use would shorten your life. How quickly depends on how extensively the power is used."

Silence fell as they absorbed this information. Lyra stared at the dormant Stone, its muted glow a pale echo of the vibrant warmth she remembered. The hollow feeling that had plagued her since its loss pulsed in time with her heartbeat—an absence that might now be filled again, but at what cost?

"And if I refuse?" she finally asked. "What happens to the Stone then?"

"It remains dormant. Protected. Until perhaps another worthy bearer emerges in some future generation." The Lady of Whispers spread her hands in a gesture of openness. "The Order will not force this burden upon you. We merely offer the choice that circumstance has placed before you."

"What about the Midnight Stone?" Elara interjected. "If Ravenna carries a fragment, could he reawaken it himself?"

"Not alone," the woman replied, her braid swinging gently as she shook her head. "The ritual requires knowledge he does not possess. But he seeks that knowledge with single-minded determination. Our watchers report his agents searching ancient sites, interrogating those with connections to the Order's history."

"How long do we have?" Kael asked.

"Months, perhaps. Weeks, possibly." The Lady's expression remained carefully neutral, though a tension in her jaw betrayed concern. "Time is not our ally in this matter."

Lyra felt the weight of all eyes upon her—her companions looking to her for a decision that would alter all their paths. The responsibility pressed down like a physical burden, forcing her to confront questions she had been avoiding since the Stone's loss.

Who was she without it? Who might she become with it restored? Was she prepared to sacrifice years of her life for the power to oppose Ravenna? And was that sacrifice truly hers alone to make, when its consequences would ripple outward to affect all those who depended on her?

"I need time," she finally said. "Not much, but... I can't decide this moment."

The Lady of Whispers nodded as if she had expected this response, her remarkable eyes softening with understanding. "Dawn will be soon enough. The chamber of awakening requires preparation in any case." She gestured toward an adjoining doorway. "There are quarters where you may rest and reflect. Food and fresh water have been provided."

"You were certain we would come," Mira observed with a touch of her usual skepticism.

"I was certain you would have the opportunity to choose," the woman corrected, that hint of a smile returning. "Certainty about choices belongs only to those who make them."

With that cryptic statement, she guided them to a series of small but comfortable rooms carved into the bedrock beneath Aetherhall's ruins. Each contained a simple pallet, a basin of clear water, and a tray of bread, cheese, and dried fruits. The blue globes provided gentle illumination that could be dimmed by a simple gesture.

As the Lady of Whispers turned to leave them, Alaric stepped forward. "A moment, if you would," he said, his voice controlled but intent. "In private."

She studied him briefly before nodding. "Of course." To the others, she added, "Rest well. The choice that awaits requires clarity of mind."

When they had gone, Lyra's companions naturally gravitated to her chamber. No one presumed to tell her what choice to make, but each offered perspective in their own way.

"The Stone chose you originally for a reason," Elara observed. "That connection existed for purpose beyond chance."

"Purpose doesn't obligate sacrifice," Rowan countered. "Especially when the terms have changed so dramatically."

"All meaningful choices involve sacrifice," Alaric said when he rejoined them some time later, his expression inscrutable after his private conversation with the Lady. "The question is whether this particular sacrifice serves the greater good effectively enough to justify its personal cost."

Mira, typically quick with an opinion, remained uncharacteristically silent until Lyra finally asked directly for her thoughts.

"I think," the alchemist said carefully, "that you've been searching for something since we lost the Stone. Not just the artifact itself, but the sense of direction it provided." She met Lyra's gaze directly. "But I also think you discovered something important in its absence—that your leadership never actually depended on the Stone's power. It came from something within you that exists independently."

"And if I do reclaim it," Lyra asked, voicing the concern that weighed most heavily, "how do I balance using its power against preserving my life? Every use would bring me closer to..." She couldn't quite finish the thought.

"We would help you," Elara said immediately. "I've been studying energy conservation techniques in my rune work. Some might be adaptable to your connection with the Stone—ways to buffer the drain, to make each use more efficient."

"And I could create elixirs," Mira added, her mind clearly already working on the problem. "Restoratives specifically designed to replenish life essence. They wouldn't prevent the drain entirely, but they might offset some of the effects."

"We would be vigilant," Rowan promised. "Watching for signs of excessive drain, ensuring you don't overextend yourself in moments of crisis."

Kael, who had been listening silently from his position near the door, finally spoke. "Whatever you decide, you won't face the consequences alone." The simple declaration carried weight beyond its words—a promise that transcended their current circumstances. "If you choose to take up this burden again, we'll share it however we can."

Their commitment moved her deeply. Even facing such a personal choice, she wasn't truly alone. Eventually they left her to her thoughts, each recognizing that this decision ultimately belonged to Lyra alone. She lay on the pallet in the dimmed light, her mind turning over possibilities like stones in a riverbed, examining each from all angles.

The Phoenix Stone had defined her journey for so long that its loss had left her adrift, questioning her purpose and place. Its restoration offered a return to certainty—a clear path forward with powers she understood how to wield. But that certainty came with a terrible price: years of her life burned away with each use of its power.

Lyra rose from the pallet and paced the small chamber, unable to find stillness as her thoughts churned. She found herself drawn to the basin of water, staring at her reflection in its perfect surface. The face that looked back seemed older than she remembered, marked by the experiences of recent months. The hollow at her throat where the Stone had once rested appeared as a shadow, a visible absence.

What would her parents advise if they could speak to her now? They had given their lives in opposition to the Syndicate's rise, choosing certain death over submission to what they considered unconscionable. Had they questioned that choice in their final moments? Had they regretted not choosing a longer life of compromise over a shorter one of principle?

She thought of Kael, who carried the weight of his sister's death like a stone in his heart. Of Mira, whose betrayal by a former friend had taught her the cost of misplaced trust. Of Elara, whose pursuit of knowledge had led her down paths that separated her from her family. Of Rowan, whose careful maps could never chart the territories of loss they had all traversed.

Each of them had made sacrifices. Each had surrendered something precious to stand where they now stood. Perhaps that was the nature of meaningful existence—not avoiding the hard choices, but making them with clear eyes and full hearts.

As the hours of night deepened around her, Lyra's thoughts gradually shifted from the question of whether to reclaim the Stone to how she might wield it if she did. The Lady of Whispers had spoken of a deeper bond, greater powers. What might those entail? And how could she use them most effectively while minimizing the drain on her life force?

The original connection had been instinctive, the Stone's powers manifesting primarily as protective energies and healing capabilities. But if the bond would be deeper now, perhaps she could channel its energies with greater precision, more conscious control. Perhaps she could set boundaries on how and when its power would flow, preserving her life force for specific confrontations rather than allowing it to drain continuously.

The idea took root, growing from vague possibility to defined intention as the night progressed. By the time exhaustion finally claimed her, dragging her into fitful sleep, a framework of decision had begun to form in her mind—not complete, but with its foundation laid.

Her dreams were vivid and strange. She stood in a field of golden light, the Phoenix Stone floating before her, its fractures glowing from within. As she reached for it, the fractures spread, branching like lightning across its surface. But instead of shattering, the Stone transformed, the fractures becoming a network of fiery veins that extended outward, connecting to similar veins that appeared in her own skin.

This is the true nature of the bond, a voice that might have been the Lady of Whispers or might have been the Stone itself whispered in her mind. *Not possession but partnership. Not mastery but mutual transformation.*

She woke with a start to find Kael kneeling beside her pallet, his hand gentle on her shoulder. The blue light in the chamber had brightened slightly, suggesting the approach of dawn though no natural light penetrated these underground rooms.

"You were speaking in your sleep," he said quietly, concern evident in his eyes. "Something about veins of fire."

Lyra sat up, the dream's images still vivid in her mind. "I was dreaming about the Stone. About what it might mean to reconnect with it." She rubbed her eyes, trying to organize her thoughts. "The Lady said the bond would be deeper, the power greater but at greater cost. But what if that deeper connection also means greater control? What if I could direct its energies more precisely, use them only when absolutely necessary?"

Kael considered this, his expression thoughtful. "Like drawing a sword only when combat is unavoidable, rather than wearing it unsheathed at all times."

"Exactly," she nodded, grateful for his immediate understanding. "The Stone responded to my intentions before, but the connection was... intuitive, almost unconscious. If I approach this new bond with clear boundaries and specific purpose, perhaps I can minimize the drain on my life force."

"A calculated risk," he observed, neither endorsing nor discouraging her line of thinking.

"Life is a calculated risk," she replied with a small smile. "None of us knows how many years we have. The question is how we use them, not how many we accumulate."

Something in her tone must have conveyed her growing resolution, for Kael's expression shifted subtly. "You've decided."

"I think I have." She rose, splashing water on her face from the basin. The cool shock helped clear the last cobwebs of sleep from her mind. "But I want to hear what the Lady of Whispers has to say about my conditions before I commit fully."

The others were already awake when they emerged into the corridor, their expressions a mixture of concern and curiosity. No one asked directly what she had decided, but their attentiveness spoke volumes.

"The Lady awaits in the chamber below," Elara informed them. "She said to join her when we were ready."

They descended together to the chamber where the Phoenix Stone floated in its crystalline container. The Lady of Whispers stood before it, her midnight blue robes exchanged for ceremonial garments of silver-white that caught the light like moonbeams on water. Her remarkable eyes—now decidedly violet in the chamber's illumination—studied Lyra's face as they entered.

Alaric's reaction to seeing the Lady in her ceremonial attire was subtle but unmistakable—a brief tightening around his eyes, a tension in his shoulders that suggested the sight awakened specific memories. Whatever history lay between them clearly ran deeper than mere acquaintance.

"You've reflected," she stated rather than asked. "And reached a decision."

"I have." Lyra squared her shoulders, drawing strength from the presence of her companions at her back. "I will reawaken the Phoenix Stone—but on my own terms."

The Lady's eyebrow rose slightly, the gesture emphasizing the perfect arch of its shape. "The ritual has requirements that cannot be negotiated."

"I'm not negotiating the ritual," Lyra clarified. "I'm establishing conditions for what follows. The Stone's power will be used specifically to counter Ravenna and the threat he poses with the Midnight Stone fragment he carries. Not for other conflicts, not for lesser threats that can be addressed through conventional means."

Understanding dawned in the woman's eyes, their color shifting subtly toward blue. "You seek to minimize the drain on your life force by limiting the Stone's use to essential confrontations."

"Exactly," Lyra confirmed. "The Stone responds to intent and necessity. If my intent is focused and specific, the bond should respect those boundaries."

The Lady of Whispers considered this for a long moment, her long fingers tracing patterns in the air as if testing invisible currents. "Your reasoning is sound. The Stone's awakening can indeed be shaped by the bearer's intentions during the ritual." A faint smile touched her lips, illuminating her face with unexpected warmth. "You understand its nature better than many who have studied it for decades."

"I carried it," Lyra said simply. "We learned each other's ways."

"Then let us proceed," the Lady replied, a new respect evident in her gaze. "The chamber is prepared. The stars are aligned. All that remains is your willing participation in the ritual of awakening."

CHAPTER SEVENTEEN

Bloodlines Revealed

Lyra stared at the ancient text spread across the monastery's library table, her fingers tracing the faded illustrations that depicted three artifacts of immense power. The Phoenix Stone—now lost in the temple collapse—glowed golden in the left illustration. The Midnight Stone—presumably still in Ravenna's possession—dominated the right in obsidian darkness. But it was the central image that had captured her attention: a crystalline structure shattered into seven distinct pieces, each containing swirling colors that seemed to move even on the static page.

"The Shattered Illusion," Alaric confirmed, noting her focus. "The original source from which both the Phoenix and Midnight Stones were derived."

The ancient library of Aetherhall had yielded this revelation just hours ago, hidden in texts so old that even Alaric had struggled to translate their archaic language. The Lady of Whispers—an enigmatic member of the Order of the Veiled Sky—had guided them to this specific tome after confirming that the

Phoenix Stone had indeed survived the temple collapse, though in a drastically altered state.

"I don't understand," Lyra admitted, frustration evident in her voice. "If the Shattered Illusion was the original artifact, why have we never heard of it? Why focus on the Phoenix Stone all this time?"

"Because history is written by those who survive to tell it," Alaric replied, his weathered hand carefully turning the brittle page to reveal additional text. "The Shattered Illusion was believed completely destroyed during the Mage Wars. Only those with the deepest knowledge of arcane history knew that fragments survived—and that two of those fragments were eventually shaped into what became known as the Phoenix and Midnight Stones."

Elara leaned closer, her scholar's interest piqued by the intricate diagrams surrounding the central illustration. "These runes suggest the Shattered Illusion possessed capabilities far beyond either derivative Stone. It could not only seal rifts but actually repair the damage to the fabric of reality."

"And perhaps more importantly," Rowan added, looking up from his own research at a neighboring table, "according to these cartographic notes, it could locate all existing rifts simultaneously. My family's Wayfinder compass was apparently modeled on this capability, though with significantly reduced power."

Kael, who had been maintaining a vigilant watch near the library entrance, joined their conversation. His face betrayed none of the turmoil that had been brewing within him since they'd arrived at Aetherhall. The revelation about the Shattered Illusion had awakened memories he'd fought to suppress—memories of his sister Lirien, and how his failure to protect her had led to her capture by the Syndicate seven years ago.

"So instead of continuing to search for the Phoenix Stone, you're suggesting we try to locate these fragments of the original artifact?" he asked, forcing his thoughts back to the present. His hand unconsciously moved to the jagged scar along his jaw—a permanent reminder of the day he'd lost Lirien.

"Not just locate them," Mira interjected, setting down a mortar and pestle where she'd been grinding herbs to treat Rowan's still-healing hands. "According to what the Lady told us, if we can gather enough fragments, they might naturally recombine—essentially reforming a version of the original Shattered Illusion."

"Which would give us power beyond what the Phoenix Stone alone could provide," Lyra concluded, her hand rising unconsciously to her throat where the Stone had once rested. The phantom warmth she occasionally felt had intensified since arriving at Aetherhall, as if responding to the knowledge they uncovered.

Alaric nodded gravely. "The Phoenix Stone was always meant to be a temporary solution—a tool to contain rifts, not heal them. The Shattered Illusion represents something far more fundamental to the structure of our world."

"But if these fragments are so powerful, why hasn't Ravenna pursued them?" Kael asked, ever focused on strategic implications. Behind his measured tone lay a deeper question that he couldn't voice aloud: Could these fragments hold the key to finding Lirien, if she still lived?

"Because he likely didn't know," Alaric replied. "This knowledge was carefully guarded by the original Wardens, of which I was the last. The Order of the Veiled Sky preserved these texts, but kept them hidden from all but their most trusted members."

"Until now," Lyra observed. "Why reveal this to us?"

"Because Veyra's influence grows stronger," came a voice from the library entrance. The Lady of Whispers stood there, her face partially concealed by the traditional veil of her Order. "The rifts widen. The barriers thin. The Phoenix Stone alone was never going to be sufficient."

She approached their table with measured steps, her movements graceful despite her apparent age. "There is something else you should know about the fragments," she continued, her voice carrying the weight of reluctant revelation. "They respond to bloodlines—to those whose ancestors once wielded the complete artifact."

Her gaze fixed on Lyra with uncomfortable intensity. "Your parents weren't simply scholars who opposed the Syndicate. They were descendants of the original Keepers of the Illusion. That's why the Phoenix Stone chose you, why it responded to your touch as it did to no other."

Lyra felt the room tilt slightly as this revelation settled over her. "My parents never mentioned anything about this."

"They likely didn't know," the Lady replied. "The knowledge was deliberately obscured generations ago, to protect those bloodlines from those who would exploit them." Her gaze shifted briefly to Alaric. "Some secrets were deemed too dangerous to preserve, even in memory."

"And Ravenna?" Lyra asked, a terrible suspicion forming. "Is that why he keeps my parents' bones? Does he share this bloodline connection?"

The Lady's expression grew troubled behind her partial veil. "No. But he has learned enough to understand that their remains might provide a magical connection to the fragments—a way to locate them through sympathetic resonance with your bloodline."

"So we're in a race," Kael concluded grimly, his mind already mapping potential strategies. "To find these fragments before Ravenna can use Lyra's parents' remains to locate them himself."

"Precisely," the Lady confirmed. "And we believe the first fragment is located at Blackspire Fortress, a Syndicate stronghold three days' journey northeast of here."

Kael's heart stuttered in his chest. Blackspire. The name struck him like a physical blow, though he maintained his outward composure through sheer force of will. Blackspire was where Lirien had been taken—the last place anyone had seen her alive. For years he'd gathered scraps of information about the fortress, planning a rescue that never materialized as the evidence of her survival grew increasingly thin.

"Blackspire?" he managed, his voice betraying none of the storm raging within. "I know it. A former military outpost that fell to the Syndicate five years ago. Heavily fortified, difficult to approach undetected."

"And you believe a fragment of the Shattered Illusion is there?" Lyra asked, skepticism evident in her tone.

The Lady nodded. "Our intelligence suggests Ravenna has been gathering resources there for months—specialized equipment, rare materials, scholars with expertise in ancient artifacts. The pattern is consistent with preparation for a major ritual."

Rowan spread his maps across the table, quickly locating the fortress. "The approach is challenging—open terrain for miles around, with the fortress itself situated on high ground. A frontal assault would be suicide."

"We're not an army," Mira pointed out. "Stealth would be our only option."

Lyra studied the map, her finger tracing the routes leading to Blackspire. Something felt wrong—a dissonance she couldn't immediately identify. The phantom warmth at her throat pulsed irregularly, as if trying to communicate a warning.

"Lady," she said slowly, "how certain are your sources about the fragment's location?"

The veiled woman tilted her head slightly. "As certain as one can be in matters of ancient power. Why do you ask?"

"Because..." Lyra hesitated, struggling to articulate her intuition. "Because something doesn't feel right. If Ravenna has my parents' remains, and they provide a connection to the fragments through my bloodline, shouldn't I feel something too? Some pull toward Blackspire?"

Alaric's eyes narrowed with sudden interest. "You're sensing something else?"

"Not exactly," Lyra admitted. "More like... an absence where there should be presence. If a fragment were at Blackspire, wouldn't my blood recognize it, just as the Lady says the fragments would recognize me?"

A thoughtful silence fell over the group as they considered this possibility. The Lady of Whispers studied Lyra with renewed intensity, her remarkable eyes visible through the partial veil seeming to shift color in the library's muted light.

"Your intuition serves you well," she finally said. "The bloodline connection is indeed a two-way resonance. If you feel no pull toward Blackspire..."

"Then either there's no fragment there," Kael finished, a complex mixture of emotions churning within him. If they weren't going to Blackspire, his chance to search for Lirien would vanish—yet another failure to add to the weight he carried. "Or something is blocking the connection."

"Or," Alaric added quietly, "our information about Blackspire is deliberate misdirection."

The Lady inclined her head slightly. "A concerning possibility. The Order's intelligence network is extensive but not infallible. Ravenna has proven adept at manipulating information channels before."

"So we could be walking into a trap," Mira concluded bluntly. "Wonderful."

Lyra closed her eyes, focusing on the phantom warmth at her throat. If it truly represented her bloodline's connection to the fragments, perhaps she could use it as a compass of sorts. She quieted her mind, letting the sensation expand through her awareness, searching for any directional pull or resonance.

For several moments, nothing happened. Then, faintly but unmistakably, she felt it—a tug that seemed to originate from somewhere northeast, but not in the direction of Blackspire as marked on Rowan's map. The sensation was subtle but definite, like a thread pulling gently but insistently on her consciousness.

"There is a fragment," she said, opening her eyes. "But not at Blackspire. It's..." She turned, orienting herself by the library's windows, then pointed. "That direction. Further east than Blackspire, and slightly more north."

Kael felt a complex mix of disappointment and relief. The possibility of finding Lirien slipped further away, yet the mission would continue on safer ground—away from the fortress where he'd failed so catastrophically before.

Rowan immediately consulted his maps, tracing a line from their current position in the direction Lyra indicated. "That would put it somewhere in the vicinity of the Sentinel Range. Rugged territory, sparsely populated."

"The Sentinel Range," Alaric repeated, recognition flaring in his eyes. "Of course. Sentinel's Reach."

"You know the place?" Kael asked, forcing himself to focus on the task at hand rather than his personal ghosts.

"An ancient watchtower, built during the earliest days of the Wardens," Alaric explained. "It stands at the convergence of forest, mountain, and plain—a natural nexus point for magical energies. We used it to monitor the boundaries between realms long before the Shattered Illusion was created."

The Lady of Whispers had gone very still, her composure momentarily disrupted by this revelation. "Sentinel's Reach," she murmured. "The archives mentioned it, but we believed it destroyed centuries ago."

"Not destroyed," Alaric corrected. "Hidden. Removed from common knowledge through selective memory manipulation—a specialty of the Order in its early days, as I recall."

A subtle tension entered the exchange, hinting at old conflicts between Alaric and the Order that had never been fully resolved. The Lady recovered her poise quickly, however.

"If a fragment is indeed at Sentinel's Reach rather than Blackspire, we must reconsider our approach entirely." She turned to Rowan. "Do your maps show the watchtower's location?"

Rowan shook his head. "No, but if Alaric can describe its position relative to known landmarks, I could approximate it."

As Alaric and Rowan bent over the maps, Lyra exchanged glances with Kael, a silent communication passing between them. She had noticed his reaction to the mention of Blackspire, the momentary tension that had crossed his face before his disciplined control reasserted itself. He nodded slightly, acknowledging her concern but indicating now was not the time to discuss it.

"What about your intelligence regarding Ravenna's activities at Blackspire?" Lyra asked the veiled woman. "If the fragment isn't there, what is he doing with the resources your sources observed?"

"A question worth investigating," the Lady conceded. "The Syndicate's interest in Blackspire remains significant, regardless of whether a fragment is present. Perhaps..." She hesitated, then continued with apparent reluctance. "Perhaps Ravenna has planted false information, knowing we would pass it to you."

"Which means he knows about our connection to the Order," Kael noted grimly. "Our movements may be compromised."

"Not necessarily," Alaric interjected, looking up from the maps. "It could be simpler than that. Ravenna may have genuine operations at Blackspire—operations important enough to protect with misinformation—while simultaneously pursuing the fragment at Sentinel's Reach."

"A diversion," Mira realized. "He wants us to focus on Blackspire while he secures the fragment elsewhere."

"Or," Elara suggested, speaking for the first time since the discussion began, "he doesn't know the fragment's true location either. Perhaps he's searching both places simultaneously."

This possibility created a momentary silence as they considered its implications. If Ravenna was as uncertain as they were, it might explain the dispersal of resources between multiple locations. It also suggested they might still have time to reach the fragment before him.

"I've located it," Rowan announced, placing a marker on his map. "Based on Alaric's description, Sentinel's Reach should be here—approximately three days' journey northeast, in the foothills where the Sentinel Range meets the Verdant Plains."

They gathered around the map, studying the terrain. Unlike Blackspire's exposed position, Sentinel's Reach appeared to be nestled among forested foothills, with multiple approach routes offering natural cover.

"The journey will be challenging," Rowan continued, tracing potential paths with his finger. "We'll need to cross the Mistwood, then navigate these highland meadows before reaching the foothills. Weather could be a factor this time of year—early storms sometimes sweep down from the mountains with little warning."

"And we must assume Ravenna has forces in the area," Kael added, his tactical mind already assessing threats despite his personal turmoil. "If he's using Lyra's parents' remains to search for the fragment, he may have detected its presence at Sentinel's Reach by now."

"Then we have no time to waste," Lyra decided, the phantom warmth at her throat pulsing in what felt like agreement. "We leave for Sentinel's Reach at dawn."

The Lady of Whispers nodded. "The Order will provide what assistance we can—supplies, maps of safe passages, protective tokens. But be warned: if Ravenna has indeed discovered the fragment's location, he will stop at nothing to claim it before you arrive."

"What about Blackspire?" Mira asked. "If something significant is happening there as well, shouldn't we investigate both locations?"

Kael's heart leapt at the suggestion, though his expression remained impassive. Perhaps there was still a chance to learn what had happened to Lirien.

"We don't have enough people to split our forces effectively," he replied after a moment's consideration, practicality overriding personal desire. "And the fragment must take priority. Whatever Ravenna is doing at Blackspire, it can't be as important as securing a piece of the Shattered Illusion."

The words tasted like ash in his mouth, but he knew they were true. The mission had to come before his personal quest—too many lives depended on their success. He'd learned that lesson at terrible cost seven years ago, when he'd abandoned his post to search for Lirien, only to fail in rescuing her while leaving others vulnerable in his absence.

"I agree," Lyra said. "The fragment is our primary objective. Once it's secured, we can turn our attention to Blackspire if necessary."

With their course decided, they spent the remaining hours before dawn in preparation—studying maps, gathering supplies, and resting as much as possible before the journey ahead. The Lady of Whispers provided them with small tokens of protection—river stones inscribed with the Order's crescent-and-line symbol, which she claimed would shield them from minor magical detection.

"Not all dangers announce themselves with drawn swords," she cautioned as she pressed the smooth stones into their palms. "These will help against subtle threats, though they cannot conceal you from direct observation."

While the others prepared, Kael found himself drawn to one of the monastery's small meditation gardens—a tranquil space where a single maple tree stood sentinel over a carefully arranged rock garden. The night air carried a hint of frost, but he welcomed the cold, using it to focus his thoughts away from memories of Lirien.

"You recognized the name Blackspire," Lyra said quietly, appearing beside him with the silent grace that had become characteristic of her movements. "More than just knowing of the fortress."

Kael didn't turn to face her immediately. Instead, he watched the gentle movement of the maple's leaves in the night breeze, considering how much to reveal. Lyra had shared her burdens with the group—her parents' deaths, her bloodline connection to the Shattered Illusion. Perhaps it was time he did the same.

"My sister Lirien was taken there," he said finally, his voice steady despite the pain the words evoked. "Seven years ago. She had magical abilities—minor compared to someone like Elara, but noticeable. The Syndicate came for her during a festival in our village."

"I didn't know you had a sister," Lyra said softly.

"Few do." Kael's hand rose unconsciously to the scar on his jaw. "I tried to stop them. Failed. This is my reminder of that failure."

"And you've been looking for her since?"

"When I could. Between assignments, during leave periods. I've gathered information, tracked rumors, bribed informants." He shook his head slightly. "The trail grew cold years ago. Most who go to Blackspire don't return."

"Yet you still hope," Lyra observed. It wasn't a question.

"Hope is a luxury I can't afford," Kael replied, though they both recognized the lie in his words. "But I need to know what happened to her. Whether she lived or died. Whether my failure was absolute or merely..." He trailed off, unable to find words that didn't sound like excuses.

"That's why you've always been so protective of our group," Lyra realized. "Why you take each threat so personally."

Kael nodded, finally turning to meet her gaze. "I failed Lirien. I won't fail again—not you, not any of you." The intensity in his eyes conveyed what he couldn't bring himself to say directly: that somewhere along their journey together, his companions had become the family he'd lost, and Lyra in particular had come to mean more to him than he dared acknowledge.

"When we've secured the fragment," she said after a moment, "we'll find a way to investigate Blackspire. I promise you that."

"The mission comes first," Kael insisted, though gratitude warmed his voice. "I've learned that lesson. Personal quests can't supersede the greater need."

"They're not always separate," Lyra countered gently. "Finding your sister—learning what Ravenna is doing at Blackspire—those things may be integral to understanding the larger pattern we're facing."

Her words offered a perspective he hadn't allowed himself to consider—that his personal quest might align with their shared mission rather than distract from it. The thought eased something within him, a knot of tension he'd carried for so long he'd forgotten it wasn't a natural part of his being.

"We should join the others," he said finally. "Dawn will come quickly, and the journey to Sentinel's Reach won't be easy."

As they returned to the monastery's main hall, Kael felt lighter than he had in years. The burden of his failure remained, but sharing it had somehow made it more bearable. For the first time since losing Lirien, he allowed himself to believe that redemption might be possible—not through self-punishment or solitary crusading, but through the bonds he'd formed with these companions who had, against all odds, become his chosen family.

They departed Aetherhall as the first rays of sunlight crested the eastern mountains, casting long shadows across the valley. The path descended through alpine meadows dotted with early morning frost, then entered the denser cover of the Mistwood as the day brightened around them. Within the forest, sound became muffled and visibility limited, creating an enclosed world of filtered light and shadow.

Rowan took the lead, his affinity for woodland navigation proving invaluable as what began as a clear trail gradually faded into game paths and then seemingly trackless underbrush. Kael positioned himself at the rear, maintaining vigilant watch for any signs of pursuit. His revelation to Lyra the previous night had left him feeling strangely vulnerable, yet also more centered—as if acknowledging his past had somehow clarified his present purpose.

By midday, they had penetrated deep into the Mistwood, where ancient trees towered overhead and moss carpeted the forest floor. During a brief rest beside a clear-running stream, Lyra found herself studying a massive oak whose trunk must have been at least twenty feet in circumference.

"That tree has witnessed more history than any living person," Rowan commented, noticing her interest. "Probably stood here since before the Mage Wars."

"You speak as if trees have consciousness," Mira observed, refilling her water flask from the stream.

"Not as we understand it," Rowan replied. "But awareness? Yes. The forest is aware in ways we've forgotten how to perceive."

The conversation drifted into philosophical territory as they resumed their journey—discussions of consciousness, perception, and humanity's estrangement from the natural world. Even Kael, typically focused on more immediate tactical concerns, contributed thoughtfully to the exchange.

"My combat instructors taught that true mastery comes when you no longer perceive yourself as separate from your weapon," he said. "Perhaps that's a shadow of what Rowan describes—the dissolution of artificial boundaries between self and other."

He thought of Lirien as he spoke, remembering how she had described her magical abilities in similar terms—not as power she wielded but as a connection she experienced, a harmony with energies that flowed through her rather than from her. At the time, he hadn't fully understood. His own training had emphasized control, discipline, the imposition of will rather than surrender to connection.

Now, after months of traveling with companions whose abilities ranged from Elara's methodical rune-casting to Lyra's intuitive channeling of the Phoenix Stone, he was beginning to grasp what Lirien had tried to explain. Perhaps if he had understood sooner, he might have better protected her—might have recognized the danger before it was too late.

"The mages of the eastern isles have a similar concept," Alaric added, drawing Kael from his thoughts. "They call it 'heart-mind unity'—the state where thought and feeling, self and surroundings, become a single flowing experience rather than fragmented pieces."

Lyra listened with interest, struck by how their disparate backgrounds and disciplines converged on similar truths. As they spoke, she felt the phantom warmth at her throat respond subtly, pulsing in a rhythm that seemed to harmonize with their conversation. Perhaps this was part of what it meant to be a Keeper—this ability to sense connections that others might miss.

They made camp that evening in a small clearing beside a brook that chattered over smooth stones. As twilight deepened into true night, the forest around them came alive with sound—owls calling, small creatures rustling through underbrush, the distant howl of what might have been wolves. The companions gathered around their modest fire, its light creating a bubble of warmth against the encroaching darkness.

"We should discuss what we know about these fragments," Kael said, breaking a comfortable silence that had settled over the group. The day's journey had helped settle his mind, focusing his thoughts on the mission ahead rather than the painful memories Blackspire had evoked. "The Lady of Whispers provided information, but much remains unclear."

"According to the texts I studied," Elara began, retrieving a small leather-bound journal from her pack, "the Shattered Illusion was divided into seven fragments during the Mage Wars. Each fragment retained a portion of the original's power, but with distinct properties."

"Properties like the Phoenix Stone's healing capabilities and the Midnight Ston e's... darker aspects?" Mira asked.

"Precisely," Alaric confirmed. "The Phoenix and Midnight Stones were actually two fragments that were further shaped and refined over centuries. The remaining five fragments were thought lost—scattered across Sylvanthia in the chaos following the wars."

"And these fragments respond to Lyra's bloodline," Rowan noted. "Which means they might reveal themselves to her in ways they wouldn't to others."

Lyra considered this. "I've felt... something since we learned about the fragments. Like an echo of the Phoenix Stone's warmth, but different. Less focused, more... potential."

"That's the resonance beginning," Alaric explained. "As we draw closer to Sentinel's Reach, it should intensify. The fragment there will recognize your approach."

"Which raises another question," Kael pointed out. "If Lyra can sense the fragments, and Ravenna has access to her parents' remains, might he not sense them as well?"

The question had been troubling him since their discovery about the bloodline connection. If Ravenna could track the fragments using Lyra's parents' remains, it created a terrible vulnerability—one that placed Lyra directly in the Syndicate leader's sights.

A troubled silence followed this observation. Finally, Alaric spoke. "It's possible, though the connection would be weaker through remains than through a living descendant. Still, we should proceed with the assumption that we are not alone in this search."

"Wonderful," Mira sighed. "A race against a homicidal sorcerer with a fondness for necromancy. Just how I hoped to spend the season."

Despite the gravity of their situation, Lyra found herself smiling at Mira's characteristic sarcasm. These moments of normalcy—of friendship and humor amid uncertainty—had become precious anchors in a world that seemed increasingly unmoored from everything familiar.

Kael watched the interaction with quiet appreciation. The bond that had formed among their group represented everything he had failed to protect with Lirien—not just physical safety but emotional connection, the sense of belonging that transcended blood relations. He had sworn to himself after losing his sister that he would never again allow himself such vulnerability, yet here he was, irrevocably tied to these companions through bonds stronger than mere duty or shared purpose.

The second day of travel brought them to the edge of the Mistwood, where the dense forest gradually gave way to rolling highland meadows. The landscape opened around them, providing expansive views of the terrain ahead—including the distant silhouette of the Sentinel Range, its peaks partially obscured by clouds. The phantom warmth at Lyra's throat had intensified noticeably, confirming they were moving in the right direction.

By midafternoon, dark clouds had begun gathering on the western horizon, promising rain before nightfall. They quickened their pace, hoping to reach more sheltered terrain before the storm broke. The highland meadows, beautiful in their autumn colors, offered little protection from the elements.

"There's a settlement ahead," Rowan announced, pointing toward a cluster of buildings nestled in a valley perhaps two miles distant. "Small, but large enough to possibly offer an inn or tavern."

"Risky," Kael cautioned, his protective instincts immediately assessing potential threats. "We don't know its allegiances."

"We also don't know if that storm will pass us by or drench us to the bone," Mira countered, eyeing the approaching weather. "I vote for potential beds and a hot meal over certainly soggy bedrolls."

After brief deliberation, they decided to approach the settlement—cautiously, with a cover story prepared and an agreement to withdraw at the first sign of trouble. As they drew closer, they could see it was indeed a small village, primarily constructed around what appeared to be a crossroads where two trade routes intersected.

"Crosshaven," Elara read from a weathered signpost at the village's edge. "I've never heard of it."

"Nor I," Alaric said, "which suggests it holds little strategic importance. That may work in our favor."

They entered the village as the first heavy drops of rain began to fall, quickening their pace toward a two-story building that bore the unmistakable signs of a tavern—warm light spilling from its windows, the sounds of conversation and occasional laughter drifting outward. A wooden sign swinging in the strengthening wind depicted a black crow perched atop a crossed pair of swords.

"The Crow and Blade," Mira read. "Charming."

The interior proved more welcoming than the name suggested. A large hearth dominated one wall, its fire casting dancing light across worn but clean floorboards. Perhaps two dozen patrons occupied tables scattered throughout the room, their conversations creating a pleasant background murmur. A long bar stretched along the opposite wall, behind which a broad-shouldered man with a neatly trimmed beard polished tankards with methodical care.

Their entrance drew some glances but no particular alarm—just the normal curiosity directed toward newcomers in a small community. They secured a table near the hearth and ordered food and drink from a serving girl whose cheerful efficiency suggested long practice.

"What brings you folks to Crosshaven?" she asked as she set down bowls of hearty stew and tankards of amber ale. "Not many travelers this time of year, what with the bandit troubles in the hills."

"We're headed northeast," Lyra replied, sticking to their agreed-upon story. "Family business in Tarlton."

The girl—who had introduced herself as Bree—nodded sympathetically. "Rough journey. The north road's not what it once was since the Syndicate expanded their territory." She lowered her voice slightly. "Between you and me, I'd consider the western route through Millerton. Longer, but less likely to encounter their patrols."

"The Syndicate has a presence in this region?" Kael asked, his tone carefully casual while his senses heightened to full alert. Any mention of the Syndicate triggered both his protective instincts and painful memories of Lirien.

"More so lately," Bree confirmed. "They've been recruiting in the outlying farms—offering protection in exchange for loyalty oaths and a share of the harvest. Some have accepted." Her expression suggested what she thought of such arrangements.

"And Crosshaven itself?" Elara inquired. "Where do its allegiances lie?"

Bree glanced around before answering. "We maintain neutrality, officially. The village is too small to resist if they decided to take it by force, but so far we've been left alone." She straightened as another patron signaled for service. "Enjoy your meal. If you need rooms for the night, we have three available upstairs."

As she moved away, they exchanged glances laden with unspoken communication. The village's precarious independence presented both opportunity and risk—a place not yet under Syndicate control, but close enough to their influence to potentially harbor sympathizers or informants.

"We should move on after the meal," Kael suggested quietly. "Find somewhere less populated to make camp."

"In this weather?" Mira gestured toward the windows, where rain now lashed against the glass panes. "We'd be miserable and exhausted by morning."

"I agree with Mira," Rowan said. "One night here poses minimal risk if we maintain our cover. We can depart at first light."

The debate continued in hushed tones until a commotion at the tavern's entrance drew their attention. Three figures had entered, shaking water from their cloaks with the casual entitlement of those accustomed to deference. Their attire marked them as soldiers of some kind—not the distinctive uniforms of the Syndicate's main forces, but something similar in design if less formal.

"Syndicate auxiliaries," Alaric murmured, recognition in his eyes. "Local recruits given limited authority to act on the organization's behalf."

The tavern's atmosphere had shifted subtly with their arrival. Conversations continued but at lower volume, and several patrons found reasons to finish their drinks and depart. The barkeeper's previously relaxed posture had tensed, though he maintained a professional smile as the newcomers approached his counter.

Kael felt his muscles coil with instinctive readiness, his hand dropping casually to rest near his sword hilt beneath the table. He'd encountered auxiliaries before during his searches for Lirien—men and women who'd traded their autonomy for the illusion of power, often becoming more zealous than full Syndicate members in their enforcement of regulations.

"Patrol went well then, Gareth?" the barkeeper asked, already reaching for clean tankards.

"Well enough," the lead soldier replied, a stocky man with a scar bisecting his left eyebrow. "Roads are quiet despite the weather. No sign of the troublemakers from Wellspring."

"Glad to hear it," the barkeeper said, sliding filled tankards across the counter. "First round's on the house, as usual."

The exchange seemed practiced, suggesting this was a regular occurrence. The auxiliaries took their drinks to a table near the door, their posture relaxed but their eyes alert as they surveyed the room. When their gaze passed over Lyra's group, Kael felt Lyra tense beside him, her hand dropping casually to rest near the dagger at her belt.

"Easy," he murmured. "We're just travelers passing through."

The next hour passed with excruciating slowness. They finished their meal and ordered a second round of drinks to avoid appearing hurried, engaging in deliberately mundane conversation about fictional relatives in Tarlton. The auxiliaries seemed content to mind their own business, though Kael noticed their leader—Gareth—glancing their way more frequently as the evening progressed.

Finally, when the tension had wound Kael's nerves to near-breaking point, they settled their bill and made arrangements for two rooms upstairs. As they rose to leave, Gareth's voice cut through the ambient noise of the tavern.

"You folks headed northeast, I hear?"

They turned to find him watching them with casual interest, one arm draped over the back of his chair. Nothing in his posture suggested immediate threat, but the deliberate nature of the question sent alarm racing through Kael's veins. He stepped slightly forward, positioning himself between the auxiliary leader and Lyra in a movement so natural it appeared coincidental.

"That's right," Kael answered, his tone neutral. "Family matters in Tarlton."

Gareth nodded slowly. "Interesting time to travel. Roads aren't as safe as they once were."

"So we've been told," Lyra replied, forcing a smile. "But some journeys can't wait for perfect conditions."

"True enough." Gareth studied them for a moment longer, his gaze lingering on Kael's scarred jaw before shifting to the others. Something in his expression made Kael's combat instincts flare—not immediate danger, but recognition. The auxiliary knew something, or thought he did. "Word of advice—stick to the main roads and travel by daylight. The hills harbor more dangers than just bandits these days."

"We appreciate the warning," Kael said with a slight nod, fighting the urge to place his hand on his sword hilt. "Good evening to you."

They ascended the narrow staircase to their rooms, maintaining composed expressions until the door closed behind them. Only then did the façade crack, tension releasing in a collective exhalation.

"He suspects something," Kael stated flatly, moving to the window to scan the street below. The rain continued unabated, sheets of water illuminated by occasional flashes of distant lightning. Perfect conditions for an ambush—poor visibility, masked sounds, limited escape routes.

"He's suspicious by nature and training," Elara countered. "That doesn't mean he knows anything specific about us."

"The way he looked at your scar," Lyra said quietly to Kael. "It was... deliberate."

Kael nodded grimly. The scar was distinctive, and if Ravenna had distributed descriptions of them to his forces, it would be an identifying feature. "We should leave before dawn," he suggested. "Avoid further interaction if possible."

"Either way, we should leave before dawn," Rowan suggested. "Avoid further interaction if possible."

They agreed on a departure time and divided into the two rooms—Lyra, Elara, and Mira taking one while Kael, Rowan, and Alaric occupied the other. Despite his exhaustion, Kael found sleep elusive. His thoughts circled between concern for their current situation and memories of Lirien—the way her eyes had widened in terror as the Syndicate soldiers dragged her away, how her outstretched hand had reached for his as he lay bleeding on the ground, unable to rise and fight.

He moved to the window, watching the rain-slick street below for any sign of movement. The revelation to Lyra about his sister had unlocked something within him—a door he'd kept firmly shut for seven years. Now memories and emotions flooded through, threatening to overwhelm the careful control he'd maintained for so long.

"You should rest," Alaric said quietly from his bedroll. "I'll take first watch."

"I'm fine," Kael replied automatically.

"You're not," the ancient mage countered gently. "You haven't been since Blackspire was mentioned. Sharing your burden with Lyra was a beginning, but healing requires more than simply speaking the words."

Kael remained silent, his gaze fixed on the empty street below. How could he explain that rest meant nightmares—Lirien's face contorted in pain, her voice calling his name as she disappeared into darkness? How could he admit that his failure haunted him not just in waking thoughts but in dreams he couldn't escape?

"She wouldn't want this for you," Alaric continued, as if reading his thoughts. "This self-punishment. This isolation even among friends."

"You didn't know her," Kael said, more sharply than he intended.

"No," Alaric agreed. "But I know what it is to lose those we love. To carry that weight across years—across centuries, in my case. And I know that the path you've chosen leads only to more pain, not redemption."

CHAPTER EIGHTEEN

Veyra's Design

T he chamber was neither here nor there—a space that existed in the interstices between realities, accessible only to those who had transcended conventional existence. Shadows moved like liquid across walls that sometimes appeared solid stone and other times seemed formed of pure energy. The air, if such a mundane term could be applied, vibrated with potential, dense with power that would have crushed a mortal mind to madness within seconds.

At the chamber's center hovered a figure both magnificent and terrible. Once human, Veyra had evolved far beyond such limitations. Her form shifted constantly, sometimes appearing as the beautiful sorceress she had been three centuries earlier, sometimes as a being of pure shadow with only the suggestion of humanoid shape, and occasionally as something so alien that even language failed to capture its essence.

Currently, she had chosen to manifest in her more human aspect—a tall woman with features of striking perfection, midnight hair cascading to her waist, eyes like twin abysses that contained swirling galaxies of violet light. She wore robes that seemed woven from the very shadows that filled the chamber, their edges blurring into the surrounding darkness.

Before her floated a viewing portal—not a physical window but a tear in reality that allowed observation of the mortal realm. Through it, she watched with cool assessment as Lyra and her companions made camp in the heart of the Eastern Wilds, beneath the ancient Heart Tree.

"How touching," she remarked, her voice carrying harmonics impossible in human speech. "My old teacher, playing mentor to a new generation of hopeful fools."

"They've proven more resilient than anticipated," observed a figure who knelt at the edge of the chamber. Corvus, leader of the shadow-binders and most favored of Veyra's Voices, maintained a respectful distance from his mistress. Unlike the other Voices who served merely as conduits for Veyra's will, Corvus retained his individual consciousness—a privilege that came with both honor and considerable risk.

"Resilience is not unexpected in those Alaric chooses to guide," Veyra replied, a hint of something almost like fondness coloring her tone. "He always did have an eye for potential. One of his few genuine talents."

She waved a hand dismissively, and the viewing portal shifted to show another location—Sentinel's Reach, where Ravenna worked feverishly over an artifact that pulsed with multicolored light. The silver-eyed man looked increasingly unwell, dark veins spreading across his visible skin as he manipulated energies beyond his full comprehension.

"And our ambitious friend continues his attempts to control what he cannot possibly understand," she observed with cold amusement. "How predictably human."

"He believes he serves you," Corvus noted, careful to keep any judgment from his tone.

Veyra's laugh held no warmth. "He serves only his own grandiose delusions. But his efforts are useful, nonetheless. The fragment responds to his manipulations, becoming increasingly unstable. Soon it will create exactly the kind of disruption we require."

"And the girl?" Corvus asked. "Lyra? She carries the Phoenix Stone. If she reaches Sentinel's Reach before the fragment fully destabilizes..."

"Oh, I'm counting on it," Veyra replied, her smile revealing teeth too sharp to be human. "The Stone's interaction with the fragment will accelerate the process beautifully. Particularly when blood is spilled in the confrontation—which it inevitably will be."

She turned from the viewing portal, her form shifting slightly as she moved, occasionally becoming transparent enough that the stars visible through her torso seemed to be part of her being rather than merely visible through it.

"You disapprove, my faithful Corvus? I can sense your hesitation."

The shadow-binder bowed his head lower, knowing better than to attempt deception. "I merely question whether Ravenna can be controlled once the fragment's power begins to transform him. He already shows signs of... independent thinking."

"Control is such a limited concept," Veyra replied, circling her kneeling servant with predatory grace. "I don't need to control Ravenna. I simply need him to create sufficient chaos at precisely the right moment. What happens to him afterward is irrelevant."

She paused, tilting her head as if listening to something beyond mortal hearing. "The convergence approaches more rapidly than even I anticipated. The Stone awakens. The fragments respond. The rifts widen." Her eyes flashed with excitement that bordered on mania. "After three centuries of preparation, the Veil thins enough for true manipulation."

Corvus remained silent, recognizing the shift in his mistress's mood. When the madness of power took her, it was safer to be overlooked than noticed.

"You think me mad," she stated, suddenly directly before him though he hadn't seen her move. One shadow-formed hand lifted his chin, forcing him to meet those abyssal eyes. "All visionaries are thought mad by those of lesser imagination. Even Alaric, with all his supposed wisdom, could never grasp the true potential of existence beyond conventional boundaries."

"I would never presume to judge, Mistress," Corvus replied carefully.

"No? Then you are unique among sentient beings." She released him, her form shifting again to something less human—taller, with limbs that bent at impossible angles and a face that seemed to contain too many features arranged in disturbing configurations. "Even the Watchers judge, from their lofty perches between realities. They observe and evaluate and occasionally interfere when they believe balance is threatened."

She spat the word "balance" as if it tasted foul. "As if stagnation were preferable to evolution. As if the natural order of existence weren't constant change, constant becoming."

With a visible effort, she composed herself, her form settling back into the more human appearance. "But I digress. You've come to report on the shadow-binders' preparations, I assume?"

Grateful for the return to practical matters, Corvus straightened slightly. "Yes, Mistress. The primary nexus points have been secured as you commanded. Our forces are positioned at the seven major rifts, ready to widen them when the signal comes. The artifacts you specified have been gathered and await your final instructions."

"And the sacrifices?"

"In place at each location. Unwilling, as you specified."

"Excellent. Fear and resistance create such useful energetic patterns during transition." Veyra's smile returned, cold and beautiful. "And what of our internal... complication?"

Corvus hesitated, knowing this was dangerous territory. "Councilor Thorne continues to advocate for more direct methods. He questions the necessity of the ritual approach, suggesting instead a simple military solution—eliminate the Stone-bearer and seize the fragments by force."

"How charmingly simplistic," Veyra remarked, though her expression hardened. "And how many support his position?"

"Three of the nine council members have expressed sympathy with his views. The others remain loyal to your vision."

"Six of nine is sufficient," she decided after a moment's consideration. "Though I dislike internal division at this critical juncture. Perhaps a demonstration of the consequences of disloyalty would be educational for the council."

"Shall I arrange something, Mistress?" Corvus offered, relieved that her displeasure wasn't directed at him.

"No need. I believe I'll attend the next council meeting personally." Her smile widened at Corvus's poorly concealed shock. It had been decades since Veyra had manifested directly in the mortal realm, preferring to work through her Voices rather than expend the considerable energy required for physical manifestation.

"But the strain—" he began, then stopped himself, realizing his presumption.

"Your concern is noted, if unnecessary," she said, her tone softening slightly. This was why she kept Corvus close—his genuine devotion was a rarity among her servants, most of whom were motivated primarily by fear or ambition. "The approaching convergence makes manifestation less taxing. The boundaries between realities grow more permeable by the day."

She turned back to the viewing portal, which now showed multiple locations simultaneously—Lyra and her companions beneath the Heart Tree, Ravenna at Sentinel's Reach, various Syndicate outposts where preparations for the coming ritual were underway, and a swirling darkness that seemed to be a rift in reality itself, widening incrementally as they watched.

"Beautiful, isn't it?" she murmured, genuine wonder in her voice. "The unraveling of artificial constraints. The return to primal chaos from which true creation emerges."

Corvus remained silent, unsure how to respond to what sounded dangerously close to religious fervor. In all his years serving Veyra, he had never fully understood her ultimate goal. Power, certainly—but power toward what end? The destruction of the current order, yes—but what did she envision rising from its ashes?

As if sensing his thoughts, she turned to him with unexpected gentleness. "You've served me faithfully for thirty years, Corvus. Longer than any other Voice. Yet you still don't comprehend what we're working toward, do you?"

"I..." He hesitated, caught between honesty and self-preservation. "I understand we seek to reshape reality according to your vision, Mistress."

"A diplomatic non-answer," she observed with a hint of amusement. "Perhaps it's time you understood more fully. Rise and approach."

Corvus obeyed with well-concealed trepidation. Closer to Veyra's shifting form, the air felt charged with potential that raised the hairs on his arms and made his shadow-enhanced senses tingle uncomfortably.

"Look," she commanded, gesturing toward the portal. The view shifted again, this time showing not the mortal realm but something far stranger—a space between realities where conventional physics held no sway. Shapes that defied description moved through environments that seemed to exist in more dimensions than the human mind could process. Colors unknown to the mortal spectrum pulsed and flowed in patterns that suggested conscious intent.

"What you see is the Interstice—the space between conventional realities," Veyra explained, her voice taking on a lecturer's cadence that eerily reminded Corvus of how Alaric sometimes spoke. "Most beings perceive reality as a single, continuous plane of existence. A few, like Alaric and his pet rune-caster, glimpse the multiple planes that exist parallel to our own. But almost none comprehend the Interstice itself—the medium in which all realities float like bubbles in a vast sea."

The view zoomed outward, revealing what appeared to be countless spheres of varying sizes, each containing what might have been an entire universe, all suspended in the strange non-space of the Interstice.

"The Veil that separates our reality from the Interstice was created—artificially imposed by beings who feared the creative chaos of unfiltered existence," Veyra continued, her eyes reflecting the swirling patterns visible in the portal. "They established rigid boundaries, fixed laws of physics, immutable rules of cause and effect. They created a cage and called it protection."

"Who were these beings?" Corvus asked, fascinated despite his unease.

"They called themselves the Shapers," Veyra replied. "Entities that evolved in the early days of our universe, when reality was still malleable. They feared the raw potential of unformed existence—the possibility that consciousness itself might reshape the foundations of reality. So they created the Veil, established the Laws, and appointed themselves guardians of their artificial order."

Her expression darkened. "For millennia, they maintained their control, presenting themselves as gods or angels or demons to primitive cultures, demanding worship and obedience while suppressing any who began to glimpse the truth. The Shattered Illusion was their masterwork—an artifact designed to maintain the Veil's integrity across all points in our reality."

"And you seek to undo their work?" Corvus asked, beginning to grasp the true scale of Veyra's ambition. "To break the Veil entirely?"

"To restore what was stolen from us," she corrected, passion infusing her voice. "The birthright of conscious beings—the ability to shape reality through will and imagination rather than being constrained by artificial limitations."

She gestured, and the portal shifted again, showing a humanoid figure manipulating the very fabric of reality around it, creating and dissolving matter through apparent thought alone.

"This is our potential, Corvus. Not merely wielding magic within the system's rules, but transcending the system entirely. Becoming true creators rather than mere inhabitants of a reality designed by others."

The vision was simultaneously glorious and terrifying. Corvus found himself torn between exhilaration at the possibilities and deep unease at the implications.

"And what of those who cannot achieve such transcendence?" he asked carefully. "What becomes of ordinary humans in this new reality?"

Veyra's expression shifted to something unreadable. "Evolution has never been kind to those who fail to adapt," she said after a moment's consideration. "But those who survive the transition will experience freedom beyond anything they can currently imagine. Some will rise to heights of creative power. Others will find their place in the new order. All will be freed from the cage they never realized imprisoned them."

There was something she wasn't saying—something about the cost of this transition that she deliberately omitted. Corvus had served her long enough to recognize when information was being selectively presented. But he knew better than to press further. The glimpse she had granted him was already more than any other servant had received.

"I am honored by your trust, Mistress," he said, bowing his head once more.

"Trust is earned, and you have earned much," she replied. With a wave of her hand, the portal closed, returning the chamber to its shadow-filled state. "Now, we have preparations to complete before the council meeting. The convergence accelerates, and we must be positioned to take full advantage when the moment comes."

"What would you have me do?" Corvus asked, grateful to return to practical matters.

"Gather the other Voices. I require their combined energy to prepare for physical manifestation." Her form began to shift again, becoming less solid, more a suggestion of presence than actual physicality. "And Corvus? Select a replacement for Councilor Thorne. Someone ambitious enough to desire promotion but intelligent enough to understand the consequences of disloyalty."

"It shall be done, Mistress."

As Corvus departed through a tear in reality that opened at his approach, Veyra allowed her form to dissolve further, spreading her consciousness throughout the chamber and beyond. Her awareness expanded, touching briefly upon each of her Voices throughout Sylvanthia, then reaching further to the rifts that had been her anchors to the mortal realm for centuries.

They were widening, just as she had planned. The fragment Ravenna foolishly thought to control was creating exactly the kind of instability she required. The Phoenix Stone's awakening provided the necessary counterpoint—light and shadow, creation and dissolution, in perfect disharmony that stressed the Veil's integrity.

Soon, very soon, the artificial boundaries would weaken enough for her true work to begin. Three centuries of patience, of careful manipulation, of incremental progress toward her ultimate goal—all coming to fruition at last.

A tendril of her consciousness brushed against the Heart Tree where Lyra and her companions made camp. The ancient entity recognized her touch, responding with what might have been sorrow or perhaps disappointment. Once, long ago, she had sat beneath those very branches with Alaric, learning the principles of balance and harmony that she would later reject as limitations rather than wisdom.

"You chose the wrong student, old friend," she whispered to her former teacher, though he could not hear her across the divide between them. "You should have recognized what I was becoming. Should have stopped me when you had the chance."

But he hadn't. His compassion, his belief in redemption, his inability to destroy what he had helped create—these had been his fatal weaknesses. By the time he finally moved against her, it had been too late. The knowledge she had gleaned, the power she had accumulated, had already set her on a path beyond his ability to counter.

Now history repeated itself with this new group of hopeful heroes. Alaric, once again guiding young talents against a threat they couldn't fully comprehend. Once again believing that balance could be restored, that the damage could be healed, that the world could return to what it had been.

"You never understood, did you?" she mused, her consciousness expanding further, touching briefly upon Ravenna's feverish work at Sentinel's Reach. "There is no returning. Only becoming. Only evolution. Only the eternal dance of creation and destruction that gives meaning to existence."

The silver-eyed man sensed something of her presence, looking up from his work with a mixture of fear and reverence. He believed himself her servant, her chosen instrument. The irony amused her. He sought godhood without realizing he was merely a tool—a catalyst for change that would ultimately consume him as surely as it would transform the world.

"Continue your work, little power-seeker," she whispered, allowing him to feel just enough of her presence to reinforce his misplaced devotion. "Break what you cannot understand. Release what you cannot control. Serve purposes beyond your comprehension."

Satisfied that all proceeded according to design, she withdrew her consciousness, consolidating once more within her chamber between realities. The convergence approached—that rare alignment when the boundaries between worlds naturally thinned, when the Veil became most vulnerable to manipulation. When combined with the destabilizing effect of the fragments and the awakening power of the Phoenix Stone, it would create the perfect conditions for her final ritual.

The Shapers had crafted their cage with remarkable skill, but even they couldn't account for the persistence of one who had glimpsed the truth, who had tasted the potential beyond their artificial constraints. For three centuries she had worked toward this moment, had sacrificed her humanity, had endured existence in the half-state between realities.

Soon, very soon, the cage would break. Reality itself would remember its original nature—fluid, responsive to consciousness, unlimited by arbitrary laws. And those who survived the transition would finally understand what true freedom meant.

As for Alaric and his newest protégés... perhaps some would adapt. Perhaps some would even thrive in the new reality she would usher in. She found herself hoping, in what remained of her once-human heart, that her old teacher might be among them. Despite everything, she retained a certain fondness for the ancient mage who had first shown her the wonders of magic, even if he had failed to understand its ultimate potential.

But sentiment would not deter her from her path. The time for hesitation had passed centuries ago, when she had faced mortality and rejected its limitations. When she had glimpsed the truth beyond the Veil and committed herself to breaking the chains that bound conscious beings to artificial order.

The chamber darkened as Veyra's consciousness fully returned to it, shadows swirling more vigorously around her manifested form. She allowed herself a moment of anticipation, of genuine excitement for what was to come. Three centuries of patience was about to be rewarded.

The game was approaching its final moves. The pieces were in position. The Veil trembled at the edge of dissolution.

And none—not Alaric, not the Stone-bearer, not even the Watchers themselves—could stop what she had set in motion.

The Syndicate's High Council chamber bore little resemblance to the governmental meeting rooms of conventional power structures. Located deep beneath the Obsidian Citadel, the circular space was designed to disorient and intimidate rather than comfort. The walls appeared to be solid black stone, yet they occasionally rippled like liquid when observed from the corner of the eye. The ceiling remained in perpetual shadow despite numerous light sources, creating the impression of infinite height. The floor was transparent, revealing swirling darkness beneath that might have been decorative or might have been an actual abyss—none were eager to test which.

Around a crescent-shaped table of polished black stone sat eight figures, each representing a different faction within the Syndicate's complex power structure. The ninth seat—directly at the table's center—remained conspicuously empty, its occupant noticeably absent.

"Councilor Thorne appears to be delayed," observed Magistra Vex, her fingers drumming impatiently on the table's surface. As head of the Syndicate's intelligence network, she valued punctuality almost as much as information. "How inconsiderate, given that he called this emergency session."

"Perhaps he's finally found the courage to match his convictions," suggested Warden Krath, a massive man whose scarred face testified to decades of military service. "Planning another coup requires significant preparation, after all."

"Your accusations border on treason, Warden," cautioned Elder Morvain, the council's oldest member and nominal moderator. "Let us not forget protocol, even in private session."

"Protocol?" Krath laughed harshly. "Was it protocol when Thorne openly questioned the Mistress's methods at our last gathering? When he suggested we abandon centuries of careful preparation in favor of brute force tactics?"

"He expressed concerns shared by many," interjected Archivist Selene, her voice soft but carrying unusual authority. As keeper of the Syndicate's historical records and magical research, she was among the few who could claim comprehensive understanding of their organization's true origins. "The convergence approaches rapidly, yet our progress in securing the fragments remains limited. One might reasonably question whether our current strategy is optimal."

"One might reasonably remember one's place," countered Magister Draven, his silver eyes—a mark of those who had undergone the Shadowing ritual—flashing with annoyance. "The Mistress's vision guides us for reason. Those who lack the capacity to comprehend her design should at least possess the wisdom to trust in it."

Further debate was interrupted as the chamber's massive doors swung open. All expected to see Councilor Thorne's distinctive figure, but instead, Corvus entered, his shadow-binder's robes seeming to absorb the light around him as he moved.

"Voice Corvus," Elder Morvain acknowledged with visible surprise. "The council did not request your presence."

"I come not by the council's request, but by higher authority," Corvus replied, his tone neutral but carrying unmistakable warning. "The Mistress herself wishes to address you."

A ripple of shock passed through the assembled councilors. None had directly communicated with Veyra in years—perhaps decades for most. Her will was typically conveyed through the Voices, with Corvus as her primary conduit.

"The Mistress? Here? Now?" Magistra Vex couldn't quite keep the disbelief from her voice. "But the energy expenditure required for physical manifestation—"

"Is her concern, not yours," Corvus finished smoothly. "Prepare yourselves. She approaches."

The warning proved insufficient for what followed. The air at the center of the chamber seemed to fold inward upon itself, reality puckering like fabric pinched between invisible fingers. Darkness poured from this distortion, not the absence of light but something more substantial—shadow given weight and presence. It pooled on the floor, rising and coalescing into a humanoid shape that gradually refined itself into Veyra's preferred manifestation.

The councilors instinctively rose from their seats, some backing away slightly despite themselves. Even those who had served the Syndicate for decades found themselves unprepared for their Mistress's direct presence. The power radiating from her form pressed against their senses like a physical weight, making breathing difficult and clear thought challenging.

"My faithful council," Veyra greeted them, her voice carrying those impossible harmonics that reminded listeners she was no longer truly human. "How pleasant to find you all gathered so conveniently."

"Mistress," Elder Morvain managed, performing a deep bow that the others hastily mimicked. "We are honored beyond expression by your presence. Had we known you intended to join us—"

"You would have what? Prepared speeches? Arranged a more impressive chamber? Rehearsed your expressions of loyalty?" Veyra's smile held no warmth. "I prefer the authenticity of surprise. It reveals so much more about one's true nature."

She moved to the empty ninth chair—Councilor Thorne's seat—and settled into it with fluid grace. The shadows of her robes spread across the table's surface like spilled ink.

"I notice we are one member short," she observed, though her tone suggested this was anything but a surprise. "Where is our esteemed Councilor Thorne?"

An uncomfortable silence fell over the chamber. Finally, Warden Krath spoke, his military directness asserting itself despite the intimidating circumstances.

"We expected him to be present, Mistress. He called this emergency session to discuss... alternative approaches to securing the fragments."

"Alternative approaches," Veyra repeated, as if tasting the words. "How interesting. And what alternatives did he wish to propose?"

The councilors exchanged uneasy glances. None wished to be perceived as aligned with potentially seditious views, yet lying to Veyra was both futile and dangerous.

"He has advocated for more direct military action," Archivist Selene finally offered, her scholarly detachment providing some insulation from the political implications. "Specifically, targeting the Stone-bearer and her companions with our full forces rather than proceeding with the ritual preparations."

"I see." Veyra's expression remained unreadable. "And how many of you found merit in this... alternative approach?"

The question hung in the air like a blade. After a moment of excruciating silence, Magistra Vex straightened her shoulders and met Veyra's gaze directly.

"I expressed support for examining all options, Mistress. The Stone-bearer has proven more capable than anticipated. Adaptability seems prudent."

"Prudence is admirable," Veyra acknowledged. "What about the rest of you? Surely Magistra Vex wasn't alone in her... prudence."

Two others reluctantly indicated their partial agreement with Thorne's position—Warden Krath and Master Ilvan, the council's youngest member and head of the Syndicate's recruitment division. The remaining four stayed silent, their loyalty to Veyra's original vision—or at least their fear of admitting otherwise—holding firm.

"How fascinating," Veyra remarked, her tone conversational despite the tension permeating the chamber. "Nearly half the council questioning the path we have followed for centuries. One might almost call it mutiny."

"Mistress, I assure you—" Magistra Vex began, but fell silent as Veyra raised a hand.

"Spare me your assurances, Magistra. I understand the situation perfectly." She leaned forward, her abyssal eyes sweeping across the assembled councilors. "You see only fragments of the design—individual pieces without comprehension of the whole. You measure progress in simplistic terms of possession and control. You fail to grasp that the fragments are means, not ends."

She rose from the chair, her form seeming to grow taller as shadows gathered around her. "Allow me to clarify our purpose, since time has apparently dulled your understanding. We do not seek merely to possess the fragments of the Shattered Illusion. We seek to use them to break the Veil itself—to release our reality from the artificial constraints imposed upon it by the Shapers."

With a gesture, she created a viewing portal similar to the one in her private chamber, though smaller and less detailed. Through it, the councilors could see the rifts that scarred Sylvanthia's landscape, pulsing with shadow energy.

"These rifts are not random tears in reality. They are pressure points—places where the Veil is naturally thinner, where the boundaries between our world and the Interstice can be most effectively manipulated." The view shifted to show Syndicate forces positioned at each major rift, preparing elaborate ritual structures. "Our preparations are not for battle but for transformation. The convergence approaches—that rare alignment when the Veil naturally thins across all points simultaneously."

The portal closed with a gesture of her hand. "When that moment comes, we will use the fragments not as weapons but as keys—to unlock the cage that has constrained conscious beings since the dawn of this reality. To restore the fluidity and responsiveness that is our birthright."

She returned her attention to the councilors, who had listened with expressions ranging from awe to horror as the true scale of her ambition became clear. "Now, does anyone still believe that a simple military solution—killing the Stone-bearer and seizing the fragments by force—addresses our actual objective?"

None spoke. Even those who had supported Thorne's position now appeared shaken by the revelation of Veyra's ultimate goal.

"I thought not," she concluded with cold satisfaction. "As for Councilor Thorne..." She gestured again, and a new portal opened, this one showing a dimly lit chamber where a figure lay strapped to an altar-like structure. Thorne's once-proud form was barely recognizable, his body twisted and partially transformed into something neither human nor shadow but some horrific combination of both. His mouth opened in a silent scream as darkness poured into him through eyes, ears, and mouth.

"He is making a contribution to our cause, in his own way," Veyra explained as the councilors watched in horrified fascination. "The ritual requires sacrifices at each major rift. Those who question my vision have volunteered to serve as vessels for the transition energies."

The portal closed, but the image remained burned into the minds of all present. The message could not have been clearer: loyalty or transformation. Service or sacrifice.

"Now then," Veyra continued, her tone shifting to something almost businesslike. "Let us discuss the final preparations for the convergence. Corvus will provide each of you with specific instructions for your divisions. The timeline has accelerated—the Stone-bearer's bonding with the fragment at Sentinel's Reach has created a cascade effect that pushes us toward the critical moment more rapidly than anticipated."

She surveyed the council once more, noting with satisfaction their properly subdued expressions. Fear was a crude tool, but an effective one when wielded with precision.

"Are there any questions? Concerns? Alternative approaches someone wishes to suggest?" Her smile was terrible in its beauty. "No? Then you are dismissed to your duties. Serve well in these final days, and you will find yourselves elevated beyond imagination in the reality to come."

As the councilors filed out, visibly shaken by both the revelations and the implicit threat they had witnessed, Veyra remained seated, shadows swirling around her manifested form. The physical projection into the mortal realm taxed even her considerable power, but the expenditure had been necessary. Sometimes personal appearance achieved what no amount of secondhand instruction could accomplish.

Corvus remained after the others had departed, waiting silently for further instructions.

"They understand now," Veyra observed, satisfaction evident in her tone. "Fear has clarified their perspective admirably."

"Indeed, Mistress," Corvus agreed. "Though I wonder if they truly comprehend the full implications of breaking the Veil."

"Comprehension is unnecessary. Compliance is sufficient." She rose, her form already beginning to lose solidity as she prepared to return to her chamber between realities. "Monitor them closely in the days ahead. Any who show signs of hesitation should join Councilor Thorne in more direct service to our cause."

"As you command." Corvus hesitated, then asked the question that had troubled him since their earlier conversation. "Mistress, when the Veil breaks and reality becomes fluid once more... what becomes of those like myself? Those enhanced by shadow but still fundamentally human?"

Veyra regarded him with an expression that might almost have been compassion, though filtered through a consciousness that had long since transcended human emotion.

"You, my faithful Corvus, will have choices that others will not," she replied. "Your years of service have attuned you to the shadows in ways that few mortals could survive. When the transition comes, you may find yourself better prepared than most to adapt to the new conditions."

It wasn't precisely an answer, but it was more reassurance than he had expected. Corvus bowed deeply, accepting what was offered.

"Prepare the Voices," Veyra instructed as her form continued to dissolve into shadow. "When Ravenna completes his transformation at Sentinel's Reach, the destabilization will accelerate dramatically. We must be positioned to channel and direct the energies that will be released."

"What of the Stone-bearer and her companions?" Corvus asked. "They move toward the Heart Tree, where the old magics might offer some protection against our influence."

"Let them believe themselves safe for the moment," Veyra replied, her voice already taking on the distant quality that indicated her consciousness was withdrawing from the physical manifestation. "Their actions serve our purpose whether they realize it or not. The Phoenix Stone awakens in response to threat, and its power creates precisely the kind of harmonic disturbance we require."

Her form had now faded to little more than an outline of shadow against the chamber's darkness. "All pieces move toward their appointed positions, Corvus. The game concludes exactly as designed—not through direct confrontation, but through the manipulation of forces beyond mortal comprehension."

With those final words, she vanished completely, leaving Corvus alone in the council chamber. He remained there for several moments, contemplating the glimpse he had been granted of Veyra's ultimate vision. Freedom from constraint. Reality responsive to consciousness. Evolution beyond current limitations.

It was glorious and terrifying in equal measure—a vision that promised either transcendence or annihilation, with little middle ground between. Yet what choice remained? The path had been set in motion centuries before his birth. The convergence approached regardless of individual doubts or fears.

All that remained was to serve as faithfully as possible and hope that when the Veil finally broke, he would be among those who adapted rather than those who perished in the transition.

With that sobering thought, he departed to prepare the Voices for what was to come. The final days of the world as they knew it had begun.

CHAPTER NINETEEN

Trust's Crucible

D awn broke reluctantly over the mountains surrounding Sentinel's Reach, pale light struggling through clouds still heavy with the previous night's storm. Lyra stood at the edge of their hastily established camp, watching as the rescued captives huddled around small fires, their faces gaunt but eyes bright with newfound freedom. The fragment of the Shattered Illusion pulsed warm in her palm, its rhythm somehow reassuring despite the bone-deep weariness that made even standing an effort.

"You should be resting," Kael said quietly, appearing at her side with his characteristic silent tread. He offered a steaming cup that smelled of Elara's healing herbs. "You pushed yourself too far during the confrontation."

"Necessity rarely consults wisdom," Lyra replied, accepting the cup gratefully. The warmth seeped into her cold fingers, a small comfort against the chill mountain air. "How are the others?"

"Recovering. Mira's inventorying what remains of her supplies—apparently while composing a detailed monologue about the unfairness of alchemical depletion rates." A hint of a smile touched his lips. "Rowan's scouting our perimeter. Elara's tending to the more severely affected captives."

"And Alaric?"

Kael's expression sobered. "Studying the fragment. He seems... concerned."

Lyra nodded, her gaze drifting back to the horizon where Sentinel's Reach's silhouette stood stark against the lightening sky. The watchtower seemed diminished somehow, its malevolent presence reduced but not eliminated. Like a predator wounded but not killed—dangerous still, perhaps more so for its injury.

"We should move soon," she said after a moment. "Ravenna may have transformed, but the Syndicate will send reinforcements once they realize what's happened."

"Agreed, but these people are in no condition for hard travel." Kael gestured toward the freed captives. "Some can barely stand, let alone march through mountain passes."

Before Lyra could respond, Rowan emerged from the tree line, moving with urgent purpose. His expression immediately put them on alert.

"Riders approaching from the north," he reported, voice low. "Six of them, well-armed but not wearing Syndicate colors."

Kael's hand moved instinctively to his sword hilt. "Bandits?"

"Too organized," Rowan shook his head. "They're following our trail deliberately, but not attempting concealment."

"Wake the others," Lyra decided. "Quietly. Let's not alarm the captives until we know what we're dealing with."

Within minutes, their core group had assembled at the camp's edge, positioned to intercept the approaching riders before they reached the vulnerable former captives. Mira stood with several potions already in hand, her dark eyes narrowed as she scanned the horizon. Her hair was pulled back in a practical braid, though several strands had escaped to frame her face, which was set in its customary expression of wary assessment.

"Just once," she muttered, tucking a stray vial into her belt pouch, "I'd like to wake up to good news. 'Good morning, Mira, breakfast is ready and no one's trying to kill us today.' Is that really too much to ask?"

Despite her complaints, her hands were steady as she arranged her potions for quick access. Mira had spent the night restocking what supplies she could, using local plants and minerals to replace the compounds depleted during their battle at Sentinel's Reach. It was meticulous work, requiring precision even under ideal conditions. In a makeshift camp with limited resources, it had been nearly impossible—yet somehow she'd managed to replenish their most critical defenses.

Elara had inscribed hasty protective runes on the ground before them, while Alaric leaned on his staff, his ancient eyes scanning the horizon with wary assessment.

The riders appeared over a ridge, silhouetted against the morning sky. As Rowan had reported, they were six in number, moving with the disciplined formation of trained soldiers rather than opportunistic raiders. Their leader raised an empty hand in what appeared to be a gesture of peace as they approached.

"That's the Green Path emblem," Alaric murmured, recognition dawning in his voice. "The intertwined leaves and roots—these are druids."

"Druids?" Mira's eyebrows rose skeptically. "Out here? I thought they rarely left their forests."

Indeed, as the riders drew closer, Lyra could make out the distinctive symbol emblazoned on their leather armor and painted across their shields. The lead rider, a woman with auburn hair braided with flowers and vines, dismounted with fluid grace once they were within speaking distance.

"Hail, Fragment Bearer," she called, her voice carrying clear authority without aggression. "I am Warden Brenna of the Green Path. We've come seeking our lost sisters—Thorn and the child Sera."

"Thorn and Sera?" Lyra exchanged surprised glances with her companions. "They were captured by Ravenna. We rescued them from the watchtower last night."

Relief washed over the druid's weathered features. "Then our visions spoke true. May we approach? We bring supplies and assistance for any who need it."

After a brief consultation, Lyra nodded her agreement. The druids approached, leading horses laden with provisions and medicinal supplies. As they entered the camp, Lyra noticed their careful movements—respectful of the land beneath their feet, eyes constantly scanning not just for threats but for signs of natural disruption.

Mira watched the druids unpack their supplies, her alchemist's eye immediately assessing the quality of their herbs and remedies. Despite her skepticism, she couldn't deny the impressive array of healing compounds they carried—some rare enough that she'd only read about them in ancient texts.

"How did you find us?" Kael asked, his posture remaining alert despite the apparent friendly overture.

"The Dream Path revealed your location," Brenna explained, unloading supplies from her mount. "When our sanctuary was breached and Thorn and Sera taken, we sought guidance through the ancient ways. The visions showed them here, in the shadow of the watchtower, and you—" her gaze fixed on Lyra, "—standing between them and darkness."

"The Dream Path?" Mira asked, unable to contain her skepticism. She crossed her arms, leaning against a nearby tree with studied casualness that belied her tension. "You followed a dream to find us? And here I've been wasting time with maps and compasses all these years."

"A druidic practice," Alaric explained before Brenna could respond. "A form of collective consciousness accessed through ritual and meditation. Powerful, though not always precise in its revelations."

"Precise enough to lead us here," Brenna countered with a slight smile, apparently unbothered by Mira's skepticism. "Though we arrived later than intended. The Syndicate's forces blocked the direct routes, forcing us to circle wide through the eastern passes."

Mira opened her mouth to deliver another sardonic comment, then closed it as she noticed a familiar herb among the druid's supplies. "Is that genuine black-root?" she asked instead, professional curiosity momentarily overriding her cynicism. "I haven't seen a living specimen in years."

"It is," Brenna confirmed, her expression warming slightly at Mira's interest. "We cultivate it in protected groves. It's becoming increasingly rare in the wild."

"It's essential for treating magical exhaustion," Mira said, almost to herself. Her fingers twitched with the desire to examine the plant more closely. "I've been substituting redvein moss, but the efficacy is barely half..."

"Perhaps we could discuss an exchange of knowledge later," Brenna suggested, recognizing a fellow practitioner despite their different approaches. "Druidic herbalism and formal alchemy rarely intersect, but when they do, the results can be... illuminating."

Something flickered in Mira's eyes—a brief, vulnerable spark of genuine interest quickly masked by her habitual guardedness. "Maybe," she conceded with feigned indifference. "If there's time."

As they spoke, two figures emerged from among the rescued captives—Thorn, supporting a still-weak Sera. The young druid's face lit with recognition at the sight of her kin, though exhaustion had left deep shadows beneath her eyes.

"Warden Brenna," she called, her voice cracking with emotion. "You came."

"Of course we came, little sister," Brenna replied, crossing the distance between them with swift strides. She embraced both Thorn and Sera gently, murmuring words in an ancient language that seemed to flow like water. "The Circle stands with its own, always."

The reunion brought a moment of warmth to the otherwise somber camp. Mira watched the interaction with an unreadable expression, her dark eyes lingering on Sera's small form. Something about the child's resilience despite obvious trauma seemed to touch something deep within the alchemist—a recognition that she quickly concealed by turning back to her inventory with renewed focus.

As the druids distributed supplies and began treating the most severely affected captives, Brenna joined Lyra and her companions to exchange information.

"The sanctuary was betrayed from within," she explained grimly, accepting a cup of tea from Elara. "One of our acolytes—his family held hostage by the

Syndicate. He revealed the hidden pathways, allowing Ravenna's forces to enter undetected."

"What happened to the acolyte?" Kael asked.

"He lives, though he will never again walk the Dream Path with us," Brenna replied, her expression troubled. "His choice was made under duress, but consequences remain. The sanctuary has been relocated, its defenses strengthened."

At the word "betrayed," Mira's hands stilled over her supplies, her body tensing almost imperceptibly. Only Elara, who had come to recognize the subtle signs of Mira's distress over their months of travel together, noticed the reaction. The rune-caster cast a concerned glance toward her friend but said nothing, respecting Mira's carefully maintained privacy.

"And what of Thorn and Sera?" Lyra asked, watching as the young druid helped distribute supplies among the other captives, her movements efficient despite her obvious fatigue. "Will you take them back with you?"

"If they wish to go," Brenna nodded. "Though Thorn may have other ideas. She has spoken often of your quest, of its importance to the balance of all things. The Circle respects individual choice, even when it leads away from our common path."

As if summoned by their discussion, Thorn approached, Sera's small hand clasped firmly in hers. The child looked better already—some color had returned to her cheeks, and her eyes were more alert than they had been since her rescue.

"Warden," Thorn addressed Brenna with respect but not subservience, "I've been speaking with Sera. We've decided to remain with Lyra and her companions, if they'll have us."

Surprise rippled through the group. Brenna studied the young druid thoughtfully before responding. "The path you propose is dangerous, sister. The Syndicate will not forget what was done here, nor will Ravenna forgive those who opposed him."

"I know," Thorn replied steadily. "But what I experienced under Ravenna's control—the violation of mind and spirit—it showed me something important. The Green Path cannot stand apart from this conflict, observing but not engaging. What the Syndicate seeks threatens the natural order itself."

"And you, little one?" Brenna knelt to address Sera directly. "What do you wish?"

The child's voice was soft but determined. "I want to stay with Thorn. And help stop the bad people from hurting others like they hurt me."

Brenna sighed, though there was pride mixed with her concern. "The wisdom of children often shames our adult caution." She rose, turning to Lyra. "Would you accept them into your company? They bring skills that may prove valuable—Thorn's connection to the Dream Path and Sera's natural affinity for sensing magical energies."

Lyra glanced at her companions, reading their responses in their expressions—Kael's cautious assessment, Elara's compassionate acceptance, Rowan's quiet approval, and Alaric's thoughtful analysis.

Mira's face betrayed more conflict than the others. She looked from Thorn to Sera, her brow furrowed. "Another child on this suicide mission," she muttered, though without her usual bite. "Wonderful." Yet when Sera's eyes met hers, something softened in Mira's expression—a reluctant recognition, perhaps, of her own younger self in the determined child.

"We would welcome them," Lyra decided, "though I must be honest about the dangers ahead. We seek the fragments of the Shattered Illusion—artifacts of immense power that the Syndicate also pursues. Our path will not be safe or easy."

"Few worthy paths are," Thorn replied with a slight smile. "And we've already faced Ravenna once and survived. With proper preparation, we can contribute rather than burden your group."

The matter settled, they turned to more immediate concerns—the care of the remaining captives and plans for their safe transport to neutral territory. The druids offered to escort them to a settlement three days' journey west, where they could find sanctuary and begin rebuilding their lives.

"Most have homes to return to, families who believe them dead," Brenna explained. "We will see them safely to their destinations, or find new havens for those who cannot return."

"And what of Ravenna?" Kael asked, the question that had hung unspoken over their discussions. "Whatever he's becoming, he's still out there."

"Changed, but not destroyed," Alaric confirmed grimly. "The transformation we witnessed was just the beginning. He's merging with powers beyond mortal comprehension—becoming a vessel for something ancient and malevolent."

"All the more reason to find the remaining fragments before he does," Lyra said, the Shattered Illusion piece warm in her hand. "This one will guide us to the others, but we need to move quickly."

As they discussed strategy, the fragment pulsed with increasing intensity, drawing Lyra's attention. She opened her palm, studying the crystalline shard as it glowed with inner light. Within its depths, swirls of color shifted and changed, occasionally forming patterns that almost resembled writing before dissolving again into chaos.

"It's trying to communicate," Alaric observed, leaning closer to study the phenomenon. "The fragments contain not just power but knowledge—memories of their original whole."

"Can you interpret it?" Lyra asked, feeling the warmth spread up her arm as the fragment's glow intensified.

"Not precisely," the ancient mage admitted. "But I believe it's responding to our discussion about the other fragments. It's... pointing."

Indeed, the light within the crystal seemed to concentrate along one edge, creating a beam that extended outward like a compass needle. As Lyra slowly turned in place, the beam remained fixed in the same direction regardless of her movement.

"East," Rowan noted, immediately consulting his maps. "Toward the coastal regions of the Old Kingdom."

"Where the second fragment waits," Lyra murmured, feeling the truth of the statement resonate through her connection to the crystal. "But there's something else too—something north. A presence that feels... familiar."

"The fragment is sensitive to its kin," Alaric explained. "What you're sensing may be another piece of the Shattered Illusion already in Syndicate possession. They've been collecting them longer than we realized."

This revelation cast a shadow over their planning. If the Syndicate already possessed other fragments, their race had begun with a significant disadvantage. The need to move quickly became even more urgent.

"We should divide our forces," Kael suggested, his tactical mind assessing their options. "Some of us pursue the coastal fragment while others investigate the northern presence."

"Divide our strength?" Mira questioned skeptically, looking up sharply from her inventory. "When facing an enemy as powerful as Ravenna?" Her voice carried a note of genuine alarm that went beyond her usual sardonic commentary. "Have we learned nothing from every tactical disaster in history?"

"Not divide—multiply," Kael clarified. "We can cover more ground, gather more information, and potentially secure multiple fragments simultaneously. Staying together limits our effectiveness."

Mira's expression remained deeply skeptical. "Right. Because smaller groups are so much harder to pick off one by one." She glanced at Sera, then back to the others, something protective flashing in her eyes. "I've seen what happens when groups fragment in the face of danger. It rarely ends well for anyone."

The vehemence in her tone caught even Lyra by surprise. Mira was often critical, but this went beyond her usual caustic commentary. There was something personal in her objection—something that made her hands clench and unclench at her sides as if physically restraining stronger emotions.

"We understand the risks," Elara said gently, moving closer to Mira with subtle support. "But the fragments must be our priority. If the Syndicate secures another before we do…"

"I know, I know," Mira interrupted, her voice tight. "The fate of the world and all that. It's always the fate of the world, isn't it?" She turned away, busying herself with reorganizing supplies that were already perfectly arranged. "Fine. Split up. It's not like my opinion has ever changed the course of these decisions anyway."

A tense silence followed her outburst. The others exchanged concerned glances, unused to seeing Mira's cynicism give way to such raw emotion. Lyra approached her carefully, aware that the alchemist often retreated further when confronted directly about her feelings.

"Your opinion matters, Mira," she said quietly. "And your concerns are valid. That's why we'll establish regular communication and a firm rendezvous point. No one gets left behind or forgotten."

Mira didn't look up from her supplies, but her shoulders lost some of their rigidity. "Pretty words," she muttered, though without her earlier heat. "Let's hope reality cooperates with your optimism."

After further discussion, they reached a reluctant consensus: they would indeed split into smaller groups, each with a specific objective, maintaining communication through magical means Alaric and Elara would establish.

"The coastal fragment first," Lyra decided, studying the directional beam from the crystal in her palm. "It's pulling more strongly, suggesting it may be more accessible. Kael, Rowan, and I will pursue it, while Alaric, Elara, and Mira investigate reports of Syndicate activity at their northern stronghold."

"And us?" Thorn asked, standing with Sera beside her.

"You'll accompany Alaric's group," Lyra replied after a moment's consideration. "Your druidic abilities will complement their magical expertise, and Sera's sensitivity to magical energies could prove invaluable in detecting hidden threats."

With their course decided, preparations began in earnest. The druids provided additional supplies and shared what knowledge they had of the coastal regions—ancient ruins where scholars had taken refuge during the Mage Wars, potentially housing forgotten artifacts and knowledge.

"The Old Kingdom's libraries were legendary," Brenna told them as they sorted provisions. "Some say entire sections were dedicated to the Shattered Illusion and its creation. If any records survived the kingdom's fall, they might provide crucial insights into the fragments' nature and purpose."

By midday, the camp had transformed into a hub of purposeful activity. The former captives, those strong enough to help, assisted with preparations for their journey west with the druids. Elara and Alaric worked together to create communication talismans—small crystals that would allow the separated groups to exchange brief messages across great distances. Mira inventoried and distributed her alchemical supplies, ensuring each group had essential remedies and defensive compounds.

As Mira worked, her movements were precise but tense, her usual running commentary notably absent. When Sera approached, offering to help sort the small vials, Mira initially stiffened, then relented with unusual gentleness.

"Careful with the blue ones," she instructed, allowing the child to arrange the safer compounds. "They don't explode or anything dramatic, but they'll turn your fingers purple for a week if they spill."

"Did that happen to you?" Sera asked, handling the vials with careful attention.

A reluctant smile tugged at Mira's lips. "More times than I care to admit. My mentor used to say he could track me by the color of my hands." Something distant and pained flickered in her eyes at the memory, quickly suppressed.

"Was your mentor nice?" Sera's innocent question struck deeper than she could know.

Mira's hands stilled momentarily. "He was... complicated," she finally answered. "Brilliant, demanding, sometimes kind. He taught me everything I know about alchemy." She resumed her work, adding more quietly, "Until he decided I was more valuable as currency than as a student."

Sera looked up, her young face showing understanding beyond her years. "Someone hurt you too."

It wasn't a question, and Mira didn't treat it as one. She merely nodded once, sharply, before changing the subject. "These green vials are for healing. Make sure Elara gets at least three—she tends to forget her own needs when caring for others."

As evening approached, they gathered for a final meal together before their paths would diverge at dawn. The mood was somber yet determined, each person acutely aware of the challenges that lay ahead and the stakes of their success or failure.

"We should establish rendezvous points," Kael suggested, spreading Rowan's maps across a flat stone that served as their table. "In case communication fails or circumstances force a change in plans."

They identified several potential meeting locations, taking into account the different routes each group would travel and possible complications they might encounter. The coastal team would head east through the mountain passes, then south along the trade routes to the ruins of the Old Kingdom. The northern team would follow the high ridges directly north, a more challenging route but one that offered greater concealment from Syndicate patrols.

"Two weeks," Lyra decided, marking the calendar Rowan had sketched in the corner of his map. "We reconvene at the Crossroads of Meren in two weeks, regardless of our success or failure in our individual missions."

As night fell, the camp gradually quieted. The druids established protective wards around the perimeter, their soft chanting blending with the natural sounds of the wilderness. Within this circle of safety, the companions sought rest before their impending separation.

Mira found herself restless despite the exhaustion that weighed on her limbs. She slipped away from the main camp, seeking solitude at a small outcropping that overlooked the valley below. The night air was crisp with approaching winter, stars brilliant in the clear mountain sky.

She withdrew a small vial from her pocket—not one of her alchemical creations but a keepsake she rarely acknowledged even to herself. Inside, suspended in clear liquid, floated a tiny silver pendant shaped like an intertwined tree and star. Taryn's gift, given the night before he betrayed her to the Syndicate for the price on her head.

The memory rose unbidden, as vivid as if it had happened yesterday rather than three years ago. Taryn's face, handsome and earnest in the lamplight of his workshop, as he fastened the pendant around her neck. "To commemorate your mastery," he had said, his fingers lingering against her skin. "I'm proud of you, Mira. More than you know."

Hours later, she had awakened to Syndicate soldiers dragging her from her bed, Taryn standing in the doorway with averted eyes as they clapped her in restraints designed to suppress alchemical abilities.

"You'll fetch a fine price," the Syndicate captain had told her, not unkindly. "Alchemists of your caliber are rare. The research facilities at Blackspire will put your talents to good use."

It was only then that she had understood—Taryn had sold her. Her mentor, her friend, perhaps almost her lover, had traded her freedom for whatever reward the Syndicate offered for gifted alchemists.

The pendant had been torn from her neck during her brief, futile struggle. Later, after her unexpected rescue by a group of mercenaries led by a grim-faced warrior named Kael, she had returned to find the workshop abandoned, Taryn gone without a trace. Only the pendant remained, dropped in a corner and forgotten in the chaos.

She had preserved it in alchemical solution—not out of sentimentality, she told herself, but as a reminder never to trust so completely again. Never to believe that connection meant loyalty, that affection guaranteed protection.

"Still carrying that, I see."

Mira startled, nearly dropping the vial as she turned to find Elara standing a few paces away, her slender form silhouetted against the starlight.

"You should announce yourself," Mira snapped, quickly pocketing the vial. "I have at least three compounds that could turn you into interesting shapes if I were startled badly enough."

"My apologies," Elara said, though her slight smile suggested she wasn't particularly concerned by the threat. "May I join you?"

Mira shrugged, which Elara correctly interpreted as permission. The rune-caster settled beside her on the rocky outcropping, her movements graceful despite her evident fatigue.

"You're troubled by our separation," Elara observed after a comfortable silence had stretched between them.

"I'm troubled by many things," Mira replied evasively. "The quality of mountain air, the scarcity of decent wine in wilderness camps, the persistent tendency of people to make spectacularly bad decisions when faced with danger..."

"Mira." Elara's voice was gentle but firm. "We've traveled together long enough that I can recognize when your sarcasm is masking genuine concern."

The alchemist sighed, her shoulders slumping slightly. "Fine. Yes, I think splitting up is a terrible idea. Happy?"

"Because of tactical considerations, or because of what happened with Taryn?"

Mira's head snapped up, her eyes narrowing. "What do you know about Taryn?"

"Only what you've mentioned in fragments over our months together," Elara replied calmly. "A mentor or partner who betrayed you to the Syndicate. Someone you trusted who sold that trust for personal gain."

"Ancient history," Mira dismissed, though her fingers unconsciously touched the pocket containing the vial.

"Not so ancient that it doesn't influence your present," Elara observed. "You resist separation because it requires trust—trust that those who go another way will return, that promises made will be kept."

Mira was silent for a long moment, her gaze fixed on the distant mountains. When she finally spoke, her voice had lost its defensive edge. "The last time I separated from someone I trusted, I ended up in a Syndicate cell waiting to be transported to one of their 'research facilities.' If Kael hadn't been pursuing a completely unrelated lead and accidentally stumbled across the transport caravan..."

She left the sentence unfinished, but its conclusion hung in the air between them. Elara reached out, her slender fingers gently touching Mira's arm in a gesture of understanding.

"We are not Taryn," she said simply.

"I know that," Mira replied, frustration evident in her tone. "Rationally, I know that. But this—" she tapped her chest, "—doesn't always listen to rational arguments."

"The heart has its own wisdom," Elara agreed. "Though sometimes it speaks from old wounds rather than present truths."

They sat in companionable silence for several minutes, watching as clouds occasionally drifted across the star-filled sky. Finally, Mira spoke again, her voice uncharacteristically vulnerable.

"What if something happens to one group while the other is too far away to help? What if we return to the meeting point in two weeks and find... no one?"

"Then we continue the mission," Elara replied, her certainty unwavering. "As they would do if our group failed to return. The fragments must be secured, regardless of personal cost."

"Just like that?" Mira's voice held a bitter edge. "Cold calculation overriding human connection?"

"Not cold," Elara corrected gently. "The deepest respect for each other's choice to be part of this quest. We all understand the risks, the potential sacrifices. To abandon the mission because of personal loss would dishonor those who fell pursuing it."

Mira considered this perspective, her clever mind turning it over like one of her experimental compounds, testing its properties and reactions. "I hadn't thought of it that way," she admitted finally.

"We each bring different strengths to this group," Elara said. "Your protective instinct—your desire to keep everyone together and safe—is valuable. But so is Kael's strategic vision and Lyra's ability to make difficult choices for the greater good."

"And what do you bring, oh wise one?" Mira asked, though the question held no malice, only genuine curiosity.

"Balance," Elara replied with a small smile. "The ability to see multiple perspectives and find harmony between opposing forces. It's the foundation of rune-craft—understanding that seemingly contradictory energies can create something greater than either alone."

Mira nodded slowly, her gaze returning to the stars above. "I'll try," she said finally. "To trust in this plan, despite my reservations. But if you get yourself killed investigating that northern stronghold, I'll be extremely annoyed."

Elara laughed softly, the sound carrying clearly in the night air. "I'll bear that in mind. Your annoyance is a powerful deterrent to death."

"It should be," Mira agreed with mock seriousness. "I've been told my irritation can wither plants and curdle milk at twenty paces."

They shared a moment of genuine laughter, the tension that had built throughout the day finally releasing. As they returned to camp, Mira felt something shift within her—not a complete transformation of her deeply ingrained caution, but perhaps the beginning of a willingness to trust despite past wounds.

Dawn arrived too soon, bringing with it the moment of separation. Final preparations were made in the gray light of early morning—packs checked, routes confirmed, communication protocols established. The druids departed first, leading the former captives westward toward safety and recovery. Brenna embraced Thorn and Sera before leaving, murmuring traditional blessings and pressing small tokens into their hands.

"The Green Path remains open to you always," she told them, her voice carrying the formal weight of her position as Warden. "May the ancient roots guide your steps and the eternal branches shelter your dreams."

The northern team departed next—Alaric, Elara, and Mira, accompanied by Thorn and Sera. Their path would take them through the highest reaches of the mountains, a challenging route but one that offered natural concealment from Syndicate patrols. Elara had prepared specialized runes to help them navigate the treacherous terrain, while Mira's alchemical compounds would provide protection against the harsher elements they would encounter.

As they prepared to leave, Mira found herself hesitating, glancing back at Lyra, Kael, and Rowan with uncharacteristic uncertainty. The familiar urge to deflect with humor rose within her, but instead, she approached Lyra directly.

"Don't do anything foolishly heroic," she said, her tone attempting lightness but failing to completely mask her concern. "I've invested too much time keeping you all alive to start over with a new group of reckless idealists."

Lyra smiled, recognizing the genuine care beneath Mira's prickly exterior. "We'll be careful," she promised. "And you watch over Thorn and Sera. They've been through enough already."

"As if I'd let anything happen to them," Mira replied, a protective edge entering her voice. She glanced at the young druid and the child, who stood ready with Alaric and Elara. Something in Sera's determined stance, her quiet courage despite all she had endured, resonated deeply with Mira's own carefully guarded past.

"Two weeks," Alaric reminded them as the groups prepared to part. "The Crossroads of Meren, regardless of outcome."

"And daily communication at sunset," Elara added, distributing the small crystals she and Alaric had prepared. "Brief reports only—the talismans' power is limited."

Final embraces were exchanged, words of caution and encouragement offered. As the northern team prepared to depart, Mira found herself unexpectedly embraced by Sera. The child's arms wrapped around her waist with surprising strength, her face turned up with an expression of complete trust that momentarily stole Mira's breath.

"I'm glad you're coming with us," Sera said simply.

Mira stood frozen for a moment, then awkwardly returned the embrace, her usual sardonic defenses completely dismantled by the child's sincerity. "Someone has to keep you out of trouble," she managed, her voice uncharacteristically gentle.

As they set off on their separate paths—Lyra's group eastward toward the coastal ruins, Mira's northward toward the Syndicate stronghold—Mira found herself walking with new purpose. The fear of separation remained, the echo of Taryn's betrayal still a shadow in her mind, but alongside it grew something unexpected: a fierce determination to protect not just herself, but these companions who had somehow slipped past her carefully constructed barriers.

She glanced back one last time, watching as Lyra, Kael, and Rowan disappeared around a bend in the eastern path. The familiar anxiety tightened her chest, but she pushed it aside, focusing instead on the path ahead and the companions beside her.

"Well," she said, adjusting her pack with determined cheerfulness, "shall we go poke the hornet's nest and see what buzzes out?"

Elara smiled, recognizing the return of Mira's characteristic humor as a sign that she was finding her balance. "Lead on, brave alchemist. The hornets await."

With Sera's small hand slipping trustingly into hers, Mira turned northward, each step carrying her further from the safety of the full group but closer to a new understanding of trust, risk, and the family one chooses rather than inherits. Behind them, Sentinel's Reach stood silent against the morning sky, its ancient stones bearing witness to yet another chapter in the eternal struggle between those who would protect the world and those who would reshape it to their will.

The northern path grew steeper as they ascended, winding through increasingly barren terrain where twisted pines clung tenaciously to rocky outcroppings. By midday, they had climbed high enough to look back upon the valley where they'd camped, now just a distant patchwork of green far below. The air had grown noticeably thinner, each breath requiring more effort, particularly for Sera whose small lungs struggled with the elevation.

"Here," Mira said, kneeling beside the child during a brief rest. She produced a small amber vial from her pack, uncorking it carefully. "Three drops under your tongue. It will help your body adjust to the altitude."

Sera complied without hesitation, her complete trust in Mira still unsettling to the alchemist. The child's face scrunched at the bitter taste, but she didn't complain.

"What is it?" Thorn asked, watching with interest.

"Mountain lotus extract with refined snowcap lichen," Mira explained, recorking the vial with practiced precision. "An old formula used by highland traders. It increases the blood's capacity to carry oxygen temporarily."

"I didn't know you were familiar with high-altitude alchemy," Elara remarked, genuine respect in her voice.

Mira shrugged, uncomfortable with the recognition. "Taryn specialized in adaptive compounds. Before he..." She trailed off, then continued more briskly, "Anyway, it should make breathing easier for all of us, but especially for Sera."

Already, color was returning to the child's cheeks as the compound took effect. She smiled up at Mira, that same unguarded gratitude that continually pierced the alchemist's carefully maintained armor.

"It tastes awful but feels wonderful," Sera declared, taking an experimental deep breath. "Like someone opened a window in my chest."

"Most effective medicines taste terrible," Mira informed her with mock solemnity. "It's an unwritten law of alchemy. If it tastes good, it probably isn't working properly."

As they resumed their journey, Alaric fell into step beside Mira, his ancient eyes studying her with quiet assessment. "You care for the child already," he observed, his voice low enough that only she could hear.

"I care about completing our mission without unnecessary complications," Mira countered, though without her usual sharp edge. "A child struggling to breathe would definitely qualify as a complication."

Alaric's weathered face creased in a knowing smile. "Of course. Purely practical considerations."

"Exactly," Mira agreed, too quickly. Then, after a pause, she added more softly, "She reminds me of someone, that's all."

"Yourself, perhaps?" Alaric suggested gently.

Mira's stride faltered momentarily before she recovered. "We should focus on reaching suitable shelter before nightfall," she said, deliberately changing the subject. "The temperature drops dangerously up here after sunset."

Alaric accepted the deflection with gracious understanding, but as they continued upward toward the distant Syndicate stronghold, Mira found herself keeping Sera within sight at all times, her protective instincts awakened in ways she hadn't experienced since before Taryn's betrayal had taught her the danger of caring too deeply.

CHAPTER TWENTY

The Forest's Embrace

The healing gardens of Aetherhall spread in concentric circles, each ring containing plants of different medicinal properties. Thorn moved through the outermost circle with practiced efficiency, her basket already half-filled with herbs for the day's remedies. Dawn had barely broken, the early light casting long shadows across the carefully tended beds as birds began their morning songs in the surrounding trees.

She paused to examine a sprig of silverleaf, her trained eye assessing its readiness before carefully cutting the stem with a small copper knife. Working with plants had always centered her, connected her to the rhythms of the natural world that had defined her life as a druid. Even here, in the ordered gardens of the Lady of Whispers' domain, she found comfort in the familiar tasks.

"You're up early again," observed a quiet voice behind her.

Thorn didn't need to turn to recognize Elara. The rune-caster's footsteps were distinctive—deliberate yet light, a scholar's measured pace. "The herbs are most potent when gathered at first light," she replied, adding the silverleaf to her basket. "And sleep remains... elusive."

Elara moved to stand beside her, the healing robes she'd adopted during their stay at Aetherhall catching the morning breeze. "The nightmares again?"

Thorn nodded, not meeting the other woman's gaze. Since their rescue from Sentinel's Reach nearly two weeks ago, her nights had been haunted by fragmented memories of Ravenna's control—the violation of having another consciousness override her own, puppet her body, silence her voice. "They're less frequent now. But still... vivid."

"I've prepared a new sleeping draught," Elara offered. "Different from the last—this one works with your natural dream patterns rather than suppressing them completely. It might help process the memories without being overwhelmed by them."

"Thank you." Thorn's response was simple but genuine. Despite her natural inclination toward solitude, she had come to appreciate Elara's quiet support during their recovery at Aetherhall. The rune-caster understood trauma in ways the others couldn't, having faced her own demons during their journeys.

They continued through the garden together, Thorn gathering herbs while Elara occasionally pointed out plants with properties she thought might be useful. The comfortable silence between them broke only when they reached the garden's innermost circle, where rare healing flowers bloomed around a small, crystal-clear pool.

"How is Sera this morning?" Thorn asked, her voice carefully neutral despite the concern that tightened her chest.

Elara's expression softened with understanding. "Better. She spoke a few words at breakfast—asked for more honey in her tea. Small steps, but progress."

Relief loosened something in Thorn's chest. The child had been nearly catatonic when they arrived at Aetherhall, the trauma of Ravenna's mind control affecting her far more severely than it had Thorn. While the druid had decades of mental discipline to draw upon, Sera had only her innate resilience—remarkable for one so young, but not inexhaustible.

"Perhaps I'll bring her to the gardens today," Thorn mused, gathering a sprig of dream-thistle whose pale blue flowers were known to soothe troubled minds. "The connection to growing things might help ground her."

"I think that would be wise," Elara agreed. "The Lady believes that healing happens in layers—body first, then mind, then spirit. Sera's physical recovery is well underway. Now her mind needs gentle encouragement to reengage with the world."

They completed their circuit of the garden as the sun cleared the eastern hills, bathing Aetherhall in golden light. The ancient structure—part fortress, part sanctuary—rose from the surrounding forest like something grown rather than built, its white stone towers seemingly an organic extension of the limestone cliffs behind it. Thorn had initially been wary of staying in such a clearly human-made environment, but the Lady of Whispers had created a rare harmony between artificial structure and natural world that even a druid could appreciate.

As they approached the east wing where the injured and recovering had been housed, Thorn noticed unusual activity near the main entrance. Figures in the distinctive blue-and-silver uniforms of the Order moved with purpose, several horses standing ready nearby.

"Messengers," Elara noted, following her gaze. "They arrived just before dawn. The Lady has been in council with them since."

"News of Lyra and Alaric?" Thorn asked, her grip tightening slightly on her basket. There had been no word from the pair since they departed for the northern mountains twelve days earlier, their mission to recover the fragments held in the Syndicate's fortress taking them beyond the range of communication crystals.

"We can hope," Elara replied, though her tone suggested she wasn't optimistic. "More likely reports from the Order's scouts about Syndicate movements. They've been unusually active since the incident at Sentinel's Reach."

They parted at the entrance to the east wing, Elara heading to the stillroom to prepare the day's medicines while Thorn continued to the quiet chamber where Sera had spent most of her time since their arrival. The child's recovery had become Thorn's primary focus during their stay—a way to channel her own healing energy outward rather than dwelling on the shadows that still lingered in her mind.

She found Sera sitting by the window, a small figure framed against the morning light. The child's dark hair had been neatly braided, likely by one of the attendants, and she wore a simple dress of pale green linen that made her seem even smaller than her eight years. Her attention was fixed on something outside—the garden perhaps, or the forest beyond.

"Good morning, little spark," Thorn said softly, using the nickname that had emerged during their earlier travels together. "I've brought fresh herbs for your room."

Sera turned at the sound of her voice, her large eyes—so dark they appeared almost black—focusing on Thorn with that unsettling directness that had survived even Ravenna's mental assault. She didn't speak, but her gaze tracked Thorn's movements as the druid arranged the herbs in small bundles around the room—silverleaf for clarity, lavender for calm, rosemary for memory, dream-thistle for peaceful sleep.

"I thought you might like to visit the gardens today," Thorn continued, keeping her voice gentle and unhurried. "The moon-roses are beginning to bloom, and there's a family of rabbits that has made a home near the west wall."

For a moment, she thought Sera might not respond at all—not unusual during these difficult days of recovery. Then, so quietly Thorn almost missed it: "I'd like that."

The simple response sent a wave of relief through Thorn that she carefully kept from showing on her face. Instead, she nodded as if this were the most normal conversation in the world. "After breakfast, then. I'll show you where the best flowers grow."

She was arranging the last of the herbs when a knock came at the door. Kael stood in the corridor, his tall frame filling the doorway, his expression a careful mask that immediately put Thorn on alert.

"The Lady of Whispers has called a council," he said without preamble. "All of us who are able. Including you," he added, his gaze moving briefly to Sera.

Thorn frowned. "The child is still recovering. Whatever news has come—"

"Concerns her directly," Kael interrupted, his voice low but firm. "The messengers brought word from the Green Path. About Sera's family."

380

The words hung in the air between them, heavy with implications. Sera had been an orphan when the Syndicate first took her—or so they had believed based on the limited information they'd gathered during her rescue from a Syndicate research facility months earlier. The child herself had spoken little of her past, and Thorn had not pressed, understanding too well how trauma could make certain memories too painful to revisit.

"I see," Thorn said carefully, aware that Sera was watching them both with those too-perceptive eyes. "When does the Lady wish to meet?"

"As soon as you're both ready," Kael replied. "In the Chamber of Echoes."

After he departed, Thorn turned to find Sera already standing, smoothing her simple dress with small hands that trembled slightly.

"We don't have to go if you don't wish to," Thorn told her, kneeling to meet the child's eyes. "Whatever news they have, it can wait until you feel stronger."

Sera shook her head, a hint of her former determination showing through the fragility of recent days. "I want to know," she said, her voice small but steady. "About my family."

Thorn nodded, respecting the child's decision despite her protective instincts urging caution. "Very well. But stay close to me, and if it becomes too much, we'll leave immediately. No one will think less of you for needing time."

They made their way through Aetherhall's winding corridors, Sera's small hand tucked securely in Thorn's larger one. The druid matched her pace to the child's, noting with concern how Sera's steps slowed as they approached the Chamber of Echoes. The room had been designed for important councils, its acoustic properties allowing even whispered words to be heard clearly by all present—but it was also imposing, with high ceilings and ancient stone walls carved with scenes from Sylvanthia's history.

"Remember," Thorn said quietly as they reached the massive oak doors, "we can leave at any time."

Sera nodded, her grip tightening on Thorn's hand as the doors swung open before them.

The Chamber of Echoes lived up to its name, their footsteps reverberating soft-ly as they entered. Around a circular table of polished stone sat the Lady of Whispers herself, regal in robes of midnight blue, her ageless face framed by silver-streaked dark hair. With her were Kael, Mira, Rowan, and two figures in the green-and-brown attire of the Green Path—druids from Thorn's own order, though not ones she recognized immediately.

"Welcome, Thorn. And young Sera." The Lady's voice carried that curious qual-ity that had earned her title—a soft tone that nonetheless reached every corner of the chamber with perfect clarity. "Please, join us. We have much to discuss."

Thorn guided Sera to the two empty chairs, noting how the child's eyes fixed im-mediately on the Green Path representatives. The druids—a middle-aged woman with copper-streaked hair and a younger man whose arm bore the distinctive scar-ring of a fire-survivor—returned her gaze with expressions that mingled recogni-tion with something more complex.

"These are Willow and Ash of the Green Path's eastern enclave," the Lady in-troduced. "They have traveled far with news that concerns us all, but especially young Sera."

The female druid—Willow—leaned forward slightly, her eyes never leaving Sera's face. "We've been searching for you for nearly a year," she said, her voice gentle but carrying unmistakable emotion. "Since the Syndicate raid on Mistwood."

Sera stiffened beside Thorn, her small body going rigid with tension. Thorn placed a protective hand on the child's shoulder, ready to remove her from the chamber at the first sign of distress.

"Mistwood was a small settlement within Green Path territory," Willow con-tinued, addressing the wider group now. "Hidden deep in the eastern forests, protected by ancient wards and natural barriers. It was home to several families with... unique bloodlines. Lineages that carried special connections to the old magics."

"Sera's family," Thorn guessed, pieces beginning to fall into place.

Willow nodded. "Her mother was a descendant of the Whisper Line—those with the ability to communicate directly with the consciousness of the forest itself. Her father came from the Stone Speakers, who could read the memories embedded in ancient rock formations. Together, they represented a rare convergence of gifts that the Syndicate has long sought to study and exploit."

"The raid came without warning," Ash added, his voice rougher, marked by emotion barely contained. "Our wards failed simultaneously—suggesting betrayal from within, though we've never identified the traitor. Most of the settlement's defenders fell in the initial assault. Those who survived scattered into the deep forest, many wounded."

"And Sera?" Thorn asked, feeling the child trembling beneath her hand.

"We believed her lost with her parents," Willow admitted, pain evident in her expression. "Their dwelling was at the center of the attack. By the time our reinforcements arrived, nothing remained but ashes. We found no survivors."

"Until rumors reached us of a child rescued from a Syndicate research facility," Ash continued. "A girl with unusual abilities who had been taken in by a druid traveling with the Phoenix Stone's bearer. The description matched what we knew of Sera, but we dared not hope too strongly."

"Then came word of Sentinel's Reach," Willow said. "Of Ravenna's capture of a druid and child. When we learned you had been brought to Aetherhall for recovery, we came as quickly as possible."

Throughout this explanation, Sera had remained utterly still, her face unreadable. Now, in a voice so small it might have been lost if not for the chamber's acoustic properties, she asked: "Are you my family?"

The question hung in the air, simultaneously simple and heartbreakingly complex. Willow's expression softened further, compassion and regret mingling in her gaze.

"Not by blood, little one," she answered gently. "But by bond and oath, yes. Your parents were our kin in the ways that matter most to the Green Path. I helped bring you into this world. Ash taught you your first words of the old tongue."

"We thought you lost to us," Ash added, his scarred hand clenching on the table's edge. "Finding you alive—it's a miracle we had stopped allowing ourselves to hope for."

Sera absorbed this information with the uncanny stillness that Thorn had come to recognize as her way of processing difficult emotions. Then, with the directness that children sometimes manage better than adults: "Did anyone else survive? From Mistwood?"

The druids exchanged glances heavy with meaning before Willow answered. "Some did. Twenty-three souls from a community of nearly a hundred. They've established a new settlement, deeper in the protected territories. They would welcome you home, Sera, if that is your wish."

The implications of this statement weren't lost on anyone present. Thorn felt a complex wave of emotions crash through her—joy that Sera might reclaim some connection to her past, mingled with a surprisingly sharp sense of loss at the thought of the child leaving her care. She had not realized how deeply attached she had become during their months together.

"This is much to consider," the Lady of Whispers interjected, her perceptive gaze moving between Sera and Thorn. "And not a decision that need be made immediately. For now, knowing that such a possibility exists is enough."

She turned her attention to the wider group. "But there is more to discuss. The Green Path's representatives bring other news—developments that concern our ongoing conflict with the Syndicate and the fragments of the Shattered Illusion."

"The Syndicate has increased activity throughout the eastern territories," Ash reported, his expression grim. "Particularly around sites of ancient power. They seem to be searching for something with increasing desperation."

"The remaining fragments," Rowan suggested. "After losing three at their northern fortress, they must be scrambling to secure those still unaccounted for."

"Perhaps," Willow agreed. "But their methods have changed. Rather than the focused excavations we've observed in the past, they're conducting rituals at multiple sites simultaneously—as if testing the resonance of the land itself."

"Resonance?" Mira asked, her alchemist's curiosity clearly piqued. "What kind of resonance?"

"That's unclear," Ash admitted. "But survivors from raided villages report strange phenomena before the Syndicate's arrival—distortions in natural magic, animals behaving erratically, plants growing in unnatural patterns. As if the very fabric of reality were becoming... unstable."

A troubled silence fell over the chamber as they absorbed these implications. Thorn felt a chill run through her that had nothing to do with the room's temperature. As a druid, she was intimately attuned to the natural flows of energy throughout Sylvanthia—and she had sensed subtle disturbances even here, in the protected sanctuary of Aetherhall. Ripples in the normally smooth currents of power, like stones dropped into a still pond.

"There's more," Willow said, her voice dropping lower. "We've received reports from our western enclaves of a figure matching Ravenna's description, though... changed. Transformed in ways that witnesses struggle to describe coherently."

"Changed how?" Kael asked sharply.

"Their accounts vary," Ash replied. "Some say his form shifts between human and shadow. Others claim he appears simultaneously solid and transparent, like a reflection in disturbed water. All agree that his presence causes physical discomfort—headaches, nausea, a sense of reality becoming less certain."

"The fragment's influence," Thorn said, remembering all too vividly the alien energies she had sensed during their captivity at Sentinel's Reach. "It's changing him, just as he intended—though perhaps not in the way he expected."

"Do we know what he seeks?" Rowan asked, the cartographer's mind already mapping possibilities and connections.

"He appears to be following a specific path," Willow answered. "Moving from one ancient site to another, seemingly testing each location for something only he can perceive. Most recently, he was sighted near the Whispering Stones—a circle of megaliths that predates even the oldest druidic settlements."

"A place of significant natural power," Thorn noted, familiar with the site from her own travels. "Where the boundaries between worlds have always been thinner than elsewhere."

Before anyone could respond to this observation, the chamber doors opened to admit Elara, her expression a mixture of excitement and concern.

"Forgive the interruption," she said, inclining her head respectfully toward the Lady of Whispers. "But word has just arrived from the northern mountains. Alaric has returned to the Order's sanctuary with the fragments from the Syndicate fortress."

A ripple of relief passed through the gathering, but Thorn noticed immediately what Elara hadn't said. "And Lyra?"

Elara's hesitation was answer enough, but she elaborated: "Alive, but gravely injured. She channeled an enormous amount of energy through the Phoenix Stone to contain a gateway the Syndicate had opened. The backlash was... severe."

"How severe?" Kael demanded, rising halfway from his seat before mastering himself.

"Alaric reports that she remains unconscious, her life force significantly depleted," Elara replied gently. "The Stone itself has undergone some kind of transformation in response to the energies it absorbed. He's requested our presence at the sanctuary as soon as possible—particularly those with healing knowledge."

The news cast a pall over the chamber. Though Thorn had spent relatively little time with Lyra compared to the others, she had developed genuine respect for the Phoenix Stone's bearer—a young woman thrust into extraordinary circumstances who had risen to meet them with courage and compassion.

"We should depart immediately," Kael stated, already moving toward the door.

"Not all of us," the Lady countered calmly. "Dividing our forces further would be unwise, given what we've learned about the Syndicate's increased activity and Ravenna's transformation."

"I won't sit idle while Lyra—" Kael began heatedly.

"No one suggests you should," the Lady interrupted, her voice still gentle but carrying unmistakable authority. "But consider carefully who will be most useful at the sanctuary versus who might serve better elsewhere."

A tense discussion followed, with Kael insisting on traveling to Lyra's side immediately while the others debated the most strategic distribution of their limited numbers. Throughout the exchange, Thorn remained silent, her attention divided between the larger crisis and the small figure beside her. Sera had withdrawn into herself again, her dark eyes distant as the adults argued around her.

Finally, a compromise was reached. Kael and Elara would depart immediately for the Order's sanctuary, their combat skills and healing knowledge respectively making them the logical choices. Mira and Rowan would remain at Aetherhall temporarily, coordinating with the Green Path representatives to analyze the pattern of Syndicate activities and Ravenna's movements.

"And what of Thorn and the child?" the Lady asked, her perceptive gaze settling on the druid.

All eyes turned to Thorn, who found herself at a crossroads she hadn't anticipated. Her duty as a druid called her to investigate the disturbances in natural energy that might threaten all of Sylvanthia. Her growing bond with Sera urged her to prioritize the child's recovery and reconnection with her surviving community. And her commitment to their shared mission demanded she contribute her unique skills where they would be most effective.

Before she could respond, a small voice broke the silence.

"I want to go home," Sera said, her words clear despite their softness. "To see if I remember it. To see who's left."

The simple statement carried the weight of decision. Thorn met the child's gaze, seeing both vulnerability and determination in those dark eyes.

"Then we shall take you home," she said simply. Turning to the Green Path representatives, she added, "If you will guide us to the new settlement, we can depart when Sera is strong enough for the journey."

Willow nodded, understanding passing between the druids. "We would be honored to escort you both. And perhaps along the way, we might investigate some of the disturbances we've reported. Your expertise would be valuable, Thorn, particularly given your recent... experiences with the Syndicate's methods."

The meeting concluded with plans made and responsibilities assigned. As the others filed out of the Chamber of Echoes, Thorn remained seated with Sera, giving the child time to process all she had learned.

"Are you certain about this journey?" she asked gently when they were alone. "It will not be easy, and what you find may not be what you remember."

Sera was silent for a long moment, her small face solemn with thought. "I dream about trees," she finally said. "Tall ones, with silver bark and leaves that sing in the wind. I don't know if they're real or just dreams. But I need to know."

The simple honesty of this response touched something deep within Thorn. She recognized in Sera's words her own lifelong connection to the natural world—that bone-deep need to understand one's place within the greater patterns of existence.

"The silver birches of the eastern forests," she confirmed softly. "They do indeed sing when the wind passes through their leaves. A high, sweet sound unlike any other tree."

Hope flickered across Sera's face—the first genuine emotion she had shown since their rescue. "Then my memories are real."

"Some of them, at least," Thorn agreed. "And perhaps the journey will help you recover more."

They sat together in companionable silence as morning light streamed through the chamber's high windows, casting patterns across the ancient stone floor. Outside, life continued—preparations being made, horses readied for different journeys, the complex machinery of response to crisis set in motion. But in this moment of quiet, Thorn found herself centered by the simple clarity of Sera's decision.

Home. Such a complicated word for those who had lost it. Yet so fundamental to healing—the need to reconnect with origins, to understand what remained and what had been irretrievably lost.

For Sera, home meant the community of her birth, the survivors who shared her heritage and might help her understand her emerging abilities. For Thorn herself, home had long been the forests and wild places of Sylvanthia rather than any fixed settlement. Yet in the months since rescuing Sera, her definition had subtly shifted to include the child herself—a connection that transcended place.

"Will you stay?" Sera asked suddenly, her question cutting to the heart of what Thorn had been contemplating. "When we find the others. Will you stay with me?"

The question held layers of meaning—fear of abandonment, hope for continuity, uncertainty about belonging. Thorn considered her answer carefully, respecting the child enough to offer truth rather than easy comfort.

"I cannot promise to stay in one place forever," she said honestly. "My path as a druid requires movement, following the needs of the land and its creatures. But I can promise this: whatever decisions lie ahead, we will make them together. I will not simply leave you."

Sera nodded, accepting this complex answer with the surprising wisdom she sometimes displayed. "Because we're family now too. Not by blood."

"But by bond and oath," Thorn confirmed, echoing Willow's earlier words. "By choice and shared journey. Sometimes those connections prove stronger than bloodlines."

The child's small hand found hers again, a gesture of trust that meant more than any verbal agreement. Together they rose, leaving the Chamber of Echoes to prepare for the journey ahead—a journey toward recovery, toward understanding, toward whatever new definition of home they might discover together.

The eastern forests spread before them like a vast green sea, ancient trees swaying gently in the afternoon breeze. From their vantage point on a hillside overlooking the valley, Thorn could trace the winding path they had followed for the past five days—a journey through increasingly wild territories as they left the settled lands behind.

Beside her stood Sera, the child's appearance transformed from the fragile figure who had spent weeks recovering at Aetherhall. Daily travel through the forests had brought color back to her cheeks and a steadiness to her movements. She had begun speaking more freely, asking questions about plants and animals they encountered, occasionally sharing fragments of memory that surfaced as they moved deeper into the territories of her birth.

"Is that it?" Sera asked, pointing toward a distant shimmer of light among the trees—too regular to be natural, suggesting structures hidden within the forest canopy.

"That's it," Willow confirmed, coming to stand beside them. The Green Path representative had proven a patient guide, setting a pace that accommodated Sera's shorter legs and frequent stops to examine interesting plants or forest creatures. "New Mistwood. Established after the Syndicate's attack on the original settlement."

"It looks... smaller than I remember," Sera observed, her brow furrowing slightly.

"It is smaller," Ash acknowledged, joining them at the overlook. The male druid had served as their scout throughout the journey, ranging ahead to ensure their path remained safe. "We lost many in the attack. Those who survived had to start again with limited resources."

Thorn studied the distant settlement with a druid's trained eye. Even from this distance, she could see that New Mistwood had been constructed with deep respect for the forest's natural patterns. Unlike most human settlements that cleared land for buildings, these structures appeared to have been grown into existing trees or built around them, creating a harmonious integration of human habitation and natural environment.

"They'll be watching our approach," Willow noted. "The settlement maintains constant vigilance since the attack. We should continue while daylight remains."

As they descended into the valley, Thorn felt a subtle change in the forest's energy—a sense of being observed that went beyond ordinary human sentries. The trees themselves seemed more aware, more deliberately arranged than in wild forest. Occasionally, she caught glimpses of movement among the branches that suggested creatures larger than ordinary birds or squirrels.

"Forest guardians," Ash explained, noticing her attention. "Creatures who have formed bonds with the Green Path over generations. They serve as our first line of defense, warning of approaching strangers."

"I remember them," Sera said suddenly, her pace quickening slightly. "Whisper-wings and branch-walkers. They used to bring me gifts—pretty stones and feathers."

Willow smiled at this recollection. "They were particularly fond of you, little one. Your mother's bloodline gave you a natural affinity with them that most children lack."

The mention of Sera's mother brought a momentary shadow to the child's expression, but it passed quickly, replaced by determination as she continued forward. Thorn remained close beside her, ready to offer support if the emotions became overwhelming, but respecting Sera's growing strength enough not to hover unnecessarily.

As they drew nearer to the settlement, figures emerged from the trees to meet them—druids in the distinctive green-and-brown attire of the Green Path, their expressions a mixture of wariness and hope as they recognized their approaching kin. Sera slowed her steps, suddenly hesitant as the reality of homecoming loomed before her.

"It's alright to be nervous," Thorn told her quietly. "Meeting people from your past—even people who care for you—can be overwhelming after all you've experienced."

Sera nodded, her small hand finding Thorn's larger one and holding tight. "Will you stay with me? When I meet them?"

"Of course," Thorn assured her. "For as long as you need."

The welcoming party approached cautiously, led by an elderly man whose white hair and beard contrasted sharply with his dark skin. He carried a staff of twisted wood that seemed to pulse faintly with inner light—a mark of significant status within the Green Path hierarchy.

"Elder Rohan," Willow greeted him with respectful inclination of her head. "We return with news both grave and joyful."

The elder's gaze moved past her to settle on Sera, his weathered face freezing in an expression of disbelief. For a long moment, he stood motionless, as if afraid any movement might dispel what he was seeing.

"It cannot be," he finally whispered, his voice rough with emotion. "Little Sera? Anaya and Terrin's daughter?"

Sera pressed closer to Thorn's side but didn't retreat. "I think so," she answered with characteristic directness. "I remember some things. Not everything."

The elder took a careful step forward, then knelt to bring himself to the child's level—a gesture of respect that seemed to ease some of Sera's tension. "We thought you lost in the attack," he said gently. "Finding you alive... it's a blessing beyond our hopes."

Others from the welcoming party had begun to react as recognition spread—gasps of surprise, murmured exclamations, a few tears from those who had clearly known Sera's family well. The child endured their attention with remarkable composure, though Thorn could feel the slight trembling of the small hand clasped in hers.

"Perhaps we might continue this reunion within the settlement," Thorn suggested, sensing Sera's growing overwhelm. "The child has traveled far and faced much. A quieter welcome might be kinder."

Elder Rohan nodded immediately, understanding in his eyes as he rose. "Of course. Forgiveness for our excitement—it's not every day the forest returns one we believed lost to the shadows." He gestured toward the settlement. "Please, come. We have prepared dwellings for you, and there will be time for proper introductions after rest and refreshment."

As they followed the elder into New Mistwood, Thorn found herself impressed by what the survivors had created in the wake of tragedy. The settlement blended seamlessly with the forest, dwellings constructed around living trees or incorporated into natural formations. Bridges of woven vines connected platforms at different heights, creating a multi-level community that utilized the forest's vertical space as effectively as its horizontal dimensions.

Sera walked beside her, dark eyes wide as she absorbed the familiar-yet-different surroundings. Occasionally she would pause, her head tilting slightly as if listening to something only she could hear.

"The trees are singing," she whispered to Thorn during one such moment. "Like in my dreams. But they sound... sad."

Thorn listened with her druidic senses and realized Sera was right. The forest here carried a melancholy note beneath its surface vitality—the lingering echo of trauma that had marked both the land and its people.

"They remember what was lost," she explained gently. "Just as you do. But they continue growing, creating new patterns, new homes. Finding ways to heal."

Sera considered this with her characteristic solemnity before nodding. "Like me."

"Yes," Thorn agreed, pride warming her chest at the child's insight. "Exactly like you."

They were shown to a dwelling that seemed to have grown organically from the junction of three massive trees, its interior surprisingly spacious and comfortable despite its unconventional structure. Woven screens provided privacy while allowing air to circulate freely, and soft mosses mixed with woven fibers created bedding that invited rest after days of travel.

"This was Keeper Liana's dwelling," Elder Rohan explained as they settled in. "She was lost in the attack, but her tree-home has been maintained in her memory. I think she would be pleased to know it shelters Sera's return."

After the elder departed, promising to return later with food and news, Thorn watched as Sera explored the dwelling with growing animation. The child moved from corner to corner, occasionally touching objects with a hesitant finger—a carved wooden figurine, a collection of stones arranged in a spiral pattern, dried herbs hanging from the ceiling beams.

"Do you remember any of this?" Thorn asked gently.

Sera shook her head, though not in negation. "Not this place. But it feels... right. The smells and the way the light comes through the leaves." She paused by a small alcove where a basin of water reflected dappled patterns. "My home had water inside too. A little stream that came through the floor and went out again."

This recollection, specific and detailed, seemed to surprise even Sera herself. She looked up at Thorn with widened eyes. "I remembered that. Really remembered."

"The mind holds more than we can access at any given moment," Thorn explained, settling on a woven mat near the child. "Especially after trauma. Being in a similar environment often helps those memories find their way back to the surface."

"Will I remember everything eventually?" Sera asked, coming to sit beside her.

Thorn considered the question carefully, unwilling to offer false hope. "Some memories may return. Others might remain hidden, or emerge only in dreams. And some..." She hesitated, then continued honestly, "Some may be lost permanently. But that doesn't diminish who you are or what you might become."

Sera absorbed this with the thoughtful silence that Thorn had come to recognize as her way of processing difficult concepts. Finally, she said, "I think I'm glad I won't remember everything. Some things were very bad."

"Yes," Thorn agreed, knowing the child referred not just to the attack on her original home but to her time in the Syndicate's custody and the more recent trauma of Ravenna's mind control. "Some memories serve us better when they remain distant."

They rested through the remainder of the afternoon, the journey's accumulated fatigue claiming them both despite the excitement of arrival. Thorn woke at dusk to find Sera still sleeping peacefully, her small face relaxed in a way it rarely appeared when awake. Careful not to disturb the child, she moved to the dwelling's entrance, where she found Elder Rohan waiting patiently.

"She sleeps," Thorn said quietly, stepping outside to join him on the small platform that served as a porch. "The journey has been taxing, especially given her recent ordeal."

The elder nodded, his weathered face solemn in the fading light. "Willow and Ash have told us some of what she endured. First the Syndicate's experiments, then Ravenna's control." His hands tightened on his staff, the only outward sign of the anger such knowledge must have provoked. "That she retains any sense of herself after such violations is testament to her strength."

"She is remarkably resilient," Thorn agreed. "Though the healing is far from complete."

They stood in companionable silence for a moment, watching as the settlement's residents lit lanterns among the trees, creating constellations of warm light throughout the forest canopy. The effect was both beautiful and practical—providing illumination while maintaining the natural rhythm of darkness that forest creatures required.

"There is something you should know," Elder Rohan said finally, his voice dropping lower. "Something about Sera that may explain why the Syndicate targeted her specifically."

Thorn turned to face him fully, sensing the weight of his words. "I've suspected there was more to their interest than simple cruelty. Her abilities seem... unusual, even for a child of the Green Path."

"They are," he confirmed. "Sera's bloodlines—both maternal and paternal—carry ancient gifts that rarely manifest in combination. The Whisper Line and the Stone Speakers have traditionally remained separate, their abilities being somewhat... incompatible in a single vessel."

"Yet they combined in her," Thorn observed.

"Yes. When her talents began emerging, even before the attack, we observed something unprecedented." The elder's expression grew distant with memory. "She could not only communicate with the forest consciousness as her mother did, but she could access the deep memories stored in stone and earth as her father could. The combination created a unique form of perception—the ability to sense patterns across time itself."

Thorn absorbed this revelation, pieces falling into place that explained both the Syndicate's interest and aspects of Sera's behavior she had observed during their months together.

"The patterns of the past informing the present and suggesting possible futures," she murmured. "No wonder the Syndicate wanted to study and control such an ability. In the wrong hands, such foresight would be a powerful weapon."

CHAPTER TWENTY-ONE

Runes of Innovation

E lara woke before dawn, her mind already racing with the day's preparations. The northern team had established a temporary camp in a sheltered valley three miles from the Syndicate stronghold, close enough for observation but far enough to avoid detection. Two days of careful reconnaissance had confirmed their suspicions—the facility was indeed conducting research on magical artifacts, with activity patterns suggesting something significant was underway.

She moved silently through their camp, checking the protective runes she had inscribed around its perimeter the previous evening. Each symbol glowed faintly in the pre-dawn darkness, their intricate patterns forming an invisible barrier against both physical intrusion and magical detection. The work had been exhausting, requiring precision that drew deeply on her scholarly training, but the security it provided was worth the effort.

"You should have woken me for the final inscriptions," Alaric said quietly, appearing beside her with the silent movement that belied his apparent age. "You pushed yourself too far."

"I needed the practice," Elara replied, offering a small smile that didn't quite mask her fatigue. "Theory and application are different beasts. The Academy taught me perfect runes under perfect conditions—controlled lighting, proper materials, unlimited time."

"And now you're learning the more valuable lesson of imperfect runes under impossible conditions," Alaric observed with approval. "Your adaptations to the terrain constraints were... innovative."

The compliment warmed her more than it should have. Despite months of traveling together, Alaric's praise remained rare and therefore precious. As the last living practitioner of certain ancient runic traditions, his assessment carried weight that no Academy certification could match.

"The northeastern quadrant concerns me," she admitted, gesturing toward a section where the runes pulsed with slightly uneven rhythm. "The bedrock there contains high concentrations of iron ore. It's interfering with the resonance pattern."

Alaric studied the section thoughtfully. "A traditional solution would involve recalibrating the entire sequence—time-consuming and potentially attention-drawing."

"Which is why I attempted a frequency modulation instead," Elara explained, pointing to additional smaller runes she had placed at strategic intervals. "These should compensate for the interference by adjusting their output to counterbalance the disruption."

"Ingenious," Alaric murmured, genuine admiration in his ancient eyes. "Unorthodox, but potentially more effective than the conventional approach. Who taught you this technique?"

"No one," she admitted. "I... improvised."

Something shifted in Alaric's expression—surprise giving way to a deeper assessment. "You created an original runic modification in field conditions, without reference materials or preparation time?"

Elara felt a flush of embarrassment at his tone. "It was necessary. The standard methods weren't viable given our constraints."

"Necessity mothers invention, indeed," Alaric said softly. "Your Academy instructors would be simultaneously impressed and horrified. Runic innovation is typically the domain of master practitioners with decades of experience."

"Or desperate scholars with no alternatives," she countered with a self-deprecating smile. "I had limited options and even more limited time."

Before Alaric could respond, movement from the center of camp drew their attention. Mira emerged from her tent, hair tousled from sleep but eyes alert as she performed her own morning ritual—checking the array of alchemical compounds arranged precisely on a flat stone outside her shelter.

"Please tell me one of you has started coffee," the alchemist called, not looking up from her inspection. "I refuse to contemplate infiltrating a Syndicate stronghold without caffeine. It's one of my few remaining principles."

"Water's heating," Elara replied, grateful for the interruption. Alaric's scrutiny had been growing uncomfortable, touching on insecurities she preferred to keep private. "Though I'm not sure Mira's definition of 'coffee' matches yours."

"As long as it's hot, dark, and makes my brain function, I'll accept whatever herbal abomination she's concocted," Mira declared, carefully repacking several vials. "Though I maintain that her so-called improvements to perfectly good coffee beans are unnecessary and possibly sacrilegious."

The easy banter continued as they prepared for the day ahead. Thorn emerged from the tent she shared with Sera, the young druid's connection to the natural world evident in the way plants seemed to lean subtly toward her as she passed. Sera followed moments later, her small face serious with the responsibility she clearly felt as their magical early-warning system.

Elara observed the group with quiet assessment as she prepared their morning meal. Each brought unique strengths to their mission—Alaric's ancient knowledge, Mira's alchemical expertise, Thorn's druidic abilities, and Sera's uncanny sensitivity to magical energies. Yet coordinating these disparate talents fell increasingly to her, a role she had assumed gradually and somewhat reluctantly in Lyra's absence.

It wasn't leadership precisely—Alaric's centuries of experience made him their natural authority on most matters—but rather facilitation. Her scholarly training had equipped her to understand enough of each discipline to serve as translator and integrator, finding connections between seemingly unrelated approaches and helping the group function as a cohesive unit.

"We should review the plan once more," she suggested as they gathered around the small cooking fire, careful to use only dry wood that produced minimal smoke. "Today's observation needs to be our most thorough yet if we're to attempt infiltration tomorrow."

The others nodded agreement, their expressions reflecting the gravity of their mission. The northern Syndicate stronghold represented their best lead on additional fragments of the Shattered Illusion—artifacts of immense power that could reshape reality itself if assembled. Their separated companions were pursuing another fragment along the coastal regions, making their success here doubly important.

"Thorn and I will take the western approach," Alaric began, indicating positions on the rough map Elara had sketched in the dirt. "The elevated ridge provides the clearest view of the facility's main entrance and the guard rotation patterns."

"Sera and I will monitor the eastern perimeter," Mira continued. "The child's sensitivity should help us identify any magical defenses or detection systems they've established. Plus, the tree cover is denser there, providing better concealment for my more... explosive preparations."

"Which leaves the southern approach to me," Elara concluded, indicating the final observation point. "The runestone formations there should allow me to establish a temporary scrying point if I can place the focus runes without detection."

"That's the most exposed position," Alaric noted, concern evident in his tone. "Perhaps I should—"

"I've already prepared the necessary inscriptions," Elara interrupted gently but firmly. "The southern approach requires runic expertise specifically. Your knowledge is better utilized on the western ridge, where you can assess the facility's architectural weaknesses."

A brief silence followed her calm assertion. In the early days of their journey, she might have deferred to Alaric's greater experience, accepting a reassignment without question. Now, however, months of field experience had given her confidence in her own assessments—and the others had come to respect her judgment.

"Very well," Alaric conceded with a slight nod that conveyed both acceptance and a certain pride in her growth. "But maintain communication through the thought-stones at regular intervals. If anything seems amiss, withdraw immediately."

The discussion continued as they finalized details—timing for observations, emergency protocols, rendezvous points if separated. Throughout it all, Elara found herself drawing on skills she'd never expected to need when she'd left the Academy's cloistered halls. Her education had focused on theoretical runic applications and historical analysis—not field operations against a powerful enemy organization.

As they dispersed to make final preparations, Mira approached her privately, voice pitched low to avoid being overheard. "You look like you haven't slept. The runes again?"

Elara nodded, unsurprised by Mira's perceptiveness. Despite the alchemist's carefully maintained façade of sardonic detachment, she missed very little—particularly where her companions' wellbeing was concerned.

"The protective circuit required more energy than I anticipated," she admitted. "The terrain complications meant each rune needed individual calibration rather than functioning as a standardized sequence."

"Mmm," Mira hummed noncommittally, rummaging in her satchel before producing a small vial of amber liquid. "Three drops under your tongue. Not a permanent solution, but it should restore your energy reserves temporarily without the jittery side effects of my usual stimulants."

Elara accepted the vial gratefully. "Thank you. What is it?"

"Something new I've been working on," Mira replied with a casual shrug that didn't quite disguise her pride. "Refined essence of mountain lotus combined with elements from those bioluminescent cave fungi we found last week. The druidic herbalism Thorn shared gave me some ideas about synergistic properties."

The casual mention of experimental alchemy might have alarmed Elara once. Now she simply uncorked the vial and administered the recommended dose, trusting Mira's expertise implicitly. The liquid tasted of honey and something sharper beneath—not unpleasant, and followed almost immediately by a gentle wave of revitalization that cleared the fog of fatigue from her mind.

"Impressive," she commented, returning the vial. "The onset is remarkably swift, but without the disorientation I'd expect from such rapid effect."

"That's the fungal component," Mira explained, her professional interest momentarily overriding her usual sarcasm. "It creates a temporary symbiotic relationship with the recipient's natural energy pathways rather than forcing stimulation through chemical means. Theoretically, it should work with your runic energies as well, enhancing conductivity without disrupting precision."

Elara raised an eyebrow, genuinely impressed. "You've been studying magical theory."

"Don't look so surprised," Mira huffed, though without real annoyance. "Some of us continue our education outside formal institutions. Besides, watching you work those runes has been... educational. There are more similarities between our disciplines than I initially assumed."

The admission—clearly difficult for someone as naturally guarded as Mira—touched Elara deeply. Before she could respond appropriately, Sera approached, her small face solemn with purpose.

"It's time," the child said simply. "I can feel the shift change at the stronghold. The guards are rotating positions."

With that reminder of their mission's urgency, personal conversations were set aside. They gathered their observation equipment—Elara's specialized runic tools, Alaric's ancient seeing-crystal, Mira's detection compounds, and the simple but effective druidic camouflage Thorn had prepared from local plants.

"Remember," Elara said as they prepared to separate, "observation only today. We need complete information before attempting infiltration. No unnecessary risks."

The others nodded agreement, though Mira couldn't resist a parting quip. "Says the woman heading to the most exposed position alone. Do try to follow your own excellent advice."

With final preparations complete, they moved out in their assigned pairs, using the pre-dawn shadows for cover as they approached the Syndicate stronghold from three different directions. Elara watched them go with a mixture of pride and concern—pride in their growing effectiveness as a team, concern for the dangers each would face in the hours ahead.

Then, securing her pack containing the precious runic implements, she set off toward the southern approach—alone with her thoughts and the weight of responsibility that had somehow settled onto her shoulders when she wasn't looking.

The southern approach proved as challenging as anticipated. Unlike the western ridge with its natural elevation or the eastern perimeter with its dense forest cover, the southern exposure offered minimal concealment—just scattered boulders and stunted vegetation clinging to thin soil. The runestone formations that made this position valuable for her purposes also made it the most difficult to approach undetected.

Elara moved with painstaking care, utilizing every scrap of cover available. Her Academy training had included theoretical courses on stealth and evasion, but those sterile classroom exercises bore little resemblance to the heart-pounding reality of field infiltration. Each exposed crossing between cover points required careful timing and precise movement, skills she had developed through necessity rather than formal instruction.

The thought-stone in her pocket vibrated gently—Alaric's signal that he and Thorn had reached their observation point safely. Moments later, a second vibration indicated Mira and Sera had also achieved their position. Elara pressed her own stone twice in acknowledgment, confirming her continued progress.

As she neared the runestone formation, the true nature of the site became clearer. What had appeared from a distance to be natural rock formations revealed themselves as ancient constructions—megalithic structures arranged in precise geometric patterns, their surfaces covered with weathered inscriptions that predated modern runic systems by centuries.

"Fascinating," she whispered to herself, scholarly interest momentarily overriding mission focus. These weren't simply convenient features for her scrying attempt—they were archaeological treasures, remnants of an early magical tradition that had clearly influenced the development of later runic practices.

The Syndicate's decision to build their stronghold near such a site was unlikely to be coincidence. These ancient stones would amplify certain types of magical workings, particularly those involving observation and divination. The facility's placement suggested their research involved similar principles—perhaps explaining their interest in the Shattered Illusion fragments, which were rumored to allow perception across realities.

Reaching the innermost circle of stones, Elara found what she had hoped for—a central altar-like slab with a shallow depression that would be perfect for establishing her scrying focus. The stone hummed with latent energy, responding to her presence in a way that confirmed its magical properties remained active despite centuries of exposure to the elements.

Working quickly but methodically, she unpacked her runic implements—chalk infused with powdered crystals for temporary inscriptions, a small silver bowl for the focusing medium, vials containing carefully prepared solutions that would enhance visual clarity and extend observational range. Each item was positioned precisely according to the ritual parameters she had mentally calculated during their planning sessions.

As she worked, her mind divided its attention between the technical requirements of the scrying preparation and broader awareness of her surroundings. Any mission involving the Syndicate carried significant risk, but their northern stronghold represented a particularly dangerous target—rumored to house not just research facilities but elite combat units specifically trained to counter magical practitioners.

The thought-stone vibrated again—three quick pulses followed by two longer ones. Mira's signal, indicating she had detected magical defenses around the eastern perimeter. Valuable information, but not immediately concerning for Elara's position unless similar protections extended to the southern approach.

She completed the basic runic circuit around the central stone, twelve interlocking symbols that would establish the foundation for her scrying attempt. Unlike the protective runes around their camp, which required substantial personal energy to maintain, these observation runes would draw power primarily from the ancient stones themselves—a more efficient approach that would preserve her strength for potential challenges ahead.

As she prepared to activate the circuit, a subtle sensation prickled at the edges of her awareness—a feeling of being watched that raised the fine hairs on her neck. Keeping her movements casual, she pretended to adjust one of the runic inscriptions while scanning her surroundings with peripheral vision.

Nothing moved among the scattered boulders. The stronghold remained a distant silhouette against the morning sky, no alarm evident in the regular patrol patterns visible along its walls. Yet the sensation persisted, growing stronger rather than fading.

The thought-stone vibrated again—a rapid series of pulses that formed their emergency signal. Sera had sensed something. Immediately following came Alaric's pattern—two long, three short—indicating they should maintain positions but heighten alertness.

Elara continued her work, outwardly focused on the runic preparations while her mind raced through possibilities. Had they been detected? Was this a trap? Should she abandon the scrying attempt and withdraw to safety?

The Academy's theoretical training offered little guidance for such situations. Standard protocol would recommend immediate withdrawal at the first sign of potential compromise—the scholarly approach that prioritized preservation of knowledge over acquisition of new information when risk factors exceeded certain thresholds.

But months in the field had taught her that such clean, clear guidelines rarely applied to real-world situations. Information was precious, opportunities limited. Sometimes calculated risks were necessary.

Decision made, she completed the runic circuit with deliberate precision, then poured the focusing solution into the silver bowl positioned at the center. The liquid—a complex mixture of purified water, powdered moonstone, and several of Mira's alchemical compounds—shimmered with subtle iridescence as it settled into the shallow vessel.

"Reveal without distortion, show without alerting, connect without compromising," she whispered, activating the runic sequence with a touch of her fingertip to the primary symbol. The inscription flared briefly with blue-white light before settling into a steady, subtle glow that spread through the entire circuit.

The solution in the bowl responded immediately, its surface becoming mirror-smooth despite the gentle breeze that had been rippling it moments before. Then, like a window opening in the liquid's surface, an image formed—the Syndicate stronghold, viewed as if from directly above, every detail rendered with perfect clarity despite the physical distance.

Elara leaned closer, careful not to disturb the delicate energies maintaining the scrying connection. The overhead perspective revealed aspects of the facility impossible to observe from ground level—the precise layout of buildings, the movement patterns of personnel, and most importantly, the heavily guarded central structure that likely housed their primary research activities.

As she studied the image, focusing the scrying view on specific areas of interest, the sensation of being watched intensified dramatically. No longer a vague impression, it now felt like a tangible presence—attention focused directly on her with uncomfortable intensity.

The thought-stone vibrated with increasing urgency—Sera's warning pattern repeated three times in rapid succession. Whatever the child was sensing, it represented immediate danger.

Elara began the shutdown sequence for her runic circuit, preparing to break the scrying connection and withdraw. Before she could complete it, however, the image in the bowl changed abruptly—no longer showing the overhead view of the stronghold but instead focusing on a single room deep within the central building.

This shift had not been her doing. Something—or someone—had hijacked her scrying connection, redirecting it to show her this specific location. A trap, certainly, but one designed to convey information rather than simply capture or harm her. The question was: what information, and to what purpose?

The room displayed in the scrying bowl contained a circular arrangement of equipment surrounding what appeared to be a containment field of some kind. Within this field floated a crystalline object that sent a shock of recognition through Elara's entire being—a fragment of the Shattered Illusion, its distinctive swirling colors unmistakable even through the scrying medium.

But it wasn't just the fragment that caused her breath to catch. It was the figure standing beside the containment field, observing the fragment with clinical detachment—a woman Elara recognized instantly despite the years that had passed since their last encounter.

"Valeria," she whispered, the name escaping her lips before she could prevent it.

As if hearing her across the magical connection, the woman in the scrying image looked up sharply, her gaze seeming to fix directly on Elara through the impossible distance between them. A slow, knowing smile spread across her face—the same smile that had once accompanied the most devastating betrayal of Elara's life.

The image dissolved abruptly, the scrying solution bubbling and then evaporating completely as the runic circuit overloaded from external interference. The ancient stones around Elara groaned with sudden strain, hairline fractures appearing in their weathered surfaces as the magical backlash sought release.

Moving with desperate speed, Elara snatched up her equipment and retreated from the stone circle, the thought-stone in her pocket now vibrating continuously with multiple overlapping warning patterns. She had barely cleared the outermost ring when the central altar stone shattered with a sound like thunder, fragments flying outward with dangerous force.

The explosion would be visible from the stronghold. Her position was compromised, her escape route potentially cut off. Worse, the presence of Valeria changed everything about their mission parameters—introducing complications that went far beyond tactical considerations into deeply personal territory.

Valeria Morvain. Once Elara's mentor at the Academy. Later, the woman who had stolen her research, claimed credit for her discoveries, and engineered her academic disgrace. And now, apparently, a high-ranking researcher for the Syndicate, working directly with a fragment of the Shattered Illusion.

The implications were staggering. Valeria's expertise in theoretical applications of runic energy made her extraordinarily dangerous—especially with access to an artifact of such power. Her presence explained the sophisticated magical defenses Mira had detected, and possibly the strange energy signatures that had drawn them to investigate this facility in the first place.

Most concerning of all was the deliberate nature of the scrying hijack. Valeria had wanted Elara to see her—to know exactly who they were facing. It was a psychological tactic, aimed at destabilizing her emotionally before the real confrontation began.

And it was working. Despite years of carefully constructed emotional barriers, the sight of her former mentor had shaken Elara to her core, unleashing memories and feelings she had believed safely contained behind scholarly discipline and the passage of time.

As she navigated the treacherous terrain toward their emergency rendezvous point, Elara fought to regain her composure. The mission had just become exponentially more complex. Her personal history with Valeria represented both a vulnerability and potentially valuable insight—if she could maintain objective perspective despite the emotional undercurrents.

The thought-stone vibrated with Alaric's pattern, followed by coordinates for the rendezvous location—different from their originally planned meeting point, adapting to the changed circumstances. At least the others had escaped detection so far, giving them options beyond immediate retreat.

Reaching a position of temporary cover behind a large boulder, Elara took a moment to center herself, drawing on the meditative techniques that had sustained her through the darkest days following Valeria's betrayal. Emotional control had always been her refuge—the ability to set aside personal feelings in favor of rational analysis and scholarly detachment.

"Not this time," she whispered to herself, making a decision that contradicted years of ingrained behavior. "This time, I use it."

The pain, the anger, the lingering sense of injustice—these weren't weaknesses to be suppressed but potential sources of strength if properly channeled. Valeria expected the reserved, controlled academic she had once manipulated so easily. She would not be prepared for the field-tested runic practitioner Elara had become—one who had learned to integrate emotion into her workings rather than separating herself from it.

With renewed purpose, Elara continued toward the rendezvous point, her mind already formulating adaptations to their infiltration plan. Valeria's presence changed the parameters, but it also provided an opportunity—one that might allow them to achieve their objective despite the increased danger.

The woman who had once betrayed her now stood between them and a fragment of the Shattered Illusion. The irony was not lost on Elara—that her most painful personal failure might ultimately lead to their most important mission success.

If she could transform that old wound from vulnerability to advantage.

The emergency rendezvous point was a natural cave formation approximately two miles from the Syndicate stronghold—far enough to provide safety, close enough to maintain operational viability. Elara arrived to find Mira and Sera already waiting, the alchemist pacing with barely contained nervous energy while the child sat cross-legged at the cave's entrance, her eyes closed in deep concentration.

"Finally," Mira exclaimed when Elara appeared, relief evident beneath her customary sarcasm. "I was about to start mixing tracking compounds, which would have been both tedious and potentially explosive."

"I encountered... complications," Elara replied, setting down her pack with hands that weren't quite steady. "The others?"

"On their way," Mira reported, her sharp eyes noting Elara's unusual discomposition but tactfully not commenting on it directly. "Thorn sensed the magical backlash from your position. What happened? Sera nearly jumped out of her skin before it even occurred."

Before Elara could formulate a response, Sera opened her eyes, her young face unusually solemn. "Someone was watching through you," she said simply. "Using your magic like a window to look back."

The child's intuitive understanding of what had occurred was remarkably accurate. Elara nodded, impressed despite her troubled thoughts. "Yes. My scrying attempt was intercepted and reversed. Someone at the facility detected my efforts and used the connection to observe me while revealing specific information they wanted me to see."

"A trap, then," Mira concluded grimly. "But why show you anything? Why not simply trace the connection back to capture you?"

"Because they—she—wanted me to know who we're facing," Elara replied, the admission difficult despite her resolution to use this emotional complication rather than suppress it. "The facility's lead researcher is Valeria Morvain. My former mentor at the Academy."

Mira's expression shifted from concern to sharp interest. "The one who stole your research on sympathetic runic resonance? The reason you left academic life?"

Elara nodded, somewhat surprised by Mira's knowledge of her past. She had mentioned Valeria only once, months ago, during a late-night conversation when exhaustion had lowered her usual guards. The fact that Mira had remembered and connected those details spoke to the alchemist's perceptiveness beneath her carefully maintained façade of detached sarcasm.

"She's working directly with a fragment of the Shattered Illusion," Elara continued, focusing on the tactical implications rather than personal history. "The scrying showed a sophisticated containment system—likely designed to harness the fragment's reality-altering properties for specific applications."

"That explains the energy signatures that drew us here," Mira mused. "But it complicates our extraction plan considerably. If she recognized you, security will be heightened."

"Or it presents an opportunity," came Alaric's voice from the cave entrance, where he and Thorn had just arrived. The ancient mage's expression was thoughtful as he joined their discussion. "Personal connection, even antagonistic ones, can be leveraged."

Elara met his gaze, understanding immediately what he was suggesting. "You think I should use our history to gain access."

"I think your history provides context that might inform strategy," he clarified carefully. "This Valeria deliberately revealed herself to you. Why? Simple intimidation seems insufficient motivation for someone of her reported intellectual capacity."

It was a valid question—one that had been troubling Elara since the scrying incident. Valeria's actions rarely had simple motivations. The betrayal at the Academy had been calculated for maximum professional advantage, timed precisely when Elara's research had reached its most promising stage but before formal publication could establish clear ownership.

"She's always been strategic," Elara acknowledged. "Every action serves multiple purposes. Revealing herself accomplishes immediate tactical objectives—warning us that she knows we're here, demonstrating her position of power—but there's likely a deeper purpose as well."

"Like what?" Thorn asked, her druidic pragmatism cutting through academic analysis to practical concerns.

Elara considered the question carefully, forcing herself to think not as Valeria's former student but as her current adversary. What would the woman she had once admired and later despised hope to accomplish with such a revelation?

"Distraction," she realized suddenly. "She expects me to be emotionally compromised by her presence—unable to think clearly or act effectively because of our history. It's a form of psychological warfare, meant to make me hesitate or make mistakes."

"Is it working?" Mira asked bluntly, though her tone held concern rather than challenge.

"It was," Elara admitted. "But understanding the tactic helps neutralize its effectiveness." She straightened, a new clarity coming to her thoughts as she embraced rather than resisted the emotional currents Valeria's appearance had unleashed. "In fact, it might work against her. She's expecting the academic she once manipulated—someone who separates emotion from intellect, who retreats into theory when confronted with personal challenges."

"And that's not who you are anymore," Alaric observed quietly.

"No," Elara agreed, a small smile forming despite the gravity of their situation. "It's not. The field has been... educational."

Sera, who had been listening intently to this exchange, suddenly stood. "She doesn't know about us," the child said with the simple certainty that often characterized her insights. "She saw you, but she doesn't know about me or Thorn. We feel... different to her kind of magic."

This observation sparked immediate tactical considerations. If Valeria remained unaware of their full group composition—particularly the unique abilities Sera and Thorn brought to their team—it represented a significant advantage.

"The druidic connection operates on different principles than academic runic traditions," Alaric confirmed, building on Sera's insight. "It might well be invisible to conventional magical detection methods."

"Which means we still have surprise elements available," Mira concluded, her clever mind already formulating possibilities. "If Valeria is focused on Elara as the primary threat, she may underestimate or entirely overlook the rest of us."

Their discussion evolved into a revised infiltration plan—one that acknowledged the new complications while identifying potential advantages. Rather than abandoning their mission in the face of increased danger, they adapted, incorporating Valeria's presence as a factor to be managed rather than an insurmountable obstacle.

Throughout this planning session, Elara found herself drawing on aspects of her experience that the Academy had never valued—intuition alongside analysis, emotional intelligence complementing technical knowledge. The balanced integration of these seemingly opposing approaches now seemed natural, though she recognized how dramatically it differed from her former rigid compartmentalization.

"The revised approach relies heavily on your ability to engage Valeria's attention," Alaric noted as they finalized details. "Are you certain you're prepared for that level of direct confrontation with someone who represents such a significant personal history?"

The question was gentle but direct—acknowledging both her capability and the legitimate emotional challenge involved. In the past, Elara might have responded with academic reassurance, citing theoretical preparation and emotional distance. Now, she offered something more honest.

"No," she admitted. "I can't be certain. Valeria knows exactly how to undermine my confidence because she helped shape it in the first place. But uncertainty doesn't equal incapacity." She smiled slightly, recognizing the growth this perspective represented. "Sometimes the most effective runes are those drawn with shaking hands—necessity focusing intention beyond technical perfection."

Alaric nodded, satisfaction evident in his ancient eyes. "Well said. The Academy's loss has been our considerable gain."

As they moved to individual preparations for the infiltration attempt scheduled for nightfall, Mira approached Elara privately, offering another vial of her specialized energizing compound.

"Different formulation," the alchemist explained. "This one's designed to enhance emotional resilience alongside physical stamina. Facing former mentors who betrayed you tends to require both."

Elara accepted the vial with a questioning look. "You sound like you speak from experience."

A shadow crossed Mira's expressive face. "Let's just say academic circles don't have a monopoly on betrayal by trusted teachers." She shrugged, visibly pushing away whatever memory had surfaced. "The compound works regardless. Three drops under the tongue about an hour before we move."

"Thank you," Elara said, recognizing both the practical help and the rare moment of personal connection from her usually guarded companion. "For the compound and the understanding."

Mira waved away the gratitude with characteristic deflection. "Save the sentiment for when we've actually succeeded. Preferably while enjoying quality wine in significantly safer surroundings."

As Mira moved away to continue her preparations, Elara found herself reflecting on how much her understanding of strength had changed since leaving the Academy. There, power had been defined by perfect technique, emotional detachment, and unwavering certainty—the scholarly ideal of control above all else.

Here, among companions who had become something close to family, she was discovering different forms of strength—the power in vulnerability acknowledged rather than denied, in adaptation rather than rigid adherence to theory, in connections that supported rather than credentials that isolated.

Valeria had once represented everything Elara aspired to be—brilliant, composed, respected within academic circles. Now, preparing to confront her former mentor as an adversary, Elara realized how thoroughly her definition of success had transformed. The reserved, cautious scholar who had left the Academy in disgrace had become something Valeria would never understand—a runic practitioner who drew power from integration rather than separation, from experience rather than theory alone.

Night would bring their confrontation, with a fragment of the Shattered Illusion hanging in the balance. The outcome remained uncertain, the dangers real. But as Elara reviewed the runic sequences she would use in their infiltration attempt, she felt a calm confidence that had nothing to do with academic certainty and everything to do with the strength she had found in the field—in herself and in the companions who now depended on her unique abilities.

Valeria had shown herself deliberately, expecting to unsettle her former student with painful memories. Instead, she had inadvertently revealed the true measure of Elara's growth—a transformation from theoretical scholar to practical adept that would soon prove more significant than either of them could have anticipated.

As evening approached, Elara found a quiet moment to prepare herself mentally for the confrontation ahead. She sat cross-legged at the mouth of the cave, watching as the sun dipped toward the distant mountains, casting long shadows across the valley between their position and the Syndicate stronghold.

From her pack, she withdrew a small wooden box she rarely opened—a relic from her Academy days containing personal items she had preserved despite their painful associations. Among them was a faded photograph: herself and Valeria standing before the Academy's grand entrance, both smiling, Elara's expression open with admiration, Valeria's more measured but seemingly genuine.

"You look different now," Sera observed quietly, appearing beside her with the silent movement that sometimes made Elara wonder if the child possessed some form of natural cloaking ability.

"It was a long time ago," Elara replied, not surprised by Sera's perceptiveness. "Before I understood what she truly valued."

"Not you," the child said simply. "Her. She looks... empty inside. Like she's wearing a person's face but there's something else underneath."

The observation was disturbingly accurate. Looking at the photograph with fresh eyes, Elara could see what her younger self had missed—the calculation behind Valeria's smile, the way her gaze assessed rather than connected.

"You see people clearly," Elara noted, carefully returning the photograph to its box.

Sera shrugged. "It's easier sometimes, when you've been hurt. You learn to look harder at what's real instead of what you wish was there."

The wisdom in the child's words struck Elara deeply. How much pain had Sera endured to develop such insight at so young an age? Yet instead of becoming bitter or withdrawn, she had channeled that experience into remarkable perceptiveness and compassion.

"When we face her tonight," Elara said, making a decision, "stay close to me. Your ability to sense what's beneath the surface might prove more valuable than any runic knowledge I possess."

Sera nodded solemnly, accepting the responsibility without hesitation. "I will. And Elara?" She reached out, her small hand covering Elara's with surprising warmth. "You're not empty inside. You're full of light—even the parts that hurt."

With that simple affirmation, the child slipped away to help Thorn with final preparations, leaving Elara to contemplate how often wisdom came from unexpected sources—and how thoroughly her journey had transformed not just her skills but her understanding of strength itself.

CHAPTER TWENTY-TWO

Veils Between Worlds

Three days had passed since the revelations in Valtoria's Chronolibrary, and Lyra had spent most of that time studying the channeling principles provided by the archivists. The complex patterns and formulations required intense concentration, but she found herself grasping the fundamentals with surprising speed—as if some part of her had been waiting for this knowledge all along.

She sat cross-legged on the floor of her quarters, the transformed Phoenix Stone resting on a silk cloth before her. Its opalescent surface shimmered with inner light, occasionally pulsing in rhythm with her breathing. According to the archivists' instructions, this synchronization was the first step toward properly channeling the Stone's reconnected energies.

A soft knock at her door broke her concentration. "Enter," she called, carefully rewrapping the Stone in its protective silk.

Elara stepped inside, carrying a tray with steaming tea and what appeared to be ancient scrolls. "The archivists provided these additional texts," she explained, setting the tray on a nearby table. "They contain more detailed explanations of the principles you've been studying."

"Thank you." Lyra accepted the cup gratefully, inhaling the aromatic steam. The tea had an unusual flavor—herbal yet somehow metallic, with undertones she couldn't quite identify. "This tastes... different."

"It's a Valtorian blend," Elara replied. "Apparently designed to enhance mental clarity and perception. The archivists claim it helps attune one's mind to the subtler vibrations of reality."

"That sounds suspiciously like mystical nonsense," Lyra observed with a small smile.

"I thought the same," Elara admitted. "Until I tried it while examining some of their ancient texts. The patterns... shifted. Became clearer somehow." She hesitated. "Have you made your decision yet? About the nexus?"

The question hung heavy in the air between them. Since learning of the destabilizing nexus beneath Valtoria and the archivists' request that she use the Phoenix Stone to reseal it, Lyra had been weighing her options carefully. The potential cost—years from her natural lifespan—was significant. Yet the consequences of inaction seemed equally grave.

"Not yet," she replied honestly. "I need to understand more about what I'd be attempting before I commit to anything."

Elara nodded, her expression thoughtful. "The others are gathered in the common area. Alaric has discovered something about the nexus that he believes is crucial to our understanding of the situation."

Lyra's pulse quickened at this news. Any additional information might provide clarity for her decision. "I'll join you shortly."

After Elara departed, Lyra finished her tea, noting with interest that the complex patterns of the channeling principles did indeed seem clearer in her mind, their relationships more apparent. Perhaps there was something to the archivists' claims after all.

She secured the Phoenix Stone around her neck, its familiar weight somehow comforting despite its transformation. Whatever decision she made, understanding the full scope of the situation was essential.

The common area bustled with activity when she arrived. Kael and Rowan were engaged in quiet conversation near the window, while Mira appeared to be interrogating a younger archivist about some aspect of Valtorian alchemy. Alaric stood at a central table where ancient maps and diagrams were spread out, his weathered finger tracing lines that connected various locations.

The lead archivist—whom they had learned was called Archivist Thale—acknowledged Lyra's arrival with a slight bow. Unlike the other archivists, whose appearances seemed to shift subtly depending on the light and angle of observation, Thale possessed a more defined presence. Tall and willowy, with skin that held an alabaster luminescence, they had features that blended masculine and feminine aspects into something elegantly androgynous. Their eyes were perhaps their most striking feature—irises of deep violet that occasionally seemed to ripple like water disturbed by an unseen force.

"You've discovered something?" Lyra asked, approaching the table where Alaric worked.

The ancient mage looked up, his expression grave yet animated with the excitement of revelation. "Indeed. Something the archivists neglected to mention about the nexus." There was a subtle edge to his voice as he glanced toward Thale.

"Not neglected," the lead archivist corrected smoothly. "Simply awaiting the appropriate moment for disclosure."

"Which conveniently arrived after I discovered it myself," Alaric countered, though without real hostility. He gestured for the others to join them around the table. "Look at this map—it shows Valtoria's location in relation to other significant magical sites across Sylvanthia."

They gathered around, studying the ancient parchment. Lines of varying thickness connected Valtoria to dozens of other locations—some familiar, others unknown to them. The pattern formed a complex web with Valtoria at its center.

"Ley lines," Elara observed immediately. "Natural channels of magical energy that flow through the land."

"More than that," Alaric said. "These are what the ancient texts call 'Veils of Convergence'—places where the boundaries between our world and others naturally thin. Valtoria sits at the intersection of seven major Veils—a conjunction unmatched anywhere else in known lands."

"And this matters because...?" Mira prompted, her practical nature asserting itself.

"Because it explains why the nexus formed here in the first place," Alaric replied. "And more importantly, why it's becoming unstable now." He turned to Thale. "The nexus isn't just a natural phenomenon that Valtoria was built around, is it? It's the reason Valtoria exists at all."

The lead archivist inclined their head slightly, neither confirming nor denying.

"The original purpose of this place wasn't primarily to preserve knowledge," Alaric continued, his voice gaining strength as he pieced together his discovery. "It was to monitor and maintain the stability of the nexus. The library was secondary—a collection of information needed to understand and control the convergence point."

"That's quite an accusation," Thale observed, their musical voice betraying no emotion.

"Not an accusation—an observation," Alaric corrected. "And one that changes our understanding of what's happening here." He pointed to specific markings on the map. "These symbols indicate disruptions along the Veils—recent ones, if I'm interpreting correctly. The nexus isn't destabilizing in isolation; it's responding to disturbances throughout the entire network."

Lyra leaned closer, studying the markings Alaric indicated. "These locations... some of them are places where we've encountered the Syndicate or found fragments of the Shattered Illusion."

"Precisely," Alaric nodded, approval in his eyes. "The Syndicate's activities—their experiments with the fragments, their attempts to manipulate reality—they've been inadvertently weakening the Veils across Sylvanthia. Each disturbance sends ripples through the network, eventually concentrating here at the convergence point."

"So the nexus is like a wound that's festering because of infections elsewhere in the body," Kael suggested, demonstrating his tactical mind's ability to grasp complex concepts through practical metaphors.

"An apt comparison," Alaric agreed. "And it means that simply resealing the nexus here, while necessary, won't address the underlying problem. The Veils will continue to weaken as long as the Syndicate's activities continue."

All eyes turned to Thale, whose expression remained unreadable. "Is this true?" Lyra asked directly. "Have you been asking me to treat a symptom while ignoring the cause?"

For the first time since they had met the lead archivist, a flicker of genuine emotion crossed their features—something like resignation mixed with respect. "Your companion's insight is... accurate, if incomplete. The nexus requires immediate attention regardless of external factors. Its collapse would be catastrophic across multiple realities. But yes, lasting stability cannot be achieved without addressing the broader pattern of disturbances."

"Which you conveniently failed to mention," Mira noted dryly.

"Our focus is necessarily on the nexus itself," Thale replied. "Valtoria's purpose has always been to maintain the convergence point. The external Veils fall outside our direct responsibility."

"Convenient division of labor," Kael muttered.

"More like deliberate compartmentalization," Alaric corrected, his ancient eyes fixed on Thale. "The original architects of Valtoria created a system where different groups maintained different aspects of the Veils, with limited knowledge of each other's work. A safeguard against any single faction gaining too much control." His expression hardened slightly. "A system that contributed to Valtoria's fall when communication between those factions broke down."

This last observation seemed to strike home. Thale's violet eyes rippled more noticeably, and when they spoke again, their voice carried a weight of history that hadn't been present before.

"The Sundering, as we call it, was indeed a failure of unity," they acknowledged. "The different Orders tasked with maintaining the Veils grew isolated, suspicious of each other. When the Mage Wars began, that suspicion turned to open conflict. Knowledge was hoarded, then weaponized. Valtoria itself became a battlefield."

"And the nexus?" Lyra pressed.

"Nearly collapsed completely," Thale admitted. "It took the sacrifice of the Seven—the original Septum—to stabilize it and create the sealing matrix that has endured until now. But their work was necessarily incomplete, as the other Veils had already been compromised."

The revelation hung in the air, reshaping their understanding of both Valtoria and the task before them. What had seemed a localized problem—significant but contained—was revealed as merely one manifestation of a much larger pattern of instability.

"Show us," Lyra said suddenly, her decision crystallizing in that moment. "Show us the nexus chamber again, but this time with complete context. If I'm to attempt this resealing, I need to understand exactly what I'm dealing with—not just the nexus itself, but its connections to the broader network of Veils."

Thale studied her for a long moment, those violet eyes seeming to peer beyond surface thoughts to deeper intentions. Finally, they nodded. "As you wish. Though I must caution that full understanding carries its own risks. Some knowledge cannot be unlearned."

"A risk I'm willing to take," Lyra replied firmly. "No more half-truths or convenient omissions. If we're to help you address this threat, we need complete transparency."

The lead archivist accepted this with another slight bow. "Very well. The chamber can be prepared to reveal the full network of connections. It will require some time—perhaps an hour. Until then, you may wish to review these." They gestured to an archivist standing nearby, who stepped forward bearing an ornate wooden box.

Inside the box lay seven small crystals, each a different color but all pulsing with the same gentle rhythm—a rhythm that matched the Phoenix Stone's current cadence exactly. Lyra felt an immediate resonance, as if the crystals were somehow attuned to her through the Stone.

"Focus stones," Thale explained. "Created by the original Septum to help channel and direct the nexus energies during the first sealing. They've remained dormant since then, but your presence seems to have awakened them."

"My presence specifically?" Lyra asked, though she already suspected the answer.

"Your bloodline," Thale confirmed. "The Phoenix Stone recognized you as a worthy bearer because of your ancestral connections. These focus stones respond to the same resonance."

"And you're only mentioning this now because...?" Mira prompted, skepticism evident in her tone.

"Because until now, they remained inert," Thale replied simply. "Their awakening in your presence was... unexpected. It suggests possibilities we had not considered."

"What possibilities?" Alaric asked sharply.

"The original sealing required seven mages working in concert, each channeling through a focus stone," Thale explained. "We believed a single bearer, even one with your connection to the Phoenix Stone, would need to compensate with greater personal sacrifice to achieve the same effect. But if the focus stones have awakened..."

"Then perhaps the cost needn't be as high as you initially claimed," Kael concluded, hope entering his voice for the first time since the nexus had been revealed to them.

"It is a possibility worth exploring," Thale acknowledged cautiously. "Though I would not raise false hopes. The sealing will still require significant energy, regardless of method."

"But potentially drawn from the focus stones rather than exclusively from Lyra's life force," Elara noted, her scholarly mind immediately grasping the implications.

The lead archivist neither confirmed nor denied this, merely inclining their head slightly before departing to oversee preparations for their return to the nexus chamber. As soon as they were out of earshot, the companions gathered closer around the crystals, examining them with newfound interest.

"Convenient timing on the revelation of these artifacts," Mira observed dryly. "Almost as if they were waiting to see how desperate we'd become before offering alternatives."

"Or they genuinely didn't know the stones would respond to Lyra," Rowan suggested, ever the voice of measured consideration. "Not everything is manipulation."

"In Valtoria? I'm not so sure," Kael muttered, though his expression had lightened considerably at the prospect of Lyra facing reduced risk.

Alaric studied the crystals with the careful assessment of one who had witnessed centuries of magical artifacts. "These are genuine," he confirmed after a moment. "And extremely old—contemporaneous with the original sealing, as Thale claimed. Their resonance with the Phoenix Stone is natural, not contrived."

"Which doesn't mean the archivists have been entirely forthcoming about their potential use," Elara pointed out. "If these focus stones can distribute the channeling burden, why not mention that possibility from the beginning?"

"Perhaps because they weren't certain," Lyra suggested, reaching out to touch one of the crystals—a deep amber stone that seemed to pulse more strongly as her fingers approached. "Or perhaps because they wanted to test my commitment before revealing all their secrets."

The moment her skin made contact with the amber crystal, a surge of energy flowed through her—not painful, but intensely present, like suddenly becoming aware of a limb that had been numb. The Phoenix Stone at her throat flared in response, creating a visible connection of light between the two artifacts.

"Fascinating," Elara breathed, watching the interaction with scholarly interest. "They're harmonizing—establishing resonance patterns that amplify each other rather than competing."

Lyra carefully withdrew her hand, the connection fading but not disappearing completely. A subtle thread of light continued to connect the Stone to the crystal, barely visible except in direct observation. "I think you're right about the distributed channeling," she said. "It felt like... like the crystal was offering to carry part of a burden. Not taking over, but sharing."

"Which changes the equation considerably," Alaric noted. "If all seven crystals function similarly, the personal cost of the resealing might be reduced to a fraction of what we initially feared."

"Assuming we can trust what these artifacts are offering," Kael cautioned, ever suspicious of too-convenient solutions. "Magic this ancient often comes with hidden costs or unexpected consequences."

"A valid concern," Alaric acknowledged. "Though in this case, I believe the greater risk would be in not utilizing them. These were created specifically for nexus management—they're designed for precisely the task at hand."

Further discussion was interrupted by the return of Archivist Thale, accompanied by two members of the Septum—the elite seven who maintained the daily rituals stabilizing the nexus. These two wore the midnight blue robes with elaborate silver embroidery that marked their status, their features more sharply defined than other archivists they had encountered.

"The chamber is prepared," Thale announced. "If you will follow us, the full network will be revealed for your inspection."

They proceeded through Valtoria's labyrinthine structure, descending via now-familiar spiral staircases and sloping corridors that seemed to fold back on themselves in ways that defied conventional geometry. The deeper they went, the more pronounced the strange qualities of Valtoria became—walls that shimmered with half-seen movement, floors that seemed solid yet somehow fluid underfoot, ceilings that appeared to open onto impossible vistas when viewed from certain angles.

Finally, they reached the massive circular door of obsidian that marked the entrance to the nexus chamber. Unlike their previous visit, when seven archivists had maintained a continuous incantation around the door, today only three remained—their voices rising and falling in that musical language that seemed to resonate with the very structure around them.

"The focus stones' awakening has reduced the maintenance burden," Thale explained, noting their observation of the reduced number. "Another unexpected benefit of your presence."

The obsidian door swung inward with its characteristic silence, revealing the chamber beyond. But where before they had seen only the central nexus—that vertical fissure shimmering with impossible colors—now the entire chamber had been transformed.

From the nexus at the center, seven distinct pathways of light extended outward, each a different color corresponding to one of the focus stones. These pathways didn't simply cross the chamber floor; they continued upward along the walls and across the ceiling, creating a three-dimensional web of luminescence that filled the entire space. Where the pathways intersected, small nodes of concentrated light pulsed with varying intensities.

"The Veils of Convergence," Thale said simply. "As they currently exist throughout Sylvanthia and beyond. The nexus serves as both connection point and regulator for the entire network."

It was a breathtaking sight—beautiful and terrifying in equal measure. The complexity of the network was immediately apparent, as was its current state of distress. Several pathways flickered erratically, their light dimming in places or flaring too brightly in others. Some of the intersection nodes pulsed with obvious instability, their rhythms chaotic rather than harmonious.

"The red pathway," Alaric observed, pointing to a particularly troubled line that flared and dimmed in rapid succession. "That corresponds to the eastern mountains—where the Syndicate established their primary research facility."

"Yes," Thale confirmed. "Each disruption along the Veils creates ripples that eventually reach the nexus. The eastern mountains have seen particularly intensive manipulation of reality through fragment experimentation."

"And this one," Elara indicated a blue pathway that seemed to fade almost to invisibility in places before strengthening again. "This matches the coastal regions where the Old Kingdom ruins are located."

"Correct again. The coastal Veil has experienced natural degradation over centuries, accelerated recently by artifact retrieval activities."

Lyra studied the entire network, her eyes drawn to the places where multiple pathways intersected. "These nodes—they're secondary nexus points, aren't they? Smaller convergences where multiple Veils cross."

"Indeed," Thale acknowledged, approval evident in their tone. "Less powerful than the primary nexus, but significant nonetheless. In the original design, each was maintained by a dedicated caretaker Order. After the Sundering, most fell into neglect."

"Which explains why the entire network is vulnerable now," Kael concluded. "With no one maintaining these secondary points, disruptions travel unchecked until they reach the primary nexus here."

"Precisely." Thale gestured toward the central fissure, where all seven pathways ultimately converged. "The nexus beneath Valtoria was designed to withstand significant disturbance, but not the sustained assault it now faces from all directions simultaneously."

Lyra approached the central platform, feeling the Phoenix Stone pulse more strongly as she drew near the convergence point. The focus stones in their wooden box, which Rowan had carefully carried down with them, began to glow more intensely as well, each resonating with its corresponding pathway in the chamber.

"If I attempt the resealing," she said slowly, piecing together the implications of what she was seeing, "it would stabilize the nexus itself, but not address these disruptions along the Veils. The problem would eventually recur."

"Yes," Thale admitted. "Though 'eventually' might mean decades or even centuries, depending on the effectiveness of the sealing and the future activities affecting the Veils."

"Not good enough," Lyra decided, her voice gaining strength as clarity emerged from complexity. "If we're going to address this, we need to do it properly—not just contain the symptom but treat the underlying cause."

"What are you suggesting?" Alaric asked, though his expression suggested he already anticipated her answer.

"The secondary nexus points," Lyra replied, pointing to the largest intersection nodes along the pathways. "They need to be stabilized as well. Not necessarily sealed completely, but at least reinforced enough to filter disruptions before they reach the primary nexus."

Thale's violet eyes rippled with what might have been surprise. "What you propose would require multiple operations, not just one. Each secondary point would need individual attention."

"Then that's what we'll do," Lyra stated simply. "The focus stones—they correspond to the seven pathways, don't they? Each designed to channel and stabilize a specific Veil?"

"Yes," Thale confirmed. "In the original system, each stone was wielded by a dedicated mage who maintained their assigned Veil."

"Then we distribute them," Lyra decided, looking around at her companions. "Not just me attempting to channel all seven simultaneously, but each of us taking responsibility for a specific stone and its corresponding Veil."

The proposal hung in the air, bold in its simplicity yet profound in its implications. Thale studied Lyra with those unsettling violet eyes, their expression unreadable. "What you suggest has not been attempted since the Sundering. The coordination required would be... challenging."

"But not impossible," Alaric interjected, a new light of understanding in his ancient eyes. "The original system was designed for exactly this kind of distributed responsibility. Seven mages, seven stones, seven Veils—all working in concert through the primary nexus."

"It would still require significant power," Thale cautioned. "Each stone draws on its bearer's life force to some degree."

"But spread across seven instead of concentrated in one," Kael pointed out, hope evident in his voice. "The cost to each would be manageable rather than potentially fatal."

Lyra nodded, conviction growing as the pieces aligned in her mind. "This is the right approach. Not just for addressing the immediate crisis, but for establishing a sustainable solution. If we can stabilize both the primary nexus and the secondary points, we create a foundation for long-term balance."

"There's just one problem," Mira observed practically. "There are seven stones but only six of us. Unless one of the archivists is volunteering to join our merry band of reality repairers."

A moment of silence followed this observation as they all realized the mathematical discrepancy. Thale's expression shifted subtly, something like reluctance crossing their features before they spoke.

"There is... another possibility," they said slowly. "One not recorded in the official histories but preserved in the personal journals of the original Septum."

"Another convenient revelation," Mira muttered, though without real heat.

"Not convenient—controversial," Thale corrected. "What I am about to share contradicts the established understanding of how the sealing matrix functions." They turned to Lyra directly. "The Phoenix Stone itself can serve as the seventh focus, channeling and coordinating the energies of the other six. Its transformation has reconnected it to the spaces between realities—the same spaces the nexus intersects."

"So Lyra would still bear the central burden," Kael concluded, his earlier hope fading.

"Not necessarily," Thale replied. "The Stone's unique properties allow it to draw power from the interstices themselves rather than solely from its bearer. With proper preparation and execution, the personal cost could be minimized."

"And you're only mentioning this possibility now because...?" Mira prompted, her skepticism returning in full force.

"Because it has never been proven," Thale admitted. "It exists only as theoretical speculation in private writings, not as established methodology. To attempt it would be to venture into unknown territory."

"Which describes most of what we've done since beginning this journey," Lyra observed with a slight smile. "Unknown territory is practically our natural habitat at this point."

The tension in the chamber eased somewhat at her wry comment, though the gravity of the situation remained. They stood surrounded by the visual representation of a network in crisis—pathways flickering, nodes pulsing irregularly, the central nexus shimmering with barely contained energies.

"If we pursue this approach," Alaric said, his voice taking on the authoritative tone of the ancient Warden he had once been, "we would need to understand precisely how each focus stone interacts with its corresponding Veil. The channeling principles would need to be adapted for multiple bearers working in concert rather than a single channeler."

"All possible," Thale confirmed. "Though it would require intensive preparation. Each bearer would need to attune to their assigned stone, learn its specific resonance patterns, and practice coordinated channeling with the others."

"How long would such preparation take?" Kael asked, ever mindful of practical timelines.

"Under normal circumstances, months at minimum," Thale replied. "But given the accelerating degradation of the nexus and your group's demonstrated aptitude for magical adaptation... perhaps two weeks. Possibly less with total dedication to the task."

"Two weeks of intensive training versus years of Lyra's life," Mira summarized bluntly. "Not a particularly difficult calculation."

"Assuming the distributed approach works as theorized," Thale cautioned. "I cannot offer guarantees where none exist."

Lyra looked around at her companions, reading their expressions—Kael's protective concern warring with strategic assessment, Mira's skepticism balanced by practical acceptance of their limited options, Elara's scholarly fascination with the magical theory involved, Rowan's quiet determination to support whatever path they chose, and Alaric's ancient wisdom recognizing patterns that echoed across centuries.

"We attempt the distributed approach," she decided. "All of us working together rather than placing the entire burden on one. It's not just pragmatically superior—it's symbolically appropriate. The nexus failed originally because the different Orders lost their sense of common purpose. We succeed now by restoring that unity."

The decision resonated through the chamber, the Phoenix Stone at her throat pulsing with increased warmth as if in approval. The focus stones in their box glowed more intensely as well, each seeming to call to a specific member of their group.

"So be it," Thale acknowledged, a new respect evident in their musical voice. "The preparation begins immediately. Each of you must select—or rather, be selected by—a focus stone. The resonance between bearer and stone is crucial to the process."

One by one, they approached the box of crystals, each experiencing a distinct reaction as they found the stone that responded to them. Kael's hand was drawn to a deep red crystal that flared with fierce energy at his touch. Mira found herself connected to a vibrant green stone that seemed to shimmer with constantly shifting patterns. Elara's fingers closed around a blue crystal that pulsed with steady, rhythmic light. Rowan selected—or was selected by—a warm amber stone that glowed with a gentle but persistent radiance. Alaric, to no one's surprise, found his match in a crystal of the deepest purple, ancient in its resonance and profound in its connection to the spaces between realities.

The final stone—a brilliant white crystal that seemed to contain all colors within its depths—remained in the box, awaiting its bearer.

"This one requires special handling," Thale explained, carefully lifting the white crystal with reverent hands. "It corresponds to the seventh Veil—the one that extends beyond Sylvanthia entirely, connecting to realms we can scarcely comprehend."

"Who will bear it?" Lyra asked, though she already suspected the answer.

"One of the Septum must," Thale replied. "Specifically, the First—our most experienced channeler. The white Veil demands specialized knowledge that only the First possesses."

With the initial selection complete, they turned their attention to practical matters. The training would need to be intensive yet carefully structured, with individual practice sessions for each bearer to master their stone's specific resonance patterns, followed by increasingly complex group exercises to establish coordination.

"The nexus chamber itself will serve as our primary training ground," Thale explained as they prepared to depart. "The proximity to the convergence point enhances the stones' responsiveness, allowing for more efficient attunement."

"And what of the Syndicate?" Kael asked, his tactical mind never far from potential threats. "If their activities along the Veils continue, won't they potentially accelerate the degradation before we're ready to act?"

"A valid concern," Thale acknowledged. "Though Valtoria's temporal nature provides some advantage. Time passes differently here—we can potentially complete weeks of training while only days elapse in the outside world."

"Convenient," Mira noted, though with less skepticism than before.

"Designed," Thale corrected. "Valtoria was created specifically to allow for intensive study and preparation while minimizing external passage of time. It is one of the few advantages we retain from the original architecture."

As they exited the nexus chamber, the obsidian door sealing silently behind them, Lyra found herself contemplating the path ahead. What had begun as a quest for knowledge about the Phoenix Stone's transformation had evolved into something far more significant—a mission to stabilize not just a single nexus point but an entire network of reality boundaries.

The weight of this responsibility was substantial, yet somehow less daunting when shared among them all. Each would bear their portion, contribute their unique strengths, and together they would address a threat that transcended individual concerns.

"Two weeks of intensive training," Kael remarked as they ascended toward their quarters. "Followed by what promises to be an extraordinarily complex magical operation affecting multiple realities. Just another typical chapter in our ongoing adventure."

His dry observation drew smiles from the others, easing the tension that had built during their time in the nexus chamber. This ability to find humor even in dire circumstances had become one of their greatest strengths as a group—a reminder that they remained human despite the cosmic scale of their undertaking.

"At least we'll be well-rested," Mira added. "Assuming Valtorian beds become more comfortable than they've been thus far. I swear mine rearranges itself while I sleep."

"That's because it does," Alaric informed her with perfect seriousness. "The furnishings here adapt to their users' subconscious preferences. If your bed seems restless, perhaps it reflects your own mental state."

Mira's expression of horrified realization caused another round of much-needed laughter as they continued their ascent. Even Thale's usually impassive features showed a flicker of amusement, suggesting that beneath their otherworldly appearance and formal manner, the archivists retained some connection to more human emotions.

As they reached the upper levels of Valtoria, Lyra found herself walking alongside Alaric, slightly separated from the others. The ancient mage's expression had grown thoughtful, his eyes distant as if seeing beyond their immediate surroundings.

"There's something you're not telling us," she observed quietly. "Something about the nexus or the Veils that you recognized but didn't mention in front of the archivists."

Alaric's gaze refocused on her, a flicker of surprise crossing his weathered features before settling into resigned acknowledgment. "Your perception grows sharper with each passing day," he noted. "Yes, there is something... something I suspected but needed to confirm before sharing."

"And have you confirmed it?"

"Partially," he admitted. "The pattern of disturbances along the Veils—it's not random, nor is it merely the result of Syndicate activities, though they have certainly contributed. There's an underlying purpose to it, a deliberate destabilization that follows ancient patterns."

"What patterns?" Lyra pressed, sensing the importance of his observation.

Alaric glanced ahead to ensure the others remained out of earshot before continuing. "During the Mage Wars, certain factions sought to... weaponize the Veils. Not merely cross them or study them, but actually use their instability as a means of attacking their enemies. They developed techniques for creating targeted disruptions—ripples that would travel along specific pathways to affect distant locations."

"And you think someone is using those techniques now?" The implications were disturbing—suggesting not just Syndicate experimentation but deliberate sabotage of reality's foundations.

"I think it's a possibility we must consider," Alaric replied carefully. "The disturbances follow patterns documented in texts I studied centuries ago—texts that were supposedly destroyed during Valtoria's fall. If someone has rediscovered those methods..."

He left the thought unfinished, but its conclusion was clear enough. They might be facing not just a natural crisis accelerated by magical experimentation, but a calculated attack on the very structure of reality itself.

"Should we tell the others?" Lyra asked, weighing the value of shared knowledge against the potential distraction it might create during their critical training period.

"Not yet," Alaric decided after a moment's consideration. "Let them focus on mastering the focus stones and preparing for the stabilization ritual. I'll continue investigating my suspicions in parallel. If I find conclusive evidence, then we can address this additional complication together."

Lyra nodded, trusting his judgment in this matter. Alaric's centuries of experience had taught him when to share information and when to verify it first. For now, their primary task remained clear—prepare to stabilize the nexus and its connected Veils, preventing immediate catastrophe while buying time to address deeper threats.

As they rejoined the others, Thale was outlining the training schedule that would begin the following morning. Each bearer would work individually with a member of the Septum to establish basic resonance with their focus stone, followed by paired exercises to develop coordination, and eventually full group sessions in the nexus chamber itself.

"The process will be demanding," the lead archivist cautioned. "Both physically and mentally. The focus stones draw on multiple levels of consciousness simultaneously, requiring integration of intuitive and analytical faculties that most individuals keep separate."

"In other words, it'll be exhausting, disorienting, and possibly painful," Mira translated bluntly. "Just another Tuesday for this group."

Her characteristic humor drew smiles from her companions, each recognizing the truth in her assessment. Their journey had indeed exposed them to experiences that defied conventional understanding and pushed the boundaries of human endurance. This new challenge, while daunting, was merely the latest in a progression that had been transforming them since their paths first converged.

"Rest well tonight," Thale advised as they reached the level containing their quarters. "Tomorrow begins a process unlike any you have experienced before—one that will forge connections not just between yourselves, but between the very fabric of realities."

With that somewhat ominous encouragement, the lead archivist departed, leaving the companions to prepare themselves for the intensive training ahead. They gathered briefly in their common area, exchanging thoughts about what they had learned and the path they had committed to following.

"So we're really doing this," Kael said, half statement and half question. "Attempting to stabilize an entire network of reality boundaries using ancient focus stones that haven't been properly utilized in centuries."

"When you put it that way, it sounds almost impossible," Elara observed with a slight smile. "But then, most of what we've accomplished since beginning this journey would have seemed equally implausible at the outset."

"True enough," Rowan agreed quietly. "From sealing rifts to confronting Ravenna, we've consistently faced challenges that exceeded conventional possibilities."

Lyra looked around at her companions, these people who had become more than friends—a chosen family forged through shared trials and mutual trust. Each held one of the focus stones now, the crystals pulsing gently in their hands with individualized rhythms that somehow harmonized when brought together.

"What concerns me," Mira said, examining her green crystal with analytical interest, "is whether these stones are truly as straightforward as the archivists claim. Ancient magical artifacts rarely come without complications or hidden properties."

"A valid concern," Alaric acknowledged. "Though in this case, the stones' purpose aligns with our own. They were created specifically to stabilize the Veils—that much is clear from their resonance patterns and the way they interact with the nexus chamber."

"Still," Kael added, "we should proceed with caution. Each of us should document any unusual effects or sensations while working with our assigned stone. Share information freely among ourselves, even details that might seem insignificant."

They agreed to this protocol, recognizing the wisdom in maintaining complete transparency within their group even as they navigated the archivists' selective disclosures. The focus stones would remain with them throughout the training period, allowing for continuous attunement and familiarization.

As they prepared to retire for the night, Lyra found herself drawn to the window of their common area—a circular opening that looked out upon Valtoria's strange landscape. From this vantage point, she could see portions of the library's exterior structure, its crystalline towers and flowing architectural lines seeming to both emerge from and merge with the surrounding terrain.

Beyond Valtoria's immediate boundaries, the land itself displayed the same fluid quality they had observed inside—features that shifted subtly when viewed from different angles, colors that seemed to contain depths beyond normal perception, horizons that curved in ways that suggested more than three dimensions.

"It's beautiful," Rowan said quietly, joining her at the window. "In an unsettling way."

"Like standing at the edge of understanding," Lyra agreed. "Seeing just enough to recognize how much remains beyond our comprehension."

The Phoenix Stone pulsed warmly at her throat, resonating with the landscape before them. In that moment, Lyra felt a profound connection not just to her companions or to Valtoria, but to the entire network of Veils they had witnessed in the nexus chamber—that vast, intricate web of reality boundaries extending far beyond Sylvanthia to realms she could scarcely imagine.

"Whatever comes of this," she said softly, "we face it together. Not just for ourselves or for Valtoria, but for all the connected realities that would suffer if the nexus fails."

Rowan nodded, his quiet presence offering reassurance without words. Together they watched as Valtoria's strange twilight deepened into a night unlike any other—stars appearing that seemed to move in complex patterns, constellations forming and dissolving in cycles that suggested meanings beyond conventional astronomy.

Tomorrow would begin their intensive training with the focus stones, a process that would challenge them individually and collectively. But tonight, in this moment of relative peace, they allowed themselves to simply exist at the convergence point of past and future, known and unknown, the world they had always known and the infinite possibilities that lay beyond.

CHAPTER TWENTY-THREE

Reforged in Fire

Lyra stood alone in the sanctuary's inner chamber, her heart pounding as she faced the pedestal where the Phoenix Stone had rested since her collapse at Sentinel's Reach. Twelve days had passed since she'd channeled the catastrophic energy backlash through the Stone—twelve days of unconsciousness followed by a week of fragile recovery. Now, finally strong enough to leave her bed for more than brief periods, she had asked for this moment of privacy to reconnect with the artifact that had become so integral to her identity.

The Stone no longer resembled the smooth amber gem she had carried since inheriting it from her parents. Its transformation was startling and complete. Where once it had been a translucent oval of warm golden-orange, it now appeared as a crystalline starburst—faceted planes radiating outward from a brilliant core, its color shifting between deep crimson and bright gold depending on how light struck its surface. Occasional flickers of blue-white energy danced along its edges like miniature lightning, especially when she moved closer.

"We've both changed, haven't we?" she whispered, stopping just short of touching it.

The room around her—a small meditation chamber within the Order's northern sanctuary—had been specially prepared for this reunion. Protective wards inscribed by Alaric himself glowed faintly on the walls, floor, and ceiling, creating a contained environment where any unpredictable energy could be safely managed. A single chair positioned near the pedestal was the room's only furniture, suggesting that even the ancient mage expected this reconnection to be taxing.

Lyra's reflection in the polished stone wall caught her attention—a young woman barely recognizable from the one who had left this sanctuary weeks earlier. Her face was thinner, cheekbones more prominent, dark circles still visible beneath eyes that held a new depth of experience. Her once-vibrant copper hair had been shorn close to her scalp after healers discovered silver streaks spreading from her temples—physical evidence of the life force the Stone had drawn from her during that desperate moment at Sentinel's Reach.

"Twelve days unconscious," she murmured, touching the silver streaks self-consciously. "Elara says I lost years of my life in those few minutes."

The knowledge should have terrified her, but instead she felt a strange calm. What were a few years compared to what might have been lost had the gateway remained open? The Syndicate woman's fate—dissolving into patterns of light and matter as the alien reality claimed her—could have been the beginning of a catastrophe beyond imagining.

Taking a deep breath, Lyra moved closer to the pedestal. The Stone responded immediately, its internal light intensifying and the miniature lightning along its edges becoming more pronounced. She could feel its energy reaching toward her like an eager pet recognizing its owner after a long absence—or perhaps more accurately, like a limb reconnecting to its body after separation.

"Alaric says you've changed fundamentally," she told it, circling the pedestal slowly. "That channeling the gateway's energy altered your very nature. He's not sure what you're capable of now, or what connecting with you might do to me."

The Stone pulsed once, brightly, as if in response to her words.

"But we don't really have a choice, do we?" she continued, a wry smile touching her lips. "The fragments are still out there. The rifts are still growing. Veyra is still moving pieces into position for whatever endgame she's planning."

Another pulse, this one accompanied by a faint harmonic tone that seemed to resonate with something deep within her chest.

Lyra stopped circling and faced the Stone directly. "I'm afraid," she admitted, voice barely above a whisper. "Not of you, exactly. But of what we might become together now. Alaric wouldn't say it directly, but I could see it in his eyes—he's concerned that your transformation might change me too, beyond the years I've already lost."

The Stone's light dimmed slightly, its lightning-like discharges calming to occasional flickers. It almost seemed to be... listening.

"But fear can't be our guide, can it? Not with so much at stake." She straightened her shoulders, resolution firming her voice. "So let's discover what we've become—together."

With that declaration, Lyra extended her hand and touched the transformed Phoenix Stone.

The connection was immediate and overwhelming—nothing like the warm comfort of their previous bond. Energy surged up her arm like liquid fire, branching through her body in pathways that mimicked the Stone's starburst pattern. She gasped, nearly pulling away, but forced herself to maintain contact as the initial shock gave way to something more complex.

Images flooded her mind—not memories exactly, but impressions too rapid and numerous to fully comprehend. She glimpsed rifts seen from the inside, experienced the sensation of reality itself as a fabric that could be rewoven, felt the presence of other fragments calling across vast distances. Most disorienting was the perception of time not as a linear progression but as a medium that could be navigated in multiple directions—like swimming through currents rather than being carried along by them.

Her knees buckled, and she barely managed to collapse into the chair rather than onto the floor. Still, she maintained contact with the Stone, instinctively understanding that breaking the connection prematurely might be more dangerous than enduring this initial overwhelming communion.

Gradually, the chaos of impressions began to organize itself, as if the Stone were learning to communicate in ways she could comprehend. The flood of images slowed to a manageable stream, the sensations of fire along her nerves moderated to a tingling warmth, and the disorienting perception of time stabilized into something closer to normal human experience—though with a new awareness of its malleability hovering at the edges of her consciousness.

"There," she gasped, sweat beading on her forehead from the effort of integration. "That's... better."

The Stone pulsed in what felt remarkably like agreement. Its physical appearance remained unchanged, but the quality of energy flowing between them had shifted—becoming more coordinated, more intentional, as if they were establishing a new language of connection.

Lyra took a moment to assess herself. Beyond the expected fatigue, she felt... different. Not dramatically transformed as she had feared, but altered in subtle yet significant ways. Her awareness had expanded, particularly her perception of the energies flowing through and around the sanctuary. She could sense the protective wards not just as visible inscriptions but as living currents of power. More distantly, she could feel the presence of her companions elsewhere in the complex—distinct patterns of energy that somehow carried the essence of their identities.

Most significantly, she could perceive the rifts—even through the sanctuary's thick stone walls and powerful protections. They registered as wrongness in the fabric of reality, tears that leaked corruption into the world like infected wounds seeping poison.

"Is this how you perceive things now?" she asked the Stone, not expecting a verbal response but feeling the question was important nonetheless. "Is this how we'll work together going forward?"

The Stone's light pulsed in patterns that suggested affirmation, though with complexity that implied the answer wasn't quite so simple. Their connection was evolving even as they communicated, each moment of contact establishing new parameters of understanding.

Carefully, Lyra lifted the Stone from its pedestal. Unlike before, when it had been a comforting weight against her skin, it now felt almost weightless—as if it existed partially in another dimension and only manifested physically in this one through effort of will. Its edges, once smooth, now felt like they might cut if handled carelessly—not physically sharp but energetically so, capable of slicing through more than mere matter.

"We need to understand what happened to you," she told it, cradling the transformed artifact in both hands. "What you've become. What we can do together now."

As if in response to this intention, a new series of impressions flowed into her mind—more coherent than the initial flood, organized almost like a narrative. She saw the moment at Sentinel's Reach when she had channeled the gateway's collapsing energy through the Stone. From this new perspective, she could perceive how the artifact had functioned not merely as a conduit but as a transformer—taking energy that would have destroyed her completely and converting it into something her human form could barely survive.

But that conversion had come at a cost. The Stone had absorbed aspects of the gateway's nature—its connection to spaces between realities, its capacity to bridge dimensions, its fundamental relationship with the fabric of existence itself. These properties had merged with the Stone's original purpose of healing and renewal, creating something unprecedented—a hybrid artifact with capabilities beyond what either the Stone's creators or the gateway's architects had intended.

"You saved me by changing yourself," Lyra realized, awe coloring her voice. "You transformed to protect me."

The Stone's light brightened in confirmation, its facets catching and refracting the chamber's illumination in complex patterns that cast prismatic reflections across the walls. The sight was beautiful but unsettling—a visual representation of how fundamentally altered their relationship had become.

With growing confidence, Lyra rose from the chair, the Stone still cradled in her hands. She felt stronger now, the initial shock of reconnection giving way to a strange harmony as their energies aligned. Moving to the center of the chamber, she held the Stone at eye level, studying its transformed appearance with newfound understanding.

"Show me," she requested simply. "Show me what we can do now."

The response was immediate—energy flowing from the Stone in controlled streams that encircled her without burning or overwhelming. Unlike before, when using the Stone's power had required intense concentration and often left her drained, this manifestation felt effortless, as natural as breathing. The energy responded to her intentions before she had fully formed them, anticipating her will rather than merely reacting to it.

Most remarkably, she could perceive how this power interacted with reality itself—not just affecting physical matter but influencing the underlying structure of existence. When she directed a tendril of energy toward a small stone figurine on a nearby shelf, she could choose whether to move it conventionally, transmute its substance, or even temporarily shift it partially out of this dimension—seeing possibilities layered like transparent overlays and selecting between them with intuitive ease.

"This is..." she whispered, words failing to capture the experience adequately. "I don't even know what to call this."

The door behind her opened, interrupting her exploration. She turned to find Alaric standing in the entrance, his ancient eyes widening at the display of energy surrounding her. Behind him stood Kael, whose expression shifted rapidly from concern to astonishment.

"I felt the change in energy patterns," Alaric explained, his voice carefully neutral despite the obvious tension in his posture. "It seemed prudent to check on you."

Lyra realized how the scene must appear to them—her slight figure engulfed in swirling energy unlike anything they had witnessed before, her eyes likely glowing with reflected power, the transformed Stone floating inches above her outstretched palm in defiance of gravity. With a thought, she dismissed the visible manifestations, though the connection with the Stone remained vibrant in her awareness.

"It's alright," she assured them, surprised by the calm certainty in her own voice. "We're... adjusting to each other. Learning what's changed."

Kael stepped into the room, his protective instincts visibly warring with his trust in her judgment. "Are you sure? That looked... intense."

"It is intense," she acknowledged with a small smile. "But not dangerous—at least, not to me. The Stone and I understand each other better than ever before."

Alaric moved further into the chamber, his gaze fixed on the transformed artifact now resting comfortably in Lyra's hand. "What have you learned?" he asked, scientific curiosity temporarily overriding caution. "About its new capabilities?"

Lyra considered how to explain experiences that transcended ordinary language. "It's become something more than it was," she began carefully. "The gateway's energy changed it fundamentally—not corrupting it, but expanding its nature. It still heals and restores, but now it also... connects. Bridges. Transforms."

"Connects to what, precisely?" Alaric pressed, his concern evident beneath the scholarly inquiry.

"To the spaces between realities," Lyra replied, the knowledge flowing from her enhanced perception rather than conscious thought. "To the fabric underlying existence itself. It can perceive the rifts more clearly now, and potentially—" She paused, the implications of what she was sensing suddenly crystallizing into understanding. "Potentially heal them more effectively than before."

This revelation shifted the atmosphere in the room. What had been perceived as a potentially dangerous transformation now appeared in a new light—as an evolution specifically suited to their ultimate mission of sealing the rifts permanently.

"How certain are you of this?" Alaric asked, hope and skepticism warring in his ancient eyes.

"Very," Lyra answered without hesitation. "I can see the rifts now, Alaric. Not just sense them, but actually perceive their structure—the way they tear reality, the patterns of their corruption. And I can see how they might be rewoven, sealed not just temporarily but permanently."

Kael moved closer, his initial wariness giving way to cautious optimism. "This changes our approach entirely. If the Stone can truly heal the rifts permanently..."

"We still need the fragments," Lyra clarified, the Stone pulsing in her hand as if emphasizing this point. "The Stone alone isn't enough—it needs the resonance patterns of the Shattered Illusion to complete the healing. But it can now serve as a... template, I suppose. A pattern for restoration that the fragments' power can follow."

Alaric nodded slowly, his expression thoughtful as he processed these implications. "The gateway's energy carried properties of dimensional manipulation—the very principles that the Shattered Illusion was created to regulate. By absorbing and integrating those properties, the Phoenix Stone has become something like a key that can interface directly with the fragments' purpose."

"Yes," Lyra agreed, grateful for his ability to articulate what she perceived intuitively. "Exactly that."

"But at what cost?" Kael asked quietly, his gaze moving to the silver streaks in her shorn hair—visible reminders of the life force already sacrificed. "This connection seems more demanding than before. What will using these new capabilities require from you?"

The question struck at concerns Lyra had been avoiding—the physical toll their enhanced connection might exact. The Stone pulsed once in her hand, and she received a clear impression that surprised her with its directness: truth.

"The Stone wants me to be honest with myself about this," she translated, a rueful smile touching her lips. "It's right, of course. There will be a cost. Using these new capabilities will draw more deeply on my life force than before—especially when working directly with the rifts or the fragments."

Kael's expression darkened with concern. "Lyra—"

"But," she continued, raising a hand to forestall his protest, "the Stone is also more... conscious of this exchange now. More deliberate in how it draws upon me. Before, it took what it needed without precision. Now, it can be more selective, more efficient." She met his worried gaze directly. "I won't pretend there's no risk. But the alternative is allowing the rifts to continue spreading corruption throughout Sylvanthia. That's not a choice I can make."

A heavy silence fell over the chamber as they absorbed the implications of her words. The transformed Stone pulsed gently in her palm, its light shifting through subtle gradations of color that seemed to reflect the complex emotions filling the room.

"We should inform the others," Alaric finally said, practical considerations asserting themselves. "They need to understand what's changed before we proceed with recovering the remaining fragments."

Lyra nodded, though a wave of fatigue suddenly reminded her that her physical recovery was far from complete. The Stone sensed her exhaustion immediately, its energy shifting to provide support rather than drawing upon her further. The sensation was novel—a reversal of their usual exchange, with the artifact actually returning some of what it had taken, stabilizing her flagging strength.

"Rest first," Kael insisted, noticing her momentary weakness despite her attempt to conceal it. "The others can wait until you've recovered your strength."

"A wise suggestion," Alaric agreed. "This reconnection has clearly been taxing, despite its apparent success. A few hours of rest before we gather the group would be prudent."

Lyra wanted to protest but found herself unable to argue against the obvious wisdom of their concern. The Stone pulsed in what felt remarkably like admonishment, reinforcing their recommendation.

"Even my own artifact is ganging up on me," she observed with a tired smile. "Fine. A few hours of rest, then we'll explain everything to everyone at once. It will be more efficient anyway."

As they helped her back to her quarters, Lyra maintained her physical contact with the transformed Stone, unwilling to break their newly established connection even temporarily. The artifact seemed equally reluctant to separate, its energy maintaining a constant, gentle flow between them that felt simultaneously foreign and deeply familiar—like returning to a childhood home to find it both changed and essentially the same.

The council chamber within the Order's northern sanctuary had been designed for strategic discussions, its circular table allowing all participants equal position and voice. Now, as Lyra's companions gathered to understand the Phoenix Stone's transformation, that egalitarian design seemed particularly appropriate. This was not a moment for hierarchy but for collective understanding of a development that would affect all their paths forward.

Elara arrived first, her healer's instincts drawing her immediately to Lyra's side to assess her condition with both conventional observation and magical sensitivity. "Your energy patterns have stabilized remarkably," she noted with professional approval. "Though they're configured differently than before—more complex, with new harmonic structures I don't fully recognize."

"That seems to be the theme of the day," Lyra replied with a small smile. "Complexity and transformation."

Mira entered next, her keen alchemist's eyes immediately fixing on the transformed Stone that now hung suspended from a fine silver chain around Lyra's neck—no longer resting against her skin as before, but hovering just above it as if reluctant to be fully bound by physical constraints.

"Well, that's certainly dramatic," she observed, dropping into a chair with her characteristic lack of ceremony. "Going for a more intimidating aesthetic? The whole 'crystal starburst of doom' look is definitely more impressive than 'smooth amber pebble.'"

"Form following function, I think," Lyra replied, appreciating Mira's ability to cut through tension with irreverence. "Though I didn't exactly get to choose the redesign."

Rowan arrived with Kael, the cartographer carrying several blank parchments and drawing tools. "Alaric suggested I document the Stone's transformation," he explained, setting up his materials with practiced efficiency. "Visual records might help us understand the changes more completely."

"Good thinking," Lyra agreed, carefully lifting the Stone slightly away from her body to give him a better angle for his sketches. "Though I'm not sure conventional drawing can capture all aspects of what it's become."

"I'll do my best," Rowan promised, already beginning preliminary outlines with quick, precise strokes. "Perhaps multiple perspectives, including attempts to represent its energy patterns as well as physical appearance."

When all had assembled, Alaric closed the chamber doors and activated privacy wards with a subtle gesture—a precaution that emphasized the significance of their discussion. Though the Order's sanctuary was considered secure, some knowledge warranted additional protection.

"As you can all see," he began without preamble, "the Phoenix Stone has undergone a fundamental transformation following the events at Sentinel's Reach. What you may not yet understand is how profoundly this changes our approach to the rifts and the remaining fragments of the Shattered Illusion."

All eyes turned to Lyra, who found herself suddenly uncertain how to articulate experiences that transcended ordinary perception. The Stone sensed her hesitation and pulsed once, sending a wave of clarity through their connection. With it came understanding of how to bridge the gap between her enhanced awareness and her companions' conventional perception.

"May I?" she asked, rising from her seat and moving to the center of the circular table.

With murmurs of assent from the others, she carefully removed the Stone from its chain and placed it on the table's surface. Immediately, it began to emit soft pulses of light that gradually increased in intensity and complexity. Under her guidance, these emanations formed a three-dimensional representation in the air above the table—a miniature model of reality as the Stone now perceived it.

Gasps of surprise and appreciation filled the chamber as her companions beheld a visualization of Sylvanthia unlike any map they had previously encountered. The land itself appeared semi-transparent, with flowing currents of energy visible beneath its surface—natural ley lines and power nexuses that formed the magical infrastructure of their world. More ominously, the rifts were clearly visible as jagged tears in this fabric, leaking corruption that spread in dark tendrils through otherwise healthy energy flows.

"This is how the Stone now perceives our reality," Lyra explained, gesturing toward the miniature representation. "Not just the physical land, but the energetic structure underlying it. The rifts aren't just physical tears—they're wounds in the fabric of existence itself, allowing corruption from between realities to seep into ours."

"Extraordinary," Elara breathed, her scholarly mind clearly racing to integrate this new perspective with her existing knowledge. "The patterns match what I've sensed through my rune-casting, but with such clarity and detail..."

"And these darker areas?" Kael asked, pointing toward regions where the corruption appeared particularly concentrated.

"Syndicate strongholds," Lyra confirmed. "Places where they've deliberately widened rifts or conducted rituals that weaken reality's natural boundaries. Their activities create resonance patterns that accelerate the spread of corruption."

Mira leaned forward, her usual sarcasm temporarily set aside in favor of genuine scientific curiosity. "Can you show us what happens when you use the Stone to heal a rift? Even just a demonstration model?"

Lyra nodded, directing her attention to a smaller rift represented in the model. The Stone responded immediately, sending a tendril of golden energy toward the tear. As they watched, this energy began to reweave the torn fabric—not simply closing the gap but actually restoring the original pattern, eliminating the corruption that had seeped through.

"Before, the Stone could temporarily seal rifts," she explained as they observed the demonstration. "Like stitching a wound closed but not actually healing the underlying tissue. Now, it can genuinely restore the damaged fabric—but only for smaller rifts, and at significant cost."

"What cost, exactly?" Mira asked, her perceptive gaze shifting from the model to Lyra herself—specifically to the silver streaks in her hair.

"Life force," Lyra acknowledged, appreciating her friend's directness. "As before, but more precisely controlled now. The Stone has become more... conscious of our exchange. More selective in what it takes and how it uses it."

"And for larger rifts?" Rowan inquired, his hands continuing to sketch rapidly even as he participated in the discussion.

In response, Lyra adjusted the model to highlight seven major rifts scattered across Sylvanthia—tears so massive that they dominated their respective regions, sources of corruption that could never be contained through conventional means.

"For these, we need the fragments of the Shattered Illusion," she explained. "The Stone can now serve as a template or guide, but only the fragments together possess enough raw power to heal tears of this magnitude."

"Which is why the Syndicate has been so determined to gather them," Alaric added, his ancient eyes grave as he studied the model. "Though I suspect their purpose is quite different from healing."

"Veyra doesn't want to heal the rifts," Lyra confirmed, knowledge flowing through her enhanced connection with the Stone. "She wants to widen them permanently—to tear down the boundaries between realities entirely."

This revelation sent a chill through the chamber. They had known the Syndicate's goals were destructive, but the scale of Veyra's ambition—the complete dissolution of the barriers protecting their reality—represented a threat beyond anything they had previously imagined.

"Why would anyone want that?" Mira demanded, genuine horror breaking through her carefully maintained cynicism. "What could possibly be worth unraveling reality itself?"

"Power beyond conventional limitations," Alaric answered quietly. "Freedom from the constraints that govern existence as we understand it. Veyra believes these boundaries are artificial impositions—cages rather than protections. She seeks to return to what she imagines was a more primal state of being, where consciousness could directly shape reality without the mediation of physical laws."

"And would kill everyone and everything in the process," Kael concluded grimly.

"Not in her view," Alaric corrected. "She would argue she's offering transcendence—evolution beyond our current limited existence. That those who survive the transition would experience freedom beyond anything we can currently comprehend."

"While those who don't are acceptable sacrifices," Elara noted with uncharacteristic bitterness.

Lyra adjusted the model again, focusing now on the fragments they had already secured and those still missing. Four glowing points represented the artifacts currently protected within the Order's sanctuaries, while three remained scattered across Sylvanthia—their approximate locations indicated by resonance patterns that the transformed Stone could now perceive.

"We've secured more than half," she observed, finding encouragement in this visual confirmation of their progress. "The remaining three are within reach, though the Syndicate is undoubtedly increasing their efforts to find them before we do."

"Speaking of which," Rowan interjected, setting aside his sketching tools to indicate a specific region on the model, "my contacts in the resistance network report increased Syndicate activity here—the western forests near what used to be Highvale territory. Their movements suggest they're closing in on something significant."

"One of the fragments," Lyra confirmed, the Stone pulsing in agreement. "I can feel its resonance pattern now, much more clearly than before. It's responding to the others we've gathered, creating a harmonic that makes it easier to locate."

"Then our next move is clear," Kael stated, military precision entering his voice as he shifted to tactical planning. "We need to secure that fragment before the Syndicate reaches it. How soon can we depart?"

All eyes turned to Lyra, the unspoken question evident—was she recovered enough for another mission so soon after her ordeal? The Stone pulsed against her skin, conveying complex information about her physical condition and the demands of the journey ahead.

"Tomorrow," she decided, balancing honesty about her limitations with the urgency of their situation. "I need one more day to fully stabilize this new connection. Then we can travel to the western forests."

"Not all of us," Alaric cautioned. "The fragments we've already secured require protection. The Syndicate will be growing desperate as we gather more pieces of the Shattered Illusion. Dividing our forces would be prudent."

A strategic discussion followed, with various configurations considered and evaluated. Eventually, they settled on a plan: Lyra, Kael, and Rowan would pursue the fragment in the western forests, while Mira and Elara remained to protect those already secured, with Alaric coordinating between the groups and maintaining communication with the Order's leadership.

As the meeting concluded and her companions departed to make preparations, Lyra remained seated at the table, the transformed Stone still projecting its model of Sylvanthia's wounded reality. She studied the visualization with mixed emotions—hope at their progress thus far, determination to complete their mission, and undeniable apprehension about the challenges ahead.

"You're concerned about something specific," Alaric observed, remaining behind after the others had left. His ancient eyes missed little, particularly when it came to the subtle signs of disquiet.

Lyra considered deflecting but decided honesty was the wiser course—especially with someone whose centuries of experience might offer genuine insight.

"The Stone is showing me something it can't show the others," she admitted, adjusting the model to highlight a particular pattern—a resonance that connected all seven fragments of the Shattered Illusion, growing stronger as more were gathered in proximity. "As we collect more fragments, their combined energy creates a kind of... beacon. One that Veyra can almost certainly perceive."

"Meaning our success makes us an increasingly obvious target," Alaric concluded, understanding immediately.

"Yes. And more concerning—" She hesitated, then continued with reluctance. "The Stone suggests that Veyra has changed since your confrontation centuries ago. That absorbing shadow magic for so long has transformed her just as the gateway's energy transformed the Stone itself. She exists partially between realities now, which gives her perception and abilities beyond conventional limitations."

"I've suspected as much," Alaric acknowledged, his weathered face solemn with the weight of old regrets. "The Voices never seemed sufficient to explain her continued influence. A more direct connection to the spaces between realities would account for much that has puzzled me about the Syndicate's activities."

"The Stone believes—and I agree—that our final confrontation won't be with her proxies or even her Voices," Lyra continued. "As we gather more fragments, we're essentially forcing her hand. She'll have to manifest directly to stop us."

"And you're concerned about facing such an entity," Alaric surmised. "Understandably so."

"Not exactly," Lyra corrected, surprising herself with the realization as she spoke it aloud. "I'm concerned about what I might have to become to defeat her."

The transformed Stone pulsed against her skin, neither confirming nor denying this fear but acknowledging its validity. Their enhanced connection had revealed possibilities that both exhilarated and terrified her—capabilities that might require surrendering aspects of her humanity to access fully.

Alaric studied her for a long moment, his ancient eyes seeing more than she had explicitly stated. "The Stone has shown you a path to victory," he guessed. "But one that requires significant sacrifice."

"Something like that," she admitted. "It's not fully formed yet—more like glimpses of potential futures where different choices lead to different outcomes. But in the scenarios where we succeed completely..." She trailed off, unable to articulate the visions that had flashed through her enhanced perception.

"You fear losing yourself," Alaric finished for her. "Becoming something other than human in the process of saving humanity."

"Is that what happened to Veyra?" Lyra asked suddenly, the parallel occurring to her with uncomfortable clarity. "Did she start with noble intentions that gradually twisted as her power and perspective changed? Is that the inevitable path of anyone who steps beyond conventional limitations?"

The question hung in the air between them, weighted with implications for Lyra's own journey. The transformed Stone pulsed once, sharply, as if objecting to the comparison.

"Veyra chose her path deliberately," Alaric replied after thoughtful consideration. "She embraced transformation not as a necessary sacrifice for others but as personal transcendence at any cost. The difference lies not in the power itself but in the intention behind its use." His gaze met hers directly, centuries of wisdom in his ancient eyes. "And in the willingness to be guided by those who remain grounded in the world you're trying to save."

The Stone pulsed again, this time in what felt remarkably like agreement. Lyra found herself smiling despite the gravity of their discussion.

"It seems my artifact concurs with your assessment," she observed. "Though I suspect its perspective isn't entirely unbiased."

"Few perspectives are," Alaric acknowledged with a small smile of his own. "But consider this: the Stone transformed to protect you, not to consume you. Its evolution appears oriented toward partnership rather than dominance. That suggests a fundamental difference from the path Veyra chose."

This observation resonated with Lyra's own intuitive understanding of the Stone's transformation. Despite its increased power and more demanding connection, it had never attempted to override her will or subvert her intentions. Their relationship had evolved toward greater integration rather than subjugation in either direction.

"Partnership," she repeated, finding comfort in the concept. "A shared journey rather than one consuming the other."

"Precisely," Alaric confirmed. "And not just between you and the Stone, but among all of us facing this challenge together. Each bringing different strengths, perspectives, and limitations that balance and complement one another."

The transformed Stone pulsed warmly against her skin, its energy patterns shifting to reflect this understanding. The model it projected above the table changed subtly, highlighting not just the rifts and fragments but also the connections between Lyra and her companions—threads of relationship and trust that formed their own kind of strength against the darkness spreading through Sylvanthia.

"I should rest," Lyra decided, dismissing the model with a gentle thought. The Stone responded immediately, its projection fading as it returned to a more quiescent state. "Tomorrow's journey will require all my strength, even with this enhanced connection."

Alaric nodded, rising from his seat with the careful movements his ancient body required. "A wise decision. I'll inform the others that preparations should proceed as planned."

As they left the council chamber together, Lyra found her apprehension balanced by newfound determination. The path ahead remained uncertain, the challenges formidable, the personal cost potentially devastating. But she would not face them alone—neither in the literal sense of her companions' presence nor in the deeper sense of the transformed Stone's partnership.

Whatever she might have to become to defeat Veyra and heal the rifts, she would not lose herself entirely as long as these connections remained. The Phoenix Stone pulsed gently against her skin, a silent promise that transformation need not mean destruction—that sometimes, like the mythical bird whose name it bore, one could emerge from fire fundamentally changed yet still essentially oneself.

Together, they would face whatever came next—reforged by trial but not consumed by it.

CHAPTER TWENTY-FOUR

Valley of Flames

The Phoenix Stone pulsed against Lyra's palm, its warmth seeping into her skin as she led her companions through the twisted valley. Ahead, the Syndicate's fortress loomed against the twilight sky—a jagged silhouette of black stone and iron that seemed to devour what little light remained in the day. The structure hadn't been built so much as carved from the mountain itself, its towers reaching toward the heavens like accusing fingers.

"We're close now," she murmured, her voice barely audible above the whisper of wind that carried the scent of ash and something metallic—like blood, but older. Ancient.

Kael moved beside her, his sword already half-drawn from its scabbard. The metal caught what little light filtered through the clouds, a gleam of defiance against the gathering gloom. "The scouts were right. No guards at the outer perimeter."

"That's what worries me," Rowan said, eyes scanning the ridgelines above. His fingers traced the edges of his map, though he'd memorized every contour and passage days ago. "Either they don't know we're coming, or—"

"—or they're waiting for us inside," Mira finished, adjusting the strap of her satchel. The glass vials clinked softly against one another, each containing concoctions she'd spent the last three nights perfecting. "I vote for the latter. The Syndicate's never been caught unprepared."

Elara remained silent, her delicate features taut with concentration as she traced invisible patterns in the air. The runes she'd inscribed along her forearms glowed with a soft blue light, illuminating the hollows beneath her cheekbones. "There's powerful magic here," she finally said. "Old magic. It feels... wrong somehow. Corrupted."

Lyra nodded, feeling the same wrongness prickling against her skin. The Phoenix Stone grew warmer in response, as though awakening to an ancient enemy. For seven years, she'd dreamed of this moment—standing at the threshold of justice for her parents. Yet now that it had arrived, doubt gnawed at her resolve.

The stone's amber light pulsed more intensely, casting dancing shadows across their faces. She'd learned much about its powers over their journey—how it could heal rifts in the fabric of reality, how it connected to the emotional threads of the past, how it responded to her intentions rather than just her commands. But its depths remained mysterious, its full potential still beyond her grasp.

"Are we really ready for this?" she asked, her voice smaller than she intended.

Kael's hand found her shoulder, his grip firm but gentle. "We've faced everything they've thrown at us. We've survived their assassins, their traps, their mind games." His eyes, usually so guarded, held a fierce certainty. "I couldn't save Lirien. But I won't fail you—any of you—today."

"We're as ready as we'll ever be," Mira added with a half-smile that didn't quite reach her eyes. "Besides, what's the worst that could happen? We all die horribly and the world plunges into darkness?"

Rowan shot her a sidelong glance. "Your optimism is truly inspiring."

"It's what keeps me so popular at parties," she quipped, but her fingers trembled slightly as she rechecked the stoppers on her vials.

Elara stepped forward, her movements graceful despite the tension radiating from her slender frame. "The path ahead will test us in ways we haven't yet faced. But remember what brought us together." She looked at each of them in turn, her gaze lingering on Lyra. "Not just vengeance or duty, but something stronger."

The unspoken word hung in the air between them. *Family*. Not by blood, but forged through trials and trust, failures and forgiveness.

Lyra took a deep breath, feeling the Phoenix Stone's power harmonize with her own. The stone had three primary aspects she'd discovered: restoration, illumination, and connection. Each required different focuses of her will, different emotional states. For what lay ahead, she would need all three.

"Then let's finish this," she said, squaring her shoulders. "Together."

They moved as one toward the fortress, shadows among shadows as the last light faded from the sky.

The entrance hall stretched before them, cavernous and eerily silent. No guards challenged their approach, no alarms sounded at their intrusion. Only rows of obsidian pillars rose to meet the vaulted ceiling, each carved with symbols that seemed to shift when viewed from the corner of one's eye.

"I don't like this," Kael muttered, sword fully drawn now. "It feels like—"

"—a trap," Rowan finished. "Definitely a trap."

Mira snorted softly. "When isn't it a trap?"

Elara raised her hand, silencing them. Her runes pulsed brighter as she closed her eyes, sensing the currents of magic that flowed through the chamber. "There," she whispered, pointing to seemingly empty air near the center of the hall. "A barrier. Invisible, but powerful."

Lyra stepped forward cautiously, the Phoenix Stone illuminating her path with its amber glow. As she approached the spot Elara had indicated, the air seemed to thicken, resistance pushing against her outstretched hand. "Can we break through it?"

"Not without alerting every Syndicate member within these walls," Elara replied. Her fingers traced complex patterns as she studied the magical construct. "But perhaps we can… slip through instead."

She knelt, removing a small pouch from her belt. With careful movements, she extracted a pinch of crystalline powder and scattered it in an arc before them. Where the dust touched the barrier, it clung and sparkled, revealing the outline of an archway.

"The barrier isn't meant to keep people out," she explained, her voice barely above a whisper. "It's designed to detect and identify those who pass through. I can modify our… signatures, for lack of a better term. Make us appear as though we belong."

"How long will that take?" Kael asked, eyes constantly scanning for movement among the shadows.

"Longer if you keep interrupting," Elara replied without looking up. Despite her words, a small smile played at the corners of her mouth.

While Elara worked, Mira moved to Lyra's side. "How's our resident Phoenix Stone bearer holding up?" she asked quietly, her usual sarcasm softened by genuine concern.

Lyra flexed her fingers, watching the stone's light pulse in rhythm with her heartbeat. "I'm fine."

"Mmm, very convincing. Almost believed you for a second there."

Lyra sighed. "I've been dreaming about this moment for seven years, Mira. Imagining what I'd say, what I'd do when I finally faced them." She glanced at the stone, its surface swirling with inner fire. "But now that we're here…"

"You're afraid," Mira finished for her. "Join the club. We meet on Tuesdays, bring your own terror."

Despite everything, Lyra felt a smile tug at her lips. "Is that what I am to you? A Tuesday?"

"More like a lifetime of Tuesdays," Mira replied, nudging her shoulder gently. "Look, being afraid doesn't make you weak. It makes you smart. Only idiots aren't scared right now."

Across the chamber, Rowan cleared his throat. "I heard that."

"And yet you didn't deny it," Mira called back softly, winking at Lyra.

"It's ready," Elara announced, rising to her feet. The powder she'd scattered now formed a glowing outline around the archway, symbols etched in light pulsing gently along its edges. "Step through quickly, one at a time. Don't hesitate in the threshold."

Kael went first, passing through the archway with a slight shimmer, like heat rising from summer stone. Rowan followed, then Mira, who gave Lyra's hand a quick squeeze before crossing.

"Your turn," Elara said, her voice steady despite the strain evident in her eyes. Maintaining the spell clearly took considerable effort.

Lyra approached the archway, the Phoenix Stone growing hotter against her skin. For a moment, she hesitated, feeling as though she stood at the edge of a precipice. Then, taking a deep breath, she stepped through.

The sensation was like walking through a waterfall—pressure against her skin, a momentary resistance, then release. On the other side, her companions waited, their expressions a mixture of relief and tension.

Elara came last, the magical outline dissolving behind her as she passed through. She swayed slightly, and Lyra caught her arm to steady her.

"I'm all right," Elara assured her, though her face had paled considerably. "Just need a moment."

"Which we don't have," Kael said grimly, pointing down the corridor that extended beyond the entrance hall. Distant footsteps echoed against stone, growing louder with each passing second.

"This way," Rowan whispered, gesturing toward a narrow passage to their left. "According to the maps, it should lead deeper into the fortress."

They slipped into the passage just as a patrol of Syndicate guards entered the hall, their black uniforms absorbing what little light filtered through the high windows. The guards passed without pause, unaware of the intruders who had breached their defenses.

As the sound of footsteps faded, Lyra released a breath she hadn't realized she was holding. "That was close."

"It's going to get closer," Rowan warned, consulting his mental map. "The inner sanctum—where the Syndicate leadership gathers—is at the heart of the fortress. We'll have to pass through at least three more guarded sections to reach it."

"Then we'd better keep moving," Kael said, taking point as they continued down the passage. "The longer we're here, the greater the chance we'll be discovered."

They proceeded in tense silence, each step bringing them deeper into enemy territory. The passage eventually opened into a broader corridor lined with doors of dark wood and iron. Rowan signaled for them to stop, consulting his memory once more.

"The archives should be through there," he whispered, indicating a set of double doors ahead. "If the intelligence is correct, we'll find information about the Syndicate's operations—and possibly the location of their leaders."

"Or another trap," Mira muttered, but she was already removing a slender tool from her belt, approaching the locked doors with practiced ease.

While Mira worked on the lock, Elara's expression suddenly sharpened. "Someone's coming," she hissed, her runes flaring in warning.

They pressed themselves against the walls as footsteps approached from an adjoining corridor. A solitary figure emerged—a woman in the distinctive black uniform of a Syndicate officer, her silver insignia marking her as someone of rank.

Before anyone could react, the woman turned, her eyes widening as she spotted them. Her hand moved toward the weapon at her belt, but Kael was faster. In a fluid motion, he crossed the distance between them, one hand clamping over her mouth while the other pressed his blade against her throat.

"Make a sound, and it will be your last," he warned, voice low and dangerous.

The woman's eyes darted between them, calculating. After a moment, she gave a slight nod.

"Bring her here," Lyra directed, moving toward an alcove where they would be less visible. "We need information."

Kael forced the woman into the alcove, keeping his blade steady. "Who are you?" he demanded.

When he removed his hand from her mouth, the woman's lips curved into a smile that held no warmth. "Someone who's been expecting you," she replied, her voice surprisingly melodic. "The Phoenix Stone's chosen bearer and her... entourage."

Lyra stepped forward, the stone glowing brighter in response to her rising emotions. "You know who I am?"

"Of course. Lyra, daughter of the traitors who stole the stone seven years ago." The woman's gaze was unflinching. "The Syndicate has been watching you for longer than you realize."

"My parents weren't traitors," Lyra snapped, anger flaring hot in her chest. "They were trying to protect the stone from being misused."

"Is that what you believe?" The woman laughed softly. "How charmingly naive. Your parents were members of the Syndicate, girl. High-ranking ones, at that. Until they decided the power of the stone should be theirs alone."

Lyra felt as though the ground had shifted beneath her feet. "You're lying."

"Am I? Ask yourself why they never told you about their past. Why they kept you isolated, moving from place to place." The woman's eyes gleamed with cruel satisfaction. "They weren't protecting the stone from the Syndicate. They were protecting their claim to it."

"Enough," Kael growled, pressing his blade more firmly against her throat. "We didn't come here for your lies."

"No, you came for answers," the woman replied, seemingly unconcerned by the steel against her skin. "I'm merely providing them. Whether you choose to accept them is your affair."

Mira stepped forward, her expression unusually serious. "If you were expecting us, why are you alone? Where are the guards, the ambush?"

The woman's smile widened. "Who says I'm alone?"

As if on cue, a low humming filled the air. The runes on Elara's arms flared brightly in warning just as the woman dissolved into shadow, slipping from Kael's grasp like smoke between fingers.

"It's an illusion!" Elara cried, her hands already weaving counterspells.

Too late. The air around them shimmered, revealing a circle of Syndicate mages who had been concealed by powerful magic. At their center stood the woman, now clothed in the elaborate robes of a Syndicate Archmagus.

"Welcome to the heart of the Syndicate," she said, her voice echoing with new-found power. "We've been waiting a very long time for the stone's return."

The battle erupted in a chaos of light and shadow. Syndicate mages launched volleys of dark energy while Kael moved like a whirlwind among them, his blade finding gaps in their defenses. Rowan darted between attackers with deadly precision, using the confined space to his advantage. Mira hurled vials that burst into clouds of disorienting smoke or splashed with caustic liquid that ate through the mages' protective wards.

Elara stood at the center of their formation, her runes blazing as she maintained a shield of energy around them, deflecting the worst of the magical assault. Sweat beaded on her forehead, her slender frame trembling with the effort of sustaining such powerful magic.

"I can't hold this much longer," she gasped, her voice strained.

Lyra felt the Phoenix Stone burning against her palm, its power surging in response to the danger. She focused on its restorative aspect, channeling its energy into Elara's shield. The blue light of the runes mingled with the stone's amber glow, strengthening the barrier even as it drained Lyra's own reserves.

The Archmagus narrowed her eyes, focusing her attention on Lyra. "The stone responds to you," she observed, her voice cutting through the chaos of battle. "But you barely understand its power. Such waste."

With a gesture, she sent a lance of shadow hurtling toward Lyra. It struck Elara's shield with such force that the barrier shattered, sending both women staggering backward. Before Lyra could recover, tendrils of darkness wrapped around her wrists and ankles, lifting her from the ground.

"Lyra!" Kael shouted, trying to fight his way toward her, but three Syndicate mages blocked his path.

The Archmagus approached, her eyes fixed on the Phoenix Stone. "Seven years we've searched," she murmured, reaching toward the glowing gem. "Seven years since your parents betrayed their oaths and fled with our greatest treasure."

Lyra struggled against the shadowy bonds, the stone pulsing frantically against her skin. "They were protecting it from you," she spat.

"They were protecting themselves," the Archmagus corrected. "Did they ever tell you what the stone truly is? What it can do in the right hands?" She smiled at Lyra's silence. "Of course not. They kept you ignorant, using you as nothing more than a vessel."

"Don't listen to her, Lyra!" Mira called, dodging a blast of energy from one of the mages. "She's trying to get in your head!"

The Archmagus ignored the interruption, her fingers hovering just above the stone. "The Phoenix Stone is more than a source of power. It's a key—one that can open the rifts between worlds." Her voice dropped to a near-whisper. "Imagine it, girl. Access to realms of magic beyond anything this world has known. Your parents understood this. They simply wanted that power for themselves."

Lyra felt doubt creeping into her mind like poison. Her parents had told her so little about the stone, about their past. What if there was truth in the Archmagus's words?

The moment of uncertainty was all the Archmagus needed. Her hand closed around the Phoenix Stone, her fingers overlapping with Lyra's. A surge of power erupted between them, a column of light that shot upward, shattering the ceiling above. Debris rained down as the energy built, a maelstrom of amber and shadow that enveloped both women.

Through the chaos, Lyra heard her companions calling her name, their voices growing distant as the power of the stone consumed her awareness. She felt the

Archmagus's presence in her mind, sifting through her memories, seeking control of the stone through her connection to it.

So much power, so little understanding, the Archmagus's voice echoed in her thoughts. *Surrender the stone, child. It was never meant for you.*

Lyra felt herself slipping, the stone's energy beginning to flow toward the Archmagus. Images flashed through her mind—her parents' faces on the night they died, their expressions not of fear but of grim determination; the years of running, of hiding; the moment she discovered the stone's power responding to her touch.

They lied to you, the Archmagus insisted. *Used you. The stone belongs to the Syndicate.*

Another memory surfaced—her mother's voice, weak but urgent in her final moments: *"The stone chose you, Lyra. Not because of us, but because of who you are. Its power has limits—it cannot create or destroy, only transform. Remember that."*

Understanding bloomed within her like a flame. The stone had never been her parents' to give. It had chosen her—not as a vessel or a guardian, but as a partner. And while its power was vast, it operated within boundaries. It could mend rifts but not create them. It could illuminate truth but not alter it. It could connect to the past but not change it.

"You're wrong," Lyra said aloud, her voice growing stronger with each word. "My parents didn't steal the stone from the Syndicate. They freed it. And they understood its true nature better than you ever could."

She closed her eyes, focusing not on fighting the Archmagus's presence but on deepening her connection to the Phoenix Stone. Instead of channeling its power outward, she opened herself to it completely, accepting its energy as part of herself.

The stone responded, its amber light suffusing her entire being. The shadowy bonds dissolved as Lyra rose into the air, suspended by the stone's power. The Archmagus's hand was torn away, her expression shifting from confidence to alarm.

"What are you doing?" she demanded, backing away as the column of light concentrated around Lyra. "Stop this at once!"

Lyra opened her eyes, which now glowed with the same amber fire as the stone. "The Phoenix Stone doesn't belong to anyone," she said, her voice resonating with newfound authority. "Least of all to those who would use it to dominate others. Its purpose is to heal, to reveal, to connect—not to conquer."

With a gesture, she released a wave of energy that swept through the chamber. The Syndicate mages were thrown backward, their spells dissipating like mist before the sun. Only the Archmagus remained standing, though she raised her arms in a defensive posture.

"You don't understand what you're interfering with," she snarled, gathering shadow between her palms. "The rifts must be opened. The power beyond must be claimed!"

"Not by you," Lyra replied simply. "Not by anyone who seeks it for selfish ends."

The Archmagus hurled her gathered shadow at Lyra, a spear of darkness aimed at her heart. Without moving, Lyra deflected it with a thought, the darkness dissolving against a shield of amber light.

For the first time, fear flickered across the Archmagus's face. "What are you?"

Lyra descended slowly until her feet touched the ground once more. The Phoenix Stone's light continued to emanate from her, illuminating the chamber with its warm glow. "I am exactly who my parents believed I could be," she answered. "The one the stone chose."

With a cry of rage, the Archmagus launched herself forward, hands outstretched to seize the stone by force. Lyra met her charge with calm resolve, capturing the woman's wrists in a gentle but unbreakable grip. The moment their skin touched, the Phoenix Stone's light flowed between them, not as a weapon but as a revelation.

The Archmagus's eyes widened as the stone's power laid bare the truth—not just about Lyra's parents, but about the Syndicate itself. Images flashed between them: the Syndicate's founding as seekers of knowledge; their gradual corruption as power became an end rather than a means; the rifts they had already opened, unleashing forces they couldn't control.

"No," the Archmagus whispered, trying to pull away. "These are lies..."

"You know they aren't," Lyra said softly. "You've always known what the Syndicate has become."

The light receded, drawing back into the Phoenix Stone as Lyra released the Archmagus's wrists. The woman stumbled backward, her face ashen, her eyes haunted by what she had seen.

Around them, the chamber had fallen silent. The Syndicate mages lay unconscious or had fled, leaving only Lyra's companions, who watched the exchange with mixtures of awe and concern.

"What did you do to her?" Kael asked, approaching cautiously, his sword still drawn.

"I showed her the truth," Lyra replied, feeling strangely calm despite the enormity of what had just occurred. "About the Syndicate, about my parents... about everything."

The Archmagus sank to her knees, her elaborate robes pooling around her like spilled ink. "All these years," she murmured, more to herself than to them. "All these sacrifices, and for what? Power that corrupts, knowledge that destroys."

Elara stepped forward, her runes still glowing faintly. "The rifts you've opened," she said urgently. "Can they be closed?"

The Archmagus looked up, her expression hollow. "Some. Not all. We went too far, too fast. The boundaries between worlds have been... weakened."

"How many rifts are there?" Rowan asked, his cartographer's mind already mapping the challenge.

"Seven major rifts," the Archmagus replied, her voice flat. "The first in the Crimson Valley, where the barrier between our world and the Realm of Flames has grown thin. The second beneath the Whispering Sea, where ancient creatures stir from slumber. The third in the Shadowpeak Mountains, where time itself has become... unstable."

She continued, describing each rift in turn—the fourth in the heart of Veilwood Forest, where reality twisted upon itself; the fifth in the Crystalline Desert, where solid matter dissolved into energy; the sixth in the ruins of Old Khalith, where the dead walked among the living.

"And the seventh?" Lyra prompted when the woman fell silent.

The Archmagus's eyes met hers, fear evident in their depths. "The seventh is in Northreach, at the ancient site of Veyra's Fall. It's the largest, the most unstable. The Syndicate High Council has gathered there, attempting to harness its power directly. If they succeed..." She shook her head. "What comes through will consume us all."

Kael's grip tightened on his sword. "Then we need to end this now. We should secure the fortress, gather whatever information we can about these rifts, and then move on Northreach immediately."

Lyra nodded, the Phoenix Stone's light dimming slightly as she allowed its power to settle. "You're right. Rowan, can you and Mira search the archives we were heading for? Look for maps, ritual details, anything that might help us understand what we're facing."

"Consider it done," Mira replied, already moving toward the double doors they'd been approaching before the ambush.

"Elara, see what you can learn from the magical artifacts here," Lyra continued. "There might be protective measures we can use against whatever comes through these rifts."

Elara nodded, her scholarly focus already engaged despite her obvious fatigue. "I'll need about an hour to properly examine everything."

"Take it," Lyra said. "We need to be thorough." She turned to the Archmagus, who remained kneeling on the floor, her confident demeanor shattered by the truth she'd witnessed. "And you're going to help us."

The woman looked up, something like hope flickering briefly in her eyes. "How?"

"By telling us everything you know about the High Council's plans. Their strengths, their weaknesses, their timeline." Lyra's voice was firm but not unkind. "Help us stop this before it's too late."

The Archmagus—Serena, she finally revealed her name to be—slowly rose to her feet. "The High Council chamber contains detailed records of all the rifts, including the specific rituals used to create them. That knowledge might help you seal them."

"Show us," Kael demanded, his sword still ready.

For the next hour, they worked methodically through the fortress. Serena led them to chambers filled with ancient texts and artifacts, each revealing more about the Syndicate's activities and the rifts they had created. Rowan and Mira returned from the archives with maps marking each rift's location, while Elara discovered protective amulets designed to shield the wearer from the worst effects of cross-dimensional energy.

As they prepared to leave, gathering the most valuable information and artifacts, a distant rumbling shook the fortress. Dust and small fragments of stone rained from the ceiling.

"What was that?" Mira asked, tensing.

Serena's expression darkened. "The High Council. They've begun the final ritual already. They're using the Northreach rift to destabilize the others."

"Can they do that?" Rowan asked, alarmed.

"With the right sacrifices, yes." Serena's voice was grim. "They're channeling life energy—hundreds of lives—to force the rifts open wider."

The implications struck them all at once. Hundreds of innocent people, their lives being drained away to fuel the Syndicate's ambitions.

"We need to go," Lyra said, her voice hardening with resolve. "Now."

They made their way through the fortress, encountering surprisingly little resistance. Most of the Syndicate forces seemed to have abandoned their posts, either fleeing the impending catastrophe or rushing to join the High Council's ritual in Northreach.

As they emerged from the fortress into the cool night air, Lyra felt the Phoenix Stone pulse with urgency. She looked to the north, where the sky had taken on an unnatural crimson hue, pulsing like a wound in the fabric of reality.

"The Northreach rift is expanding," Serena confirmed, following Lyra's gaze. "We have days at most before it tears open completely."

"And the other rifts?" Elara asked.

"They'll follow, one by one. The Crimson Valley first, then the others in sequence."

Rowan was already calculating distances, routes, possibilities. "Even if we ride without rest, we can't reach Northreach in time to stop the ritual."

"We don't need to reach Northreach," Lyra said, an idea forming as she felt the Phoenix Stone's power thrumming through her. "Not directly. If the rifts are connected as Serena says, then perhaps we can use that connection to our advantage."

Elara caught on immediately, her eyes widening. "The Crimson Valley rift. It's closest to us."

"Exactly," Lyra nodded. "If we can stabilize that rift using the Phoenix Stone..."

"...it might disrupt the High Council's ritual," Serena finished, a spark of hope lighting her eyes. "It could work. The stone's power is fundamentally opposed to what they're attempting."

Kael's expression remained doubtful. "And if it doesn't work? If we waste time at the Crimson Valley while the Northreach rift continues to grow?"

"Then we'll have tried," Lyra said simply. "And we'll face what comes next together, as we always have."

The decision made, they gathered what supplies they could and set off toward the Crimson Valley, a journey of two days if they pushed themselves to the limit.

The path to the Crimson Valley took them through treacherous terrain—jagged mountain passes where the air grew thin and bitter cold, followed by barren lowlands where sulfurous vents belched noxious fumes. The closer they came to the rift, the more the landscape bore signs of corruption—withered vegetation, strange crystalline growths erupting from the soil, animals twisted into unnatural forms.

By the end of the first day, exhaustion dragged at their limbs. They made camp in the shelter of a stone outcropping, the distant glow of the Crimson Valley visible on the horizon like a wound in the night sky.

"We should reach the valley by tomorrow evening," Rowan said, consulting his maps by the light of their small fire. The flames cast flickering shadows across his face, deepening the lines of fatigue around his eyes. "If we push hard."

"And if we don't collapse first," Mira muttered, massaging her blistered feet. Her usual sarcasm couldn't quite hide her exhaustion. "Not all of us have Kael's inexhaustible stamina."

Kael, who was keeping watch at the edge of their camp, didn't respond. His silhouette remained vigilant despite the day's grueling march, though Lyra noticed how he leaned more heavily on his sword than usual.

Elara sat cross-legged near the fire, her eyes closed in meditation as she replenished her magical reserves. The runes on her arms glowed faintly, their light dimmer than normal—a sign of how much energy she had expended maintaining protective wards during their journey. The closer they came to the rift, the more essential those wards became, shielding them from the worst effects of the corrupted environment.

Serena kept to herself, seated slightly apart from the others. Though she had proven helpful since her confrontation with Lyra, the others maintained a wary distance. Trust would take time to build, if it ever could.

As the others settled into uneasy sleep, Lyra took her turn at watch, the Phoenix Stone warm against her palm. Its light pulsed gently, almost like a heartbeat, as if it were alive and aware just as Serena had said.

"What do you want from me?" she whispered to it, too softly for anyone else to hear.

The stone's light intensified briefly, and Lyra felt a sensation that wasn't quite words but carried meaning nonetheless: *Balance. Healing. Truth.*

Simple concepts, yet the weight of worlds hung upon them.

The second day of travel proved even more arduous than the first. The terrain grew increasingly unstable as they approached the Crimson Valley—the ground itself seeming to shift beneath their feet, fissures opening without warning, releasing bursts of superheated air that could scald exposed skin in seconds.

By midday, they were forced to don protective gear fashioned from supplies taken from the Syndicate fortress—cloth masks soaked in Mira's alchemical solutions to filter the toxic air, gloves to protect against caustic minerals that seemed to crystallize out of nothing.

The physical toll mounted with each step. Rowan developed a persistent cough that he tried and failed to hide. Elara's slender frame trembled with the effort of maintaining their protective wards. Mira's usual quips grew fewer and more strained. Even Kael showed signs of wear, a slight limp developing where a sudden ground-shift had wrenched his knee.

Lyra felt the drain as well, a bone-deep weariness that made each step an act of will. Yet the Phoenix Stone seemed to sustain her, its warmth flowing through her veins like liquid strength when her own reserves faltered.

"We need to rest," she finally said as Rowan stumbled for the third time in as many minutes.

"No time," Serena replied, her voice muffled by her mask. "Look ahead."

On the horizon, the crimson glow had intensified dramatically since morning, pulsating with increasing frequency. Streaks of darker red shot through the glow like veins in an inflamed eye.

"The rift is destabilizing faster than I expected," Serena continued. "The High Council's ritual must be progressing more quickly than we thought."

"Then we push on," Kael said grimly, offering Rowan a steadying hand. "Together."

They reached the Crimson Valley as the second day waned, the sky above them shifting from azure to deep crimson as they approached the rift. The valley itself had been transformed by the rift's presence—the once-verdant landscape now scorched and barren, the air shimmering with heat that emanated from a tear in reality at the valley's center.

Through this tear, Lyra could glimpse another world—a realm of perpetual flame and stone, where massive shapes moved through rivers of molten rock. The sight filled her with both awe and dread.

"The Realm of Flames," Serena murmured, her voice hushed. "One of the seven outer realms that border our own."

Elara studied the rift with professional interest despite the danger, her runes glowing in response to the powerful magic. "The tear isn't complete yet," she observed. "It's still... stretching, for lack of a better term."

"That gives us a chance," Lyra said, feeling the Phoenix Stone grow warmer as they approached the rift. "I need to get closer."

Kael stepped in front of her, his expression resolute. "Not alone."

"None of us goes alone," Mira added, already preparing her alchemical compounds. "That's kind of our whole thing, remember?"

They approached the rift together, the heat growing more intense with each step. At fifty paces, the air became difficult to breathe. At thirty, their skin began to blister despite Elara's protective runes. At twenty, Lyra felt the Phoenix Stone vibrating against her palm, its power surging in response to the rift's chaotic energy.

"I can't go any further," Serena gasped, falling to her knees as the heat overwhelmed her.

"None of us can," Rowan said, his face reddened from the heat. "Except perha ps..."

All eyes turned to Lyra, who stood with the Phoenix Stone held before her like a shield. The stone's amber light formed a protective bubble around her, keeping the worst of the heat at bay.

"I have to go alone from here," she realized, meeting each of their gazes in turn. "The stone will protect me."

Kael's expression was anguished. "Lyra—"

"I'll be all right," she assured him, trying to project more confidence than she felt. "The stone won't let me fail. Not now."

Before anyone could argue further, she turned and continued toward the rift, each step requiring more effort than the last as the very air seemed to resist her passage.

The Phoenix Stone's light intensified, enveloping her in a cocoon of amber energy that pushed back against the rift's crimson glare.

At the very edge of the tear, Lyra could feel the barrier between worlds—thin as gossamer yet resilient as steel. Through it pulsed the power of the Realm of Flames, ancient and hungry, seeking to consume everything in its path.

She raised the Phoenix Stone, focusing on its restorative aspect. *Mend what is broken,* she thought, channeling her will through the stone. *Restore what has been torn.*

The stone's light surged outward, meeting the rift's crimson energy in a spectacular collision of power. For a moment, nothing seemed to happen. Then, slowly, the edges of the tear began to draw together, the glimpse of the fiery realm beyond growing narrower.

But as the rift began to close, Lyra felt resistance—not just from the rift itself, but from elsewhere. A distant power pulling against her efforts, trying to keep the tear open. The High Council in Northreach, she realized. They were fighting her through the connection between rifts, pouring their combined power into maintaining the tear.

Lyra gritted her teeth, pushing back with everything she had. The Phoenix Stone burned against her palm, its power flowing through her in waves that made her bones ache and her vision blur. Still, the rift resisted, hovering in a precarious balance between closing and tearing wider.

I need more, she thought desperately. *More power, more focus...*

As if in answer, she felt a hand on her shoulder. Turning, she found Elara beside her, the rune-caster's delicate features strained but determined.

"You're not alone," Elara reminded her, her runes blazing with blue fire that somehow withstood the rift's heat.

Then Kael was there, his sword planted in the ground before them, its metal glowing white-hot but unmelting. "Never alone," he echoed.

Mira appeared at her other side, her alchemical pouches emptied but her spirit unbroken. Rowan joined them, his keen eyes focused on the rift as if mapping its weaknesses. Even Serena dragged herself forward, adding her knowledge of the Syndicate's magic to their united effort.

Lyra felt their strength flowing into her, not as raw power but as something deeper—trust, belief, love. The Phoenix Stone responded, its light expanding to encompass them all, drawing from their unified purpose.

With a final surge of will, Lyra directed the stone's full power at the rift. "Close!" she commanded, her voice carrying the weight of not just her own determination but that of all her companions.

The rift shuddered, resistance faltering as the Phoenix Stone's light overwhelmed the distant pull of the High Council. With a sound like thunder, the tear sealed itself, reality knitting back together in a cascade of amber and crimson light.

The backlash sent them all sprawling, the superheated air around them suddenly cooling as the connection to the Realm of Flames was severed. For several moments, they lay gasping, their bodies and spirits drained by the effort.

Lyra was the first to rise, the Phoenix Stone still clutched in her trembling hand. Its light had dimmed to a gentle pulse, but she could feel its satisfaction—if such a thing were possible for an artifact of power.

"We did it," she breathed, helping Elara to her feet. "The rift is closed."

"Not just closed," Serena said, her voice filled with wonder as she stared at the spot where the tear had been. "Healed. The boundary between worlds is stronger now than before the rift was opened."

Kael retrieved his sword, the metal now cooled to its normal state. "And Northreach? The High Council?"

As if in answer, a distant rumble shook the ground beneath their feet. To the north, the crimson glow in the sky flared brilliantly, then began to fade.

"The ritual has been disrupted," Serena confirmed, her expression a mixture of relief and concern. "But not stopped entirely. The High Council will regroup, adapt their approach."

"And the other rifts?" Rowan asked, his cartographer's mind already calculating their next move.

"Temporarily stabilized," Serena replied, "but not sealed. Each exists in its own unique relationship to the barriers between worlds. The Crimson Valley was perhaps the most straightforward—a direct tear between our realm and the Realm of Flames. The others will require... different approaches."

"Then we go to Northreach," Lyra decided, her voice stronger now. "We face the High Council directly, end this once and for all."

As they gathered their strength and prepared for the journey ahead, none of them noticed the small fragment that had broken from the Phoenix Stone during the sealing of the rift. It lay half-buried in the scorched earth, its amber light pulsing with a rhythm slightly out of sync with the stone Lyra carried.

Nor did they see the shadowy figure that emerged from behind a distant outcropping once they had departed, moving with careful precision to retrieve the fragment. The figure—cloaked and hooded against recognition—held the shard up to the fading light, a smile playing across lips that had not known joy in centuries.

"At last," Veyra whispered, her voice like dry leaves rustling in autumn wind. "A beginning."

She closed her ancient fingers around the fragment, feeling its power resonate with her own. The Phoenix Stone had rejected her long ago, deemed her unworthy of its gifts. But this shard, separated from the whole, had no such discernment.

As Lyra and her companions journeyed toward Northreach and their final confrontation with the Syndicate's High Council, Veyra turned in the opposite direction, the shard guiding her toward a different destiny altogether.

The game had changed. New pieces were in play. And the balance of worlds hung in the balance.

CHAPTER TWENTY-FIVE

Epilogue

T he game had changed. New pieces were in play. And the balance of worlds hung in the balance.

Veyra studied the Phoenix Stone fragment in her palm, watching how its amber light pulsed with a rhythm slightly out of sync with the greater cosmos. Such a small thing to hold such potential. Where Lyra and her companions saw only a tool for sealing rifts, Veyra recognized something far more profound—a key that could unlock possibilities beyond mortal comprehension.

She closed her ancient fingers around the shard, feeling its power resonate with her own transformed essence. The Phoenix Stone had rejected her centuries ago, deemed her unworthy of its gifts. But this fragment, separated from the whole during that tremendous expenditure of power at the Crimson Valley rift, had no such discernment. It responded to her will, hungry for direction after being severed from its purpose.

"We are alike, you and I," she whispered to the shard. "Both broken from our original design. Both seeking a new path."

The wind shifted across the scorched valley, carrying the distant sounds of Lyra's group as they departed toward Northreach. Such determination they showed, such conviction in their righteous cause. Veyra might have admired their unity if she hadn't recognized its fundamental naivety. They still believed in absolutes—in clear divisions between right and wrong, in the sanctity of boundaries between realms, in the necessity of order over chaos.

They hadn't yet learned what she had discovered through centuries of existence between realities: that all boundaries were ultimately artificial, all order eventually gave way to entropy, all certainty was illusion.

Veyra turned away from their path, the shard guiding her toward a different destination. The High Council's ritual at Northreach had been disrupted, but not destroyed. Their crude attempts to force the rifts open wider would ultimately fail, with or without Lyra's intervention. They lacked the fundamental understanding required for true transformation of reality.

But Veyra had patience. She had perspective. And now, she had a fragment of the very artifact designed to mend the tears between worlds—an irony that brought a cold smile to lips that had not known joy in centuries.

Where others saw endings, she recognized beginnings. Where they sought to restore barriers, she would find new ways to dissolve them. Where they fought to preserve a reality they understood, she would usher in one they couldn't begin to comprehend.

As twilight deepened over the Crimson Valley, Veyra slipped between shadows, moving with the fluid grace of one no longer fully bound by physical laws. The fragment pulsed against her palm, its light dimming as if trying to hide from distant eyes that might sense its presence.

"Soon," she promised it, her voice like dry leaves rustling in autumn wind. "Soon we will find the others like you. And together, we will rewrite the very foundations of existence."

The ancient being who had once been human vanished into the gathering darkness, leaving no footprints on the scorched earth to mark her passing. Behind her, the sealed rift in the Crimson Valley held firm, its boundaries stronger than before—a temporary victory in a war whose true scope remained hidden from those who had won it.

The confrontation with the Syndicate's High Council would come and go. Rifts would be sealed, lives would be saved, heroes would be celebrated. But beneath these visible currents, deeper patterns were forming, ancient powers awakening.

The true game was just beginning.

www.ingramcontent.com/pod-product-compliance
Lightning Source LLC
Chambersburg PA
CBHW020825030726
47496CB00001B/103